IN A
WORLD
JUST
RIGHT

IN A
WORLD
JUST
RIGHT

Jen Brooks

SIMON & SCHUSTER BFYR

NEW YORK   LONDON   TORONTO   SYDNEY   NEW DELHI

SIMON & SCHUSTER BFYR

An imprint of Simon & Schuster Children's Publishing Division

1230 Avenue of the Americas, New York, New York 10020

SIMON & SCHUSTER BFYR is a trademark of Simon & Schuster, Inc.

For information about special discounts for bulk purchases, please contact Simon & Schuster Special Sales at 1-866-506-1949 or business@simonandschuster.com.

The Simon & Schuster Speakers Bureau can bring authors to your live event. For more information or to book an event, contact the Simon & Schuster Speakers Bureau at 1-866-248-3049 or visit our website at www.simonspeakers.com.

Jacket design by Lizzy Bromley

Interior design by Hilary Zarycky

The text for this book is set in Fairfield.

Manufactured in the United States of America

2 4 6 8 10 9 7 5 3 1

Library of Congress Cataloging-in-Publication Data

Brooks, Jen, 1971–

In a world just right / Jen Brooks.—First edition.

pages cm

Summary: Eighteen-year-old Jonathan Aubrey, a scarred loner, escapes at will into other worlds of his making but suddenly, the world where a popular girl is his long-term girlfriend is intersecting reality in startling ways.

ISBN 978-1-4814-1660-3 (hardcover : alk. paper)

ISBN 978-1-4814-1662-7 (eBook)

[1. Disfigured persons—Fiction. 2. Supernatural—Fiction. 3. High schools—Fiction. 4. Schools—Fiction. 5. Dating (Social customs)—Fiction. 6. Orphans—Fiction.] I. Title.

PZ7.B79447In 2015

[Fic]—dc23

2013051336

MAY - - 2015

FIRST
EDITION

For Chris,
with all my love

IN A WORLD JUST RIGHT

CHAPTER 1

IT'S TWO O'CLOCK IN THE MORNING, AND THE STREETLIGHT stretches my shadow across Kylie's lawn up into her mother's English garden. My shadow's head is where the fat yellow lilies will bloom after graduation this summer. Bunches of smaller flowers her mom planted yesterday, a rainbow of color in sunlight, sleep under a blanket of moonlight gray.

I glance up and down the street at a neighborhood of unlit windows, to confirm no one saw me appear out of thin air.

Without crushing anything, I navigate Kylie's garden and squeeze between bushes to reach the window. Her curtains are drawn, so I can't see inside. With a kick to the mulch, I uncover the butter knife we hid there and slide it along the window's edge to unhitch the screen. I push the unlocked window up, then part the curtains to see into the room.

Kylie's sitting up in bed. Awake. Startled. Watching me come through the window.

She relaxes when she figures out it's just me, Jonathan, the messed-up boyfriend.

I crash into the room as quietly as I can and slip off my sneakers. Kylie slides over and pulls back the covers for me to lie down. She won't ask if I'm okay, because clearly I'm not. I don't make surprise nighttime visits casually.

"Did I scare you?" I ask.

"A little."

"Sorry."

She props her head on her hand, her long red-brown hair looking black as it trails to the pillow. The darkness smooths her face, gives her two wide eyes over a bump of nose and kissable lips. Lips denied me in the real world. She presses closer, and our lips meet. For a few glorious moments we kiss each other, and I start to feel better. She's warm and smells like she showered before bed, all coconutty or pineappley or something.

Then she pulls away. Her eyes search my face, waiting.

I don't actually want to talk. I want more kissing. I want more *her*. I reach for her hand, separate out her index finger, and draw it down the left side of my face, from my eye practically to my jaw. She doesn't flinch, and that is exactly what I need. I pull up my shirt and place her hand on my chest, where the scarring is the worst. She moves her fingers over the snarls and craters, caresses them, then replaces my shirt and kisses the scar on my face.

Her eyes look into mine. Most people can't look me in the eyes. The real Kylie has never looked me in the eyes, but this Kylie seeps into me with a gaze. She is not disgusted by me. She loves me.

She puts a finger to the scar on my face. "Is this bothering you again?"

"I don't know." Actually, that's a lie. What's bothering me is the weird cosmic whisper I got just before I came here, which scared me more than my near-death memories, but I do not discuss cosmic topics with Kylie.

Thankfully, she rolls with my faked ignorance and stays focused on my scar. "It's just a line." She moves a little deeper into the covers and puts her head on my chest, ear to my heart. "And evidence that you're a miracle."

I enfold her in my arms and say nothing. No one in the real world cares that I'm a miracle, not since the doctors congratulated themselves and discharged me.

"Seriously," she says, and I can feel her words vibrate against my chest. "Do you want to talk about it?"

Talking won't help. Sometimes the truth cannot set you free. Sometimes, when the night is bad and the universe taunts me, I just need to be with my girlfriend.

"I feel better now," I say.

Kylie breathes a contented sigh and snuggles against me. My body practically shivers with the ecstasy of being with her. She's everything I need to live, and she's not even real.

Here's a story for you. Once upon a time there was this kid named Jonathan Aubrey. He was eight years old. He had a mom and a dad and a six-year-old sister, Tess, and an Auntie Carrie and Uncle Joey. One day they all got on a plane to Disney World. Except for Uncle Joey, who was on some business trip or other. It was going to be the funnest, most perfect trip of a lifetime. The airplane took off . . . and fell out of the sky into Boston Harbor. (Yes, the Tragedy in the Harbor, the famous crash they contrasted with the Miracle on the Hudson.)

Little Jonathan was one of three people who survived. He spent three months at Massachusetts General Hospital in a coma, and when he woke up, they sent him home. Except there wasn't anyone at home anymore. They were in the ground at Pine Street Cemetery, and he had missed all the funerals and everything.

He went to live at Uncle Joey's house instead. Uncle Joey tried to be good to Jonathan, but there was that business thing that often kept him away, and Uncle Joey was grieving just as bad because he'd lost Auntie Carrie.

Jonathan didn't come out of that coma the same way he

went in. He had a little lag in his speech. He limped. He had burns and scars on parts of his body. Most of the ugly skin he kept covered with long sleeves and pants, even on days when it got to be almost a hundred degrees. But one uncoverable, ragged red scar ran from his eye to his jaw, and the marks of the stitches made a railroad track on his face. When he returned to school, kids were afraid of him. Teachers tried to be nice, but they just couldn't stop every kid who whispered "Frankenstein." Jonathan learned to take it quietly. At recess he'd sit on the monkey bars pretending he was part of everyone's play, even though he got thoroughly ignored. He paid attention in school and liked his teachers, but teachers' attention wasn't enough, and they tried too hard to make him feel normal. He wanted so much to be asked to play kickball. The closest he got was when Hunter LeRoy made him fetch the ball out of some poison ivy, saying that if he got a rash, it couldn't make him any uglier. He really said that. Hunter LeRoy is a jerk to this day.

Jonathan would sit in his room in Uncle Joey's house and stare out the window. Sometimes he would pretend the street crawled with kids fighting some kind of rebellion against alien invaders, and he was their leader. He would have friends and daring escapades with a healthy dose of heroics, and his scar would be a badge of honor, a war wound.

One day he squeezed his eyes shut so tightly with longing that when he opened them . . . he was standing in the middle of a battle with a gun in his hands. There were people and aliens running in the street. Laser blasts shot craters into the manicured lawns. Tanks, helicopters, bodysuits full of gadgetry everywhere. He was wearing a bodysuit full of gadgetry. "Commander Aubrey!" someone yelled. Jonathan made a motion with his arm, and a dozen kid soldiers followed him down the street to fight the alien invaders.

This new world was Jonathan-is-a-hero. He went there a lot. Until he figured out it was not the only world he could make.

I'm awake before Kylie, watching the red digital numbers count down the time till her alarm. Two more minutes.

She has rolled away from me, forehead pressing against the wall, and most of the covers are bunched in her curled arms. I'm on my back, lying at the other edge of the bed, not touching her with my disturbed thoughts.

I am here because something happened last night—a breath, a murmur, a shift in the earth, like everything under me slid a millimeter off center from where it should be, which is a weird feeling when everything looks perfectly normal and no sound at all has been made. But I got all creeped-out in a way I feel silly trying to explain, and the shiver I got was so powerful, it sent me scrambling out of bed and over to Kylie's, just so she could put right the world.

To a certain extent I just have to put up with weirdness in my totally weird life. Kylie fixed my mood, so all's quiet on the western front this morning.

I can't reward her for her good deed by letting the squawk of the alarm wake her, so I carefully turn it off and roll myself over to fit my body to hers. She makes a little groany wake-up noise and pulls my arm over her.

"What time is it?" she whispers.

"Would you believe me if I said school's canceled?"

She takes a deep breath and sighs it out, and we lie there together, content for a moment before we roll back the covers and rise. We exchange a few kisses laced with morning breath, which are sweet anyway.

"You okay?" she asks.

"All better." I convince her with a smile. She reflects it back at me, magnified by her beautifulness, and I come *this close* to dragging her back under the covers.

With a final kiss she leaves for the bathroom. I slip out the window, replace the screen, and rebury the butter knife. Since witnesses are waking in the surrounding houses, I crouch in the bushes to vanish back to reality.

Step one: Squeeze eyes closed.

Step two: Picture world. (That would be the real world this time.)

Step three: Open eyes.

That's all there is to it.

I'm standing perfectly still in the woods behind Pennington High School, sensing the world around me. Nothing seems out of place. Relief carries away my tension like rain washing down a roof. Whatever was worrying me last night has passed.

I trudge up a path through the woods to the school. Because my house is pretty far away, there wasn't enough time to walk here and still get to class by the bell, so my sacrifice for a few hours earlier with Kylie is a shower at school.

The back door is always open in the morning, so I sneak inside, grab stuff from my gym locker, and clean up. My shampoo's not coconutty or pineappley, but it squelches any thoughts my scalp might have about starting a dandruff habit. I wore (mostly) clean jeans to Kylie's last night, so they're good to go again today, and the T-shirt I pull out of my backpack smells much better than the one I slept in. Okay. Ready to face another day.

I push open the locker room door as someone else yanks from the outside. There's a second of shock before I recognize the other guy and try to lighten things with a "Hey, Mark," but he brushes past me like I'm not there. Not even a grunt of acknowledgment from the kid voted this year's class chatterbox.

This real-world invisible treatment, after so many years, has lost its sting. The locker room door shuts behind me, sealing me in the empty hallway. I shortcut to my E-Hall locker through the weight room, and a wall of mirrors announces that I, Jonathan Aubrey, do in fact exist. I create a reflection in a real mirror in the real world, so I can only assume I'm not actually invisible.

Granted, invisibility would be a great superpower to have, but world-making will have to do, since it's the power I got.

There's still about ten minutes before first period, so I take my time at my yellow-over-blue-over-brown-over-orange-painted locker. There are so many layers, the lockers stick when you open and close the doors. Pennington High School is something like sixty years old, a building that's out of date without being charming. The desks and chairs are chiseled, and graffitied, and covered in the grime from thousands of student bodies. About half the windows are Plexiglas replacements that've yellowed with time.

Fellow seniors in this hallway grab books and move on, talking about college plans, sports practice, homework they need to copy. When I feel that stalling another second at my locker will be overkill loser-ish, I slam the door shut and head off for a walk around the more crowded halls of freshmen, sophomores, and juniors, who take the bus and therefore arrive sooner. I'll be just another anonymous walker until it's safely late enough to grab my seat in first period.

As usual, no one greets me in passing. No one looks at me in their rush to do whatever they need to do. I could be here or not, and the school day would go on just the same. I'm missed only by the computer that adds up the absences my teachers input when I'm gone to Kylie-Simms-is-my-girlfriend.

I'm halfway up B-Hall when I see her talking to a teacher at the far end.

The real Kylie Simms.

She looks exactly like my Kylie, from her ponytail to the toes poking out of her sandals. Gorgeous. Athletic. Smart. Confident. Kind. A million other adjectives to fall in love with. She's wearing a royal-blue T-shirt with a winged-foot logo and *Pennington Track and Field* in white. There's a meet today, so all the track girls will be wearing them. Kylie is team captain and one of the top sprinters in the state. Her devotion to the sport is the reason I joined the track team myself in Kylie-Simms-is-my-girlfriend.

I try not to stare at her, but I can't help myself. One would think that having an exact Kylie copy all to myself in another world would satisfy my craving for her, but one would be dead wrong. My curiosity knows no bounds.

She doesn't spare a glance in my direction as I walk by. Not that I expect her to. Kylie Simms might be a nice girl, but she doesn't have much reason to talk to a loner like me. As I keep going down the hall, forcing myself not to look back, I feel the small thrill of potential fading away. Whenever I see Kylie, there's always the chance she'll notice me, but I haven't hit that lottery yet.

How would she feel to know that in another world not only does Jonathan Aubrey love her but she loves him right back?

It's sick, I know. What I've done. But it's all I have for happiness, and just thinking about Kylie in Kylie-Simms-is-my-girlfriend makes me realize I forgot to give her the yearbook form I picked up for her that's due today. I look at my watch. Six minutes to first period is enough time for a quick errand.

I duck into the nearest bathroom, second stall, and find it empty. Without wasting time I squeeze my eyes shut, picture the same exact bathroom in Kylie-Simms-is-my-girlfriend, and open them.

I'm crouching on top of the toilet. Since this stall's been locked for ages due to a broken flusher, it's the safest place to switch worlds in a hurry. Before I can crawl out, the main door creaks open and then bangs closed. I'm stuck listening to the sounds of someone doing their business while at least a minute ticks by. When whoever it is finally finishes washing his hands and exits, I look again at my watch. I can still make it.

After a careful listen to make sure I'm really alone, I climb off the toilet and under the locked stall door, ready to find Kylie.

It doesn't take long. School in Kylie-Simms-is-my-girlfriend appears pretty much the same as it does in the real world, so I'm not surprised to see a lot of the same people in this hallway as I did a moment ago. I expected to search for Kylie by her locker in D-Hall, but she's here, in B-Hall not far from the doorway where real Kylie was talking to the teacher. She's with Lilly DeMarco, who is also dressed in the blue-and-white Pennington High track shirt, and they're headed my way. Some teeny part of my brain finds this odd, since Kylie isn't usually this early for class, but I dismiss it so I can get back to the real world in time for my own class.

Locker doors slam. Cell phone screens flash as students shield them from teachers. The hallway is backpacks and hair and books and voices. Arms brush in passing. I hold my books a little more tightly and prepare to greet Kylie with our usual peck on the lips. Her red-brown hair, tied up in a ponytail, sweeps back and forth with her stride. She flashes a smile at another track girl pulling books out of a locker. Lilly says something to make Kylie laugh.

I'm smiling myself. I know I just saw her this morning, but sappy smiles just burst out whenever I see her. I slow my stride to meet up with them and offer that kiss. Kylie doesn't take any notice of me. I'm right in front of her, but she keeps talking to Lilly as if I'm just another kid going to class. I've moved into the middle of the hallway to join her, and I get bumped by a freshman with an enormous backpack. I take a step to catch myself, and I'm touching Kylie. She finally looks at me and my smile, and as I lean toward her face, I sense that something is very, very not okay. I pull away, kiss aborted, and register the shock on her face. It might even be horror as her eyes travel down my scar.

Lilly takes her arm and pulls her down the hall away from me. They giggle, exchange a few words I can't hear. Kylie looks back at me strangely. Then they sort themselves into their separate classrooms.

Slowly the realization of what has happened dawns on me. I think I've just done something I've never, ever done before. But how? HOW? I started the day in the real world and switched in the bathroom. I know I did. But somehow, maybe, I didn't.

I mixed up my worlds.

I check the hallway for the truth, but my two school worlds are mostly the same except for track and Kylie. Maybe today they are a little too identical. Although my worlds contain the same people, they're rarely doing the same exact things at the same exact times. The answer comes when Rob Finkelstein passes me. Rob is in my running group and a good friend in Kylie-Simms-is-my-girlfriend. He totally ignores me on his way down the hall.

Oh, God. How did this happen?

My gut twists and my tether to the real world goes slack. I

lean against a locker and take a shaky breath. I just tried to kiss the real Kylie Simms. Lilly will tell the whole school by third period.

Later I'll have to go to real creative writing class and face Kylie. I think of how much we mean to each other in Kylie-Simms-is-my-girlfriend, how good it feels to run side by side for a few miles, to make out on the couch with the TV on mute, to talk for hours over hot chocolate at Lacy Pastry. The reminder that in reality I mean nothing to her at all makes me sick. I stumble back into the bathroom.

I'm pretty sure nobody notices.

CHAPTER 2

SINCE HIDING IN THE BATHROOM ISN'T THE BEST WAY TO deal with a colossal screw-up, I decide to write myself a dismissal note. (I'm eighteen, and my school lets us "adults" do this.) I stumble home to Uncle Joey's house, replaying my morning, my last night, trying to figure out what I did to end up in the real world trying to kiss the real Kylie Simms, dreading what she thinks of me. I'm sure I started school in the real world. In the bathroom I'm sure I switched worlds. Maybe I've gotten so casual about flipping back and forth that I forgot to do something I normally do. I can't think what. I can't think of a single thing I did wrong.

My guess is that this is related to the creeped-out feelings that led me to Kylie's last night, if only because I don't believe in coincidences. Still, I managed to switch from Kylie-Simms-is-my-girlfriend to the real world just fine this morning. Why would things get messed up after that?

Unless whatever I felt was the beginning of the end of something. Like when a person's very sick, they might have this moment when they realize something's wrong, and from that point on they have good days and bad days until the end. What if my world-making powers are dying, and instead of disappearing all at once, they'll sputter and jerk through good days and bad days until they reach their end? In two short months, I'll leave the Neverland that is high school and have to grow up. What if world-making works only for a kid?

I'll have to wait until I'm in my room to test that theory. If I blink out of this world while walking down the street, someone might see.

When I reach home, I glance at the car Uncle Joey bought me, which sits in the driveway all red and shiny. In Kylie-Simms-is-my-girlfriend my car gets me a lot of attention, but I never drive it to school in the real world. I'd feel too weird showing up with a car that's better than everyone else's. It would beg people to talk about me behind my back.

I press the key fob button to deactivate the house alarm, and enter through the mudroom. Uncle Joey's house is something like four thousand square feet with five bedrooms and no people. Auntie Carrie was a few months pregnant when the plane crashed, so there's a half-finished baby room upstairs. Uncle Joey has a first-floor master bedroom wing with an office and a marble bathroom, and I get the whole upstairs to rattle around in myself. The sum total of my stuff fills a medium-size moving box, so there are three rooms up there whose doors never get opened.

As if I'm on my regular after-school routine, I pick up the home phone to check for the stuttering dial tone that means there's a message, but it's clear. I grab a cold slice of last night's pizza from the fridge and sit at the breakfast bar. The whole kitchen reflects in the gleaming granite countertop. Although I'm not hungry, eating is something I can control, so I start to feel better.

Because they're staring at me, I thumb through the small stack of college applications on the breakfast bar. The idea of college—open minds and starting over—is very appealing. It's like making a new world, except it would be real.

Uncle Joey, who's a Princeton grad and a Harvard MBA, has been helping me collect these applications. Since it's April, I've missed practically all the deadlines, but it doesn't matter much anyway. If I want to go to college, I've got to do summer school or a year of prep school to make up for the classes I've failed due to absences I've accrued by traveling to Kylie-Simms-is-my-girlfriend. Uncle Joey's lawyer's been fighting the school board about this, saying I've done enough satisfactory work to pass all my classes grade-wise.

I've finished my pizza.

By now my screwup will be all over the school.

I want to go to Kylie-Simms-is-my-girlfriend just so I can talk with the Kylie who loves me about what happened, but of course I can't do that. I talk to girlfriend Kylie about a great many things, but the real world is not one of them. She thinks Kylie-Simms-is-my-girlfriend *is* the real world, and I'm not sure what would happen if I told her it wasn't.

But enough of this. I can't believe how nervous I am as I climb up the stairs and flop onto my unmade bed. The sun streams through the picture window over my desk and my unused computer. Most kids my age spend half their lives in that virtual world. They can't make the worlds I do.

Or did. I'm about to find out.

I kick off my shoes and slide under the covers. I squeeze my eyes shut, hold them closed for several seconds of concentration, and open them on a world of gyrating bodies with low-cut tops and high-cut bottoms. In leather and vinyl and eyeliner, they grind away to the rhythm, flashing suggestive movements at one another.

The scared part of me cries with relief. I can still switch worlds! The logical part says if I can, I need another explanation for what happened this morning.

A vision of Kylie's horrified, almost-kissed face comes to

mind, but drains quickly away, like I'm watching her through a television darkening. My worry evaporates even as I try to hold on to it, reaching with all I am to keep focused. It's been a while, so I forgot this would happen if I chose this world, but the creeping euphoria replaces everything else.

Music pounds through the speakers and becomes my pulse. There is a camera crew and a sophisticated light and sound setup enhancing the dancing, increasing the sex factor, as the pop singer rounds her mouth over a tune. There are no takes. No breaks in the filming like there are in the real world. Just nonstop dancing and singing and rolling around on satin sheets. This world is simply Jonathan's-smokin'-hot-dance-club. I made it when I was thirteen and crazy for "experience," which would explain the embarrassing name. I hardly go here since I made Kylie-Simms-is-my-girlfriend. There isn't any need.

It takes only a few seconds for the first dancer to notice me. A wet-skinned woman with straight black hair and an outfit the size of an orange peel. She puts a finger under my chin and guides me forward. Sensation overwhelms me.

Besides the rhythm, the dancing, the groping, there's the intoxication. The world drowns my thoughts, like losing myself without the need to do drugs. The room tips a little to the side, but no one falls. We are all writhing and swinging, strobe lights and beat. Thick air weighs on my eyelids. I try to remember why I came to this world just now.

It's impossible to think clearly. So I don't.

The alarm beeps way too early. After a long afternoon, a late night, and only a few hours' sleep, my body aches with the spent effort of my visit to Jonathan's-smokin'-hot-dance-club. I roll onto my side and pull the covers up to my chin. Now that I'm back in the real world, I'm feeling all kinds of awful.

Regret for indulging in Jonathan's-smokin'-hot-dance-club.

Regret for yesterday in the hallway.

Lucky me to awaken with the Kylie incident in my head. What hurts more than anything else is the way she looked at my scar, like it was contagious or something. How could I not have seen she wasn't the right Kylie?

Lying in bed is just an invitation for the nightmare to continue, so I drag myself from under the covers and go into my bathroom. While the water warms for a shower, I stare at my scar in the mirror. A pale, faded reminder of what the real world took and will never return.

The shower feels good, like my layer of awfulness sloughs away and circles the drain. I towel off and throw on a long-sleeved shirt and jeans. When I reach for the sneakers I threw into the closet last night, I rest my hand on the silver shoebox instead. It lies on the floor, a little coffin for a pair of shoes Uncle Joey somehow ended up with and I stole back. My eight-year-old-me shoes. Dried now after their washing in the harbor when I was underwater for God knows how long. Every time I touch that box, I think of the mall, of my mom pressing down on my toes through the sneakers to see if the shoes fit.

I don't disturb the grave by opening the lid. I grab my eighteen-year-old-me shoes, tie them on, and head downstairs.

I find a bottle of water to throw into my backpack with the books I brought home to do no homework last night. Uncle Joey hasn't eaten the last green apple, so I swipe it on my way out the door for the walk to school.

The morning is actually kind of beautiful. Mornings in April come earlier as the days lengthen, and there's a cloud-reflected sunrise firing the sky. It's a good omen against my hopelessness, and somewhere along the road I decide I'm going only to first and second period in the real world, just long enough to see the real Kylie in class and get whatever's going to happen over with. Then I'll finish the day in Kylie-Simms-is-my-girlfriend. Today is relay day at practice, and Kylie and I have finagled a way to be on the same team.

At my E-Hall locker the door pops open on a gym bag swollen with clothes. My stomach sinks as I realize I skipped yesterday's track meet in Kylie-Simms-is-my-girlfriend when I fled home. This is not good, even if the meet was in a world I made. Suddenly, seeing the real Kylie in class doesn't seem as big a deal. I'll be suspended from today's practice for sure, and girl-friend Kylie will have to find someone else for her relay team. My penance for indulging yesterday in Jonathan's-smokin'-hot-dance-club.

Now I have two unpleasant situations scheduled for today—the real Kylie during second period, and Coach Pereira after school.

Here is where one might think: If he made Kylie-Simms-is-my-girlfriend, why can't he make the coach in that world blow off his absence? Answer: It doesn't work that way. Once I make a world, it runs on its own. I could make a new Kylie-Simms-is-my-girlfriend with everything the same, except with a coach who loves his athletes to skip track meets, but it would get exhausting keeping track of every new world I made just because I messed something up. I don't make worlds because I can't take responsibility for my actions. I make them because I'm a sad, pathetic loner. There's a difference.

I grab my history book and creative writing notebook and begin the trek to Non-Western History with Ms. Sawyer. It's an okay class that might be interesting if it weren't full of non-college types who never do any work but somehow still pass. (Yes, I took the class because that description fits me.) In

Kylie-Simms-is-my-girlfriend, by contrast, I have first period AP Economics with Ms. Palumbo, my favorite class and teacher ever, which I'm barred from in the real world because I've failed too many classes due to absences.

I'm one of the first to get to Non-Western History. Even though we're seniors, we have assigned seats like we're in first grade. Mine's in the front by the door. That means everyone in the class gets the chance to walk by and totally ignore me. I've given up trying to catch their eyes on the way in. No one ever says hi.

Class goes by in a whir of terms on the board, definitions in the notebook, a pop quiz on the reading no one did. As the clock ticks closer to the end bell, I get more and more nervous. What will Kylie do about the incident in the hall yesterday? I don't know which would be worse, me finally making her radar or me still being gum on the floor of her control room.

The bell rings. I'm about to find out.

When I enter the hall, it's stuffed with kids. A bunch of gossiping girls clogs the flow like a ten-car pileup. Somehow I get by them and through the busy crossroads of ramps and staircases between the original high school building and the addition. As I enter D-Hall, I'm on the lookout for Kylie. I'm maybe a few seconds later than usual, but in a world of bells and regular routes, it's enough time to get a glimpse of Kylie before class.

She's at the classroom door. She scans the hallway, and her gaze lands on . . . me.

Incapable of staring back at her, I find an important club notice on the wall to pseudo-read. I slow down as I walk by it, mentally kicking myself for having zero guts. When I'm too far to read any more without stopping, I turn toward Kylie, but she's disappeared into the depths of creative writing.

I cross the hall and slide into class. Finding a seat in here is always a challenge because Mr. Eckhart switches up the desk arrangement every day. Today, mercifully, the desks are in formal rows. He must have given a test last period. Kylie has grabbed a seat by the window next to her usual critique partners, Emily Eilson and Zach Odanhu. She's greeting them, but her eyes catch mine in the instant before she sits. That's twice now. I choose the desk farthest away from her in the corner by the book closet.

In Kylie-Simms-is-my-girlfriend I sit with Kylie, Emily, and Zach.

From here I can see her profile against the backdrop of the courtyard beyond the wall of windows. She thumbs through her notebook and opens it to a page that might be the poem we were supposed to polish for homework last night. Damn. I dig through my backpack for my own draft as the late bell rings. I find my notebook and my page of scribbled words and cross-outs. It's not a poem for the ages, but if I had just copied it over neatly, I could have handed it in for credit. Mr. Eckhart is closing the door, his signal that class is beginning. I wish I had thought enough ahead to copy the poem over in Non-Western History, but now it's too late.

Mr. Eckhart is an older teacher, not about-to-retire older but not fresh out of teaching school either. He still has the energy to rearrange his classroom on a period by period basis, and he turns to us now and says, "Okay, writers. Circle it up." I groan inwardly, but everyone else hops into action to help Eckhart make a giant circle of desks for the twenty or so people in the room. Because of our relative positions in the rows, Kylie and I end up on opposite sides of the circle. We are stuck for the whole class having each other in direct sight.

"We'll start with what we finished last night," Eckhart says. He points to four pictures still taped to the board. The first is a lighthouse, the second a carousel, the third a plate of spaghetti, the fourth a gravestone. We had to choose one yesterday and write a poem about it in class using a set of figurative language rules. Then we were supposed to clean up the poem however we liked last night. "I'll give you fifteen minutes to pair up with someone who did not choose the same picture you did. Give feedback, make notes, and we'll come back together and talk about what you've written."

If I had known creative writing would involve so much find-ing of your own partners, I never would've taken the class. I usu-ally end up with Kaitlyn Frost, who in the eyes of Pennington High School is an even bigger pathetic loser than me, and her writing is all about faeries and other stuff that third graders think about. Personally I don't mind her, because I feel we both have a little understanding of loneliness, but I really, really have a hard time finding positive stuff to say about her writing.

So, as usual, Kaitlyn asks me to partner with her, but she's written about the lighthouse, same as me, and isn't allowed to be my partner. She goes off to ask Luis Alves what picture he picked, and suddenly I'm alone. Everyone else is in pairs or threes exchanging poems. Eckhart sees me standing there, waits a few seconds to see what I and the class do, and then clears his throat. He's always encouraging us to watch out for one another, not simply to fall into the safety of choosing our best friends for critique and forget about the rest of the class. The throat clearing means, *Look up, class. Someone's partnerless.* It doesn't happen often. Last time he cleared his throat was for Kaitlyn. As everyone's attention focuses on me, I wish I could squeeze my eyes shut and wake up in a world without worlds.

"Which picture did you pick?" someone asks. I think it's Luis.

"The lighthouse," I say, knowing I won't be able to work with him because Kaitlyn and her lighthouse have already claimed him. Why didn't I just write about the spaghetti? Why didn't I just lie and say I wrote about spaghetti so I could sit down and no one would be staring at me right now?

Kylie, Emily, and Zach whisper to one another. Then Kylie stands up. "I did the gravestone."

Kylie Simms gathers her things to come partner with me.

Kylie Simms smiles reassuringly at Emily and Zach as she leaves to come partner with me.

Kylie Simms moves closer to me.

We sit down in desks that touch each other.

Her legs, her runner's legs, are long and beautiful under her short skirt, and all but one sandal-clad foot disappears under the desktop when she sits and crosses her legs. I know those legs but I don't know them. I know the hands that pass me a poem about a gravestone. They touched me just yesterday morning, but they've never touched me at all. I gave Kylie a ring for her seventeenth birthday, but there are no rings on these fingers.

"Thanks," I say, both for the poem she has passed me and for rescuing me from total annihilation.

"Did you finish yours?" she asks, because she sees that my draft is scribbles.

"Sort of." I rip out the poem and hand it to her. She doesn't say anything, just picks a few fringes off the edge and makes a tiny pile of them in the corner of her desk. If she'd entertained for a second the notion that I might be worth getting to know, I've spoiled it by being a complete and utter slob. She glances at her old critique partners, and I know she'd rather be sitting somewhere else.

Everyone is already reading poems out loud to each other. Eckhart believes in hearing our words out loud. "Do you want me to go first?" Kylie asks.

"Doesn't matter." Why can't I be friendlier? I can't believe how much this Kylie resembles my Kylie. Right down to the tropical scent in her hair, something I couldn't have known when I made my Kylie, because I've never been close enough to smell her real hair before today.

She squints at my scribbles and makes out the title. "The Lighthouse." She huffs a little air through her nose as if commenting on my lack of title cleverness.

THE LIGHTHOUSE
by Jonathan Aubrey

I see a lighthouse on the shore.
I've never seen it lit before.
Today, however, it is bright

With guiding, misty lighthouse light.
The boats go by it one by one,
The fisherpeople having fun.
They leave on time like floating clocks
But do not dash upon the rocks
Because they have the lighthouse lit
They're safe because they pass by it.

She pauses to read it again to herself. I'm a little impressed she's made out all the words through my editing marks. "I like 'guiding, misty lighthouse light,'" she says, and I recognize the tone as the one I use with Kaitlyn Frost when she writes a unicorn poem.

"Yeah, I surprised myself with that bit of brilliance."

She looks up from the page. Her eyes go to my scar, then move away. She reveals no awful reaction, just another person checking themselves in the act of staring at the mark of Frankenstein. "You don't think much of your poem."

"There isn't a lot of thinking to do about it. I mean, I tried, but I'm no poet."

"Well, it's not the waste you think it is." She holds the paper up between us and reads it aloud again. It's so short, it takes only a few seconds. "You don't hear that?"

"Hear what?"

"The rhyme, the meter. It's good. Most people who try to

write a poem with rhyme and rhythm mess up a beat or can't find a word that exactly rhymes. Yours is perfect."

"Great. I have a career ahead of me as Dr. Seuss."

"That's not what I mean."

"You can say it's no good. I can take it. 'Honesty is essential in critique.'" Eckhart's mantra.

"I am being honest."

She is. I know. It's a bad poem, but she's managed to find two good things to say about it. "Okay. So what should I do to improve it?"

She stares at the words again, points to the last two lines. "This sounds a little weird without any punctuation and the two 'because'es. All four of your last lines make a sentence, but the last line should be by itself. I would put a period after 'lit.' That way you have, 'They're safe because they pass by it' as one sharp sentence ending the poem. It's your message."

I take in the advice. It's good. In Kylie-Simms-is-my-girlfriend I get this kind of advice all the time, but I thought for some reason I made Kylie smarter in my world than she is in the real world. Like the smell of her hair, it's another thing I got right without knowing it.

I take the paper from her and put in the suggested period. I don't want to talk about my poem anymore. "Let's do yours," I say, and adjust the angle of her poem on my desk.

MY TREE
by Kylie Simms

I brush fallen acorns from the hollow
between root bumps where I sit sometimes
sharing my day with you
holding you.
I squeeze my eyes closed
and you are sharing your day with me
holding me.
Acorns need more like six inches
than six feet.
I dig the dirt and plant something,
but you're too deep to sprout back.

"Wow," I say, because I can't say what I'm really thinking. I'm stuck on lines five through seven: "I squeeze my eyes closed / and you are sharing your day with me / holding me."

She's making a world.

The idea of Kylie Simms being a world-maker stops me cold. I know she can't be, that in the poem the speaker is merely imagining that the dead person is with her, but Kylie could have used a million ways to describe it other than "I squeeze my eyes closed."

She's waiting for me to say something constructive. "Wow" isn't exactly helpful critique. I mentally shake myself and point to the title, which might be simple but is a hell of a lot more clever than mine. "I like 'My Tree.' At first you think the title means the tree she sits under, but then you come to the end, and the tree is the dead person. Her tree is what would grow from the acorn. Her lover is buried in the ground, and she wants him to grow back."

"What makes you think it's a *she* talking about a *lover?*"

It's obvious, isn't it? But I scan the poem and don't find any gender-specific pronouns. Eckhart has told us over and over not to confuse an author with a speaker, but I just made Kylie the speaker of a poem that could have been about anybody. "Okay. Sorry. It could be a he, but whoever he or she is, there's two mentions of holding each other."

"That doesn't make them lovers."

"Are you saying they're *technically* not lovers because maybe he or she loves him or her from afar? Fine. The speaker is in love with the dead person, whom he or she may or may not have slept with."

Kylie makes some kind of half snort, half laugh. "Can't you think of any other people who might want to hold each other?"

Now that she's mentioned it, I guess there are other people who can hold each other. A parent and child. A sibling and sibling.

Two best friends. Suddenly I'm overwhelmed by a memory of being very small and very sick, my mother and father letting me snuggle in their bed while we watch cartoons and they take turns pressing a cold cloth to my head. There was a time when people in the real world might have wanted to hold me, but I forgot how people can touch each other all the time. The only person who touches me lately is the girl sitting next to me, and it's in the way I assumed when I read the poem.

"So who's the speaker?" I ask. "And who's the dead person?"

She reaches for her poem to take it back. Eckhart is in full hover mode, a sign that time's almost up. Kylie simply shrugs. Whether she doesn't know or just doesn't want to share, I can't tell.

Eckhart claps his hands together. "Let's re-circle, folks."

Kylie smiles like she's apologizing for having to go, but she wastes no time gathering her things and returns to her faraway seat by Emily and Zach.

The various pairs and threes grab desks and shift back into position. Eckhart claims his spot in the circle and starts on his left, asking for summaries of critique discussions. He mows through four people before getting to me.

"Jonathan, let's hear the poems from your group."

I hate reading my stuff out loud, but I'm used to it in this class. Everyone knows by now that I'm no writing star, that

33

my work gets it done but isn't an example of awesomeness. I read "The Lighthouse," then Kylie reads "My Tree," and then Eckhart asks her to talk about my poem.

"'The lighthouse keeps fisherpeople safe,'" she begins. "'Fisherpeople,' besides being a nod to political correctness, shows kind of a carefree attitude from the speaker. The rhyme and rhythm reinforce that, make it whimsical, like the poem shouldn't be taken seriously. But the poem is very serious. It's about a caring force out there keeping people safe. I think the most important line is 'I've never seen it lit before.' That says that for some reason the speaker feels he hasn't been kept safe. The fact that he sees it lit today means he hopes he's finally come under protection. The whole poem's like a defense mechanism. The speaker uses a childish rhyme and meter to make it seem like protection is kind of a joke, but he's hiding behind a carefree attitude only to make it seem like it's no big deal to him if the lighthouse doesn't protect him after all."

I'm stunned. That's pretty deep psycho-crap from someone who didn't say any of this to me in partners. I don't even bring up the fact that my poem doesn't have gender-specific pronouns either, so my speaker isn't necessarily a *he*.

The class takes Kylie's reading and digests it thoughtfully with a few comments. Apparently they didn't realize, as she did, that the poem is about my inner self longing for a lighthouse in my life.

I don't think it's true, but I'm a little uneasy.

Now it's my turn to talk about Kylie's poem. "It's about a person sitting under a tree by a grave. The title is partly about the tree and partly about the dead person sprouting back to life like an acorn. The speaker may or may not be a she and may or not be the dead person's lover."

It's a little sarcastic, the way I say it, but I'm edgy and annoyed about the analysis I've just received, and I want this to be over. The class ignores my tone and does its chitchat thing about what the poem means and who the speaker and dead person could be, and Kylie graciously participates. Finally Eckhart asks, "How many of you have done something like Kylie describes, gone to a cemetery alone to be with a loved one?"

A couple of people actually raise their hands. "My grandmother," says one. "My dad," says the other. A few people look at me. With my whole family in the ground, it might make sense that I'd visit them alone because there's no one else left, but I never have. I've never visited them at all, not even with Uncle Joey. I can't explain why.

Mr. Eckhart, I think, doesn't know about the plane crash, but he must sense the shift in mood, because he changes the subject. "Who did you intend as the speaker and person being mourned?" It's the same question I asked, but she doesn't shrug it off this time. She looks at me. The whole class can see where she's focusing. An awkward couple of seconds pass. I think she's going to say my name. That she put me in a graveyard to be with Mom and Dad and Tess and Auntie Carrie. Her eyes hold mine, and I stop breathing. Can't swallow. She seems to be searching for her answer in my face. Her brow furrows in confusion. Her lips part slightly as she inhales with some inner revelation.

"I . . . don't know."

Everyone seems satisfied with that, so Eckhart moves on to the next poems, but Kylie won't stop looking at me. She wrote a poem about me, and for some reason I feel guilty.

CHAPTER 3

AFTER SCHOOL I GO TO KYLIE–SIMMS–IS–MY–GIRLFRIEND and knock on Coach Pereira's office door. There are dozens of kids in the gym hallway coming and going from the locker rooms. A bunch of runners at the far end review the relay lineup for today's workout. Sprinters and distance runners, throwers and jumpers, boys and girls, all mixed up together. Yesterday's meet was against a weak team, so for mercy's sake some of our top people didn't run, while others tried out events they'd never done before. Between yesterday and today the point is to get in some team bonding through understanding one another's events.

Even though yesterday's meet wasn't tough, we were all supposed to be there. I knock again, and this time Coach answers. "It's open."

I turn the handle and walk in on a meeting he's having with the girls' head coach and the assistant coaches. They hold clipboards with rosters for the various field events.

"Shut the door, Aubrey," Coach says. I stand in the little nook behind it while the coaches finish their game plan for who officiates what today, and when the meeting breaks up, Coach and I are alone. I sit on his famous twill couch and brace myself.

"What happened yesterday?" he asks.

I haven't really prepared an answer. How do you tell your coach you forgot your track meet because you confused your worlds?

"I don't know, Coach. I just . . . I just messed up."

He studies me. He's not the kind of person who takes excuses, even good ones. Mine is a very far cry from a good one.

Besides girlfriend Kylie, Coach Pereira is the only person, even in this world, who can look at my scar and not turn away for shame or pity or whatever else people feel when they see it. He looks at it now, stares at it, really, not shy that I know what he sees or can guess what he's thinking. He's making an excuse for me, and it has something to do with how messed up I am.

"You want to talk about it?" he says.

For the second time today I feel guilty. I shake my head and fight to maintain eye contact. Coach respects eye contact.

He waits a few seconds in case I change my mind, then reaches for a clipboard. "We need someone to pick up the high jump bar today. I already put Jefferson in your relay spot."

"Okay, Coach."

"You know I'm always in this office if you want to talk."

"Okay, Coach." When he rises, it's my cue to get out. I pause with my hand on the door. The high jump bar punishment is embarrassing but generous, coming from him. "Thanks, Coach." I head straight out to the track.

Usually the boys' team and the girls' team warm up separately, two massive swarms of kids, with slower runners petering out in the back like comet tails. Today everyone's been told to warm up and stretch in relay teams, so there are small-group satellites with batons circling the track. Some are doing passing drills with the stick.

Although there's more than a hundred kids out here, I spot Kylie right away. She, Paul Jefferson, Ginny Hamleigh, and Nathan Chen finish their warm-up jog and sit on the infield to stretch. I want to sit with them, but they're doing the team bonding thing, and I'm an outcast for the day. Instead I go over to the high jump to help Coach Tambini, who is adjusting the standards to set the bar at starting height.

"I got the bar today, Coach," I say.

He pretends like he doesn't know I'm in trouble for skipping yesterday, even though he just saw me in Pereira's office. "Thanks," he says, like I'm doing him a favor.

The warm-up period ends. Teams are called to the starting line and arranged in heats for the first race, the four-by-one-hundred meters. High jump designees from several teams start arriving and getting their steps. I volunteer to hold the tape measure for some and spot takeoffs for others. I'm so busy helping, I almost miss Kylie marking off her own steps in the track's third passing zone just meters away. She makes a disappointed face at me and puffs out her lower lip in sympathy for my doghouse status. It should be me passing the baton to her, but I see Paul Jefferson in the second exchange zone ready to go.

The starting gun fires, and Ginny Hamleigh emerges somewhere in the middle of the stagger. She gains ground on the runners to her outside but gets passed by Tom Aguirre, one of the top boy sprinters at Pennington. Nathan Chen takes the baton from Ginny in the first exchange zone, almost running away from her, but thankfully they don't drop it. In a real meet teams keep a decently consistent pace all the way around, but this race has people in it who aren't normally sprinters. Nathan Chen is a two-miler, and he doesn't have sprint wheels. By the time he gets to Paul Jefferson, a javelin thrower, their team is in fourth or fifth place.

Paul doesn't know how to get off the line, so Nathan plows right into him. The baton clanks to the track. Paul has to run back to retrieve it. He's pretty fast, though, for a thrower who never runs, and since no one else had a good handoff either, when he approaches Kylie, he's back in the thick of things. Kylie times her takeoff perfectly and reaches back for the baton without breaking stride. She passes two teams in the exchange zone and sets off after the leaders.

She has only a hundred meters to close a considerable gap, but she's doing it. People run down the infield shouting at the racers. The finish line is at the opposite side of the track from the high jump, so I don't see the finish in the mass of people. A cheer goes up.

Coach Tambini marks off someone's clear of the bar and smiles at me. Impressed that I managed to snag such a fine girlfriend. For the moment I puff with pride.

The relay pseudo-meet takes about an hour and a half, and when the equipment is all picked up, I wait for Kylie in my fancy red Uncle Joey car. By the time she plops down in the passenger seat, there are only a few athletes left in the senior lot. She clicks her seat belt firmly into place. I haven't fastened mine. I rarely do, despite the law. Seat belts make me feel trapped.

I start the car and let it idle, not ready to drive her home.

"We could've used you on the four-by-eight," she says. She means she missed me.

I place my hands on the steering wheel and watch a couple

of sophomores walk over to the rotary to wait for their ride. "I'm sorry. I screwed up."

She settles back into her seat and watches the sophomores too. "I worried the whole meet and all night when you didn't answer your phone," she says. "Why didn't you at least call me?"

I would have called her if I'd been in her world, but my real-world phone just doesn't reach this far, and Jonathan's-smokin'-hot-dance-club made me forget anyway. She thinks that when I disappear I'm taking depressed alone time. She thinks I need solitude to deal with life. I don't correct her, because the alternative is to tell her I'm in a different world.

"Do you have your creative writing notebook with you?" I ask.

"What does that have to do with you not calling me?"

"Do you have your poem you wrote for today?"

She exhales impatiently. "Yes."

"Can I see it?"

She turns and gets up on her knees to dig through the backpack she flung into the backseat. Her body fills the space between the front seats, brushes against me, and I smell the sweat and dirt of the track meet mixed with that tropical something both Kylies like putting in their hair.

She pulls out a piece of notebook paper and falls back into the passenger seat. "Why do you want this?"

I'm not sure I do, but I need to check. I reach for it, but she pulls it toward the window, away from me. "Jonathan, what's wrong?"

"Nothing."

"You tell me not to worry when you disappear, but you've never missed a meet."

"I'm fine."

"Are you really?"

"I will be when you let me see that." I point to the poem.

She sighs and hands it over. I unfold it and read.

MY TREE

by Kylie Simms

I brush fallen acorns from the hollow
between root bumps where I sit sometimes
sharing my day with you
holding you.
I squeeze my eyes closed
and you are sharing your day with me
holding me.
Acorns need more like six inches
than six feet.
I dig the dirt and plant something,
But you're too deep to sprout back.

Although I don't have the other Kylie's poem for comparison, it appears that this version, which was written by my totally separate girlfriend in a totally separate world, is an exact match. Nothing like this has ever happened before.

CHAPTER 4

KYLIE DOESN'T ASK ANY MORE QUESTIONS. "AWKWARD silence" describes the whole ride to her house.

I turn into her driveway and shift into park. She gets out and pulls the seat forward to reach her pack. She walks around the back of the car over to my window. I wind it all the way down.

"Why did you freak out about my poem?"

"I didn't freak out."

"Yes, you did." She rests her hands on the open window, leans in.

"I have to know," I say. "Who is it about?"

She chews her lip, making me wait for the answer because I won't explain why her poem bothered me. "No one in particular. Some woman by the grave of her husband."

"A she and a dead lover."

"What?"

"Never mind. As long as it's not about me."

"I only write love poems for you." She smiles. The ice breaks. We're both thinking of the Valentine's Day poem she wrote a couple of months ago.

"Okay," I say.

"Okay?"

I nod as she leans all the way in and kisses me on the cheek. "I'll call you later. Please pick up." When I nod again, she seems satisfied and goes up the walk to her door. At least to her, everything is all right. I really am freaked out.

I pull out of the driveway and head to Uncle Joey's, overwhelmed by questions. What does it mean that both Kylies wrote the same exact poem? Which Kylie wrote the poem first? It has to be my world mix-up. I was worried about the real Kylie hating me, but this poem thing is the actual fallout. How could almost kissing someone in one world make people in two different worlds share a poetry brain?

When I get to Uncle Joey's, the driveway is blocked by an unfamiliar car—silver, midsize, a little worn. I have to park along the curb.

I don't see the driver anywhere, so I head inside and find the front door open a sliver. My mental warning bells start clanging. I push the door open and notice that the keypad on the security system is still glowing. It reads *System Disabled*. Someone has entered the correct code.

It must be Uncle Joey, but the car outside isn't his, and it's parked all askew like the driver was in a hurry.

I don't call out. Instead I creep through the foyer and peek into the kitchen. No one there. I pass through the kitchen and the living room toward Uncle Joey's wing. He's not in his bedroom, his bathroom, or his massive closet. Then I hear footsteps above. Someone's on my floor.

Terror seizes me. An intruder is in my house. No way could it be Uncle Joey, who never ventures upstairs. My first instinct is to hide, and my second is to run. I should just blink out and go back to the real world. Deal later with the aftermath of whatever's occurring, when I come back to wait for Kylie's call.

I don't do any of those things. I have to know who's up there, so I steal back through the living room and kitchen, grabbing a knife just in case, and round the corner so I can see the landing above. A figure pauses at the top of the stairs. I clutch the knife a little tighter and retreat a step. A pair of legs scrambles into view, and I see a girl, a high school girl with long black hair and a heart-pumping figure shown off by her tight jeans and tight tank top. She has a tattoo on her shoulder I can't clearly make out.

In her hands is the silver shoebox I keep in my closet.

I drop the knife, and jump back when it hits my foot.

She turns toward my racket, and I see her face. I don't know her, but I'm hit with déjà vu stronger than a baseball bat to the head. She dashes down the stairs and out the front door. I run after her, but she's fast. She's already at her car and throws the door open. I'm able to grab it before she can seal herself in. She tries to yank it closed while jamming her keys into the ignition, and as the car starts, she puts both hands to the door and pulls. I let go because I want to keep my fingers, and she puts the car in reverse and hits the gas.

I'm only a distance runner, but I surprise myself with how quickly I sprint to my own car, start it up, and pull it onto the road. She's already at the end of my street, but she's stopped at the stop sign because of traffic. I'm almost to her bumper when she peels out, and I barely slow down before swinging my car out into the traffic behind her.

She puts her hand to her rearview mirror and gawks back at me. We're on Marberry Road, which is fairly busy, since it's the main access to west Pennington. She goes the speed of the traffic, and I get a twinge of disappointment she's not good enough to make this a high-speed chase. Marberry connects to Main Street via a fork, and we both merge into the greater traffic. I cut someone off to stay directly behind her, and get the blare of a horn for thanks.

No problem, buddy.

Why did some girl just steal my old shoes? Did she break

into my house with the intent to steal them? And *who is she?* Combine this with the Kylie questions, and I might have to hire a private investigator.

The girl puts on her directional and turns right onto Pine Street. I stick to her bumper, concentrating on being too close for her comfort. At the end of the street, it takes me a moment to register the stone archway—Pine Street Cemetery. I hit the brake and skid to a stop. I can't follow. Not in there.

This is the only entrance I know of. I cut the ignition, stay in the car, and wait.

An hour later the girl still hasn't come out, and I realize I've just wasted sixty minutes of my life. I drive back to Uncle Joey's and reset the alarm code. Though the thief girl looked familiar, I don't have a name to put with the face. I can't think of a single reason why she'd want my shoes, and I can't think of a single way she'd even know they were in my closet. Not even Uncle Joey knows I have them, but she must have been searching for them specifically. No one surprises themselves by taking a pair of ratty sneakers during a break-in, not when there are so many more attractive things in Uncle Joey's house.

I wait downstairs for girlfriend Kylie's call and grab a glass of milk before sitting on the couch. Shows blur past as I scan the channels, worlds birthing and dying. Something in my head is on fast-forward. I realize I have an ear cocked to hear if the girl intruder returns.

The phone rings.

"Hello?"

"You picked up!" Kylie says.

"I said I would."

"I wasn't sure I believed you."

"I am one hundred percent capable of being trusted today."

"So you're feeling better?"

"Mostly."

"Wanna do something tonight?"

"How about Lacy Pastry for a hot chocolate?"

"Will you pick me up?"

"Give me ten minutes. And, Kylie?"

"Yeah?"

"Bring your creative writing notebook. I need you to write a poem."

CHAPTER 5

WE PICK A SPOT BY THE WALL AND ARRANGE OUR HOT chocolates and plates of pastry on the glass table. She's chosen a triangle of baklava, and I've picked a fat éclair absolutely smothered in chocolate.

Lacy Pastry is a girlie shop when it comes to decor. Doilies sit under the napkin holders on each table. Thick, protective plastic wraps the white chairs upholstered in lace. Every inch of wall space is covered in a Victorian mural—ladies with wide lacy skirts, lacy gloves, lacy parasols, men in top hats carrying canes, roads peppered with horse-drawn carriages and lined with flower gardens. Every time I look at that mural, I think it might be interesting to make it into a world, but then I ask myself what I'd even do if I got there.

Kylie takes the lid off her hot chocolate, stirs the whipped cream into the cup, and blows on it before venturing a sip. I put the cup to my lips and take a slog through the hole in the cover, then pick up my éclair. It's so damn good, it's worth braving the girlie decor time after time.

"So you want me to write a poem," she says. She picks up her baklava and bites. Honey drips onto her chin, and she catches it with the tip of a finger.

"It doesn't have to be a good one, but I think it has to be about me."

"You think?"

"It doesn't have to be a love poem."

"Where are you getting these rules?"

"God."

She smiles. "Uh, doubtful."

"You doubt that God talks to me?"

"I doubt you'd listen if He did."

"Fair point." We've done the religion talk. Kylie was raised in a churchgoing Catholic family with rather liberal religious views. She did CCD and First Communion and all that but goes to church only on Christmas and Easter. Despite the fact that she's a questioner of religion, she's the most spiritual person I know. I kind of envy that about her.

I, on the other hand, have had such a considerable amount of crap happen in my life that I prefer to think there's no such thing as God. If there were, He or She would have a lot to answer for.

"Okay, the voice of the Almighty is not in my head. I'd rather not explain, but I need to do a test, and you're the only one who can help me."

"By writing a poem about you."

"Yes."

"And not a love poem."

"Maybe not this time."

"There'll be a next time?"

"Depends on the voices."

She shakes her head and rolls her eyes, but she is smiling. She's so going along with my craziness. I want to reach out and give her a great, big bear hug, that's how much I love her at this moment.

"So what kind of poem?"

"Something about how I like éclairs?" I pose with the pastry in front of my open mouth.

She pretends to consider this possibility. "I'm not sure éclairs provide sufficient poetical inspiration."

"That's a shame." I take a huge bite. Éclairs inspire me.

"How about running? I think I could do a little something about running."

"That should work."

She opens her notebook, then fishes in her purse for a pen. I sit silently, polishing off my dessert while hers goes untouched for the moment. "Do you want serious or funny?" she asks.

I shrug. "Your call."

She sips her cocoa and gets to work. Her right hand scribbles words on the paper, pauses, crosses words out, replaces scratches with new words. I'm tempted to read across the table, but the truth is I'd rather be surprised, so I shift in my seat so my back's against the wall and I'm facing the inside of the shop. Two other tables host solitary coffee drinkers, and one table by the window holds a giggly group of middle schoolers all sharing a giant slushy drink. The germophobe in me cringes as the one straw gets sucked by so many different mouths one after the other.

A man at the counter orders a coffee and a dozen cookies. He's dressed in a suit, like the ones Uncle Joey wears, or maybe even my dad used to wear, and I wonder how old the kids are who'll be eating chocolate chip and oatmeal raisin cookies with him tonight.

As far as I can remember, my dad didn't bring me home cookies this late at night. He was always home when I got back from school. If I were a kid again, I wonder if I would prefer cookies from a late dad to no cookies from a dad who was always there. Knowing what happened to my dad, I'm ashamed to think that the stupid little kid me might have wanted the cookies. I give that regret half a second and push it away.

I drain my hot chocolate. Kylie takes a quick bite of baklava and a sip of cocoa, but her pen keeps moving. The germ-sharing preteens leave in a flurry of voices, and in the silence following their exit, Kylie puts down the pen. "Done."

I scooch my chair so I'm facing her again. "Is it serious or funny?"

"It's done." She turns the notebook so I can read right-side up, then stuffs the remaining baklava into her mouth.

JONATHAN AUBREY
by Kylie Simms

He runs the mile,
Sometimes the half- or the two-mile.
It's so much better
To have a distance runner boyfriend
Than a sprinter,
Because I get to savor his race
A lap at a time,
Watching his stride,
The swing of his arms,
The determination on his face,
And cheer for him each time he passes.
But nothing is finer

Than running beside him
Casual mile after mile
With no particular finish line.
Just him and me
And our breathing
And the trail,
And I wish running could be done
Holding hands.

"Jeez, Kylie."

"I know. I'll edit it at home if you want."

"No, no, don't change a thing. But you wrote a love poem."

"I didn't set out to, but I didn't have a choice, with you sitting right there."

It's a compliment. That remark, the poem. I'm seized again with the urge to hug her. She licks the last of the honey from her fingers and pulls a napkin from the dispenser on the doily. For a second I'm a voyeur watching her through a one-way glass. Her beautiful brown eyes shift to the door as some new customer jangles the bell by coming in. I have a flash of memory from earlier in the day—that girl who stole my shoes had nice eyes too, but hers were smothered in makeup.

"Can I take this?" I make like I'm going to tear the sheet out of her notebook.

"That's why I wrote it, right?" Rip. Out it comes.

"Do you have a lot of homework tonight?" I ask.

"A little. Why?"

"Wanna bring it over? I have a little too."

Of course, we both know that means quality time on the couch. At least until Uncle Joey gets home.

I drive Kylie home a little after ten. Uncle Joey's still not home, but she's tired and I'm tired, and we did manage to get our homework done before moving on to more intimate pursuits. But all good things must come to an end.

After I take the car back to Uncle Joey's, I squeeze my eyes shut and emerge in my bedroom in the real world. I check my closet to make sure my real-world little Jonathan sneakers haven't been snatched. They're resting peacefully at the back. I drop Kylie's poem onto the nightstand and collapse into bed, not bothering to get undressed.

Sleep comes quickly, but I wake several times in the night, chasing the leftovers of dreams I can't remember. It's the kind of night I have every so often, and I'm not surprised when I wake up exhausted to the alarm clock radio. Kylie's poem still sits on my nightstand. I fold it and put it into my backpack, take my shower, dress, and head to school.

First period Non-Western History goes by in its usual blur of notes and anecdotes. I didn't have creative writing homework last night, so I have nothing to copy over. I'm so tired, I catch myself falling asleep a couple of times. By the time the bell rings, I'm fully awake, though. The anxiety of seeing real Kylie grips me like mortal fear.

I wind my way through the halls, navigating clusters of people stopped at lockers or doorways, and get to creative writing early. To my surprise Kylie's already there, just settling into a seat. Today the desks are arranged in groups of four. Only three other kids have arrived, and they're sitting with one another in a grouping at the front. I shuffle along the wall to the grouping farthest away from Kylie.

I pull my notebook and pen and girlfriend Kylie's running poem out of my backpack. I tuck the poem into the back of the notebook, not sure what I intend to do with it. It's not like I can show it to real Kylie. It's in her handwriting, assuming her hand-writing is the same in both worlds, and the title has my name followed by the attribution of her name. If someone showed me a romantic running poem that my double wrote in another world, I think my head would explode. My purpose today is not to make Kylie lose her head. It's to see if she wrote the same poem last night. I want to know if yesterday's matching grave poems were an isolated incident I can chalk up to cosmic weird-ness, or if the Kylies really have been connected somehow.

I don't know how I'll find out. If she wrote a poem on her own last night, it's not like she'd show me, is it? *Oh, Jonathan, by the way, I wrote a poem about us running together. Wanna see?*

Emily and Zach come crashing into the quiet of the room Kylie's head pops up. Her eyes find me, and she looks quickly away. I try not to stare, but I can't help but notice the color rising in her cheeks.

Kaitlyn Frost arrives and sits across from me, effectively blocking my view of Kylie. I resist the urge to strain around her to see, but I'm annoyed. Luis Alves plunks himself down as well, and we almost have a full four. That last seat is very likely to remain empty.

The rest of the class comes in right before the late bell and settles into seats. Mr. Eckhart clears his throat and rubs his hands together like they're cold. "Today is group day," he says. "Count off by fives, please."

We do so. Kylie is a two, and I'm a three. I'm not sure whether to be disappointed or relieved that we're not in the same group. People grab their stuff and reorganize according to the count-off. I move toward the window and one of my new group mates, Zach, while Kylie ends up with Luis back where I came from. I try to sit facing Kylie, but Amber Hirsch sneaks in before me, and I'm left with a seat overlooking the courtyard.

My group is me, Zach, Amber, and Claude Arsenault. Overall

not bad, though I'm sure they see me as the weakest writer. Zach is my friend in Kylie-Simms-is-my-girlfriend. Amber is one of those girls with glasses who's mousy but not bad-looking and has her own group of friends. Claude is quiet and a little overweight, and one of creative writing's stars because everything he writes is sarcastic-hilarious.

"Okay," begins Eckhart. He rubs his hands together again. "In addition to group day, today is also contest day."

A ripple of excitement runs through the room. We've had two contest days so far, and the prizes were gift cards to a local bookstore/coffee shop. Only ten dollars, but hey, that's a date over two fancy hot drinks, unless you want to buy half a book.

"You have eight minutes to write a descriptive paragraph of no more than one hundred words," Eckhart says. "The catch is that you may not use visual imagery. You must rely solely on the other senses. When time's up, you will share your piece with your group for critique, then print out an anonymous, improved version for posting around the room. The class will then read one another's paragraphs and vote for the piece that evokes the strongest sensory images. Questions?"

No one raises a hand. A few are already writing. I'm totally blank on things to describe without using the sense of sight, so I'm certain I'm not taking a date for coffee tonight. My group mates and I all exchange looks and then get to work.

Let's see. I could write about love. You can't see that and you can feel it, but I can't think of any sensory images that don't include seeing or clichés. I'm pretty sure cliché won't work, unless I go over-the-top cliché for effect, but that's been done before. By Claude Arsenault, actually, about a rap star trying to talk to a wall.

I rest my forehead on my hand and try to imagine what I might hear or smell if I were somewhere else. In Jonathan-is-a-hero it's all laser blast burns, alien squeals, and human shouts. I haven't been there in so long, it might be fun to write about it. In Jonathan's-smokin'-hot-dance-club the music is so loud, it hurts, and there's a whole bunch of touching I don't think Eckhart would approve of writing about in class.

Maybe a track meet.

Maybe this classroom.

I bet I could win if I did the crashing airplane.

The screaming, the heat of the fire, the plunge into the icy harbor. Salt in my throat.

Maybe the hospital bed after?

No. No. No. It's not that I'll fall apart if I think about it. Enough time has passed that I don't break down blubbering with every remembrance. It's just . . . no one at school cared about the details back when it happened. I'm not going to gratify any curiosity now.

Swinging on monkey bars might do. Cold metal on the hands and nothing but air beneath the feet. Kids screaming all around. It's as good an idea as any, and since I'm the last one to start writing, it'll have to do.

Several silent minutes tick by while the only sound in the room is rustling paper and scratching pens. Although I was the last to start, I'm the first done in my group, mostly because I care the least about getting every last word sparkly perfect. Zach finishes second. Claude, smirking to himself over what is undoubtedly a paragraph worth smirking at, finishes third. Amber is still tweaking things when Mr. Eckhart calls the class to attention.

"You have twenty minutes to exchange, critique, print, and post. Starting now." Amber dashes off some final correction.

"Should we just read our own?" asks Claude.

We all nod. One by one we read our paragraphs out loud. Claude's is hilarious. It's about the tastes and smells in a Pokémon game. Amber's is about lying in grass. Zach's is about driving a car. My monkey bars win moderate praise. We give one another feedback and then head for the computers at the back of the room to type and print. The class trickles up to Eckhart's desk for scotch tape to post our masterpieces on the wall.

Eckhart goes around with a red pen writing a number on each anonymous paper. "Remember, no choosing someone in your own group. Write the number of your favorite on one of these." He holds up little squares of blue paper. "And drop it in here." He holds up an empty tissue box we've used for voting before. "Begin."

We all head for different starting places. Kylie chooses a spot by Eckhart's desk, and I land three or four papers down from her. I know where Claude's masterpiece is posted, because of the laughter already erupting on the next wall. As I go around the room, I can guess, with decent accuracy, the author of each paragraph. We've been reading and listening to one another's work for months now, and we have this sort of familiarity with one another's words. It's the closest thing I have to friends in the real world, and I'm surprised at how strongly I like these people all of a sudden.

Kylie slides one entry closer to me, and suddenly I'm holding up the line. I read the words in front of me quickly and move on. Apple picking. A circus. Dinnertime. The beach. Kylie glances my way with more and more frequency as I round the corner and begin my third wall. Then I come to this:

What I hear is rhythm. Step, step, huff, step, step, huff. Stones crunch, twigs snap, fallen leaves crackle. The air is rubbed pine needles and early frost; the ground is soft on soles of

air, or gel. We match strides perfectly, the beat
of seasons and earth running through us. The
autumn sun, at its low angle, is as useless as a
flame in a picture. But a new warmth flushes
more strongly than miles of covered trail—
step, step, huff, swing, swing—he holds my
hand.

Wow. Just . . . wow.

I don't like it quite as much as the poem folded in my notebook, but there is no doubt in my mind that Kylie wrote this.
There is no doubt it's about me. I inhale some courage and turn
toward her, acknowledging openly that she has been monitoring
my progress.

She studies again the paragraph posted before her, but then
she takes her own breath of courage and looks back at me.
There are a couple of students busy reading between us, so
we're partly protected by a shield of their bodies, but we are
unquestionably, unequivocally looking at each other. The skin
on my neck prickles. I can't imagine what she's thinking or feeling, but for me the wash of emotion is strong enough to stop my
heart, like a near-death experience, or meeting God. Something
life-changing happened when she made the decision to meet
my eyes. We're going to have to talk about this. I am not only on

Kylie Simms's radar. I am holding her hand in the control room.

The rest of the class is unaware that the earth just moved beneath them. The students between us are ready to read Kylie's paragraph, and I'm in the way. I step back to let them pass. Kylie's expression is uncertain, maybe even scared. I imagine she's a little messed up over this.

I find my voice first. "Can I talk to you after practice today?"

She closes her mouth. I think her lips came unsealed with a gasp when we looked at each other. She chews on her upper lip and nods. "Five o'clock in the senior lot."

CHAPTER 6

I ARRIVE EARLY TO WATCH THE END OF PRACTICE, BUT there are only a few pole vaulters and a hurdler still on the track. I assume Kylie's in either the weight room or the locker room, so I sit on the curb where I can see the gym door and the senior lot at the same time. I don't see Kylie's car, and it occurs to me she may have changed her mind.

I really hope that's not the case.

I'm usually in Kylie-Simms-is-my-girlfriend this time of day, finishing up my own workout. Today I made a lame excuse to girlfriend Kylie, which she accepted without question. Then I hurried through a locker room shower so I could be here for real Kylie. Practice didn't go so well because I was agonizing over what, exactly, would happen at this meeting.

I only know what I want to happen—to learn how real Kylie is getting her poetry inspiration from my girlfriend—but it's not the kind of thing I can just ask her. What I *don't* want to happen is to scare her away with crazy-strange questions. It'll be better to talk with her a little before I decide what to say, and that's what has my adrenaline level at flood stage. How can I talk to this girl I've admired from afar for so long? Especially since she already knows something weird is going on? Maybe she's only a little curious. Maybe she's completely freaked out. Maybe she wants to ask specific questions. I can't make a plan of attack before I know where she's coming from.

"Hey, Jonathan."

I jump. It's Luis Alves from creative writing. He's hauling a gigantic duffel bag, and I vaguely remember he's on the baseball team.

"Hey."

I want him to keep walking, but he stops right in front of me. This is awkward because I can't recall a single time someone from school engaged me in a conversation outside the classroom. Does this mean we're kind of friends? Is he just being polite?

"I've never seen you around after school," he says.

"Yeah."

"Somethin' up?"

"No."

He looks at me like he can't understand my monosyllabic English. I'm being rude, but I want him to go away. Kylie's car just pulled into the parking lot, and I don't want him to know I'm meeting her. Plus my adrenaline's starting to give me the shakes.

"Okay, man." Because I just glanced behind him, he looks over his shoulder toward Kylie, then back at me. "See you tomorrow."

"See you in class," I say, proud to have mostly completed a sentence. Luis greets Kylie on his way across the lot, and she must have asked him if he'd seen me, because he turns and points a finger. Okay, so he knows. Whatever.

Luis heads out of the picture as Kylie—the real, honest-to-God Kylie—walks up to me. She's obviously been home to shower and change, and although the reason might be other plans after this, it's nice to think that she cleaned up just for me. Her hair flows softly over her shoulders. Rarely do I get to see her hair when it's not tied up, even in Kylie-Simms-is-my-girlfriend.

I stand and offer my traditional witty greeting. "Hey."

"Hey."

I can't read her emotion. A little nervousness maybe, but I get the sense she's annoyed. Does Jonathan Aubrey annoy Kylie Simms? If so, we're off to a bad start. Vaguely I wonder if the other Kylie in my made-up world is annoyed with me because I'm not around. They share a poetry brain, why not an annoyed-with-Jonathan brain? My gut says that whatever Kylie's feeling right now has nothing to do with her otherworld twin and everything to do with something the matter with me.

"So?" she says. "What did you want to talk about?"

I hoped we'd do this somewhere other than the student parking lot. I don't know this Kylie well enough to invite myself into her car, and I didn't bring my own car—not that this Kylie would be comfortable inside it. We could go sit in the stands by the track, but the pole vaulters are still there.

"I just . . . I wanted . . ." She folds her arms and settles her weight on one foot. This is killing me. "I thought we should talk about what you wrote today." Not the subtlest start, but her impatience is urging me to get to the point faster than I'd hoped.

"What about it?"

It was about me. "I thought it should have won." Duh. Did I just say that?

She says nothing. Kylie really isn't one to put up with nonsense.

"Okay." I take a deep breath and spit out some truth. "I thought you were watching me as we went around the room. Something weird happened when I read your piece. Maybe I was imagining it, but if something weird didn't happen, we wouldn't be standing here, right?"

Her shoulders drop about a quarter inch. She sucks some of the gloss off her lip and watches her foot play with some sand on the asphalt. "So?"

"I just thought you might want to talk about it. Maybe that and your tree poem from before."

Her head snaps up. "What's that got to do with anything?"

"I don't know."

The bang of shed doors announces that the pole vault equipment has been put away. Finally. "I don't want to stand here by the road," I say. "Can we sit in the bleachers for a few minutes?"

She nods and turns. An awkward silence settles between us. Usually silence with girlfriend Kylie is comfortable, companionable, but this silence trembles. I'm conscious of the need to keep appropriate distance between our bodies. We climb the tiers of benches and sit at the top in the middle. We aren't alone on the track. Some middle-aged guy is walk-jogging laps, but for now he's opposite us on the far turn. Kylie and I sit side by side—I can't believe I'm sitting here next to her after all these years—and watch him.

She perches her feet on the bench below and leans back into the rail. "Have you ever gone running, Jonathan?"

A hundred times with you. She must be thinking about the piece she wrote today. Maybe her inspiration for writing it. "Not really."

"Does that mean never?"

"I guess so."

"So I wouldn't have seen you running in town or anything?"

"Not likely."

The walk-jogger reaches the top of the straightaway. In another minute or so he'll pass in front of us. His face is obscured by shadows. The track doesn't surround a football field, as it does in so many other schools, so it doesn't have stadium lights. Simply one orange sulfur thing that buzzes when lit. The sun's late afternoon glow comes to us through a tangle of bud-branched trees opposite.

"Kylie," I start. I think I'm about to say stuff I might want to take back, but she's on the edge of what she really wants to ask. If this conversation bombs, I can always go hide in my made-up world until final exams are over. I'm not graduating anyway. "I almost bumped into you the other day in the hall. Do you remember that?"

She nods.

"Since then—please don't take this the wrong way—you kinda keep popping into my head."

Her intake of breath is slow but audible. "What kinds of things pop into your head?"

I'm lying at this point, so I have to guess what's been happening in her headspace. It could be anything from subconscious poetry topics to, well—is it conceited to hope she might dream about me? "I think that lighthouse poem I wrote might have been about you." It wasn't, but it seems an easy-ish place to start.

"How so?"

What was it she said in class? I need the lighthouse's protection. Well, if I tell her she's my lighthouse, I would expect us both to heave our lunches over the corniness of it. She liked the "fisherpeople having fun" line, but I don't remember why. Probably she wouldn't think it a compliment to be told she's the happy fisher. "Maybe 'about you' isn't right. I think it's more I pictured you while I wrote it, how you would react if you ever read it. I wanted to impress you. But I don't remember needing to impress you so much before that incident in the hall."

"Hmph," is all she answers. I'm grateful walk-jogger is down there, because he's something to look at while our conversation stalls for half a lap.

Since I offered the tidbit, however untrue, about me writing a poem for her, she should tell me about her poem, but she doesn't. Instead she asks, "Do you have a girlfriend?"

"Uh . . ." I have to clear my throat in surprise. "Not really."

"Like you don't 'really' go running?"

"This world hasn't been too good for either my running or my bachelor status."

She goes ultra-still, the way people do when they realize they've said something to dredge up memories of a dead family and a coma. I meant that to be funny, mostly a joke to myself because I run and date Kylie in another world, but I realize too late that she takes it to mean because of the airplane crash.

We sit for a long time, unable to pierce the cocoon of self-consciousness that forms around us, separating the experience of our conversation from the almost empty track and the dropping temperature as the sunlight filters through the trees. I fold my arms over my torso in defense against the April chill. Kylie remains motionless.

Walk-jogger stops at a gate not far below and reaches for his toes. He circles his arms a few times and leans side to side, then glances up at us as he swings through the gate and disappears into the parking lot. Kylie and I are alone with the orange sulfur lamp and swelling shadows.

"When we were in third grade . . . ," Kylie says slowly. Her gaze remains fixed on the infield below. "I wanted to be your friend. Hunter LeRoy shoved me once, and you told Zach not to pick him for dodgeball at recess. Since you and Zach were always captains, Hunter didn't get to play until he said sorry to me. Do you remember that?"

I have a vague recollection of Kylie in a dodgeball circle. I don't remember defending her against Hunter LeRoy.

Hunter LeRoy was always *my* bully. "I wish I could say I did."

"Then a few weeks later, you didn't come to school. Mrs. Costa said you were in the hospital and might not be back for a long time. I made you a card but didn't know how to send it."

This is all news to me. I don't talk much with my girlfriend Kylie about the past because her past is just a bunch of memories she woke up with when I made her. I've assumed she carried a copy of the real Kylie's childhood with her, but maybe that's not true.

"When you finally did come back," Kylie continues, "you were different. You walked funny and couldn't play dodgeball. You didn't talk to anyone, not even Zach. People made fun of you because of your face, and I hated that I didn't have a dodgeball game to take away from them. When you started staying inside for recess, I asked Mrs. Costa if I could stay in one day, but when I did, you ignored me. I didn't understand. It was third grade. You just became like a statue after a while. No one even made fun of you anymore because you just sat there in your own world and didn't respond to anything."

Although I'm not lying when I say I'm basically okay on the subject of the crash, this is not one of those okay times. My hands are trembling. Kylie is throwing little-kid memories at me that I haven't examined in many, many years. Usually I have jumbled flashbacks of the plane going down, or being smothered by water, or yearnings for my family to be alive. The idea that there was a kid in my third-grade class who wanted to reach out to me is painful to hear, especially because that kid was Kylie. And I don't remember her doing it.

"The truth is," she continues, "when you almost bumped into me in the hallway, I had dreamed about you the night before. In the dream I walked to your house and went up to your room to watch you sleeping. It was so weird when our paths crossed later at school. Like fate or something. Maybe God's giving me a chance to apologize for not trying hard enough in third grade."

If she were my girlfriend Kylie, I'd make a God crack, but I've never had the religion talk with this girl. Plus, I'm a little in awe that she actually did have a dream about me. "So was the cemetery poem because of your guilt?"

She folds her arms like I'm doing, as if she has suddenly realized it's cold. "I don't know. I was thinking about how you were before the accident, and how you put Hunter LeRoy in his place to defend me. Back then all I wanted was to be your friend." She pauses and takes a big, shoulder-moving breath. "Then last night I got this idea about running with you in the woods. It came out in the piece I wrote today."

We both know the hand-holding run was romantic, not third-grade friendly. She's just admitted that, for at least the time it took to write that piece, she had romantic feelings about me. It doesn't seem, however, that she understands them. But who does? Who can explain what causes you all of a sudden to feel something for another person?

Except I know it's not spontaneous love. I made a world where I made Kylie love me, and somehow that's affecting this Kylie. It's not natural and it's not sweet. I can't tell if this Kylie is trying to tell me she'd like to start something, but I don't know if that's a good idea. For years I've been, as she says, nothing but a statue, devoid of personhood to an entire population of my peers.

It's an identity I've come to accept. It's an identity that's been safe for a really long time, and I don't want to give it up. I have what I need in Kylie-Simms-is-my-girlfriend even if that world isn't real.

But this isn't real either. This Kylie wouldn't be having romantic running thoughts if it weren't for the other Kylie. Take that world away, and would this Kylie still write me a poem? I don't know, but I wish she would.

What I really want is to dive into her and soak up her thoughts, the excitement of getting to know her all over again for real. She's different from girlfriend Kylie. Less perfect? More substantial? Harder to decipher than my ever-compliant girlfriend. She's talking to me with the same frankness my girlfriend does, but that frankness feels less warm, more analytical.

She's not being unfriendly, but I'm surprised by how much she can talk about feelings without expressing many.

Her demeanor is more distant than my girlfriend's, but maybe "guarded" is the better word, because she's choosing how to word her frankness, not just pouring out uncensored thoughts. Not knowing what she's holding back is unfamiliar territory because my girlfriend holds back nothing.

"I loved what you wrote today," I say. "It means a lot that someone can think of me like I'm alive."

For the first time since we sat down, she actually looks at me. I wish it were love in her eyes, but it's sympathy. Sympathy, at this point, sucks.

"I wish I had come back for another indoor recess," she says, and I imagine she's picturing how transformed my life would have been if only we had shared crayon sessions in elementary school. I don't know if she's envisioning herself as my savior or my friend. There's a huge difference.

I also don't know if she means she's sad it took this long to finally notice me again, or if she can't be my friend now that I've grown up to be such a freak.

She reaches inside her jacket pocket and pulls out a folded manila envelope. Then she stands. I stand too.

"I don't want to makes things difficult," she says. "I might have led you to think something about my feelings for you. The truth is, I thought of you when I wrote a couple of things. I don't know why." She puts the envelope into my hand and closes my fingers over the edge. She turns to go, but hesitates, still clasping my hand under hers.

It's a magical heartbeat of contact. Not at all what I expected after the farewell words she just delivered. We both stare at her hand folded over mine and the envelope, and I don't bat an eyelash for fear of scaring her off.

It's probably only a few seconds that pass, but since I don't know how many seconds there'll be, the time expands. I abandon focus on everything but her hand. She has long fingers like my girlfriend's, warmer than I expected in the April chill. I can see only her thumbnail since the other fingers are curled under, and it's polished a pale pink. My girlfriend never wears colors on her nails.

Kylie gives the side of my hand the tiniest caress with that thumb, so small I could pretend it didn't happen, except for the sparks that shoot through me.

She pulls her hand away like she's the one who got shocked. "Um . . . yeah . . . Good night, Jonathan."

What could this mean?

She heads down the bleachers, but this whole moment is ending too soon for me. My hand wants hers back. "Kylie." She turns around. "I don't assume anything at all. Thanks for coming tonight."

She gives me a good-bye wave as she works her way to the bottom seats, then glides down the few stairs to the ground. I'm still not ready to let her go.

"Kylie." She looks up and puts her hands on the rail, a gesture that says she's okay lingering. My confidence soars. "Will you go running with me? Maybe this weekend? Just a couple of miles."

She sighs, considering my request. "I'll have to think about it. Maybe Sunday. Give me your number, and I'll call you." She pulls out her phone, and I tell her what numbers to punch in. Today is Friday. I wish tomorrow were a school day so I didn't have to wait two days to see her again.

"I'll call tomorrow night," she says.

"Okay. Thanks."

I watch her disappear into the parking lot, wishing I felt invited to escort her, but stoked that she put my digits into her phone and promised to call.

Her car groans to life, navigates the parking lot, and putters off down the driveway. The envelope in my hand commands me to sit back down and open it.

Inside is a piece of yellow construction paper folded in half. A Crayola rainbow spans the sky over a building with the word "hospitel" printed above it. The inside of the card has a drawing that looks like a tree with flowers. *Get well soon your frend Kylie.*

CHAPTER 7

BY THE TIME I WALK HOME, IT'S A LITTLE AFTER SIX. UNCLE Joey's been here and gone. There are dishes in the sink and a note that he left me pizza in the fridge. It's pepperoni, which is my favorite, but I'm just not in the mood to eat right now.

Any other day I'd be done with dinner and on my way back to Kylie-Simms-is-my-girlfriend. For the first time since I can remember, I don't want to go. I don't want to taint the conversation in the bleachers by going to a made-up world. I feel guilty in a tired sort of way.

I grab my backpack and haul it up toward my room, but stop short at the top of the stairs. There is light spilling through my doorway into the hall. I never leave the lamp on. A shadow crosses the light, and my bed creaks as if someone just sat on it. I freeze with both fear and the absurd worry that I didn't make my bed.

This time I don't run downstairs for a knife, but I put my bag down so I'm ready to hightail it out of here, just in case.

I inch along the hall until another step would put me in the doorway. I stop breathing as I slowly peek beyond the frame, expecting to see that girl sitting on the bed. No one is there. I step into the room to find it empty, as neat as a room with an unmade bed can look. No drawers lie open and rummaged through. No papers have been flung across the floor. I bend to check under the bed, and find it clear. I open the closet door, and there's no one inside, though I do note that my silver shoe-box is still there. I check my bathroom—empty.

Only the lit bedside lamp gives away the fact that someone was here.

This whole thing unnerves me and isn't what I want to be thinking about after talking with real Kylie. Someone was in this room less than one minute ago. My gut says it was that girl. She couldn't have gone out a window, could she? I would have heard that, but I check the bedroom and bathroom windows, all of which are locked from the inside. The only option is one that seems more and more likely the more I think about it. . . .

Another world-maker?

Could it be I'm not the only one?

The first time I saw her wasn't in this world. It was in Kylie-Simms-is-my-girlfriend, a world I *made*. Someone is popping through my worlds, and I'm so exponentially creeped-out by this thought that I do what I always do—run to girlfriend Kylie.

I squeeze my eyes shut and open them standing in the same exact room, except the light isn't on. I take out my cell phone, feeling guilty because I blew Kylie off earlier and wouldn't be here now if not for all the breaking and entering. She doesn't know why I blew her off, so I swallow my guilt and dial. She picks up on the third ring.

"Hi, Jonathan." She sounds so normal, when the universe right now is anything but.

"You busy?"

"Just helping my mom. You wanna come over?"

I don't. I want to be with Kylie but not while she's helping her mom. "Wanna go to the mall with me? Nothing to eat here."

"You can have some leftover chicken and potatoes we had for supper."

"I would, but I'm in taco mode."

She hesitates. Whatever she and her mom are doing must be kind of important. The right thing to do here would be to say, *Forget it. I'll see you tomorrow.* It's hard when I want to see her so badly, but I fake some nonchalance.

"Never mind. It's okay. I'll swing through the drive-through on Route One."

"No, wait!" she hollers before I can hang up. She covers the receiver so all I can hear is her muffled voice presumably talking to her mom. She's making excuses so we can see each other, and I should be pleased, but I feel only sad for some reason. She returns shortly. "I'll be ready in ten minutes."

We find a decent parking spot near the food court, and I order two tacos and a large nachos, which Kylie likes to share. We get fruit smoothies from the counter next to the taco place and sit at a round table in the middle of the food court.

Kylie's hair is tied back again, low at her neck instead of up high like she does for track practice. The low ponytail looks nice with the earrings I gave her—studs of red crystal I wish were rubies but still cost a lot for a kid in high school living on last summer's pizza delivery money. She's also wearing the ring I gave her that matches. Kylie isn't fancy, but she likes jewelry that sparkles without being all in-your-face. I wonder, insanely, if there will come a time when I'm comfortable buying real Kylie a piece of jewelry.

I nurse my smoothie along with my guilt as I consider that in my heart I'm cheating on my girlfriend with my girlfriend.

I've been kind of quiet since I picked Kylie up at her house. She knows me well enough to know that quiet happens sometimes with me, but I don't want her thinking anything's wrong, so I hand her the cheese dip with a smile, and we each shovel a chip into the yellow smoothness.

"So, what were you helping your mom with?" I ask.

She crunches on her chip before answering. "She's putting together a scrapbook for my great aunt's retirement party."

"When's the party?"

"Memorial Day weekend. My mom doesn't believe in waiting till the last minute."

"That's a safe policy."

"I wish I could apply it to writing papers."

"Procrastination only makes your papers better."

She smiles and dips another chip.

Around us the mall is filled with Friday night shoppers, families out for a cheap dinner, and preteens who can't get permission to do anything better. This is not where I would take Kylie on an official date, but we've been together so long, official dates don't happen that often. Our time usually passes in moments like this—easy togetherness, the security of being with a best friend I don't have to work to impress. Again I think of real Kylie and how if I meet her to run on Sunday, it will not be comfortable. It will be work, as relationships are when they start out.

As Kylie munches more chips and I unwrap my first taco, my gaze slips over the people around us, searching for couples. There's a pair at the doughnut counter, both holding shopping bags. Another couple sits a few tables back, feeding each other cannolis. Another couple strolls by, perusing each eatery's menu as they pass. I guess that the cannoli sharers are fairly new to each other, the menu studiers are a couple years in, and the shopping baggers probably have kids all grown up. I wonder if I'll still be sitting here with one Kylie or the other twenty-five years from now.

That's when I see her. The girl I think was in my room. She's way over by the restrooms and is staring right at me. When our eyes lock, she looks away, pretending she hasn't been watching. She starts moving across the far end of the food court, and I watch, unsure what to do. Kylie notices and turns around. "What are you looking at?"

"Nothing. I have to go to the bathroom," I say. Lame, I know, and I think Kylie has seen the girl, but I can't let her get away. Not after she was just in my room in the real world, and now she's shown up in Kylie-Simms-is-my-girlfriend again.

"Jonathan—"

"I'll be right back."

I don't wait to hear her response. I'm halfway across the food court, eyes on the girl as she rounds the corner into the mall proper. I don't blink, in case she suddenly pops out of this world, but since I never pop in and out where others can see me, I'm hoping she maintains a similar policy.

Her hot-pink sweater is easy to track in the crowd. She's

not window-shopping. Her long strides say she's trying to look casual while covering distance quickly. I don't know if she knows for sure I'm following her.

I'm half jogging while I dodge women with baby-strollers and groups of preteens walking side by side. I bump one girl standing with her friends at the window of a sexy underwear store. She swears at me, but I've already moved on.

Pink-sweater girl has only a two-mall-cart lead. I'm passing a smokeless-cigarette stand and a bonsai-tree stand, gaining ground, when she suddenly stops, eyes riveted just to the left ahead of her. I pause too, and see a woman, not old so much as grandmotherly, leaning against the window of a candle store, but she's not looking inside at the candles. Everything about her screams cosmic weirdness, except that she's simply standing there, pleasant-seeming, an ordinary woman at the mall.

Pink-sweater girl digs in her heels at the sight of the woman and glances back at me, undeniably aware I've been following. The old woman's eyes turn to me as well, and I'm struck by how blue they seem from such a distance, as if they are made of pure sky. The girl gives the woman a small shake of her head, turns to the north wing of the mall, and bolts, her black hair swaying side to side over her hot-pink back.

The old woman sighs and turns toward the candle store. I break into a run after the girl.

Suddenly it's like shoppers are throwing themselves between us. I have to dodge a family with little kids, a grandmother with a cane, and some high schoolers sucking smoothies. I collide with a woman coming out of a clothing store, and pause to pick up her bag and thrust it at her. Pink-sweater girl gains a little ground, but I still have a chance. We pass the quarter-drop kiddie cars and round a corner into a department store. People point at our chase scene, and I think the hollering behind us might be a security guard. The girl doesn't slow at all, just rockets down an aisle and weaves in and out of the clothes racks, brushing blouse sleeves and pant legs and knocking over a pile of T-shirts.

I can almost reach her if I dive, and I'm going to have to, because she's headed for a women's dressing room. With a heave I leap forward and catch her sweater. She jerks backward and tumbles into me, kicking and rolling to free herself, but I will not let go.

Other people are upon us. Hands try to pull me away. She fights me hard with fists and kicks, then ducks her head, throws up her arms, and wriggles free of the sweater I'm left clutching. She scampers into the dressing room, in a pink bra with her black jeans. I kick whoever is holding me and get free long enough to plunge into the dressing room and catch the stall door before she can close it. We push in opposite directions, but I get enough of an opening to force my shoulder through. She smashes herself against the door, and I smash back, throwing the door wide. I slam into her, and we hit the mirror on the back wall. The glass cracks. We fall through it and thud together to the ground.

The ground is beach sand.

She is beneath me. We both breathe heavily from the chase, and our chests press back and forth against each other. Her shoulder, covered only with a satiny bra strap, is all I can see from this position. She shoves me off, and I throw her the pink sweater before flipping onto my back to see the undersides of coconut trees. When I stand up to look at her, she's not wearing the sweater or her jeans but a string bikini.

The coconut branches sway in a light breeze. The turquoise sea scents the air with salt. Waves roll casually into the sand. The sun is far hotter than the one we left behind in Pennington. For miles in either direction the beach stretches, completely devoid of people but big on seashells you could sell to tourists.

"Who are you?" I ask.

She stops brushing sand off herself and gestures to the landscape. "Now, this is a world to be lived in, huh, Jonathan?" She smiles, a bit know-it-all-like, and I'm seized again with the feeling that I might actually know her.

She pulls her hair back and frowns. Like when she was

walking in the mall, I get the sense she's trying to be casual, but something is urgent. "Go back to Kylie. She's probably pissed by now."

She finishes some magic move to tie her hair back, steps forward, and shoves me in the chest real, real hard. . . .

I'm lying on the floor of a public restroom. A pair of legs stands at a urinal, and a zipper zips. Shoes jump back. "What the—" A deep breath. "I didn't see you, kid. Are you okay?"

I don't know if I am, but I nod and stand up. I don't want this man calling security, not after the chase down the mall.

"You sure?"

"It happens sometimes. Doctor says I'm okay."

He shakes his head and leaves, and I'm alone. I stick my hands under the automatic faucet and wash off whatever I might have picked up on the bathroom floor. I rest against the counter and reassure my reflection in the mirror. *It's okay. It's okay. You're okay.*

CHAPTER 8

LAUGH, AND THE WORLD LAUGHS WITH YOU. LAUGH *alone, and the world thinks you're an idiot.*

Time flies like an arrow. Fruit flies like a banana.

My karma ran over your dogma.

What happens if you get scared half to death twice?

If you ate pasta and antipasto, would you still be hungry?

So I'm feeling philosophical. Kylie's sitting beside me in the passenger seat as I drive her home. We've said four words to each other since I rejoined her at the food court. I started with "I'm sorry," and she ended with "Let's go."

If she knew my thoughts were skirting the borders where philosophy meets humor, I think she'd be mad. I don't know exactly what she's feeling, but I don't think it's mad. I mean "mad" as in angry, not crazy. Let's reserve the word "crazy" for me right now.

I've come a tad bit unglued. It's quite an emotional ride to go, in a matter of hours, from talking to your dream girl in real life, to bringing your made-up dream girl out for tacos, to chasing some world-hopping girl through the mall into a dream world.

I wish I could reassure Kylie I wasn't hounding some hot chick through the mall for fun, but I'm not sure what she thinks I was doing when I ran off. She sits in stubborn silence, or contemplative silence, energy focused, while my energy bounces throughout the car. This is the closest we've come to a fight in the three years since I made this world.

Just because you're paranoid doesn't mean they're not after you.

Enough, brain. We pull into Kylie's driveway, the car stops, and I shift into park. Kylie makes no move to get out, so we sit for a moment while the car idles and I reconnect my tongue to the few neurons I can trust not to say the wrong thing.

"Kylie," I manage to say.

She looks over the dashboard out into the world lit by headlights. "Something weird's happening with you," she says. "I feel weird around you today."

"I'm sorry."

"I don't like feeling icky like this."

I put my hands on the steering wheel, like pretending to drive somewhere gives me control. "How can I fix it?"

"You can start by telling me why you went after that girl."

"It's not what you think."

"What do I think?"

"I recognized her, or thought I did, but it turned out she was somebody else."

She sighs. "In all the time I've known you, I've never heard you give a lame excuse instead of the truth."

"It's not a lame . . ." But it is, and denying it only makes it lamer. Plus, I can't help but reflect that I've given her plenty of lame excuses over the years for my odd behavior, and she's only just now noticing this one?

The colon separating minutes from hours on the digital clock blinks by the seconds as I sit there, helpless, completely unable to tell her anything that will make things right. Kylie is patient for a very long time.

"Never mind," she finally says. "Don't worry. I just . . . I'm going in." She opens the door and steps out, lingers a moment before closing it.

"I'll call you tomorrow," I say.

"Okay."

She shuts the door and waves as she crosses in front of the headlights. When her front door closes behind her and the entry light winks out, I feel as alone as I've ever felt. I wish that I could confide in her, but I don't see how. Some girls, maybe all girls, would throw a fit if their boyfriend ran after a hot girl in the mall and then lied about why. She didn't even ask why I

returned from the bathroom when I set off in the other direction. Kylie might be a little subdued, but she took it all so well.
I'm grateful that no matter what I do, she seems to take it well.
A teeny tiny part of me, though, wishes she would kick and
scream a little. It would be more normal.

Laugh, and the world laughs with you.

Cry, and the world couldn't care less.

Driving home is like driving through a void. I park the car
in Uncle Joey's driveway and squeeze my eyes shut to return
to the real world. I emerge in the kitchen. All the lights are out
except for the one by the front door that comes on with a timer.
Uncle Joey isn't home, and although I often prefer having the
house to myself, I really wish he were here right now. I need
parental guidance, or at least the feeling that someone's looking
after me.

The house stands, big and silent. I'd give anything for the
sounds of that girl breaking and entering upstairs. I wouldn't
even go up and scare her off. I'd just sit down here and listen to
the footsteps and the creaks.

I'm drawn to the only light in the house, the one by the front
door. To reach it I have to go through the living room. I pick
my way through the semidarkness in slow motion. Sitting on
the mantel is a small photo tucked behind a vase—me with my
mom, dad, and Tess. My sister is in my mom's lap, set before

a cake with one candle on it. I'm three years old sitting beside them, ready to blow the candle out. My dad stands behind us, the top of his head cut off by whoever took the picture. There was a time when the place I lived in was a house where I was never alone. At Uncle Joey's the cold sofa, love seat, recliner, coffee table, rug, lamps, and tasteful accessories all are arranged as if for a photo shoot. No one actually lives among them. There is no life here.

I've gotten myself into a mood, and usually the thing I do at times like these is visit a world. I could even make a new world.

I won't, though. All I want right now is what's real. And what's real is a Kylie who barely knows me, an uncle who's still not home, and a family who's still dead. I need to wallow in self-pity for a while, and I know the best way to do it.

In the dark I go upstairs and down the hallway, straight past my room to the one at the end. I open the door and fumble inside for the light switch. I almost never come in here and don't think I've ever turned on the light, but the switch is where switches usually are, and a stark overhead globe brightens as I flip the lever.

I step farther inside an almost empty room with neutral cream wall paint and neutral beige carpeting. Nothing has ever been hung on the walls. It is the same as the day the builders declared the house finished. Except for the bins.

A dozen green plastic bins sit double-stacked against the wall, each labeled in permanent marker: Jonathan's room, Tess's room, Mark and Christine's room, silver and crystal, china, trophies, Mark's work (two bins), Christine's work (two bins), photos, Mom and Dad (my grandparents, who were Uncle Joey and my mom's parents; both died when I was a baby).

I have done this before, come in here and rummaged through the bins, but it's been at least four years. I was in middle school the last time, lost in my loneliness after an incident with kids at school, wishing for the protective love of my family. I start with the bin for Mark and Christine's room, my mom and dad's stuff. I reach for a purple velvet pouch, open it, and spill my dad's coin collection onto the rug. He had a couple hundred coins, mostly from other countries he had visited, coins worth no more than the value stamped on them, but there are a few more valuable, older coins sealed in plastic that tumble out too. I run my hand through them, spread them out and remember how proud my dad was of this little collection, how he'd started it when he was a boy, with a single Canadian penny he'd gotten at the store as change for a candy bar. I find the penny, picturing him holding it in his palm and telling me how he went straight home and washed it with soap to try to make it shiny. Some of the older coins came from his own father's collection when he died. Dying early is the rule in our family. I never met my dad's dad.

I put the coins back into the velvet pouch and reach into the bin. I pull out a two-pocket school folder, frayed and browned at the top. It's a small collection of things my mother kept from her school days. On top is a computer printout, three sheets I have to unfold because they're attached by perforations. The sheets have a column of holes punched out on either side, where they were fed into a printer. On these sheets is the first computer program my mom ever wrote. It's in BASIC, and it's the directions to make a Christmas scene with flashing tree lights and snow falling outside a window. She reproduced the scene years later for me and Tess, to show us that graphics had come a long way.

I riffle through my mom's papers. She once took creative writing, like me, and I read a few of her poems. She was better than me, but not nearly as good as Kylie. She also saved a few tests with perfect scores, some papers she wrote for history and English class, a copy of her school newspaper that includes an article she wrote about the gymnastics team. My mom did gymnastics from age three until she graduated college.

My dad has no similar folder. He wasn't quite as into school as my mom was, which is weird, since he ended up a teacher. Instead there is a shoebox with a few memories from the middle school where he worked. I open it and touch the newspaper articles and kid-drawn pictures and thank-you notes. One note, my favorite, is written on a folded piece of yellow composition paper:

> *Dear Mr. Aubrey,*
> *Thanks for helping me get out of the locker yesterday. I wish you were my dad. I hope I wrote this letter in the write form for a letter.*
> *Sincerely,*
> *Justin Mably*

I wonder how many of his students wished my dad were their dad. He taught sixth grade, so his kids were three years older than I was when he died. I wish I had had three extra years to get to know him. A lot of my memories of him are really just things I've found in these bins.

I put my mom's and dad's things away and take out Tess's bin. This one opens on a collection of Lil Miss dolls. I don't bother to take them out, just paw through to the layer of stuffed animals underneath and find Meow Meow, a cat drawn on an hourglass-shaped pillow. It's wearing its third skin, hand-sewn by my mom because Tess loved it so much that she wore through the original stuffing cover and mom's first replacement attempt. Around its middle Tess tied on a shawl my mom knitted that last Christmas. I don't remember much about Tess's toys, but Meow Meow stands out because Tess had a big fight with mom over bringing it on the plane. Mom wanted it to stay home, I guess, because she thought it would be lost or ruined. Turns out she was right.

I put the cover back on Tess's bin and prepare to torture myself with photos, but first I lift the lid of my own bin. I don't want to touch anything inside it, just want to check on my things. Most of them didn't get packed for a few years because I was still playing with them. My Game Boy is on top of my Thunderbirds Island play set and Where's Waldo books. I distinctly remember how it felt to spread out this stuff on my bedroom floor in my old house. Tess made daily attempts to play with it, but I stopped letting her in my room after she broke a palm tree off my Thunderbirds Island ramp.

I put the lid back on and settle in with the photos.

Most of them are in albums. A few from my family's last months are in envelopes from the developer because Mom didn't have the chance to sort them. A separate bin within the bin contains the professional photos that were on the wall and mantel in our old house. I open that bin and pull out my school picture from third grade. I was a cute kid, I have to admit. I pull the backing off the frame and find my pictures from second grade, first grade, and kindergarten. The one thing all four little boys have in common is a smiling, unscarred face.

I reassemble my picture frame and pull out Tess's. Hers is a first-grade picture, and she's missing a front tooth. She's wearing a purple velvet dress I actually remember. Under Tess's picture is a family portrait taken at the mall. We're dressed in Christmas colors with a white-lit tree in the background. My dad and mom pose like catalogue models in their red crew-neck shirts and black pants. Tess wears a green-and-black dress, and I wear a green sweater with black pants. We're a color-coordinated, Christmas-perfect family.

Looking at us, though, I feel a little disturbed. Not because I'm longing for those good old days—well, I am, but that's not what's disturbing me—but because the picture reminds me of something I can't remember, if that makes sense. I study the four faces, search the nooks and crannies of the Christmas tree, but the thing I need to see eludes me. I decide to leave the picture out and go through a few of the albums.

The albums come in all shapes, sizes, and textures. My mom kept a distinct album for each major vacation, and then a chronological, numbered set containing photos of our daily lives. (Her life had reached album number thirty-one.) I open album thirty-one, the one whose events I most remember, and flip through the last year of our lives. I had a birthday party at an indoor playground. Tess had a birthday party in the backyard. Dad got his Teacher of the Year award. Mom painted the kitchen. Tess and I played at the beach. Mom and Dad played golf with Auntie Carrie and Uncle Joey. Dad helped Tess ride her bike. Mom hugged me. It's when I'm near the end of the album that I see it.

A picture of Mom and Tess sitting on the front doorstep. There are carved pumpkins to their right and to their left and a scattering of fall leaves under their feet. They're wearing light jackets, and the wind is blowing their similarly long, dark hair. Mom has her arm around Tess, who smiles for the camera like she wants the world to see how many teeth she's lost. And my mom. Her face.

Looks very much like the pink-sweater girl's.

Though Mom's face is older, I'm struck by how surely I know I saw it only hours ago. I grab the Christmas picture and study it again, this time concentrating on Mom, whose pose is less casual than in the pumpkin picture. The formality makes her appear less familiar, the angle a little off, but the same formality that makes Mom's face more distant makes Tess's face look older. Like in a few years she could look very much like our mother.

It's been ten years since these pictures were taken. Ten years to become a young woman.

I'm reeling with the idea of it.

A ghost? Resurrected? Never dead at all?

I know with a certainty I've felt very few times in my life that that girl I chased in the mall is my sister.

Tess.

CHAPTER 9

AFTER AN HOUR RUMMAGING THROUGH MORE PICTURES
and all of Tess's bin, I put everything away and start wandering
around Uncle Joey's dark house, hoping for Tess to reappear.
She disappoints me. I watch TV downstairs for a while, though
"watching" is a generous way to describe it. I'm remembering
Tess in all her sisteryness, both fond and irritating memories of
growing up together for her short six years. I hoped Uncle Joey
would come home, but when he doesn't appear by the eleven
o'clock news, I go to bed.

I guess I sleep okay, because the next thing I know my alarm
is going off. It's Saturday morning, seven thirty, and I have eight
o'clock track practice in Kylie-Simms-is-my-girlfriend. I pull on
my running stuff, eat a piece of toast and drink a small glass of
OJ, switch worlds, and head to the track.

Kylie-Simms-is-my-girlfriend feels different this morning.
The track, the trees, the sky, the rock I kick off lane six, the

sound of hurdles being dragged into position, the spring-thaw smell of the damp infield—all are tainted by the idea that Tess might be alive. My whole concern has shifted from enjoying made-up world stuff to figuring out real-world stuff.

Kylie stands with her coach by the triple jump pit. I'm struck with the thought that, judging from their serious postures, they're probably discussing next week's championship meet with Dunford High, and whereas yesterday it would have mattered a great deal to me that Pennington win, today I have trouble seeing how it matters. I've never had a thought like this before, and I know it's because I expect Tess to intrude on this world at any moment. Tess has become very real, even if I don't know what she is or how she is alive.

I head for the opposite end of the long straightaway, to the starting line for the hundred and hundred hurdles, where the boys' team stretches. The gray day threatens rain, and there is a sense that we'll have to get practice in quickly before the sky opens. The girls' and boys' teams remain pretty separate during most practices, except for hurdlers and jumpers, who work with the same coach, so I don't get to do much more than wave at Kylie during the warm-up before I'm off on the roads with my distance pack for a seven-mile run. By the time I get back, a light rain is falling, but Kylie's sprinter group isn't finished with their workout. They're doing this thing called pacer chasers, where they pair up and run two hundreds, alternating who runs first and who has to wait a few seconds before chasing the partner down. It's a workout that takes a while because they walk the opposite two hundred to get back to the starting line.

Kylie is chasing down Mandy Breuger, the second leg on the four-by-one-hundred relay that Kylie anchors. The pair of them are well known at the state level, and to watch them battle down the straightaway—Kylie gaining after Mandy's huge head start, Mandy fighting her off because she's supposed to keep from getting caught—is a little like watching superheroes do battle.

Again, I'm awash with this impression that nothing matters, like they could run world records tomorrow and it wouldn't mean a thing because they aren't real. They cross the line together and fold over with hands on knees, each catching her breath. It must have been their last one, because they stay there at the finish, collecting more and more pairs of sprinters as they come in. Then everyone does a two-lap jog and some quick stretching at the fence because the rain is falling a little more steadily.

I spend the wait doing extra stretches and getting extra rained on with Rob Finkelstein. He's waiting for his girlfriend to be done too. After running and sweating in the rain, though, we can't get more soaked through than we are already. Eventually the girls start collecting their spikes and extra layers and go their separate ways. Rob says good-bye, leaving me standing at the fence alone, and for one horrible second I have the fear that Kylie isn't going to come over. But she does, like always, and my body floods with relief. Kylie wanting to be with me still matters, no matter how much my attitude is off today.

She tosses her wet sweatshirt over her shoulder. "Have a nice run?" she asks.

"LSD," I say. That's "long, slow, distance" to us distance runner types.

"How far?"

"Seven. How many pacer chasers?"

"Ten."

The coaches are still on the track timing latecomers only partway through their workouts. Maybe twenty people are still training around us, but no one hangs out casually by the fence like we are doing. The rain's a little cold at this point.

"Are you still mad at me?" I ask.

"I told you I wasn't mad."

"Are you still feeling icky?"

She pauses, maybe to assess the state of her ickiness, then kicks my toe playfully. "Not so icky."

"Then I'd like to go on a date today." And make it up to her for yesterday at the mall.

"Oh yeah? With who?"

I wish she hadn't said that. It makes me think she believes I'm yearning after pink-sweater girl, which there is no way I can tell her is my sister. "I was thinking of asking you. Wanna go out with me?"

"Where to?"

"It's a surprise."

"Only if it involves hot chocolate."

"What quality date wouldn't involve hot chocolate?"

We walk up to our cars together. She has a couple of towels in her trunk, and she lets me borrow one to keep my seat from getting soaked. I promise to pick her up in half an hour, and we drive to our separate showers to get clean and warm.

Miraculously, Uncle Joey's home. He's in his office by the looks of the light spilling from the doorway. I would peek in and say good morning, but I'll have to work pretty quick to be at Kylie's on time, so I run up the stairs, trying not to leave muddy drips on too much of the pristine carpet.

When I emerge dressed in sneakers, jeans, and a brown sweater, I'm making okay time. "Bye, Uncle. Be home later!" I holler as I dash out the door.

Kylie is waiting in her doorway and comes running when I pull up. The rain has turned into a fine mist that doesn't splash around but still requires windshield wipers. We go to the drive-through at the closest coffee place and get our hot chocolates, then head into the city.

"Where are we going?"

"I told you, it's a surprise."

We talk a little about the track team and about the big meet next week, news at school and news in Kylie's family. It's all pleasant conversation, but there is the sense that we're avoiding what we really need to talk about. For Kylie that would be the incident in the mall. For me, it's Tess as well, but also this strange new unease about Kylie-Simms-is-my-girlfriend not being real.

We rarely go into the city even though it's only a thirty-minute ride. City traffic intimidates me, not because the people cut you off or forget they have turn signals, but because they all seem to know where they're going, and I need a split second at each intersection to make a decision. City drivers are not forgiving of people who need to think while they drive.

We do make it to our destination, though, and I offer up a kidney to pay for a three-hour spot in the nearest garage. The only spaces left are on the roof. I take Kylie's hand in mine, and we navigate the stairwells and streets until we're approaching the Fine Arts Museum.

Kylie and I have never gone to an art museum together. Neither of us is particularly artsy, and I have no idea if coming here is a nice surprise or if she's inwardly groaning. I just wanted to do something different, something grown-up, something that would expand our world.

"Cool" is all she says as we go up the steps and push open the huge glass doors. Inside we find a multistory rotunda filled with voices echoing into the frescoes of mythological figures on clouds and mountaintops. For a moment the sound is like prayers wafting up to the painted gods. I lead Kylie over to take our place in line for tickets.

"Is this okay?" I ask. "Do you want to stay?"

"Yeah. I've always wanted to come here. I'm surprised to find myself here today, though."

"What if I told you I'm secretly an artist and the third floor is exhibiting my stuff right now?"

"If that's true, there'd better be a painting of me up there."

"If it were true, they'd all be of you."

"Don't be such a sap."

The line moves pretty quickly, and soon we have our entry badges and maps and are standing at the foot of the massive granite staircase. Grand columns to either side sweep the eye up toward the balconies of the second and third floors.

"What do you want to see?" Kylie asks.

"I've never seen any of it, so I'm up for anything."

She studies the map, flipping back and forth to see the collection and exhibition descriptions and their locations. I watch her, my awesome girlfriend Kylie, and I'm thinking about the day I created her. The darkness in my bedroom. The loneliness I felt.

It was the start of sophomore year, before driver's licenses and R-rated movies, and I spent that whole summer in Jonathan's-smokin'-hot-dance-club trying to keep myself from thinking of Kylie, from doing what I was about to do. Then I squeezed my eyes shut, and Kylie-Simms-is-my-girlfriend formed around me. I was in her bedroom, her bed actually, and she let me put my arms around her, and we kissed and explored each other, and I remember so clearly how warm I felt afterward, Kylie falling back to sleep, me never to sleep again because of insane happiness, and the softness of her, and me secure in the knowledge that making her world had not been a mistake.

Now as I watch her study the map, mulling over her decision, I'm highly aware that I made her what she is. I'm less her boyfriend than her keeper. Her creator. And this change in how I see her sickens me, frightens me, because all this time I thought I loved her.

Oh God. I do love her. That's not what I meant.

Is it?

She looks up from the map, blanches a little at something she sees in my face, and recovers quickly. We're still pretending something weird isn't going on between us. "If I had to pick one thing to see before I leave, it's the medieval art collection."

"Medieval art it is."

Turns out medieval art is about as far from where we're

standing as you can get, so we chart a course and get moving. On the way I'm surprised to find out how many worlds one can travel to in an art museum. The modern collection appeals to me with its room after room of sculptures made of the strangest things—such as bottle caps or a giant cheese grater. There's this one painting that's just a purple square, an orange square, and a yellow square with a tiny red circle inside it. I'm fairly certain I could reproduce this particular painting, but I would never think to give it the meaning described in the plaque beside it. Kylie pauses over a few life-size figures made of copper pipes but is generally unimpressed with modern art. When we enter the watercolors collection, she examines a number of pictures with pinks, greens, blues, and yellows. Pond scenes. Park scenes. Seascapes. I recognize the names of a few artists.

I think we're having a good time. I'm trying not to dwell on the question of Tess and the fact that my girlfriend isn't real, and Kylie's doing a pretty decent job being cheery, even if she is keeping at least three feet of distance between us at all times.

"I never realized 'art' covered so many things," Kylie says as we pass the peace quilt made by local schoolchildren. We see totem poles and Egyptian bracelets, ancient lutes and ceramic pitchers, ceremonial masks and children's dolls. Things start to blend together after a while, because the more we look at stuff, the more we realize everything humans make can be considered art.

The entrance to the medieval section is a towering stone archway reassembled from a cathedral in Europe. Set into wooden timbers on either side are huge stained-glass windows backlit to reveal crucifixion scenes. I sense Kylie's excitement level rise as she draws a breath and passes under the arch. Inside, a round room contains seven stained-glass windows. I don't need the plaques to tell me what they depict: night and day; sky and sea; land and plants; stars, sun, and moon; fish and birds; animals and man; an eye at rest. The seven days of Creation.

"I love castles," Kylie says, which is a weird thing to say, since these windows are clearly from churches, not castles. She bops from one day of Creation to the next, oblivious to the fact that I, her anonymous creator, have gone still as I imagine what a stained-glass window depicting her creation would look like among these others. Smaller, I think, less colorful, less majestic. Just my dark bedroom and Kylie springing from my forehead.

Of course I'm no god, but for the first time *ever*, I feel a little like one, an awkward god. Here stands Kylie, raising her eyes to each of seven windows for a thoughtless second, unaware that the truth of her origin is not debatable in creationist-versus-evolutionist circles. I could tell her with certainty how she was made. What's unknowable is the origin of my power to make her. This is obviously not the first time I've asked myself why I can do what I do. I falter in this room because I feel like the answer might be behind the stained glass, if only I had the courage to shatter it.

Kylie's experience of this same moment is less profound. With her gawking done, she patters from the room as though it were any other. I watch her go, feeling all the while like a giant spotlight beams down on me, fixing me in place. A room away she glances at icons of Jesus, Mary, angels, saints, all stylized with gold halos or pointy beards or symbolic staffs and whatnot. Those things are less threatening, more like the display of the first rough clay figurines ever fashioned by human hands, or the modern female statue made out of single-serving coffee thingies. Kylie, moving among the art, becomes indistinguishable, something molded from clay and breathed on.

She apparently forgets me when she sneaks a peek into yet another room beyond. As she disappears through the doorway, I finally find my feet and chase her down. The room is draped in tapestries, this time from the castles she loves. The largest depicts a medieval hunting scene, with a bloody deer. Kylie studies the tapestry with more interest than she spared the religious stuff, and she practically swoons over the ceremonial armor standing beneath it, plated in gold and stamped with medieval designs.

"This is so cool," she says, and her hand slides into mine. It's warm and squeezes my hand with gratitude. I hate that as I feel a distance swelling between us, she has felt the gap shrink. This medieval expedition has definitely turned out differently for each of us.

To find the exit we cross through a gallery of Pre-Raphaelite paintings and are confronted with a temporary exhibition of Arthurian pictures. Kylie makes a little happy noise and squeezes my hand harder.

"Why didn't you just say this is where you wanted to go?" I ask.

"Do you think I knew what 'Pre-Raphaelite' meant?"

I follow Kylie around the room as she studies the details of knights being knighted, dead ladies floating around in boats, and Holy Grails touched by the most worthy champions of faith. I don't think she even knows much about the legend besides what she has seen in a couple of old movies like *First Knight* or *King Arthur*, which I suspect don't tell the whole of it, by the looks of this art all around us. Still, the exhibit is a nice way to end our museum experience.

We take the elevator down, and emerge by the gift shop. While Kylie's off browsing, I search through the posters for a reproduction of one of those Arthurian pictures. I don't find one, but I do pass a T-shirt display with a colorful print of an

Arthur and Guinevere painting and a caption on the back about Pre-Raphaelites. I buy a medium for Kylie and a large for myself and tuck them into my jacket before she can see. Then we head out of the museum to find somewhere to eat, and end up in a little burger place a block away.

I order a fancy chicken sandwich, and Kylie chooses a turkey burger. We split a fries and onion ring platter, which comes on a bed of lettuce, as if putting a piece of salad at the bottom is going to change the fact that we're eating grease. Because we're runners, we're usually a little careful about what we eat, but this is a special occasion. It's a date.

As if reading my mind, Kylie says, "Chicken and turkey count as a healthy decision."

"We do have to get protein," I agree. "Just don't give me that crap about fried potatoes and fried onions counting as vegetables." I munch happily on a giant, crispy onion ring.

"They do, though."

"We should have gotten a salad," I say.

"Isn't the boy supposed to be the defender of junk food and the girl the health food junkie?"

"It's more like sprinters defend junk food and distance runners eat right."

"Is that so?" She takes a bite out of her turkey burger. When she does, a tomato wedge slides partway out the back. We both eat, concentrating on our chewing and the comings and goings at the tables around us. Someone ordered a brownie sundae that I'm tempted to go over and sample.

Kylie puts down her turkey burger to take a sip of strawberry lemonade. She casts her glance down at the table as she drinks. I can tell she wants to get down to talking about something, but the changes in her expression tell me she's not sure how to proceed. She goes for something safe. "So, what was your favorite thing you saw today?"

I'm midchew, so I get a few seconds to think about it before swallowing. We can talk about art if that's what she wants. "I guess the rocket ship made out of rocks with those caveman paintings on them."

"I didn't see that."

"It was in the modern room. You weren't too into it, remember?"

"Yeah, I don't get modern art."

"So, what was your favorite thing you saw today?"

She smiles. She can't help but let her happiness over having a favorite trump everything else for the moment. "The whole King Arthur room. I think I'm a girlie girl in love with romantic stories."

"I seriously did not know that."

"My mom used to read to me from *Le Morte d'Arthur* when I was younger. The Round Table. The Lady of the Lake.

Excalibur. A lot of love stories that didn't end so well. A lot of knights in disguise accidentally killing their friends because no one could recognize anyone. A lot of weirdness surrounding the quest for the Holy Grail."

"Sounds a lot like Monty Python," I say.

"Only, real tales of King Arthur aren't meant to be funny."

"Who said Monty Python was funny?"

"You did. About a thousand times after we watched it in eighth grade."

Eighth grade is two years before this Kylie began her existence, but she has memories going back further than that, and of course I have to pretend it all happened. She's told me about Monty Python before. In this world Kylie and I have been friends since birth and in love since we were old enough to be in love.

The onion ring pile dwindles faster than the french fry pile, so I start eating fries to even it out. Kylie puts down her burger and sits kind of still, watching me dip the fries in ketchup and stick them into my mouth. Eventually I get that she's waiting for me to stop eating, so I wash down my food with some cola and give her my full attention.

"What's going on, Jonathan?"

I clamp down on a *What do you mean?* because playing dumb isn't going to help anything. I was hoping we could finish out this date pretending nothing was wrong.

"I mean," she says, "besides that girl last night. You looked at me weird when we were starting out in the museum. I know sometimes you get distant, but I always know the reason is something else. I get the feeling this time your distance is because of me."

"It's not."

"Well, what, then?"

How do I tell her the problem is that she isn't real and that's not as okay as it used to be?

"When we were in third grade," I say, "and the crash happened. Do you remember if we were friends?"

"Of course we were friends. We've never not been friends."

"What was I like after the crash? You know, when I went back to school."

She senses we're entering dangerous ground, that she has to be careful not to say the wrong thing. "Uh . . . you were . . ." Her eyes scan the plates and silverware on the table. "I don't know. You had the scar, and you were obviously sad because your family had died."

"But was I different in other ways? Did I change enough to make people act differently toward me?"

"Well, yeah. Everyone felt bad for you. Don't you remember the party the class threw on the one-week anniversary of you coming back to school? Those first few weeks, you had so many people inviting you over to their houses that I didn't see you much."

I don't remember any of this, of course, because it never happened, and I sit in silence for a moment, mulling over her version of the truth.

"Were you jealous?" I ask.

"As jealous as a person can be when their best friend is suddenly everyone else's best friend."

"But did you know, even then, that you wanted to be more than friends?"

"In third grade?"

"In third grade."

"Yeah." She answers, blushing. I'm seeing Kylie blush more and more these days. "In third grade."

"You couldn't possibly know you loved me in third grade."

"Don't tell me what I knew and didn't know. Don't ask me a question if you're not gonna take my answer seriously."

"I take you seriously. It's just that . . ."

"Why? When did you first know you loved me?" she asks, a daring note in her voice.

"I honestly can't remember."

"That's such a cop-out."

I am not dodging her question. Although this Kylie isn't the one I originally fell for, I can't remember when I first started loving the other Kylie. It could have been third grade. It probably was third grade if I made this Kylie to think she loved me starting then. "I guess I'll put it this way. You are the kindest person I've ever met. More important, you're kind to me. You're generous, and loyal, and have a way of making me feel better about myself. You make me a better person because I want to be good enough to deserve you. I love all this about you, and since you've been this way your whole life, it makes sense I've always loved you. The part where I realized you were hot came later."

She takes a long sip of her strawberry lemonade. She might be embarrassed. She might not believe me.

"What I don't get," I say, "is what you see in me."

I need to hear her catalogue my specific lovable qualities, to hear there are reasons she loves me besides the fact that I made her do it. Her answer is a little spirit-crushing in its vagueness. "I love everything about you, Jonathan. Just . . . everything." She says it with a familiar tremble in her voice so full of sincerity. Her pure affection has given me comfort so many times before, so why not today?

My eyes lock on hers. I want to feel the old cliché of drowning in her eyes, but my mood makes me see nothing but shallows. "We've been together for so long. Haven't you wondered what it would be like to go out with someone else?"

Her lips retreat from the lemonade straw, her eyes reflecting the glass below. "Never once have I wanted to go out with someone else, but . . ." Her face darkens. "I'm guessing you have."

"No, no, no. That's not what I meant."

"What else could you mean? We've been together forever, and you want to try something new. Is that what's been bugging you? Is that why you took off after that girl?"

"I didn't mean *I* wanted to try something new. I just can't believe *you* don't. I'm not very lovable these days. I'm mopey. I almost never take you on dates anymore. Why aren't you tired of me? Bored of me?"

"Love doesn't get tired or bored."

"Sure it does."

"Do you know this because you're tired and bored of me?" Her tone sounds angry, but her eyes glisten, and I wish this conversation had never started.

"Of course I'm not tired or bored with you." But this is a pseudo-lie. I'm *unsatisfied* with her because I've recently started to question whether a made-up girlfriend is real enough to satisfy me.

"I don't believe you. What aren't you telling me?"

I bite my lower lip, deciding whether to feed her more pseudo-lies. Here and now isn't the place for truth, especially since I don't actually want to lose her. Perhaps I can't lose her. Perhaps I created her love to be so strong that no matter what I do, I can't lose her. I'm the closest I've ever come to testing those waters, and I won't wade in. Not today.

"Kylie." I reach a hand across the table, and she puts her hand in mine. I'm fairly sure most other girls wouldn't do that while wondering if they are about to get broken up with. "I know our years together should make me secure about you, but the truth is, they don't. I've been insecure since third grade. Not just about you, about everything. That it all can be taken away. Now that high school's ending in a couple of months, things are going to change. I'm worrying because I think that's part of what you do when you're about to graduate. I look at you and look at me and think about what might happen when we go to college, and I'm insecure."

"Is that why you were so worried about your scar the other night?"

I do think the other night started all this. She's smart enough to have made the connection without knowing what the connection is. "Yes."

"So why the girl in the mall? You shrug that off, but it means something."

I am on the border of hating myself, but I fill my mouth with more lies and spit them out. "When I saw that girl last night, I wasn't lying to you, I thought I recognized her. I recognized her from the crash. I had to see if I was right."

Kylie's expression says this surprises her, but she's buying it. "Did you talk to her?"

"For, like, three seconds. I asked if she was on flight 4460."

"Was she?"

"She didn't say, but she got annoyed like I was feeding her a pickup line. If she had been on the plane, she would have had a different reaction."

"What did you do?"

"I said I was sorry and came back to you."

"So why didn't you tell me this before? I worried all night over it."

"I was afraid you'd say I was ridiculous. It was ridiculous to think, after all, that I'd see someone that young from the plane, when it's a fact that only two other people survived, and they were both a lot older than me."

"It's not ridiculous. I never think you're ridiculous."

"You tell me I am all the time."

"Okay. Sometimes you're ridiculous. Like right now. It's ridiculous that you're insecure about me and ridiculous that you'd think I would think you're ridiculous because you thought you saw someone from the crash."

Believe it or not, I followed that.

Her hand squeezes mine. "Jonathan, if you're being both-ered by the crash, you can talk to me. If you don't want to talk, at least tell me it's because you're bothered by the crash. But telling me nothing just leaves me to make my own guesses, and that's left me very insecure about *you* these last couple of days."

"I'm sorry."

She holds my hand a minute longer, her thumb caressing my fingers until the waitress comes to clear our mostly-eaten meals and hand over the check. It's done. This almost-fight. It's over, and she's forgiven me. Her unconditional love is my rock, and it's also my problem.

We gather our things and head out the door, down the street, and up the stairs to the roof of the garage. When we're in the car and I've started the engine, I remember the shirts I bought at the museum.

"Here's a little something to remember great art by," I say, and hand her the size medium. She unfolds it and holds it to her front, looking down at the reproduction of Arthur and Guinevere.

"Perfect," she says, her eyes lighting up. As I move my hand to shift the car into gear, she lays hers on top of mine. "Don't ever be insecure of me. I love you more than anything."

Despite the awful things I've been thinking about her being not real, her touch still sends shivers up my arm. That's real. I lean over and kiss her on the mouth. She kisses back. We let the clock's colon flash for a bit while we make up.

When we separate, she puts her seat belt on and I back out of our spot. She looks out the window as we descend floor by floor through the parking garage, her new shirt folded in her lap.

I think about how I'm going to wear mine tomorrow when I go running with real Kylie.

CHAPTER 10

I TRY TO REMEMBER THE DREAM I HAD LAST NIGHT, BUT I can't.

I do remember waking up with a jolt, panting and scared.

I usually roll my eyes when I see this in a movie, some character screaming as they shoot straight to a sitting position in bed. Who does that in real life?

Although I wasn't exactly screaming when I woke up, and I didn't bolt upright, a noise in my throat was clawing to get out. I think I might even have been whimpering, but the vision of what scared me dissolved into a blue-and-black nothingness before I could will myself to remember.

I couldn't go back to sleep.

Now it's eight o'clock on Sunday morning, and I'm waiting for Kylie at Hargrove State Park. I'm in my artsy T-shirt, though it's buried under a sweatshirt because the morning is cold. I'm stretching by the entrance, mourning the loss of half a night's sleep. I'll be able to run, but I'm not so charming when I'm tired, and that worries me.

A lot is riding on this morning's outing. I still have no clear sense of the extent of the two Kylies' thought-sharing and no idea how they're doing it. If I can push the conversation a little, I might get some insight.

More important, I'm about to have a workout date with the *original* Kylie Simms. I don't want her to like me because she's connected to the other Kylie. I want to use this opportunity to see if she can like me because I'm me.

I rewind to the scene in the stands when I last talked to her. She told me she wanted to be my friend in third grade and left me holding a ten-year-old get-well card in a hand she'd held longer than necessary. I hope that was a good sign and not an isolated incident.

Apparently sleep deprivation and deep thoughts have killed my alertness, because I hear "Hey there" before I even see Kylie approach.

"Morning."

She sits across from me and puts her water bottle on the ground. "Brrrrrrr," she says. Wasting no time, she bends one leg and puts the other out straight for a hamstring stretch. "I was thinking we'd do the pond loop."

That's a little less than three miles of flat pine-needley terrain. "Sounds good."

I've already done my hamstrings, so I lean back and get my right quad. She gives no sign that a repeat hand holding is in today's plan, but it's hard to tell for sure because she's guarding herself again, putting all her focus on the business of running preparation.

If her brain is still attached to the other Kylie's, I figure I'll get a reaction to my museum shirt, so despite the temperature, I pull off my outer layer. A few scars show under the short sleeves, but they're not my worst scars. Besides, I long ago had to conquer my bare arm fear in order to run on the track team. She doesn't look at me right away because she's on her way to stretch her calves against a tree. I stretch my own against another tree.

When the stretching is done and we drop the rest of our overclothes into a pile, I'm relieved that her gaze fixes, not on my arms, but on the Arthur and Guinevere painting. She plays it cool.

"Nice shirt," she says. "Where'd you get it?"

"Fine Arts Museum."

"Is it new?"

"It's been there longer than I've been alive."

"I meant the shirt."

She's not quite as skilled as the other Kylie in the language of smart aleck. The other Kylie would have sarcasmed me back. "I got it yesterday."

She nods. She expected that answer.

Kylie might not understand this cosmic weirdness that's happening, but it seems she's rolling with it. Without announcing our intention to start running, we turn toward the pond loop trail and begin.

Our start is in a wide field rimmed by stately oak trees. The park here is big enough to hold soccer tournaments, and there are at least four marked fields with standing goals. No one plays this early on a Sunday, though. The only other people in the park just after eight a.m. are joggers and dog walkers. We are the only people I see not of retirement age.

About a quarter mile across the fields, we enter the trail system. The pond loop diverges only a few yards in, and we follow it into the woods, where it's quiet and naturey, and squirrels dodge into the fallen leaves at our approach.

We go slow, maybe nine-minute miles, so neither of us is struggling for breath. Her gait is smoother than mine, her arms low, whereas my hands tend to curl up at an odd angle. It's not much different from running with girlfriend Kylie, except for the fact that real Kylie is not as sure of my pace or ability as I am of hers. She's running a little more slowly than my girlfriend usually does, but it could be because she's tired from yesterday's workout. Technically our coaches don't expect either of us to be running today. Her coach might not be thrilled that she's doing distance at all, since she won't be running anything longer than a two-hundred in the big meets.

"Wanna do some intervals?" I ask. Usually girlfriend Kylie likes to do a mile or so of intervals in a distance run.

"Intervals?" she puffs.

"Unless you're too tired from the pacer chasers yesterday," I puff back, chancing my first push, to see what Kylie will reveal.

"How do you know I did pacer chasers?"

I jump over a root. Puff. Puff. "I saw you do them."

"Were you stalking me at practice?"

"Uh-uh," I say in my firmest denial voice. "I've never been to your track practice."

"Then how do you know what pacer chasers are, and how do you know I did them yesterday?"

"The same way you knew I got this T-shirt yesterday."

She doesn't deny it, just keeps thumping down the trail beside me. I guess it's a clue. Experiences beyond writing assignments are passing between the Kylies. At the next junction we stay on the pond loop by going left and up a small rise. The wind picks up, stirring the bare branches and making the occasional trunk creak. "Okay," she says.

"Okay what?"

"Thirty seconds." She raises her wrist and pushes a button on her stopwatch. "Go."

We pick up the pace considerably. Kylie is in her element, ponytail swishing, arms pumping. Her stride is smooth and open. I'm not an awkward runner, but next to her I feel like one.

"Stop," she says, and punches her stopwatch. We slow to a recovery jog and wind around a turn to find a straight stretch of trail. "Sixty?"

"Sure."

She presses her watch, and we're off again, this time for sixty seconds. We keep alternating between thirty seconds and sixty seconds for about ten minutes, and by the end all we can do is walk-jog. We're both breathing heavily, so we go a few minutes real slow before we recover enough to get back to normal jogging. We've rounded the pond, and for the first time I notice all the little green things around us. The growth of early spring.

"Didn't you tell me you don't go running?" she asks.

I admit, I do a mental victory pump because my athleticism has impressed her. "I believe I said you wouldn't see me running in town."

"Meaning you travel to exotic places, or you wear your invisibility cloak?"

Touché. So she speaks smart aleck after all. "Would you

believe I've been running with you a hundred times?"

She ducks to avoid a low-hanging branch. "Back to that awkward place where we acknowledge that something weird's going on but don't talk about what it is."

"You're right," I say. "Enough of awkward. Let's just run."

"No. I want to know how you've been running with me a hundred times."

Obviously I can't tell her. That will lead us down a path that has the truth of my world-making at the end. It's way premature to go there, so I backtrack. "I only asked if you'd *believe* we'd been running together before. I didn't mean anything by it."

Kylie flashes me a sideways *You're so full of it* look, narrow eyes and all, but thankfully doesn't push me for another answer. As much as I want her to tell me what wonkiness has been happening in her head, she apparently won't, unless I confess as well. Until I'm ready to do that, I'll have to settle for hints and clues and hope she keeps wanting to spend time together.

It does not escape me that the last poem girlfriend Kylie wrote was a romantic one about running through the woods together, and here we are. Now that the intervals are over and the pace has slowed, we find a new rhythm. The synchronicity of our steps and the way we jump roots together and hold wayward branches back for the other creates an energy that wasn't there at the start of the run. We laugh at two ridiculous squirrels circling a tree trunk. I yield to her over a footbridge that we have to take single file. She grabs ahold of my arm to save me when I stumble over a rock.

The run takes on a different kind of awkwardness. It becomes slightly more than friendly. I hear it in the strain of her voice, and to be honest, my voice as well, as we test each other with small talk about the path and the weather. I feel it in the inch or two closer to each other that we're traveling now. There's a chemistry building, and although I want to believe she's attracted to me, I can't help but worry.

Because what happens with me and girlfriend Kylie is romantic, this Kylie must be getting a bunch of romantic crossover in the same way she's getting poetry and info about art museum dates. That means whatever she feels right now probably has nothing to do with my questionable charm and more to do with girlfriend Kylie's feelings. The crossover must have her wondering what she's doing here with the biggest loner at Pennington High. I can't imagine what it's like to be her around me. Confused? Embarrassed? The teeniest bit happy?

My greatest fear: Even if I manage to purge the bits coming from girlfriend Kylie, I won't be sure of this Kylie because her feelings didn't start in a natural way. Do I want her to fall for me? Of course I do. She's the real Kylie, the one I wanted badly enough to create a world around. Maybe if I launch a campaign of Jonathan Aubrey awesomeness at her, and we get to know each other as well as I know my girlfriend, it won't matter how things started.

That's a really big maybe.

Except for our footsteps on the trail and our heavy breathing, we finish our run in silence. We get across the field with a burst of speed that always comes at the end of a run. Only a couple of dog walkers are in sight as we sit back down to stretch and Kylie takes a swig from her water bottle.

Despite the cool April morning, we're both sweating. We each sit in a hurdler stretch and reach for our toes. Her legs are the perfect length for a runner. The perfect length for a girl.

"Why haven't you ever gone out for the track team?" Kylie asks.

"Don't know."

"You could talk to Coach Pereira tomorrow."

"No point in that. There's only a month or so left in the season, and I'm a senior, sort of, who won't be back next year."

"How are you 'sort of' a senior?"

"I don't have enough credits to graduate. Too many absences."

She changes to a quad stretch and leans back on her elbows. "Yeah, you do miss school a lot."

"You've noticed."

"I think everyone notices."

"Everyone is paying attention to whether or not I show up for school?"

"Well . . . it's more like . . . You know how people have certain reputations? Yours is that you skip a lot."

"I *skip school*?" I'm offended to be known school-wide as a skipper, even though that's exactly what I am.

Her voice drops suddenly, like she doesn't want to be over-heard. "You're not in therapy all those days, are you?"

"No, not in therapy."

"Okay, well, people just assume it's a posttraumatic airplane disaster thing. That you can't deal with people. You have an uncle who makes you go to school, but you don't talk to anyone when you're there."

I try to decide if she's one of those people who think I can't deal. I picture her with friends, whispering diagnoses of me as I shuffle by, staring at the floor. I didn't realize Kylie noticed me at all, never mind that she's been speculating about my mental health. "That's quite a lot people think they know about me."

"That's all you let people know about you."

"I let them know I'm a walking advertisement for posttraumatic stress? No, I don't. That's an assumption people made. You can spread the newsflash that I'm not depressed, and I'm not mentally unbalanced." Am I?

"I didn't mean to offend you." Her tone says I might have overreacted in my response.

"If all these people all these years actually thought I was suffering, why did they do nothing but talk behind my back and ignore me face-to-face?"

She shifts uncomfortably under the weight of that accusation. Kylie, after all, is one of those people who did nothing all those years.

The thing is, I've never blamed anyone for keeping their distance from me. Except maybe when it first happened, I was mad at my parents for leaving me and at God for taking them. I wasn't angry when Hunter LeRoy told me to fetch the ball out of the poison ivy. I wasn't angry at the whispers of "Frankenstein" or the way I was never invited back into dodgeball games after all that physical therapy helped me walk normally again. I wasn't angry when I moved up to middle school and I ate lunch in the cafeteria by myself, or in high school when I went to Kylie-Simms-is-my-girlfriend to avoid eating lunch in the cafeteria by myself. I simply grew used to being invisible and sought what I needed in my other worlds. None of my classmates could know I chose to make worlds when they chose not to help me. It makes sense what Kylie's saying, that they would think I skip school so I can hide from the world. That's exactly what I do.

Kylie squints at me through a sunbeam falling between

the branches above. I'm afraid she sees anger in my face, an unreasonable anger at her third-grade self of ten years ago. She says, "It's hard for people who can't understand what you went through. I don't think anyone knew what to do to help you."

She means *she* didn't know what to do, which is so weird coming from her, because my girlfriend Kylie would never have been insecure about that. She would have known exactly how to drag me out of isolation and would have been confident while she was doing it. I've seen her do similar things a thousand times for other people.

Is kindness a quality I got wrong? Something I added when I made her?

But this Kylie isn't insensitive or unkind. She made an effort in third grade, and she's making an effort now. I can't judge her for not knowing how to help me. *I* didn't even know how to help me.

A piece of her hair has come loose from the ponytail and clings sweatily to the side of her face. Her cheeks are pink from the run and the cold. Her mouth is wide but not too wide, lips full but not too full. My gaze shifts down her body, that long, lean, feminine shape I have lain against so many times. In real life she let me suffer alone, but she was the only one I know of who tried when we were small. That truth conquers all.

As my eyes take her in, I notice, with a little satisfaction, her eyes sweep over me as well. Since I haven't answered, she speaks again. "You want to know the truth? When you didn't let me be your friend, way back when, I thought you hated me. Not hated everyone, just me, because I must have said or done something wrong. I've been afraid of you all this time, thinking you have a long memory and I'm the last person you'd want to talk to."

"You're afraid of me?"

"Well, not if you tell me you don't hate me."

"I don't hate you, Kylie."

"Yeah, but maybe you did a little, back then?"

"I've never, ever hated you. I can't believe you thought I did."

"Even if you don't hate me, I'm still sad."

"Why on earth would you be sad?"

She draws a deep breath and blows it out. "'Cause I'm sitting here with you and you're a totally normal human being, and all along you were never tragically, irreversibly ruined by a horrible accident."

"Who says I'm not ruined?" A drop of sweat beads at her throat. I want to whisk it away before it soaks into the collar of her shirt.

"You're not ruined, Jonathan. You're something, but it's not ruined." Her eyes appraise me again, except this time I don't think it's the outside she's searching. She pauses at the sleeve barely covering the scars on my upper arm and then at the line on my face, but she doesn't shift away like she's afraid to be caught staring. She takes her time with the scars, then moves to my shoulders, my chest, my face, my eyes, all equal parts of me. She's *seeing* me. She's really seeing me as a person instead of a tragic disaster. I assume she's adding up all she's learned recently about the real Jonathan and comparing it to the Jonathan she thought she knew, much like I've been comparing her to the image of her I turned into girlfriend Kylie. It's ironic that the only other person who's ever looked at me this way, who's ever really seen me, is my girlfriend.

I'm distracted by the flush that deepens her already pink face. I'm hypnotized by the rise and fall of her chest, gentle because she's long since caught her breath. I'm enchanted by the way she's tucked stray hairs behind her ears, an invitation for my lips to press a whisper there.

Her eyes on me say she feels it too, the urge to be closer even though we're leaning away from each other in our stretching poses.

She sighs. "I feel like we're making up after, like, a ten-year fight."

Slowly we unbend and sit up like normal people while time does its own little stretch between us. She swallows nervously. I'm so tense, my lungs can't loosen enough to get me air.

"Kylie," I say. "Would you let me do something?"

"What?"

"Close your eyes."

"I am not closing my eyes."

"Okay, then."

I slide forward until I'm about two feet away and get up on my knees. I'm in her personal space, and she leans back, an instinct to keep the distance right. I lean in, and she realizes what I want to do.

She licks her lips. The running has made them dry. I've already taken care of mine, so now that we're both ready, I put my mouth to hers, as gently as I can. She flinches backward, so I freeze where I am, and she looks at me, uncertainty and something else—desire?—in her expression. I've pushed her where she didn't expect to go, but I can't tell if she wants me to back away. Better to be safe than sorry, so I retreat a few inches. She rises back up to meet me, and the pressure of her kiss meets mine, and everything turns warm and soft and salty (we've been running, after all), and her lips part just a little so we can kiss more deeply, which we do for about three breaths, and then we're not mouths, only lips brushing once, twice.

We don't withdraw. Inches separate our faces, too close to look into each other's eyes, but looking isn't what matters. We're experiencing what it means to be this close to each other, our breath heating each other's cheeks, the sound of life rushing in and out of our lungs like the vitality of a swift run. Her body rose to meet mine, but now she recedes slowly. I fall back as well until we are sitting side by side.

I will never forget this moment. My first real kiss.

She clears her throat and shifts position, a signal for me to give her breathing room. The sun is warm and bright, and it shines on her face. She doesn't run from me but stays, thoughtful, by my side.

Campaign Jonathan Aubrey awesomeness begins.

I'm going to write her a poem.

CHAPTER 11

ON MONDAY MORNING I CAN'T WAIT TO GET TO SCHOOL in the real world. I've got a poem in my pocket, printed in my neatest writing and folded in an envelope with "Kylie" written on it. The envelope is sealed, so I can give it to her at the end of creative writing for opening later.

I don't see Kylie before school starts, but I never normally do. I decide it would be best not to stalk her at her locker, so I go straight to Non-Western History and start counting seconds until the bell for creative writing.

Not halfway through class, the classroom phone rings and Ms. Sawyer answers it. "They want you in guidance, Jonathan."

"Me?"

"They said you're late for your appointment."

I have a fuzzy recollection of making a springtime appointment, along with all the other seniors, just before February vacation. Two months is a long time to keep a guidance appointment slip.

I pack my things as quietly as possible while Ms. Sawyer returns to her lecture on Siddhārtha Gautama. I travel two long hallways and past the cafeteria to get to the guidance office, where the secretary greets me warmly, and Mr. Diamond, my counselor, waves me into his tiny office in the line of counselor offices along the wall.

"Hello, Jonathan. Good to see you."

"Good to see you, too, Mr. Diamond." I like my guidance counselor well enough. Because of my special circumstances—not just being the victim of a plane crash but being the plaintiff in a lawsuit to get my credits for graduation—I've met with Mr. Diamond more than the average student.

Mr. Diamond has a file open on his desk. I sit in the chair opposite him and read the top paper upside down. It's my transcript.

"I've spoken to your teachers, Jonathan. Ms. Sawyer says one more absence will put you over the limit. Mr. Eckhart says you have two absences to go. Ms. Perez and Mr. Papadakis say you've got more than twenty in their classes and have already lost credit."

Ms. Perez teaches Spanish and Mr. Papadakis teaches astronomy. I like them both fine, and their classes are okay, but I spend a lot of afternoons in Kylie-Simms-is-my-girlfriend.

"Your uncle argues your special circumstances justify the

truancy, and as far as I'm concerned, since your case is already before the law, my role isn't to play authoritarian with you. I want to talk to you about what you plan to do once this school year ends. We discussed some possibilities last time I saw you. Have you made any decisions?"

"No, sir."

"What options are you considering?"

I can't tell him that answer honestly. The only option I have on the table is to go to college in Kylie-Simms-is-my-girlfriend, since that's the only place where I have enough high school credits to attend college and have actually gone through the motions to apply and be accepted. I wish I could transfer my credits from that world to this one. I'm smart enough to have kept up my grades in both worlds even when absent. The difference is that Kylie-Simms-is-my-girlfriend accepts my grades despite my absences. The real world, for right or wrong, won't credit me for classes I've passed when my absences go over the limit, so I can't graduate. I've legitimately done all the work and passed all the tests in two separate worlds. I've put in the right number of class hours, too, even though they're half in one world and half in the other. It's more than your average high school graduate, so it really sucks that I won't get a real-world diploma.

I chose to split my time, and this is the consequence of that choice. "My uncle wants me to go to a four-year school. So I guess I'm considering any options where I can earn back the credit I've lost."

"Summer school will help a lot, since it's only attendance, not grades, that is the problem. Have you considered an application to Northern Mass. Community College? One semester there after summer school should be enough to earn your diploma."

"I have the application. My uncle still thinks I'll be going directly to college, though."

"Community college is college."

"Tell that to my uncle."

"Look, Jonathan. Your uncle's an intelligent, well-informed man who certainly has your best interests at heart. BUT. Ultimately you have to take responsibility for decisions regarding your education. For decisions regarding your life."

"Yes, sir." My plan to get an education in Kylie-Simms-is-my-girlfriend has always been only a backup. If I don't go to college in the real world, my life here and my life there will diverge so drastically that I don't know if I'll be able to straddle worlds as I've been doing so far. How could I be a PhD in one world and a pizza delivery guy in the other?

"Do you consider summer school and community college your best option? Or do you have something else in mind?"

"My uncle mentioned a school for gap years."

"Boxton Academy."

"Yes, sir."

"It's more expensive, and will take the full school year, but it's another good option. The trick is that they have a very rigorous attendance policy. You don't want to find yourself at the end of an expensive private school year still without a diploma."

"I realize that, sir. It's not like I'm just goofing around when I miss school."

"No one knows what you do when you miss school. Not even your uncle. None of your teachers can name a friend here you might be spending time with."

That stings a little. My teachers actually spent a few moments considering my friendships and could come up with nothing. I consider that they may actually have opinions about me, and I doubt they're very positive ones.

"I'm not doing drugs or drinking or making destructive decisions."

"You don't think skipping school on a regular basis is a destructive decision?"

Of course, to someone who has only the real world to live in, all my skipping would seem destructive. To me, having other worlds is the only thing that's kept me alive. Since I can't make that argument, I simply say, "I do, sir."

Mr. Diamond sighs. He's a guidance counselor who takes

his job very seriously. He wants to help me, and I guess he has helped in a lot of little ways throughout the years. It's not his fault I have a secret I won't tell.

The bell rings for the end of first period. In less than a second the sounds of kids bursting forth from classrooms fill the hall beyond the guidance office. Mr. Diamond ignores the ruckus to concentrate on me.

"You told me once you wanted to be a doctor. Is this still the case?"

"I don't think that's possible now, even if I did want it."

"What makes being a doctor impossible?"

"No awesome college is going to accept someone who barely squeaks out a diploma after an extra year. No medical school is going to accept someone who doesn't go to an awesome college."

"I'm not sure of your definition of 'awesome college.'"

"You know, a big-name school. Not Northern Mass. Community College."

"For you NMCC is a stepping stone to a 'big-name school.' It's a good place to start and does not have to be the end of your education."

I know this. I know my professional life isn't necessarily doomed at eighteen. If I stick to the real world and get done what needs to be done, I can have a career. I've never wanted to be a doctor, though. That's just something you say to a guidance counselor who asks what you want to be when you grow up. If only I knew what I wanted to be. Come to think of it, I probably am doomed.

But a little whisper says, *Jonathan, maybe you have real Kylie now. Maybe you can live in the real world.*

It's the first time since waking from the coma that I ever, ever thought maybe, possibly there could be something for me here. The epiphany stops me cold, like I've just found out I'm going to die tomorrow. No, like I just found out the doctor was mistaken about telling me I'm going to die tomorrow. Something pretty awesome wells up inside me. Possibilities.

Mr. Diamond is trying so hard that I want to leave him believing he's done some good. "I'll talk to my uncle and let you know as soon as we make a decision. I know what I have to do. Can I just have another summer school application?"

Mr. Diamond obliges with a copy sitting on his desk, as if he knew I'd ask for it. "You never have to make an appointment to see me, Jonathan. Just stop by whenever you want to talk, whether for a minute or an hour."

"Thank you, sir. I appreciate it."

I hold up the summer school application to indicate my thanks, and leave his office. Another student is waiting for him in the common area. She smiles at me as if I am a regular human being instead of an invisible man. I think her name is Candice.

The hallway crowds are thinning as I step out of guidance. Mr. Diamond forgot to give me a late pass, and I don't want to interrupt the beginning of his meeting with Candice, so I hurry to creative writing, hoping Mr. Eckhart forgives a few seconds' lateness. I've never seen him issue a detention, but I've never known anyone to need one in his class either.

The late bell rings just as I reach the door. I have to stop Mr. Eckhart from closing it on me. I slide into the classroom and see the desks arranged in groups again. As usual Kylie is sitting by the window with Zach and Emily, but there's one empty desk in their group. My usual group mates, Kaitlyn and Luis, are sitting with two empty desks.

I want to sit with Kylie, but she doesn't end my awkward pause by waving me over. She glances up at me, but Emily is talking to her, and she shifts her attention back to her friend.

I am, to use a good creative writing word, crestfallen. I thought yesterday's outing meant Kylie would publicly acknowledge me today. Without an invitation I can't just join them, so I go to my usual spot with Kaitlyn and Luis and sit facing Kylie. She glances over again but gives no hint that I should have chosen to sit with her. I wonder if she wanted me to, or if she's afraid what Emily and Zach would think, or if she's had a change of heart since our kiss. Now I have eighty-four minutes of hell to worry about it in a class where I hoped I'd be in heaven.

Mr. Eckhart begins class with a rare lecture. Today it's classic and not-so-classic ways to deal with meter. Iambic pentameter and all that. I open my notebook to write down his examples of stressed and unstressed syllables and the famous poets who arranged them to make brilliant verse. As I thumb through to a fresh page, I pass the draft of the poem I wrote for Kylie last night. It's crossed out and written over with words in the margins. It's not Keats or Shelley, but its final draft is sitting in my backpack waiting to be delivered to Kylie at the end of class.

COSMIC MYSTERIES
by Jonathan Aubrey

Who is God,
And what is His plan?
What is truth,
And how do we know it?
When will it all end,
And what will come after?
Where is consciousness,
And what is a dream?
Why does the universe exist,
And are we alone in it?

How are you here

And let me be with you?

Okay. It's really, really not Keats or Shelley, but it's the best I could do, and in Kylie-Simms-is-my-girlfriend it's exactly the kind of poem that would make Kylie tear up because she would know how much affection went into it. The thought of girlfriend Kylie triggers some guilt, but if real Kylie's behavior today means she's dumping me before we even go out, I have the rest of eternity to repent for the sin of cheating on my girlfriend. I flip past "Cosmic Mysteries" and smooth out the blank page that follows, but my thoughts wander away from Eckhart's lecture.

The idea of summer school makes me weary. Kylie won't be summer schooling in either world. Instead she'll be working her summer job before going off to college. In Kylie-Simms-is-my-girlfriend, that means the University of Massachusetts at Amherst. I don't know where real Kylie is going to school.

In Kylie-Simms-is-my-girlfriend, with credits intact and good SATs, I've also been accepted at UMass Amherst. Kylie thinks we're going off to college together, and I suppose we could, but I suspect it won't be as easy to catch up on material in college as it has been in high school. I'll have to miss a lot of college classes in Kylie-Simms-is-my-girlfriend if I'm simultaneously trying to make up high school classes to get a diploma in the real world.

The bigger question here is what Mr. Diamond was asking me in his guidance office. What do I want to do with my life?

I've totally been avoiding the answer. There's this little birdie or guardian angel or scrap of conscience telling me to make something of my life, to stop escaping into made-up worlds because it's the easy way out.

Well, little birdie/angel/conscience, I'm happy in my other worlds. Since when is it a sin to be happy? Huh? The real world is nothing but pain and disappointment, so get off my case about my drug of choice. My crappy life has earned me the right to be an addict of world-making.

What's that, little birdie? If my other worlds are so great and the real world so awful, how come I keep coming back?

I don't know!

I don't know why I haven't cut the cord and chosen life in Kylie-Simms-is-my-girlfriend. With a girlfriend's love and a college education secured, it should be a no-brainer, right? Right? Why don't I close my eyes to the real world and disappear forever into happiness?

Because despite all my misery, I want to be real. Real is *real.* Some primal part of me understands that the worlds I make can't substitute for the real thing. They are a consolation for everything I've lost. They keep me just happy enough that I can bear coming back to the real world time and time again. Ironically, my worlds are my tether to reality. Without them I might not have the will to live.

I thought I could get away with this come-and-go existence, but the desire to be real has become so strong since I made that mix-up in the hall when I almost kissed Kylie. It's no longer good enough to have scattered happiness across a bunch of worlds. I want the best parts of my life to be here, in the real world, to the point where I don't need to make other worlds anymore. I want Kylie's love for real. I want friends. I want family. I want my life to have a purpose.

But the real world denies me all of this, so I don't know what to do but flit back and forth from one made-up place to the next, gathering bits of each into a chopped-up pile of life. I don't know how to transfer all the pieces into this one real world to complete a picture, and no one can help me. I am utterly, utterly alone in this.

I probably should start considering plans that don't include Kylie—life plans for how to get a degree and a job and a real life. But when I try to do that, my soul cries out for her.

And my soul cries out for something else, too. Something lost when I was eight years old that I want more than anything, more than even Kylie, to have back.

I'm pissed at Mr. Diamond for doing this to me. Today of all days when I have to figure out what yesterday meant for me and Kylie. I don't want to think about the future, because at this moment everything feels like it hinges on the next thing Kylie does.

The clock says ten minutes have passed, and my notebook is still blank. I've been watching Kylie the whole time. Kind of openly. She's caught me doing it but hasn't smiled. She hasn't frowned either, so I don't know what to think.

People are putting their notebooks away, and I realize Eckhart has given us a direction I didn't hear. I close my notebook and wait for the handout he's delivering group by group. It turns out to be a worksheet on poetic meter. Luckily, after forcing us to take a crack at the answers independently, he lets us discuss with our group mates. Kaitlyn and Luis have observed that I took no notes and graciously help me with my answers. By the tentative way they speak, they know something's wrong. I wonder if they think I'm doing a posttraumatic crash freak-out.

As class nears its end, Eckhart gives a homework assignment and we pack up. There is an awkward two minutes when we sit waiting for the bell, and Kylie doesn't come over to talk to me. Even though others are traveling about, she stays parked with Emily and Zach.

I take out my sealed envelope containing "Cosmic Mysteries"

and debate whether to deliver it on the way out. I was so sure of Kylie when I kissed her yesterday, but an entire class's worth of cold shoulder has shot my confidence.

"Are you okay?" Kaitlyn asks. Her eyebrows are raised in worry for me. It's touching, but a little weird coming from Kaitlyn Frost of the unicorns and rainbows.

"Yeah. Just tired. Thanks for helping me today."

Then the bell rings and we're all headed for the door.

I hold the poem in my hand and rise slowly, trying to time my exit to coincide with Kylie's. She looks at me and lets Emily and Zach move ahead of her. I take this as encouragement.

Instead of meeting me at the doorway, though, she stops to talk to Mr. Eckhart. She doesn't indicate in any way that she wants me to stay, but unwilling to give up just yet, I go out the door and stand in the hallway. The classroom empties, and a moment later Kylie emerges.

"Oh," she says, like we've just bumped into each other in an elevator she thought would be empty.

I think my hand is sweating. The envelope I'm holding feels slick.

"I didn't know if I should wait for you," I say.

Her cheeks pinken, and she gets flustered. "Oh, I, uh, I'm sorry. I had to talk to Mr. Eckhart about something."

"Okay, well . . ." I don't know what else to say. The halls

are crowded with kids. Eckhart is coming toward the door, and we're blocking his exit. I can't read Kylie's emotion. "I guess I'll see you later." Some vague, maybe-in-class-tomorrow later. I turn to go.

She grabs my arm. "No, wait." Her fingers fall away when I turn. "What class do you have next?"

"Spanish, Perez, E-Hall."

"I'm headed to F-Hall. We can walk partway."

Eckhart is almost upon us, and he clearly sees us talking. I wonder if he's the kind of teacher who has an opinion of me, and what he thinks as I walk away with Kylie Simms.

It's not far from creative writing to the place where E- and F-Hall split, and it's a conversation-free journey. I doubt anyone passing would believe that we're walking together. When we reach the stairs she has to climb to F-Hall, we pause.

While trying to empty my voice of all pleading and desperation, I ask her, "Do you think we could get together later?"

She pulls her upper lip in. Thinking about it. Then she nods. Without another word, without any concrete plan, she slips by me and up to her class. I'm left standing there with the envelope still in my hand.

This weird sensation comes over me. As the chaos of changing classes swirls all around, I get this impression that everything in my world is a painting on a window, and if I walk up and scratch some paint away with a thumbnail, I'll see a great, wide something else beyond. Something foreign and not so nice—the real, real world I've never had to face. Is this what it means to hit a milestone—like high school ending—in your life? To come one step closer to adulthood? Is that great, wide something else the world of responsibility Mr. Diamond was talking about? I reach out to a post holding up the staircase and scratch some paint off it. Brown flecks fall away and expose the royal-blue layer of some year past.

After track practice in Kylie-Simms-is-my-girlfriend, I give "Cosmic Mysteries" to girlfriend Kylie. She reads it with the usual ardor she brings to all my poetry, and gives me a great big hug for thanks.

"What's the occasion?" she asks.

"Just another day in love."

Cheesy, I know, but I get a kiss for that. And another kiss. And I'm glad it was my girlfriend who got the poem from my hand.

I'm guessing that somehow real Kylie will feel this moment, just like she's felt the others lately. It's almost like giving the poem directly to her, too.

CHAPTER 12

GIRLFRIEND KYLIE HAS TO BUCKLE DOWN AND GET AN English paper written, so I luckily don't have to make an excuse for not seeing her tonight. I go back to the real world and dial up real Kylie to see if she meant it earlier about getting together. She doesn't pick up her cell, so I call her house number.

Her mother answers. "Hello?"

"Hi. Is Kylie there, please?"

"Who's calling?"

"Jonathan."

"Sure. Just a minute." A microsecond pause. "Jonathan . . . Aubrey?"

"Yes, ma'am."

"Okay, sure. Just a minute, Jonathan." She calls to Kylie, and I hear the click of another phone picking up.

"Hello?"

"Hi, Kylie. It's Jonathan." Another click tells me Mrs. Simms has hung up her handset.

"I know. Caller ID."

"Yeah." Now that we have that out of the way. "I didn't know if you still wanted to get together tonight."

"Well . . ." I feel an excuse coming on. *I have too much homework,* or *my mom needs me to do something,* but instead she sighs like she's resigned to fate. "Okay. Have you eaten yet?"

"Uh-uh."

"How about Mexican Station?"

Does she know I love tacos, or is that just a lucky guess?

"Should I pick you up?" I ask.

"If you want. I can go whenever."

She's not reluctant, but she's certainly not thrilled. "Be there in a few minutes."

When I get to her house, she emerges in jeans, sneakers, and a Windbreaker. Her hair is pulled back in her signature ponytail. She makes no comment on my shiny red car, which is good because I'm a little embarrassed about it. I know high school boys are supposed to appreciate nice cars, but that's because high school boys driving them want people to notice how cool they are. As I've said, I strongly prefer going unnoticed.

Because it's a Monday night, there isn't a wait at Mexican Station. We're shown to a table by the window where we have a view of the parking lot. At least if my car's stolen, I'll be able to ID the culprit.

I haven't done any of those gentlemanly things like open Kylie's car door or pull out her seat, because I get the sense that fawning over her will only increase the distance I want to bridge.

"What are you getting?" she asks as she peeks over her menu. She's noticed I'm not reading mine.

"I always get steak tacos."

I'm curious to see what she picks, because girlfriend Kylie is physically incapable of eating something other than a chicken burrito in a Mexican restaurant. She closes the menu as our server approaches, and sure enough, we order steak tacos and a chicken burrito. When our server leaves, we start crunching on the free chips and salsa.

"Let's play hypothetical questions," Kylie says.

"Huh?"

"You know, questions with situations that could never happen, but you give an answer anyway."

"I know what hypothetical questions are." There's mariachi music blaring over the PA system, so I wasn't sure I heard her correctly. The idea of playing a game is weird, but her face is deadly serious. "Okay, I guess." Girlfriend Kylie has never asked me to play hypothetical questions.

"Do you want to go first?" she asks.

"No, you."

"Okay." She scoops salsa onto a chip and stuffs it into her mouth before it drips. "If you had to live in one season—spring, summer, fall, or winter—for the rest of your life, what would you pick?"

"Hmmmm." She'd probably say summer. Girlfriend Kylie has always been in love with summer. "I'd pick fall."

"Why?"

"I like leaves."

"Because of the colors? Or you like jumping into a big, raked pile?"

"Everything about leaves." I crunch down two chips loaded with salsa. "And you?"

"Winter, definitely."

I finish chewing and swallowing my bite while I deal with my surprise. "What do you mean, winter?"

"You know, snow and Christmas and two school vacations."

"But you hate winter."

Her head tilts in surprise. "Winter has always been my favorite season. What makes you think I hate it?"

"Uh, lots of people hate winter in New England, so I just assumed."

She narrows her eyes. "Don't assume things about me, Jonathan. I think you've been making a few assumptions lately."

The verbal slap warms my face with embarrassment. "Sorry."

"You pick a question now."

"Okay." I'm not supergood at this, so I say the first thing that pops into my head. "If you could talk to any one person, dead or alive, for five minutes, who would it be and what would you talk about?"

"That is so not original."

"And your question was somehow the awesomest hypothetical ever?"

"At least it's not asked in every English class I've ever taken."

"So what's your answer in every English class you've ever taken?"

She sits a little straighter in her chair and crosses her forearms on the table. "Once I picked Jesus. Once I picked JFK. Once I picked Amelia Earhart. And once, the very first time I ever was asked, I picked *you*." Her tone dares me to be surprised about that.

I guess I should be surprised. Or startled or something, but that kind of admission seems par for the course these days. "What could you possibly want to talk to me about?"

"That's privileged information between me and my English teacher."

"Isn't there a rule that the askee has to answer the whole question?"

She caves with a quick shrug. "I wanted to ask if you were mad at me."

"Why on earth would I be mad at you?"

"I was in fourth grade. Remember I told you I thought you ignored me in third grade because you were mad at me?"

"Jeez, I hope you're over that by now."

"I don't know. You seem a little irritated."

"I *kissed* you yesterday, Kylie. I thought we left the park on a good note. What happened between yesterday and today?"

The server appears and lowers a giant lemonade in front of each of us. We wait silently for him to disappear. Kylie's brows knit together as she sips. I don't touch my drink because I'm waiting for an answer.

She puts her lemonade down and asks another question instead. "If you could be a superhero, what superpower would you pick?"

"The make-Kylie-answer-my-questions power."

"I'm serious."

"So am I."

"Really. What would you pick?" She smiles the teeniest bit and raises her eyebrows. The expression says that if I play along, things might turn out okay. I give her my best if-you-insist sigh.

"I would pick . . ." I'm about to say flight, which isn't so clever but would be pretty cool, but I change my mind at the last second. "I'd be Legalman."

"Is that a superpower?"

"It is if I get to change the law instantly whenever I want."

"You mean like what crimes get the death penalty?"

"I was thinking more like what crimes don't deserve having credits taken away."

It takes her a second to catch on. "You mean your credits for graduation."

"Yep."

I glance out the window at my shiny red car and think it's my substitute prize for all the work I put into high school in two worlds. At least I'll have the best pizza delivery vehicle on the planet for the rest of my life.

After a complaint like that, girlfriend Kylie would have given me a pep talk about how I can rally up the credits and save graduation. Real Kylie munches a chip with salsa and lets my moment of self-pity slide. "Your turn to ask again."

My creative energy is not up to the task of designing witty questions. The only questions I want to ask aren't hypothetical, and I'm still waiting for an answer to what happened with Kylie between yesterday and today. I pick around in the chip basket as I think. "If you won the lottery, what would you do with a hundred million dollars?"

She rolls her eyes. Another unoriginal one. Girlfriend Kylie and I have actually done this question before, though. I would give some to my uncle, and she would parcel out gifts to her rather large and extended family. Then we would both start charitable foundations right after we went on a vacation around the world—part private jet, part private yacht.

That's not what this Kylie says. "I'd keep a bunch for myself, of course, to buy a house and send kids to college and all that. Then I think I'd build a super state-of-the-art research facility and hire the best scientists."

"To research what?"

"Cancer. Genetic diseases. Spinal cord injuries. Coma."

I let that "coma" slip by just as she let pass my bit about getting back my credits. "I didn't know you were into medical research."

"Why does that surprise you?"

Girlfriend Kylie is not scientific in any way. She doesn't know what she wants to do with her life, but the only things she's talked about have to do with running or writing. The Peace Corps has come up a few times. Maybe a world-class journalist reporting on wars and world events. Girlfriend Kylie is a humanities/social studies girl all the way and has taken the bare minimum of science classes she could get away with.

"So do you want to be an actual scientist or just run the business of the lab?"

"I want to be working on cures. I've wanted to ever since I was young."

"So you're in, like, AP Chemistry now?"

"Last year, along with AP Bio. It's physics this year."

I can't believe what I'm hearing. Of course, it's fabulous that Kylie wants to be a medical researcher, but it's so un-Kylie.

"If you're into science, why take creative writing?"

"It was the only decent thing that fit into my schedule after I picked all my major classes."

My jaw hits the floor. Girlfriend Kylie had been aching to take creative writing since she was a freshman. It's open to juniors, but she couldn't schedule it last year around her two history classes.

"You don't like creative writing?"

"I do, now that I'm in it. I just don't want to be a writer."

"So you're going to major in science in college."

"I'm thinking biochemistry."

"Where did you apply?"

"Actually, I got my acceptance to Stanford the other day."

"In *California*?" My heart skips a beat, warning me what it will do if she goes so far away. She's leaving me for *California*.

"I'm pretty sure Stanford hasn't opened a Massachusetts campus."

"Why can't you just go to MIT?"

"I can't go to MIT if they don't accept me."

"So you applied?"

"I didn't get in."

"But you got into Stanford."

"I haven't heard from everywhere I applied, but Stanford's always been my first choice."

"Is your second choice in Massachusetts?"

For an instant I see heartache bleeding in her eyes. She lowers them. "Jonathan, my second choice doesn't matter anymore."

Oh God. California? How could she be going to California?

Her shoulders soften, and she sighs like she's sorry for breaking the news of the apocalypse. "I made these plans long before this happened." She gestures back and forth over the table to indicate "us."

I nod. It's all I can do, since I think my language skills are dying along with the rest of me. *California.*

"What are you going to do next year?" she asks. "Can you earn your credits back?"

"Mr. Diamond wants me to do summer school and a semester at NMCC. My uncle wants me to do a year at Boxton Academy. Either way should be enough to get a diploma. If all goes right, I'll only be a year behind."

"What do you want to do after that?"

"College, I guess."

"To study what?"

"Philosophy." I don't mean that. Maybe I do. I guess if I figure out the meaning of life, it'll be at least as important as Kylie
finding a cure for comas.

She doesn't know if my answer's serious, but she moves right
to the point. Even if she likes winter (then why *Stanford*?) and
wants to be a biochemist, she and girlfriend Kylie both possess
directness when it matters. "So we won't be near each other
next year."

"Do you want us to be near each other?"

She closes her eyes. Her knees must be moving back and
forth under the table, because it's causing her upper body to
shake. The server picks that exact moment to deliver steak
tacos and a chicken burrito. It smells so good, my mouth waters
even though my stomach currently can't stand the thought of
eating. "Can I get anything else for you?" he asks, though he
must sense he's interrupting. *Yeah, get us a way to be together in
California.*

Kylie opens her eyes but is still shaking. I send the server
away with a "No, thank you" and watch while he crosses the
room, away from our conversation.

"I don't feel like myself lately," Kylie says. "And it's your
fault." She goes quiet, but my mental alarms start clanging so

loudly, my ears actually hear them. I stand accused. I shrink a little in my seat and brace myself. This is, after all, what I wanted her to talk about.

She folds her hands in her lap and starts again. "I have to ask you. The other day, in the hall at school, did you bump into me on purpose?"

"No. I really didn't." At least at the last minute I aimed to avoid her. I hoped she'd let that particular humiliating moment go.

"I told you I had a dream the night before that I was in your room watching you sleep. It wasn't some sexy dream or anything, just me watching and you sleeping. I woke up and thought how weird that was, to do nothing in a dream but stand there. It was even weirder that you were the one I picked to watch. We aren't exactly close, as we both know, so it's not like I thought about you superfrequently."

I stifle a great big *Ouch* at that.

"The next morning we met in the hall," she continues. "Lilly laughed and joked that you were trying to kiss me, and ever since then I've been obsessed—I'm totally going to embarrass myself here—with the idea of kissing you." Her glance falls to her chicken burrito, the courage to meet my eye lost for a moment. She has finally let her guard down.

"If it helps, I've been obsessed with kissing you for years and years," I say lightly, so she'll lighten up, and she shakes her head like I just said the stupidest thing imaginable.

"Oh yeah?" she asks, and then the quirk of a smile she almost showed disappears. Of course it's true. Even if I can never convince her of how perfectly I love her, she has to know everyone sees her as a beautiful girl with a lot going for her. She can't find it all that ridiculous that some boy has had a crush on her from afar. I'm probably not the only one. Is it more awkward to admit a few days' worth of thinking about someone, or years of a crush?

"Yesterday, after the run, when you really did kiss me . . ." Her voice shushes so no one will overhear. "I don't know what I expected. I was curious. What would it be like to kiss Jonathan Aubrey, whom I used to know as this outgoing kid but who's turned himself into this . . . shadow? What would it be like to kiss Jonathan, who once had the most terrible tragedy happen to him and who won't let anyone past the scars?" Her eyes dart to the scar on my face, then down to my lips, and I remember how deeply she tried to see me yesterday right before I kissed her. I can't help but look at her lips in return. If there weren't a table between us, I don't think it's too crazy to say she would kiss me again right now.

But there is a table, and there are people all around. I'm trying to play it cool, but there's all this *need* radiating off Kylie.

She sits very composed, very politely, a perfectly self-controlled dinner companion, but pulses of her unseen emotion rush at me and make me picture wild eyes and hands clawing at a face.

"So how did it feel to kiss 'Frankenstein'?" I ask. It hurts to call myself the name that once dogged me in elementary school, but Kylie's body language says she doesn't see me as a monster. The way she just described me shows she's bright enough to tell the difference between a face and a person. Even as a little girl she saw the difference in me.

"Well," she says, ignoring the monster slur, "since the hallway, I've felt slammed by all these . . . thoughts. I've had crushes before. But this is different. It's like something's forcing me to obsess about you, and I don't know whether to just enjoy it or fight like hell. I know that's an awful thing to say."

Yeah, it's pretty awful to hear, even though I understand more than she knows. "Don't worry about it," I tell her.

"But for that moment yesterday, when you leaned over, the slammy feelings went away, and you kiss so sweet, Jonathan, and I felt like I was born to have that moment with you, like I found this whole layer of you that never shows. I didn't feel obsessed. I felt something more genuine, and . . . Huh, I guess I'm on the edge of making some kind of poem here, it seems." The change in her demeanor is so abrupt, it's like someone flipped her confession switch off. Her face goes lobster red.

I guess she's reached the limit of embarrassing things she can admit for one day. "Anyway, it's back to obsession for me. Like you're this great big magnet and I can't get away wearing my chain mail and armor."

Her medieval metaphor reminds me of girlfriend Kylie in the art museum. I'm heartened by her nice description of us kissing, but I wonder why that intimate moment would be *less* creepy than the rest of the time, instead of more. Does this mean she really could love me for real?

It's true I mixed up my worlds one day, but I didn't do it on purpose to change this Kylie. I was happy in my made-up world. Girlfriend Kylie was happy in my made-up world. Real Kylie was blissful while ignoring me in the real world.

Kylie presses her fingers to her forehead like she has a headache. She slides her palms to her hot cheeks. "I can't believe I said all that. I just couldn't stop myself. It's like I'm on truth serum or something."

She takes her cup and inspects the lemonade inside. "You didn't put something in here, did you?"

I've withdrawn a little because I feel so damn guilty, but the question snaps me back to attention. Her eyebrows are raised, and she's wearing the tentative smile of someone who's cracked a joke at a very unfunny moment. The last of her bright aura of neediness dissipates as she takes an exaggerated sip.

"I hope that's a rhetorical question," I say, trying my best to show I'm grateful she chose to share all she did.

"As opposed to a hypothetical one."

"You don't have to feel funny about being truthful with me."

"Sure I do. I barely know you."

"Do you want to know me? Or would it be better for me to just go away?"

Her fork is in her hand, and it pushes the rice around her burrito. "I don't want you to go away, but . . ."

I'm tempted to finish her sentence for her—*but I think you should.*

". . . I need to be careful."

Careful. That's better than "Go away." "Do you want to try just being friends?"

Her head slowly shakes. "I don't think that would work."

"So you want to try being together? See what happens?"

She's still not looking at me. The rice is now mixed with her beans in a lumpy slop. "I don't know if that would work either."

What I strongly suspect this moment requires is me putting my arms around her and telling her it will be okay, but there's that table between us, and there's mariachi music playing over the chatter of other guests we've been ignoring since we sat down. If we were alone, sitting on the seawall at the beach, for example, I think she would want me to touch her, but instead we start tentatively picking at our meals. Our previous conversation drops entirely, and I wonder how much she regrets.

When her burrito is half-gone, she looks around the restaurant as if noticing for the first time there is a world out there. "It's busy tonight," she says. The color of her cheeks has mostly returned to normal.

"Yeah."

"If you could visit any place in the world, any time in history, where would you go?"

I polish off a taco as I decide my response. The honest answer is Logan airport ten years ago, just before my family boarded the plane of doom. It's not the first time I imagine calling in a bomb threat or setting off a fire alarm or something so the plane can't take off. I won't tell Kylie that, though. Our conversation is still recovering from its serious moment. "I think it would be great to be on Mount Olympus a couple thousand years ago."

"You know you'd be alone and a little cold."

"Not if I were in charge of keeping Zeus's thunderbolts warm."

"I meant any non-fictitious place and time."

"Well, you should have said that up front. I'm sticking to my answer."

Her shoulders have lost most of their tension, though her face is still more anxious than relaxed. I dive in with my own question. "Would you rather be famous and poor, or rich and unknown?"

"Hmmm. I think I'd just rather be famous and rich." Her smile widens just enough to make clear this isn't true.

"That's cheating," I say.

"I never cheat. What would you rather be?"

"Is that your question?"

"Yeah. Would you rather be rich and unknown or poor and famous?"

"That depends."

"On what?"

"On which you find more attractive." I'm pushing it with that answer, but she only rolls her eyes.

"You think I care? I just admitted I'm obsessed with you."

"Okay, then. You can be rich and famous, and I'll be poor and unknown."

"Deal." The server notices we've put down our forks and knives. He comes to clear the plates and offer dessert. When we turn him down, he hands me the bill.

Kylie makes a grab for it as soon as he turns away. I don't let her touch it.

"C'mon," she says. "I want to pay my share."

"When you're rich and famous, you can pay me back."

Since she can't see the total, she takes out her wallet and

throws a twenty at me. I pick it up and give it back. "Seriously, Kylie. Let me pay. It's just dinner, and it'll make me feel better about torturing you."

"You don't owe me."

"No. I just want to do something nice for you. Please let me."

She puts the twenty back into her wallet. "Thank you, then."

I tuck some cash into the receipt folder and balance it on the edge of the table for the server when he comes back. Kylie sits patiently with me for the wrap-up of our restaurant experience. It's a familiar wait, like I'm sitting with girlfriend Kylie instead of this other person who has favorite seasons and life goals I never knew until tonight.

"If you could ask your future self," I offer, "say twenty years from now, any question, what would you ask?"

Her beautiful brown eyes meet mine, and at this moment they're full of doubt. "That's easy." She blinks and shifts focus to something in the distance. "I'd ask if I should have gone to Mexican Station tonight with Jonathan Aubrey."

CHAPTER 13

UNCLE JOEY'S HOUSE IS DARK WHEN I GET HOME, EXCEPT for the light on the timer in the foyer. I stop in the kitchen for a glass of water. The Mexican food was salty and has left me thirsty.

I climb the stairs and go into my room. I leave the lights off and sit on my bed thinking of Kylie. Both Kylies.

I love my girlfriend. My recent attitude about her lack of realness bothers me. So what if I made her? So what if I made her to love me? She's been my rock for most of high school, always cheering me up when I need it, always a part of my good times. She's ready to share her whole life with me starting with college next year, which is awesome to think about, except for that teeny problem of my conscience telling me not to disappear into a made-up world.

I don't love real Kylie the same way I love my girlfriend. I am undeniably attracted to her, fascinated by the differences between her and my girlfriend, in love with the prospect of her loving me, but we have not put in the years together—the long runs, the dinners, all the other intimacies—that my girlfriend and I have to make what we have love. That said, I don't think it would take very much to be in love with real Kylie. I'm most of the way there.

My feelings aside, cheating on girlfriend Kylie is not okay, and neither is making real Kylie miserable. This can't go on indefinitely.

I don't know what to do. What I feel for both Kylies is painfully real, and I hate that they didn't come by their feelings for me naturally, as I did for them. I'm seized by an urge to cry. I need someone to talk to who isn't Kylie, but I have no one else in my life but Uncle Joey. Maybe he's home, in bed early. I must really be desperate, because I decide to go check.

I let the banister guide me back downstairs. I go through the living room and into Uncle Joey's wing. His bedroom door is open, and when I look inside, I see his bed is still made. Just in case he's sitting in his office in the dark, I check there, too, and find I am as alone as I thought in this empty, empty house.

I slog back upstairs, but this time pass my bedroom and head for the room at the end of the hall. I open the door but leave the light off. Instead of re-examining the contents of the boxes, I open the closet. Some of my mom's and dad's best clothes hang inside here—Mom's wedding dress and some evening wear, Dad's suits and ties. Not the sweaters they used to wear apple picking, the jeans for the playground, or the T-shirts and shorts for painting the house one summer.

The everyday clothes are all gone now. Bagged up and left in a drop box years ago. This black dress and gray suit aren't what I really want right now, but they'll do. I take them into my arms and sit under the window holding them, just holding these things that my mom and dad marked important occasions with, hopefully laughed in, maybe were wearing when they pulled out their wallets and showed off pictures of me and Tess. My cheeks are wet, and I'm sniffling every few seconds because I'm hugging the clothes tight to my chest. Maybe I'm ruining them with my tears, but I can't imagine my mom and dad would mind at this point. I don't mean to be over-sentimental, but for some reason I'm compelled to just start talking to them.

"Hi, Mom. Hi, Dad. It's me."

They don't answer.

"I just wanted to tell you I miss you. That's all. And that I don't know what to do about Kylie. And I'm failing high school. And everything's all screwed up and I'm a little short on people to talk about it with. That's all."

The clothes smell like dust from a closet, not the warm, vibrant smells of two people who used soap, detergent, and other perfumey things in life. They're soft, though. If my parents were here to hug me, it would be through two layers of clothes, theirs and mine, so it's partly satisfying. In the dark it's easier to imagine they're here.

"When you were alive," I say, "did you picture what you wanted me to be someday? Did you want your kid to be a doctor? A philosopher? A medical researcher? Before the crash was there anything I was kinda good at? Anything I can choose to make you proud?"

I heard of a movie once where some mom who was dying made a video for her kids for after she was gone. A professor dying of cancer wrote a book for his kids. My parents didn't leave me anything. Not even clues. Of course, they didn't know they were going to die suddenly, but it would have been helpful if they'd planned for the unexpected.

Once, not long after I made Jonathan-is-a-hero, I wanted to make another world called The-crash-never-happened. The night I almost did was a night a lot like this. Only, I was crying on my bed instead of in this cold room, and I was holding the picture from the mantel instead of dusty clothes. I had The-crash-never-happened all worked out, what day it would start (a sunny day in summer), what we would do that day (go to the beach), what we would pack for lunch (peanut butter and jelly sandwiches), even what towels we would bring (the circus-themed ones Auntie Carrie had given us). The cry I'm having right now is nothing compared to the one I had that night. I was still pretty young, still talking to God back then, and I prayed so hard that He would just give me back my family without my having to do it by making a world. He could send their souls back from heaven anytime He wanted, but He didn't.

In the end I couldn't do it either. There is a difference between creating a world from nothing, like Jonathan-is-a-hero, or copying a living person I barely knew, like Kylie, and bringing the three people who meant the most to me back from the dead. It was too much to bear. I hated myself for a long time after that night. Since I had been granted world-making powers, what better way to use them than to give my family back the lives that were stolen away? Drowning in my guilt over the decision to leave them dead was more painful than almost drowning in a sinking plane in Boston Harbor.

If I had made The-crash-never-happened, I would have a mom and dad right now to tell me what to do. About Kylie. About everything. I wipe my slobbery face on the gray suit and sit, tearless in the dark. I'm all dried up. And I'm very tired.

"It's not so bad as all that." The light snaps on, and I hit my head on the windowsill as I jump with shock. Standing at the switch is the pink-sweater girl. Only, she's wearing a black leather vest over a brown turtleneck.

"Tess?"

She's chewing gum. Her jaw drops and rises with the chomping of it. Then she blows and snaps a quick bubble. "Yep."

I rise and brush the wrinkles out of Mom's and Dad's clothes to hang them back in the closet, never taking my eyes off Tess. My dead little sister.

She just watches with her arms crossed, leaning against the wall. "Honestly, I didn't think you'd be the type to hold a pity-fest."

My eyes are still swollen, so there's no use pretending they weren't full of tears. "I would think, of all people, you'd understand."

"Oh, I understand perfectly."

I hang Mom's and Dad's clothes nicely in their place, and now I have nothing to do with my hands but shove them into my jeans pockets while I confront this strangely hostile, grown-up person who says she's Tess. "Have you returned from the dead to torment me?"

She scoffs at that. "Yeah, I was restless in my grave because I never had the chance to get you back for tormenting *me*."

"I never tormented you."

"As the big brother, you made torment a priority."

"I think you—"

She holds up a hand like a police officer halting traffic. "Shut up. I'm not here to argue with you."

The room turns chilly all of a sudden, like they say it does when a ghost is in the room. I'm just shy of scared right now— my arguing with her was a way to keep my nerves in check. "Then why are you here? What are you?"

"I thought you recognized me."

"How can you possibly be Tess?"

"That's for me to know and you to find out."

What a lousy thing to say. I can't believe she said that at a moment like this. "Who are you, really?"

She pushes off the wall and steps closer to me. "C'mon, Bro. This room is creepy." She takes my hand, and a shudder runs through me. Her touch is warm, like a living person's, but she can't be my Tess and be living.

Since she's evasive with her answers, I stop asking questions and let her lead me out of the room. Her straight black hair hangs to the middle of her back. A couple of metal bracelets clink together as she sways her free hand with her stride. She's all womanly figure, which makes it even harder to believe she's the same person who did her hair in pigtails and played shirtless at the beach with me.

Shouldn't a reunion between a long-lost sister and brother require, at minimum, a great big hug? She doesn't seem too moved by seeing me, and the emotional distance makes an even bigger tangle of my emotions. This might really be Tess. My Tess. Alive Tess.

She takes me into my room and sits me on the bed, then plops down beside me and checks her wristwatch. I glance over at my alarm clock to see it's almost ten p.m. "Usually," Tess says, "she's asleep by now, but she's writing that damned paper."

Writing a paper. "Are you talking about Kylie?"

"Of course I'm talking about Kylie. Isn't that why you're all weepy and such?"

"Your pleasant attitude's making me happier by the minute."

"Don't flatter me."

She checks her watch again, like it will say something different even though it has been only a few seconds. She leans back on my bed, pulling her legs up so the bottoms of her boots are on the edge of the mattress, and puts her hands behind her head. Since I don't move, all I can see of her now are her black leather boots. "Tell me, Big Brother, if you could have only one Kylie, which would you pick?"

"I'm not discussing Kylie with you."

"Sure you are."

"No, I'm not."

"Not even if I can solve your problem?"

"I don't have a problem."

"Sure you do."

She shifts position again, and her boots disappear behind me. "I'm here to help you solve it." She moves around on the bed, and the next thing I know, her fingers are massaging my shoulders. Where she touches me, warmth radiates down in deep circles, like her hands are heating pads, or even heating guns. Ironically, it makes me shiver at first, but as she kneads and presses and digs with her thumbs, I realize my shoulders have been holding a lot of tension. I melt into a slouch, and Tess pushes me down onto the bed so she can reach my middle back, my lower back. I sink into the bedcovers, and she straddles me, pushing me deeper into the mattress while her warm fingers find tension and rub it away. I think vaguely that having my sister do this is not appropriate, but the heat spreads quickly from my back into my chest, arms, and legs. My head grows heavy like I'm half-asleep, and with my eyes closed all I can do is absorb the deep circles she's making from my spine out, then from my lower back up. Long, slow, rhythmic movements. Penetrating knots and cares and untying them until I feel something like an ice cream cone that's melted to the summer pavement.

She changes technique and starts running her fingers up and down with a feathery touch. My skin prickles, and all my little alarms go off because I can't move. She pauses at my lower back and lifts my shirt a few inches, running her fingers left and right on the bare skin. I try to fight it but sink deeper and deeper into that dreamy state. Her hands slide up under my shirt, and the weight of her shifts forward. With an increasing warmth she lowers herself to reach up to my bare shoulders. The tension is gone, and I'm about as able to shake her off me as a puddle can shake off a towel. Every movement of her fingers soaks some of me up, and I'm drawn inside her, like her flesh and blood and bone are my flesh and blood and bone. I open my mouth to protest, but all I hear is a moan stifled by the blanket. Everything is wrong.

Her chest presses against my back, and her head settles on my neck. Her fingers stroke gently up and down behind my ears, even the ear turned to the mattress. She reaches under my jaw and rubs circles to loosen the clench I've apparently been holding. The unnatural warmth of her hands and her body covers me like the world's heaviest down comforter, and I'm sweating even as my skin remains prickled all over. She moves my arms so they stretch out over my head, intertwines her fingers with mine, and my softened muscles don't resist. She's massaged herself into me so deeply, I can only lie there beneath her.

In this position her mouth is near my upturned ear. "This is merging," she says. "This is your answer."

My mouth forms the words as she says them. Her words, my

words, I'm not sure anymore. My fingers grasp my own fingers; her leather boots crowd my own toes; her leather vest pulls tight over my own chest; her feminine, flowery scent becomes my scent. When she breathes, it's my breath. Our hearts thump with one pulse. I am still me, but she is also me. Her calm control interlaces with my panic and makes it feel like I'm yelling to myself from a mountaintop far, far away.

"If this were the Kylies," she says, but I hear my own voice, "they'd become everything you want." Our arms come down, and she's no longer on top of me. She has descended into me. We roll to our side and curl into the covers, breathing, slowly breathing. "One new Kylie to want you and love you and remember everything you've shared in your made-up world. But she'd be here, in your real world."

I hear the quiet of my room like an echo. Her ear, my ear, one ear. The desk, dresser, and closet all stand, solid and timeless, while I see them with echoing vision. Old Jonathan's room. I am old Jonathan no longer.

We curl a little more tightly, grasping the covers with our shared hands, and all these thoughts that aren't mine mix themselves in. Memories combine. Two perspectives of what it meant for an older brother and younger sister to witness the same snowfall through the windowpane. Of the jealously one felt while the other blew out birthday candles and opened presents. Of running, simply running through the yard and down the street. Of one falling from a tree and breaking on the ground and the other screaming for Mom and Dad to come help. Of one pushing the other into the deep end of the neigh-bor's pool. Of petting sheep and using crayons and hiking in woods and watching cartoons. Magic, speed, singing, anger, whiteness, joy. Seizing with panic when the cabin alarm goes off and Mom clutches one of us and Dad the other and the fire rolls across the ceiling. Seat belts choke our bellies and Mom burns black and Dad yanks our buckles, and windows darken with sea, and the minutes, the endless minutes, while water rises from the front of the cabin and we hold on to seat backs to climb to the place where someone has opened a door at the back, and seat belts are stuck, all the seat belts are stuck except for ours, and hands can't unstick them, and the pressure of the water on our chests and the cold and the moment when we can hold out no longer and breathe the water in.

Kylie. Either I think of her or Tess thinks of her. I'm with Kylie on the very first day I made Kylie-Simms-is-my-girlfriend. She smiles at me. Even though I willed her to love me as part of my world-making, I gasp with surprise when she kisses me for the first time. It's awkward to gasp while someone's lips are touching yours, and I panic that I've just given her the worst kiss ever. She doesn't take notice, just tries again, and this time

I do a little better, even manage to move my hands along her back.

I dredge up real Kylie at Mexican Station, shaky and awkward as she describes her "obsession" with me. Tess mentally smirks at the idea of someone enthralled by my pathetic case, and her callous response flits amid my own embarrassment over Kylie's weird feelings. The Fine Arts Museum emerges next, complete with my dissatisfaction with my girlfriend's lack of realness and my girlfriend's perception that something's not right between us.

More images, more sensations, rise and recede intermixed with shadows from Tess, as if certain thoughts wither and die before they can reach me, whereas my thoughts can't move into her fast enough. In a flash of insight, I realize most of what's coming from her is really an echo of what's coming from me— not really a sister's perspective at all but my own framed in a stranger's set of eyes. I try to see Tess herself, but get only shadow. She, by contrast, soaks up everything I am, down to my guilt over whatever is happening to Kylie in both worlds.

The bed shifts beneath me, and Tess's fingers are kneading at my back again. Thoughts of Kylie subside, and I flex my fingers, the first movement I've been able to make for some minutes. I check to see that I can curl my toes. My abdomen contracts on command. My eyes open and close. Tess's warmth leaks away as I test more and more parts and remaster my thoughts, feel my liquid self grow solid again.

Tess squeezes my arm, then lies down behind me. As before, her touch makes me shiver, though she is as warm as a furnace.

I lie still, reliving the past few moments, thinking of that movie where the guy goes into a chamber with a fly and comes out with the fly's genetics all mixed up in him. That's not too far off from how I feel. Only, instead of becoming part fly, I've become doubly myself.

She pats me on the arm and then shifts again as if moving to sit up. I slip away from her and perch at the end of the bed, far enough so she can't confuse me with another touch.

"What just happened?"

"I told you. It's merging. It's your answer."

"My answer to what?"

"What to do about Kylie."

"I'm not doing that with Kylie." No way.

"*You* don't merge with her. She has to merge with herself. You know, the real Kylie with the extra special version you created."

"That's sick."

"Well, she wouldn't be quite so relaxed. I was just trying to help you out."

"That's sick," I say again. I wouldn't have had the experience myself if I'd been given a choice.

"Oh, get over yourself, Jonathan."

"No, you get over yourself, Tess. If you really are Tess." I'm remembering how part of what just happened was sharing the experience of drowning in the crash. Something about those memories now seems more like the echo I sensed just before she finished with me. Did she steal my memories and then send them back like they were hers, too?

"If you have a problem with me, I don't have to help you," she says.

"I don't see any help here."

"I just merged with you, Jonathan, to show you what has to be done."

"You're not listening. There's no way I'm letting that happen to Kylie."

"Well, sorry to be the bringer of bad news, but you don't have a choice."

"Like hell I don't."

"You sure need everything spelled out for you." She rolls her eyes and sighs mightily. "This is what's wrong with Kylie and Kylie. You mixed up your worlds and the Kylies have started to merge. If you don't help them finish, it won't be pretty."

CHAPTER 14

TESS SITS CROSS-LEGGED ON THE OTHER SIDE OF MY bed, all smug in the extra knowledge she has that I don't. Her hands rest on her knees in a meditation pose. Her face, though, is anything but meditative. The scowl there speaks volumes about what she thinks of me at this moment.

I'm not quite sure how to act around her. I don't feel like the big brother in this scenario. She knows how to do all this stuff I don't, like merge people and flit around through my worlds. I suppose we once had a sibling rivalry, which could be hostile sometimes, but that's what children do. Tess's teenage antagonism is over-the-top, and kind of mean, and really intimidating, and makes me wonder if the crash messed her up as much as it messed up me. I may have gotten all the physical scars, but inside I changed only into a self-pitying loser, while she might have changed into an actual monster.

"You're so full of it," I say, because I'm so upset, it's all I can say. She scares me. Plus, what if she's right about merging Kylie?

"You know, I'm getting pretty close to letting you deal with this on your own."

I squint my eyes at her, and she squints back. It's the kind of thing we might have done when we were six and eight years old back in the day. "If you really want to help me, you need to back up and explain a few things."

She rounds her fingers and her thumbs to make Os on the tops of her knees, and she replaces her scowl with a creepy smirk that makes my blood shudder. "Okay, shoot," she says.

I'm tempted to do that little-kid thing where you mimic someone you want to drive up a wall—*Okay, shoot*—but I don't, because it's possible she'll be straight with me if I behave.

It's a mighty effort to project composure with my voice. "First of all, what exactly is merging?"

She inhales impatiently and looks to the ceiling as if summoning help from the Almighty to deal with this stupid question, but when she looks back down at me, it's with the same restraint I'm exercising too. "Merging is exactly what it sounds like. Two different bodies merge into one."

"And the result is one person."

"Yes."

"But whatever you just did to me, we're still two people."

"Well, that's because I don't want to be half me, half you, forever. I was just giving you a taste of what it would be like."

"But . . . I felt like I was wearing your clothes. I was thinking thoughts that didn't come from me."

"We were close to being merged, you and I, but I unmerged us."

"Well, why can't you 'unmerge' Kylie?"

"I can't unmerge someone else any more than I can merge them. I can control only what happens to me."

"Then teach Kylie how to unmerge herself."

"I can't."

"Can't? Or won't?"

"She's not a world-maker, Brother Jonathan. Both Kylies have lived blissful, tragedy-free existences."

"So, it's definite." Though, until now I didn't realize I'd had any doubt. "We both got our powers from the plane crash?"

"Duh," she says, but her face darkens. Just a split-second cloud, but that lost beat tells me she's not saying something she should.

Now I'm curious as hell.

She must sense her slip, because she shifts out of her meditational pose and crosses her arms, firmly entrenching herself in a *You can't touch me with a ten-foot pole* attitude so surly, I wonder why she even came here in the first place. I decide to chip away in a slightly different direction. "How can you show up in *my* made-up worlds?"

"I can be in any world I want. It goes with the merging ability."

"Does that mean I can go into your worlds too?"

"Someday we'll test that theory."

"This seems like a great day for a test. How about a field trip to the beach? That was your world, wasn't it? Back at the mall?"

"We have far more important errands tonight than visiting my little worlds."

"You still haven't told me what world you come from, exactly."

She drops her arms and whips on an offended expression. "Your world, silly."

"Then why is this the first time you've ever come to talk to me? Where do you get off knowing oh so much more about all this than I do? Why am I under the impression you're buried in a grave with Mom and Dad?"

"You've never actually seen that plot, have you? Never been to visit the graves of your dearly departed family you profess to miss so much."

She's got me there, and I can't stand it that my fear is the only reason I can't say for sure if her name is on a gravestone.

She scoots off the bed and stands in front of me, hands on hips. "I bet your girlfriend's done with her paper by now."

"So?"

"We could go fix your problem."

"You mean now?"

"Will there be a better time?"

"You still haven't answered my questions."

"I'm tactfully changing the subject."

All her knowing and not telling makes it hard not to loathe her with a fiery passion. "I still don't understand how merging Kylie will make anything better."

"For one thing, you won't have to go world-hopping all the time. You'll have your girlfriend with you in your real world, and you can finish the year earning back credit in your classes."

"I don't need to make things better for me. I meant for Kylie."

"Oh, you mean the I'm-obsessing-over-you-and-it's-freaking-me-out thing?" She flutters her eyelashes in a bad imitation of a flirty Kylie. "You know you like it."

"Shut up, Tess."

"Would you still want to change things if she were obsessing over you and *she* liked it?"

"What part of 'shut up' was tricky for you?"

She takes a breath and shifts her weight to her other foot. Her shoulders drop and give her a less hostile posture, which sort of resets the conversation. She sits down next to me again. I cringe when she lays her heat gun fingers on my leg, a peace offering of sorts. "In all seriousness," she says, "if you don't help

Kylie, her obsession will get crazy worse. Your girlfriend Kylie is already starting to wonder what she ever saw in you, but her world is still forcing her to love you, and that's an internal conflict you don't want escalating. They'll merge a little more and a little more each day but never be able to finish because they can't touch.

"But if they do touch, once merging is complete, they'll be one totally normal person, maybe even a better person. That's because merging is an opportunity. When you merge, you feel like you just remembered a bunch of things you'd forgotten. You get to use extra brain space that normally goes unused, but you don't have extra leg space or lung space, so you keep what's healthier. Like if real Kylie has a weak ankle from a sprain, merging will give her your girlfriend's ankle 'cause it's healthier.

"She'll have to reconcile conflicting memories, like how she spent the last few years with or without you, but I'm betting the memories with you win out since they're pretty happy ones."

I hope that's true, but it's not the only thing that will have to go one way or the other. "Will she want to be a journalist or a medical researcher?"

"I don't know."

"Won't her parents mind when she comes home with a totally new set of life goals and a boyfriend she claims she's been seeing for all of high school that they know nothing about? When they start questioning her sanity, won't that make her question it too?"

"Eh." She waves a casual hand in the air. "She's going to college in a few months. No one there will question her."

"But what about those few months she's home?"

"You could merge her parents, too."

"Absolutely not."

"Then Kylie will just have to deal with it. It might suck for her till she leaves for school, but it will suck for the rest of her life if you don't help her."

"Okay. If I choose to do this, what do I do?"

"You pick which world you want Kylie to live in, and you take the other Kylie to her. Then they touch."

"What do you mean, 'they touch'?" I do not want to think about the back rubbing scenario and two Kylies, but the image forms anyway.

"I mean this." She points a finger and pokes me in the forearm. A burning hot jolt goes up to my shoulder.

"And then what happens?"

"Two become one and you're done."

"And she's happy again?"

"Happier."

"And there's no aftereffects?"

"Nope, except for the teeny possibility of homesickness for her other world, but that won't be a problem if you close it."

"Close it? I can't close a world."

"Sure you can."

This is news to me. I have only ever been a world-maker. I have never ended a world. "Okay, smartie. How do you close a world?"

"Same way you open one."

That makes no sense. To make a world I squeeze my eyes shut and think real hard on what I want to open them on.

"You will it closed," she says. "That's all. You just convince yourself that you want it closed, and it will close. Plus a little destructive imagery."

"That's not how I make a world."

"Sure it is. You just think the squeezey-eye move has something to do with it. What opens a world is your will to have it be and your images of creation."

"And Jonathan said, 'Let there be a Kylie who loves me,' and there she was."

Tess cocks her head and gives me a sideways glance. "Yeah. Kinda like that."

"But if I can close a world, why do I even have to merge the Kylies? Can't I just close Kylie-Simms-is-my-girlfriend and let the real Kylie live in peace?"

"That would be the worst possible thing, if you're trying to save her."

"Why?"

"Because she's already partly merged with your girlfriend. If you kill off the girlfriend, it'll kill off the parts of real Kylie that have merged already."

"But they haven't touched."

"Their thoughts have. Their emotions have. You've seen that for yourself."

"Enough." I feel like my guts are coming out of my head. "I have to think about this. I need you to leave me alone for a while."

"Fine." She rolls away from me and climbs off the bed. "But the longer you wait, the worse it gets."

"I get it, okay? Just go."

I expect a sharp comeback, but she disappoints me. "I'll come back tomorrow night. I have some things to teach you that you'll need to know in order to do this right." It's the least sarcastic her tone has been since she appeared down the hall. I'm almost thankful for her help. Almost. I don't feel even one percent right about any of this, and I don't know whether it's because I don't trust Tess to be giving me good advice or I don't trust me to take it.

"I'll see you tomorrow, then," I say.

Without an actual "Good-bye," she blinks out of existence, and I burn to know where she went. Another world? Another place in this world? The afterworld? The grave? Speculation will drive me mad, so I do the only thing I can do. Lace up my sneakers and go for a run.

I don't want to run to Kylie's house, but my feet start moving in that direction. When I get there, I'll just look at her through the window. Or I can run by without stopping at her house at all. I don't have the heart to ruin her peaceful night's sleep just because I'm not sleeping.

The streets are full of solitude, a perfect setting for a restless mind. No cars pass me as I hop over tree roots that've grown up through the sidewalk. Very few windows are backlit through curtains. It's cold enough that I can see my breath.

Tess has sprung to life after all these years, at the same time two Kylies begin haunting each other. Of course this can't be coincidence. I trace the chain of events: a strange disturbance sent me running to girlfriend' Kylie's, I almost kissed real Kylie when I thought I was in Kylie-Simms-is-my-girlfriend, the Kylies started to merge, Tess appeared in order to help me fix it. Is Tess connected to that initial cosmic weirdness? Or has she been watching me all along and appeared only because I'm in trouble?

Tess wants me to merge two Kylies into one. Does that, essentially, mean they both die? Does that mean they both live? Will Kylie understand what's happened to her? Will I lose her?

A critical part of me, one I'm trying real hard to relegate to the background of my fear, insists that this is what I get for messing in world-making. Maybe the power has finally caught up with me. I'm not strong enough or wise enough to use it properly, and now I've made a mistake only a better person can fix.

The exclamation point on all my thoughts is this: my world got turned inside out when I was eight. It's not fair to have everything inside out again.

I need Kylie right now. There is no way I'm going to make it through what remains of the night without her. I know I said that I wouldn't invade her peaceful sleep, but she won't mind. She never minds, not in Kylie-Simms-is-my-girlfriend.

Tess said changing worlds is a matter of will, not eye-squeezing, so I try it. I keep my eyes as open as possible, which is necessary anyway, since I don't intend to slow my pace and the tree roots are doing their best to send me sprawling. I will myself into my other world, but for the first time with eyes wide open, I see what I never saw before. Blackness stretches away from me in all directions. It's scattered with spheres, hundreds and hundreds of spheres, visible only in the tiniest slivers, like very new moons. Dark corridors weave among the spheres, joining them, outlined by whatever obscure light forms the crescents. The scene is breathtaking in its vastness, cosmic in ambiance, like looking at a universe without stars or solar systems or galaxies, but rich with worlds. So many worlds. I try to linger, but it takes only a split second to slip through the corridor to Kylie-Simms-is-my-girlfriend, or rather, for the corridor to slip over me. The impossible distance between worlds shrinks like a stretched coil that has suddenly snapped back. One quick breath and a blink of the eye, and my journey's over. I stand in the shadows between the bushes outside Kylie's house, panting from the run and the anxiety of watching my own shift between worlds.

There is so much I don't understand.

I catch my breath and let my heart rate return to normal, trying to convince myself that being here is a good idea, and that I should still worry about my small problems in the face of the vastness I just crossed. I open her window and crawl through without her even stirring.

I toe my shoes off and stand watching Kylie. Her back is to me, and her hair is spread over the pillow. Her feet, cozied in thick purple socks, stick out from the bottom of her covers. In the corner her fan whirs, a sign that she was having trouble sleeping, which normally would make me want to cuddle up and offer comfort, but tonight I have a feeling I'm the reason she needed the fan.

If that's the case, coming here was a huge mistake. I go to pick up my shoes so I can cross back to the real world, when Kylie stops me with a word. "Jonathan."

She doesn't roll over, and my name sounded like it was spoken into her comforter. She's still asleep. Half-bent toward my shoes, I freeze to listen.

Her breathing is quick and shallow, like she's running maybe, but nothing of her stirs beyond the rise and fall of her covers with her breath. "Jonathan," she says again, and it sounds like she's trying to scream it out.

I go to the bed and gently rouse her with a hand on her shoulder.

She rolls toward me and says my name again. "Shhhhh," I say. "It's okay."

Her eyes open to my face, and it takes a moment before she apparently comprehends that she's awake and I'm here in the flesh. She cringes back and cries out with enough volume that I hope her parents don't hear. I listen for telltale signs of them running down the hall.

"You scared the crap out of me," she whispers, more loudly than I would like.

"You were dreaming."

"Yeah," is all she says. I can't tell if she's forgotten her dream or if she knows she was calling my name. "What are you doing here?"

"I needed to see you."

"In the middle of the night?"

"I guess it was a bad idea." I hope this is the aftereffects of the dream, because she has never given me such a cold reception.

She rubs something out of the corner of her eye with a fingertip. "What time is it?"

"Three seventeen."

She flops onto her back. She's in the middle of the bed. There's no room for me, so I continue standing awkwardly beside her.

"Is something wrong?" she asks.

Only everything. "No. I think I'd better go." When I turn, she reaches over and grabs my arm.

"Don't. I'm sorry. I was having a nightmare."

"Yeah. About me."

"Why would you think that?"

"I heard you say my name."

She ruminates on that for a moment. "You were dragging me somewhere. I didn't like it."

"I would never take you somewhere you didn't want to go." That's not a lie, not yet.

At last she scoots over to the wall. "It was just a dream," she says, and lifts up the covers for me. I am so relieved, I jump right in and put my arms around her.

She snuggles into me, soft and mostly relaxed, considering the last few minutes. For the moment, anyway, this Kylie is comfortable with me. This Kylie wants to be with me. I kiss her hair, secure that she appreciates the affection.

"Have you been running? You're wearing running stuff," she asks.

"Yeah."

"Why would you run all the way over here?"

"Maybe I just missed you." Her hand moves to my chest and makes mini caresses through my shirt, right where the worst of my scars live, over my heart.

"This is twice in a week. Should I be worried?"

"No worries." I kiss her again on the head. We lie there for a while, her fingers gently caressing, my arm wrapped tightly around her. She slides a leg over mine. I shift a little to face her. She props herself on an elbow, and soon we're kissing. Slow kisses so filled with devotion, I wonder if Tess is wrong. Kylie is not conflicted. She loves me as she always has.

We cover a few bases in silence, moving hands and bodies under the covers. I wish I weren't doing this after getting sweaty from running, but she doesn't seem to care. Neither of us is sweating now. We are not aflame with violent passion. Our touches are soft and unhurried, like each stroke of the fingers or brush of the lips whispers, *I love you* or *I'm content being this close to you.*

Kylie and I have done violent passion, but tonight that's not what I need, and she has always excelled at giving me what I need. Tonight I need *I love you* more than anything else in the world.

I lose track of time—five minutes, ten minutes, more, less. We finish with a deep kiss. She plants a peck on the tip of my nose and says what she has just shown me with the gentleness of her body. "I love you, Jonathan."

I smile. It's been a while since the corners of my mouth turned up instead of down. "I love you, too. Always." What I really want to say is *Thank you. Thank you for being the only person in the world who loves me.* But that's not what the moment calls for.

She cuddles into the soft space between my shoulder and my neck, ready to find sleep together. All my time with Kylie has built this special easiness between us. When I first created her, we couldn't mess around and then snuggle in for the night so quickly. It's beautiful, really, the way we are so comfortable now, and before I let her dream, I cast off my final doubts with a question.

"Kylie, did you ever want to be a medical researcher?"

She lazily drapes an arm over me. "A long time ago, I think I did. I wanted to cure you, but, then, you didn't need curing."

"Was winter ever your favorite season?"

"Maybe on snow days from school." Her voice is sleepy, and she stifles a yawn as she nestles closer. "Why the random questions?"

I want to tell her. I really want to tell her, because she deserves to know, but I don't think three in the morning, just roused from a nightmare and reconciled with intimacy, is the best time to do it. Plus I don't think I can make myself say the words.

"Are you okay?" she asks.

"I'm fine, now." And I am. Except I don't ever want to be without her, and I fear, one way or the other, soon I will be.

CHAPTER 15

I LIE AWAKE IN KYLIE'S BED, BUT SHE ISN'T HERE. HER ALARM clock says 6:04 a.m., so I assume she's in the shower. Since she chose not to wake me, I figure it's okay to linger long enough to say good-bye.

I close my eyes, so tired that I'm almost asleep again when I hear the door click open. For one panicky second I think it's Kylie's mom, but it's not. Kylie glides over to me wearing a fluffy white towel, her wet hair clinging to her head and shoulders. "Morning," she says, and sits on the edge of the bed.

I sit up with her, noting the difference between my rumpled sleepiness and her fresh showeredness. Her long legs are smooth and shiny like she just shaved them. In the semi-lit room the white scar on her knee glows. It's just a short line, earned when she hit a hurdle in practice last year. It bled a red rivulet down to her sock, and when the scab peeled, she was proud of the evidence left behind. Now we both had scars.

I only note it now because I'm remembering something Tess said. If one Kylie had a sprained ankle and the other didn't, a merged Kylie would end up with the good ankle. So a merged Kylie, it follows, would end up with a scar-less knee. We'd no longer be "scar buddies," as Kylie once called us. Irrationally, I'm devastated by this thought.

Kylie notices me staring at her scar, but she doesn't say anything. Last night was so nice, I really am wondering if Tess's merging scenario disaster is highly exaggerated. One way to check is to spend time with real Kylie and see how she's recovering from her confessions at Mexican Station. If she seems as normal as this Kylie, things might be okay after all. The only problem with that is that it means spending today in the real world, not with my girlfriend.

"I might not see you in school," I tell Kylie.

"How come?"

"I have to take care of something. Nothing bad, but it has to be during school hours. I'm going in to talk to Coach Pereira just in case I'm not back by practice."

She doesn't like this idea. I note a faint wrinkle in her mood. "You want to tell me about it?"

"Maybe later."

"Tonight?"

"I don't know. I might have to do something for Uncle Joey."

That sounds like one excuse too many, and the excuses are only going to pile up the longer I split my Kylie time.

"Fine," she says, and storms over to her dresser. She picks up a hairbrush, turns on a blow-dryer, and gets to work in the mirror. She glares at my reflection as I put on my shoes. Only then do I notice the circles under her eyes, like maybe she didn't sleep well the rest of the night.

I wave to her, unable to say good-bye because I don't want to shout in her parents' house over the hair dryer. I've never seen her act hostile before. As I climb out the window and crouch in the bushes to go back to the real world, I'm worried that maybe she's not altogether normal after all.

My nerves are shot as I walk into creative writing. The desks are arranged in a circle today, so I park a few seats down from two girls who arrived before me. Mr. Eckhart is out of the room, and the doors to the adjoining rooms are open. The noise of hyperactive freshmen comes pouring through the door to the front.

A few more people arrive, including Emily and Zach, who sit directly opposite me and start unloading their materials for class. I reach down to unzip my bag and pull out my notebook and pen. While I'm bent over, someone claims the seat next to me. I recognize the shoes. It's Kylie.

"Hi," she says, and it comes out like a little-girl squeal. In fact, she bounces a couple of times in her seat like an excited kid. Out of the corner of my eye, I see Zach and Emily look up at us. They frown, and I feel like I've done something wrong.

"Hi." I'm not a blusher like Kylie, but I feel a twinge of blood rising to my face.

She's dropped her backpack onto her desk and is rummaging through it. In a few seconds she's got a notebook and pen and has stuffed the bag under her chair. She reaches over and grabs my notebook right off my desk, flips through the pages until she finds a blank one, and writes, *Dear Jonathan, I'm sorry about last night. Love, Kylie.* Although Emily can't see what's written, I swear her jaw drops when Kylie gives the notebook back to me. Zach just looks amused.

Eckhart chooses that moment to walk in, and the bell sounds behind him. He closes all the classroom doors and announces it's a free writing day. "Let's put up a few topics," he says.

The class sits and thinks for a moment before people start raising their hands. Eckhart chalks their suggestions onto the board.

"Write about what it would be like to be the last of the unicorns." That was Kaitlyn Frost.

"Write a conversation between the ghost of a person who got killed by a drunk driver and the person in jail who killed them." Mitchell Hoversley.

"Make a list of things you can use a tissue box for." Sherri Grace Pearce.

"Make as many stupid similes as you can." Claude Arsenault.

"Make up a college major and describe the classes." Zach.

Eckhart adds a couple of his own and sets us to writing independently for fifty minutes. Students relocate from their desks to their favorite inspirational spots, but I never change positions for free writing. Kylie usually sits by the window, but today she doesn't budge.

She grins at me like we're sharing a secret plan to collaborate on a masterpiece, and opens her notebook. Before long she's writing, so I get to it.

I decide to make a college major in world-making. If I had to read this to the class, or if I thought Eckhart would actually take it seriously when he reads it, I wouldn't do this, but with Kylie all giddy beside me I feel a little reckless.

Courses:

World-making 101: Will it. Don't squeeze it.

World-making 102:

Um, World-making 102 . . .

As for that World-making 102 . . .

There are plenty of things I think of writing but just can't bring myself to. *World-making 102: Living without a family.* Or *Creating the love of your life.* Or *When your dead sister shows up.* Or *What to do when your girlfriend and the girl you want to be your girlfriend start to merge.* Nothing is lighthearted enough to match my original intent. The last thing I want is Eckhart reporting me to Mr. Diamond.

So I flip the notebook page to start something new. I'd rip the page out, except that would make a noise in the silent room.

What to do now?

My writer's brain is like a pig, covered in slop. There's one stupid simile, but I don't think Claude Arsenault would be impressed.

The rule in free writing is that you keep your pen in motion as much as possible. Even if you're stuck, you commit words to paper, so I raise my pen and start committing words.

Fainthearted.

Singularity.

Indefatigable.

Corroded.

Zealous.

Supercalifragilisticexpialidocious.

New Zealand.

Metamorphosis.

Antidisestablishmentarianism.

Paradoxical.

Another notebook slides onto my desk. Kylie has written

me another note. *Dear Jonathan, Want to trade notebooks?*

I look up at Eckhart, who's working at his desk. Sometimes he free writes with us, but today he's grading papers. Kylie stares at me expectantly.

With a slight cringe because I don't know how we'll get credit for this session if we don't write in our own notebooks, I pass mine over. The draft of "Cosmic Mysteries" is in there, but since I intended to give it to her before, and since I'm guessing its content will be familiar to her because girlfriend Kylie has read it, I don't worry too much. Most everything else is as bland as can be. She doesn't flip through the pages, though. She just starts writing in my notebook as if it's hers and she's following directions.

I turn to the next page of her notebook, thinking I'll write something too, but the next page is full. It's a poem titled "Jonathan."

> *he spent the night*
> *in my head*
> *in my room*
> *warm under the covers*
> *a dream but not a dream*
> *this need*
> *like thirst*

like starvation

his presence a feast

are you here, jonathan

i can't tell anymore

please come to me

i'm shivering

Beside me her pen stops moving. She's frozen, gauging my reaction. The room keeps writing, oblivious to what Kylie and I are doing. Emily looks up, eyes unfocused, and returns to her page having found the word or idea she was searching for. Claude smirks to himself in the corner. Claude is always smirking.

Kylie's poem sounds desperate, but the person beside me is giddy. I don't think I've ever known a manic-depressive, but that diagnosis comes to mind. I switch the pen to my left hand to fake that I'm still writing and slowly move my right hand to cover Kylie's. I want to calm and reassure her. She makes a sound—half giggle, half sigh—and to my mortification, several people look up. I'm too afraid to make the sudden movement to detract my hand, just in case the onlookers haven't noticed yet. Kylie and I move our pens like the sound didn't come from us, and the temporary distraction passes.

I can't write with my left hand, so what comes out are strange markings like some ancient language. I wonder if I can get credit for that. Kylie's pen flies down the lines of my notebook, her mood still overexcited, her hand tight beneath mine. Since my touch is not helping anything, I carefully pick my hand up, but she's quick to grab it back, her hand now on mine, clutching it tightly. Mr. Eckhart notices. His eyes narrow on our clasped hands. He doesn't give away any disapproval by his expression, but he does meet my eyes. I'm sure I appear distraught, because that's how I feel. I peek at the notebook Kylie's furiously writing in. The page is covered in the same four words written over and over: "Jonathan Aubrey Kylie Simms, Jonathan Aubrey Kylie Simms." She doesn't notice that she's being watched. Her fingernails dig and undig into my fingers while she writes.

Mr. Eckhart goes back to his work, and I'm guessing he's chosen not to interrupt class by making a big scene out of a relatively small one. Emily is gaping at us now. She pokes Zach in the leg, and he looks up to see us too. Kylie comes to the end of the page and stops. I look sideways at her to see if she's okay, and she looks sideways back at me, then down at our hands. Her nails retreat from my skin, and she pulls my hand under her desk. While she holds my wrist, she rubs out the nail marks with her other hand. "Sorry," she barely whispers.

Her energy subsides a bit, and she returns almost to baseline again, except for the fact that she doesn't let go of my hand. Instead she clasps it just a little more tightly while with her other hand she slowly raises the hem of her jeans. She has to let go of me to get the pant leg up over her knee, but she manages the task, then places my hand on her knee so my index finger touches the smooth skin. Emily and Zach are about to fall out of their chairs.

She shifts in her seat, and between my finger and my eye it's clear that she has no scar there. Eckhart clears his throat at us. Several heads pop up out of their notebooks, several voices snicker, and Kylie drops her pant leg.

She doesn't let go of my hand, though, and although I'm dying because this incident will ruin my obscurity as soon as the ending bell puts the gossip mill in motion, I squeeze her hand back in solidarity.

Mr. Eckhart keeps Kylie and me after class to ask if everything is okay. He makes it clear that future distractions during writing time won't be welcome, but I can tell he's more curious than angry about whatever's going on.

He releases us to the changing of classes. Kylie managed to separate her hand from mine long enough to be scolded by Eckhart, but as we emerge from the room into a small gathering of spies who've already heard, she reattaches herself and pulls me down the hall. I hear someone sneer under their breath, "I wouldn't believe it if I didn't see it."

"What is she thinking?" someone says, and then giggles.

I want to melt through the floor.

Although I planned to stay in the real world today, I can't bear to go through with it now. The truth is that most kids don't give us a second glance because underclassmen probably don't know how unusual it is for Kylie to be with me, but it still *feels* like every eyeball swivels in its socket as we pass.

At her next classroom door Kylie mercifully says good-bye with nothing gushier than a smile and a "Thanks for walking me to class." I run straight to the office to dismiss myself. The secretaries don't even tsk-tsk me anymore. They just take my note and let the administration deal with me.

I endure the final two classes in Kylie-Simms-is-my-girlfriend before heading to track practice. I'm so looking forward to just being out on the roads with my running friends. I need a good heart-pumping, head-clearing distance run and the chatter of other guys talking about normal things.

But when I get down to the gym, the workout posted on the wall is a light two miles on the track. I can't believe I forgot that tomorrow is the big meet against Dunford High School. I didn't expect to be on the track today.

I usually love track days because Kylie's sprint workouts are on the track.

I go out for the team warm-up and stretch next to Rob Finkelstein. He's in a good mood and fills most of the stretch with a story about a girl in his history class whose choice of outfit "left little to the imagination." Kids snapped cell phone pictures every time the teacher turned to add notes to the board. I try not to compare his laughter at this scandal to the other laughter surely spreading over me and real Kylie in the real world. A hundred meters away girlfriend Kylie's leading her team in a stretch, her back to me. I watch her through most of Rob's chatter, hoping she's still the normal Kylie I was with last night, not the unsettled one from this morning.

Coach Pereira comes to collect the distance runners after we finish our stride-outs. He talks to us briefly about the competition tomorrow, who will run what and which points he hopes we'll score in each event. When he's done, we start jogging, and I pass Kylie coming up the track with a pair of starting blocks. The usual bounce in her step is missing. She acknowledges me with a "Hey" as we pass each other, the businesslike delivery not unusual in the middle of practice, but considering everything, not a good sign.

Kylie and Mandy Breuger do starts for their pre-meet workout. I have eight slow laps, so I watch them race each other, over and over, to their coach's mock starting gun. Kylie, who's the best starter on the team, gets beat by Mandy almost every time.

My workout finishes first, like usual. When the sprinters' workout eventually ends, I get the feeling Kylie deliberately avoids me. She goes off with Mandy to stretch by the shed. I sit with Rob and his girlfriend, Jessie, while Jessie finishes her stretch. When Kylie stands up as if done, she goes into the shed. All the hurdles, blocks, cones, etc., are stored in there, and she might be checking over some equipment. I decide it's time to go see her, so I wander over, casually, though I sense disaster coming.

When I round the door to see her talking with Mandy inside, I put on my most confident boyfriend smile.

Kylie ignores my entrance. She stops talking to Mandy and goes over to a set of tape measures, inspects how well each is rolled up. The field event officials are famous for tangling the plastic measuring lines on the wind up. Before big meets the captains sometimes take it upon themselves to check the shed equipment and perform little fixes, but Mandy makes no move to help Kylie. I don't think they're in here to check equipment, and Mandy's giving me a bit of the stink eye.

"Hey, Mandy," I say.

"Hey, Jonathan."

"You guys all set, or should I wait up in the parking lot?"

Kylie starts rerolling a tape measure. "I'm gonna be here a little bit. You can go without me."

That never, ever, ever, ever, ever happens.

Mandy takes that as her cue to leave. "See you tomorrow," she says with one more glance at each of us as she goes out the door.

"Have I done something wrong?" I ask.

"No," Kylie answers a little too quickly.

"Why are you doing your best to half ignore me?"

"I'm not ignoring you." She pulls out another tape and unwinds the mangled part.

"I said *half* ignore."

"Whatever."

She just whatevered me. My heart sinks.

"Kylie, what's wrong?"

"Nothing. I just have to do a few things and there's no need for you to wait."

"Can I help? You could get done faster."

"Uh-uh." She shakes her head for emphasis. "I'm fine. Really. You can go."

"You're getting rid of me."

Her hand pulls length after length, spinning the remaining tape around its axis. I think she's about to deny it, when she stops pulling and sighs. "Maybe I am."

The admission means we're getting somewhere. Since we're

on opposite sides of the shed, I take a few steps closer. "Is it because of this morning?"

She shakes her head.

"What, then?"

"I don't know. Just . . . I need a little space."

The words no boyfriend wants to hear. "Did something happen?"

"No. . . . I don't know." I'm pretty sure I'm wearing an expression of utter devastation, but with no remorse she plows right past me to put the tape measure into the triple jump crate. "Just don't come over tonight, okay? I have to sleep for the meet tomorrow."

"I understand," I say. She does look tired. She tries to plow back past me to get another tape. I reach for her shoulder, mostly to show her I'm still here for her when she's ready. She draws a startled breath and yanks away. She realizes a second later what she's just done.

"I'm sorry, Jonathan. I didn't mean that."

The damage, however, is done. I saw the appalled expression on her face, though it morphs quickly into something that begs me to forgive her. I'd begun to think Kylie wasn't capable of breaking up with me because of how I made her world. Looks like merging with your counterpart who has no loving-Jonathan requirement might change all that. Hurt as I am, I'm mindful enough to remember this is all my fault, not hers.

"It's okay," I say. I don't make another move to touch her, just back slowly away. "See you in school tomorrow."

Her hands are fisted at her sides, and her eyes glisten as she watches me go. "Yeah. See you tomorrow."

CHAPTER 16

I SHOOT TO THE SITTING-UP-AFTER-A-NIGHTMARE position, shivering all over even though the sheets are soaked with sweat. I have this lingering image of seat belts in a tangle, arms and legs and necks strapped to a chair like in an execution, the buckles on those seat belts rising up and floating away. In the shadows I might even detect the echo of a scream I think I made.

I've thrown my comforter to the side, and the sweat on my body cools in the bare air, only making me shiver harder. I pull the bedcover back around me and hunker down against the mattress, working through the shivers and calming my breathing. I check the clock and find it's just after two a.m. The dream recedes as dreams do, and my body slowly rediscovers its own warmth.

Apparently my body also thinks it's slept long enough, because my brain clicks into worry mode, assaulting me with memories of the previous day. One Kylie's pseudo-affection in creative writing, one Kylie's pseudo-rejection in the shed. The snickering in the hallway. Is it really so bad for people to think real Kylie might like me? Shouldn't I go to school tomorrow and strut around all proud or something? Maybe it's time to finally show up in my fancy red car. If I'm seeing Kylie, that should bring me only good attention, right?

But the dark side of my soul says no one in the real world could think it's natural for Kylie to like freakish Jonathan Aubrey with the faded scar and the BEWARE OF LONER sign. In the real world people won't be happy for me. They'll be horrified for Kylie. And they'll be right. What's happening to her is not natural.

A movement of air behind me causes my warmed skin to prickle again. Someone is in my room.

"If you're gonna be awake all hours of the night, you may as well be productive, Big Brother."

My first instinct is to tell her to go back to wherever she came from, but my second instinct wins out. I roll over.

"So . . . are you ready?" she asks.

"Ready for what?"

Tess smiles and flips some of her gorgeous dark hair. "Only the most important lessons you'll ever get in your life."

"And that means . . ."

"I'm going to show you the full power of being a world-maker."

"Does that mean I get to visit your make-believe worlds?"

"Not even in your dreams."

"But that time at the mall, when we ended up at the beach, that was your world, right?"

"That's for me to know and you to find out."

"That answer gets less and less funny with time."

"Forget my worlds, Jonathan. I'll teach you what I can to help you save Kylie. That's it. Most of what I'm going to show you is stuff you should have figured out on your own already. You're just too chicken to experiment."

"What? I've experimented."

"Yeah, right. You made your first world by accident. The rest was just the same exercise over and over. Get up and get dressed," she commands.

"Turn around," I say, because I'm wearing boxers and a T-shirt. She obliges me, and I slide my sweatpants back on. "Ready."

She raises her eyebrows at my ruffledness. I was sleeping, after all. "What?" I say. "I have to dress up or something?"

"No, the slob look suits you."

"Go climb up a tree and branch off."

She laughs out loud, and as she laughs, her skin and clothes change color. They become a uniform, scaly brown as her arms lengthen and her legs fuse together. Her fingers split and elongate into tree branches, complete with bushy green leaves. Several more branches sprout from her head and shoulders, and soon the plaster on my ceiling is chipping away behind the thick canopy of a tree.

For my part I fall rather inelegantly back onto my bed with a shriek.

Tess's laugh echoes through the branches as though each leaf is a mouth emitting sound.

"It's not funny!"

The leaves shrivel and contract along with the branches, and Tess morphs back into the human being she was a moment before. "You have no sense of humor."

"No, I have no sense of *your* humor."

"Same thing."

A piece of plaster about the size of a quarter falls to the carpet between us. We both look up, and the ceiling blinks. One second it's tree-damaged; the next it's like new.

"What are you?" I say.

"I'm not doing anything you can't do."

"I can turn myself into a tree?"

"Yep."

"I can fix broken ceilings?"

"Yep. Your first lesson this evening is how to manipulate objects within a world. Let's take a little trip to

Jonathan's-smokin'-hot-dance-club, shall we?"

Before I can consent, I'm whisked through that moon-slivered, sphere-filled vastness between worlds, and my bedroom is replaced by an enormous sound stage. The familiar intoxication seeps through me and dulls my ability to think. This place is not for thinking. It's for moving and for doing.

Boom. Boom. Boom.

A dancer slinks up to me, a bleached-blonde with leather suspenders and a turquoise tank top. Her lips blow me a kiss as she arrives, and she slides one glossy red fingernail down my cheek, my neck, my chest. Then she latches on to me from behind and starts grinding to the music.

I created this world so I could do this kind of thing, and through a druglike haze I inevitably absorb the beat into my muscles. The music in the air and the bodies writhing all around are fast-acting intoxicants, and although I'm seriously embarrassed about being here with Tess, I can't help but move with the dancer. No one here cares that I stick out like a sore thumb with my T-shirt and sweatpants. Nor do they care that I'm a terrible dancer. With the world in my blood, I have rhythm, if not moves.

Blondie's hands caress my hips, and I close my eyes. We push and pull against each other as the music changes to a new song and a woman's voice starts crying out about the "Dance,

dance, dance." Rolls of satin drop around us like banners from the rafters, and a red sea of fabric billows all around in the fan-made wind. Blondie turns me around, and I see her face and stop breathing.

Blondie is Kylie.

Her red-brown hair is curled and styled with about seven inches' more volume than normal. Her lips are Valentine-red with lipstick. She's wearing a black leather bra and bikini bottom with black leather boots that reach halfway up her thighs. Her hips slink side to side as she dances in place.

But what has me cold is her eyes. The Kylie brown is covered with bright violet contacts. Purple and silver makeup covers her eyelids and flares out to her temples like a butterfly wing mask. She's wearing thick black eyeliner and fake lashes so long, I can't believe she can hold her lids open.

To the beat she moves her arms up to her head and slinks around some more—like a pole dancer without a pole. I can feel the conflict in my core—the intoxication I've made a parameter of this world versus the revulsion of seeing Kylie turned into this thing I picture walking the streets soliciting Johns, not Jonathans.

Boom. Boom. Boom.

"A little much, isn't she?"

Tess is at my ear. Kylie reaches an arm out to me and caresses my cheek with the back of her hand. Tess's head bobs with the beat, and when Kylie steps back and gyrates a little more, Tess imitates her.

I can't stop my body from finding all this a little stimulating, so I do what I always do when I lose control. I skip out of the world.

Poof.

My bedroom in the real world is remarkably silent compared to the blaring bass and soprano of Jonathan's-smokin'-hot-dance-club. My head is also remarkably clearer. I stand in the center, waiting for Tess, but she doesn't follow right away. Maybe that same high I jumped home to escape has enthralled her. Somehow, though, I think Tess is immune to that kind of stuff.

With a flash of strobe light Tess whirls out of thin air. Her hair is done up in the seven-inch style Kylie wore, and her makeup and outfit match Kylie's too. Tess's body is curvier and fuller than Kylie's, so the skimpy leather is even less able to hide what needs hiding.

She still moves to a beat, and the creak of her leather boots echoes in the room.

"Stop that," I say.

"Oh, you're just jealous."

"What could I possibly be jealous of?"

"That I make this look good. But don't worry, Brother dear . . ." She reaches a hand toward me and flicks it like a magician. One second I'm in comfy grays, and the next I'm sporting formal black suit pants, shiny leather shoes, and a white dress shirt unbuttoned to the waist. By instinct I turn away from Tess because my scars are exposed.

"I can fix that," she says, and when I look down, my skin is beautiful. Having the old weight gone leaves me lighter, airy almost.

The bedroom booms with Jonathan's-smokin'-hot-dance-club again, and I'm lying on a mattress covered in pink silk. Somehow I've acquired a pink bow tie at my neck. Tess smiles down at me and says, "In that outfit you definitely look *smokin'* hot." She licks a finger, touches it to the air, and makes a sizzling sound.

Not funny. I don't want to look smokin' or any other kind of hot. Already the dancers are converging on me like zombies from a horror movie. It doesn't take more than a second for the high of Jonathan's-smokin'-hot-dance-club to kick in, and I find myself reaching for them as they undulate closer with the music. Parting two especially buxom dancers with a delicate shove is Kylie, coming at me like a predator for the kill.

I have never had this problem before. I have never come here without wanting this. The conflict between the sensuality

I created in this world and the rationality I need to hold on to actually hurts my brain. Kylie climbs on top of me, her movements a weird slow motion because of the strobe light. I can't stop any of this, so I get ready to blink back to my room.

Then the last functioning part of my mind remembers Tess saying this was a lesson and something about manipulating objects within a world. "What do I do?" I cry out to Tess, whom I've lost track of but assume isn't too far away.

"Whatever you want," she calls from the dance floor.

That advice is not exactly helpful.

Kylie is pawing me like a cat, and I hear the words of the song comparing a woman to a lioness. Other dancers on the edges of the bed start pawing around too, and grooming their arms with their tongues. When Kylie opens her mouth to do the same, it's clear that there are two things I want to be different: (1) I want Kylie to disappear from this world, and (2) I want to turn off the world parameter that makes me—well, not want Kylie to disappear from this world.

I think of Tess sprouting leaves and sporting a tree trunk, and the assurance that she did such an impossible thing gives me the confidence that I can make these two changes to Jonathan's-smokin'-hot-dance-club. I concentrate with the core of my being and will Kylie away, then will myself a little self-control, and suddenly the person about to groom my face is

the bleached-blonde, and I shove her off me. I roll off the bed and watch her stumble backward into the crowd.

This changes the mood of Jonathan's-smokin'-hot-dance-club, and instead of continuing the prowling cat dance, the dancers begin to growl. The strobe lights turn crimson, and the scene looks like it's being shot in a fog of blood. I spot Tess jerking back and forth with a partner.

Instead of a place where desire and music converge into what I used to think was healthy teenage escapism, Jonathan's-smokin'-hot-dance-club has become nothing but animal savagery with leather boots and cheap pink bow ties. I remember the ridiculous outfit I'm wearing and change that back into my comfy T-shirt and sweatpants. None of the dancers comes my way. I stand alone while they claw and bite one another. The spell is broken for me. I go back to my room.

Tess doesn't make me wait for her.

She arrives with a feline nose and mouth and furry pointed ears adorned with pink bows. Her skin, which I can see almost all of because she's wearing that skimpy dancer outfit, is a mottled tan and white. I think that's a tail twitching behind her.

"Not bad, hon," she says, and licks the back of her hand. "That's two lessons in one."

I stare at her while she finishes the cat-grooming thing. She makes a little meow with her cat mouth and crawls onto my

bed. I stand in the middle of the room giving her my best death stare. Then it occurs to me . . . I might be able to change Tess.

I concentrate with my inner being, and instantly she's in pigtails and a frilly yellow dress with white kneesocks and white patent leather shoes. Her face is cat-makeup free and cutesy like a doll's.

She inhales sharply with surprise and switches back to a more Tess-like outfit of jeans and a hot-pink tank top. I, however, end up in the frilly yellow dress with white kneesocks. Ha-ha.

I switch myself back to the T-shirt and sweatpants.

"You learn quick," Tess says. "I guess that's good."

The last thing I care about right now is Tess's assessment of my progress. "Please tell me that wasn't Kylie back there."

"That wasn't Kylie back there."

"Really, I need to know whether that was Kylie."

"Relax, Brother. In order for Kylie to appear in Jonathan's-smokin'-hot-dance-club, you would have to physically bring her, which is lesson number three."

"What were lessons one and two again?"

"Manipulating objects and changing parameters. When you make a world, it comes with a certain set of rules. In Jonathan's-smokin'-hot-dance-club, one of the rules was the power buzz you set up for yourself so you could relax to what those girls do.

You were pretty young when you made that world, so you were probably nervous. I'm betting you didn't make that parameter on purpose, but it still set itself up according to your need."

She's right. I was too young to dream up intoxicating myself. Even now I'm not sure I would have chosen that parameter. It's bizarre to think of my worlds anticipating my needs, and maybe knowing me better than I know myself.

Tess continues. "Same in Kylie-Simms-is-your-girlfriend. You certainly did make one parameter on purpose—that Kylie love you. She has loved you all this time because she's bound by that parameter. But there are other parameters you set up, again probably without meaning to. Like the fact that you don't lose class credit for being absent.

"Just now you changed the parameter of intoxication in Jonathan's-smokin'-hot-dance-club, just like you can change any rule about any world. You can add rules too. Like if you want your smokin' hot dancers to prefer break dancing, they'll do head spins to 'Rockit.'"

I'm still stuck on the Kylie-loving-me parameter. What would happen if I went to Kylie-Simms-is-my-girlfriend and changed it?

"Changing parameters is actually a trickier skill than simply manipulating objects," Tess continues, "which was the more basic lesson that I was trying to teach you by putting a Kylie clone in the dance club. I changed the first dancer who approached you, and you changed her back. Lesson accomplished."

"Tess . . ." I have a question, but the asking of it has me extremely nervous. I concentrate on the yellow frilly dress with kneesocks, and Tess's clothes change again.

This time she leaves them on and just draws up her feet so she sits cross-legged on the bed.

"How can I do that?" I ask.

She knows that what I'm asking is not, How do I have this ability? She knows I'm asking, How come I can do it in the real world?

"You're a world-maker. You can do certain things."

"But I didn't make this world."

"True."

"I don't understand."

"You don't have to understand, Brother dear. You just have to know what you can do."

"Why can't you be straight with me?"

"I'm being as straight as I can be. Some things are just the greater mysteries of the universe. Now, do you want your other two lessons?"

"What if I said no?"

"Then I would go. It's entirely your choice." She hasn't changed out of the little-girl dress and pigtails.

"Whatever," I say.

"Maybe you've had enough for tonight."

I don't confirm or deny that, but all the energy has gone out of me.

Tess scoots off the bed, and when her shiny shoes land on the floor, she's shrunk about two feet. She looks up at me with a little girl's face, the one that she wore when she was six.

"Everything will be okay, Jonathan." Even the pitch of her voice is raised like a little girl's. "I'll show you everything you'll need." She clasps her small arms around my thighs and gives me a squeeze. My hands find her pigtailed head and awkwardly return the hug.

Then she's gone.

I'm alone with my fears in the dark, wondering again what Tess is.

CHAPTER 17

NO MATTER WHAT HAPPENS THE NIGHT BEFORE, THE SUN always rises.

I wonder if sunrise is a parameter I can control in one of my worlds. Not going to try it today, though, in case I make the earth crack in half or something.

I get showered and dressed like I do every morning, check the contents of my backpack, and stop in the kitchen on my way out because something smells yummy. Uncle Joey has made French toast, which he does from time to time, and now he's down the hall getting ready for work. He's left me three pieces on a plate next to the bottle of syrup. I planned on grabbing a muffin and eating while I walked, but I never pass up a hot breakfast.

I eat quickly because the first bell rings in half an hour, and it takes me twenty minutes to walk there. Uncle Joey doesn't emerge, so I holler a good-bye and slip out the door with a plastic cup full of OJ.

As I trudge up the sidewalk along the high school's drive-way, a car full of students slows beside me. I risk a split-second glance to see who's doing the staring, but I only vaguely recognize a bunch of junior girls. As seconds pass and I get farther in, buses that stop for every speed bump begin clogging up the flow, so it feels like every car is slowing to gawk at me, Jonathan Aubrey, the guy Kylie Simms went all funny over in class yesterday.

When I reach the building, I'm invisible, as always. People have eyes only for spotting their friends or dashing final visits to lockers when it's this close to the bell. I'm indescribably relieved that there isn't a gang of gossips assembled at the door.

I endure first-period Non-Western History, then hurry to creative writing. I hope to beat Kylie and pick a seat without having to worry whether or not to sit next to her. Turns out I'm the first to arrive. The desks are in rows, so I claim my usual back corner away from the window. Other students file in and take seats. I cringe when Kaitlyn Frost sits next to me, but I didn't exactly put a SAVED JUST IN CASE KYLIE WANTS IT sign on the seat.

The class fills up and the bell rings. Kylie is not here, and the seat in front of me remains disappointingly open.

Kylie's had practically perfect attendance since kindergarten. And this afternoon is a track meet. Today is not a Kylie-like day to miss school. Could she have her guidance appointment?

The minutes tick by, and it's all I can do not to worry about her as Eckhart drones on about descriptive characterization and characterized description.

Finally, with twenty minutes to go, Kylie comes in with a note for Mr. Eckhart. A seat is open next to Emily and Zach, which she looks at while Eckhart reads the note. "Thank you, Kylie," he says, and places the note on his desk.

Kylie turns directly toward me. My pulse quickens as she glides up my row and settles in the empty desk in front of me. Mr. Eckhart has lost the class's attention as several people outright turn their heads to watch her. Kylie's face gives nothing away as she quietly takes out her notebook. When the class goes back to listening to Eckhart, my cell phone buzzes. I jolt but manage not to make a scene. Eckhart doesn't notice.

Kaitlyn Frost watches me take out my phone. I want to tell her to turn around and mind her own business, but she catches herself staring and scribbles in her notebook. I've received a text: *Are you coming to the meet today?* I actually love that she spelled out all the words.

I have to be at the meet happening in Kylie-Simms-is-my-girlfriend. I'm scheduled to run the two-mile, which is the first event. Maybe I can work it so I get back to the real world in time to watch Kylie run, if that's what she's asking.

I text back, *What are you running?* and hear the muffled vibration of her phone.

After a minute my phone jolts me again. I think I startle Kaitlyn out of her newfound concentration on the teacher.

Triple jump, 100, 4 x 100.

I don't know if girlfriend Kylie is competing in the same events in her world. I've never had a reason to stay in the real world on a track meet day, so I don't know how closely related the two meets are. The triple jump usually happens during the two-mile, so I often miss Kylie triple-jumping. The hundred is after the hundred hurdles, which is after the two-mile. I could make it back here to watch the hundred as long as the other Kylie isn't running it at the same time. Then is the four-hundred, then the four-by-one-hundred. All practically in a row. Kylie will be done when the meet is only half over.

I send my reply: *I'll definitely be around for the 4 x 100.*

Today's meet is only sort of important for the boys' team, but Dunford's girls' team is really strong. Dunford and Pennington always treat this meet like it will determine the conference title, because most years it does. The four-by-one-hundred will be important to win because the relay winners take all the points, unlike in a regular event, where there are points for second and third.

Kylie doesn't text again, so I assume her original intent was to see if I was going to watch her run. We sit the remainder of class while Eckhart reads examples of good characterization and description and asks the class to comment. Kylie's chair touches the front of my desk, which means that as I try to catch up on the notes Eckhart has written on the board, her hair is about twelve tiny inches from my hand. It's all I can do not to reach out and touch it.

When the bell rings, Kylie turns around. "Are you sure you'll come?"

"I'll pick a spot by the third exchange to cheer for you."

Technically there is no way I should know that's where she'd want me to stand, but she's not bothered by my special knowledge.

She smiles like I've just made her whole day, the way girlfriend Kylie smiles at me, or did until yesterday. I walk Kylie to where E-Hall and F-Hall split and stay for my last two classes in the real world. The other Kylie asked for space, and staying out of her world is the most space I can give.

After school I go to Kylie-Simms-is-my-girlfriend. I try to avoid Kylie before my race, and I'm pretty sure I'm successful only because she's doing her part to avoid me right back. She doesn't even come to the line before the gun to wish me luck. She doesn't look up from the triple jump—which is a total of two feet away from the track—in order to cheer as I run by. Eight times.

I finish the race in third, so I earn us a point that Coach wasn't counting on. That makes me happy even though I don't think we're going to need the point.

I do a hasty cooldown so I can spend a minute or two in the background watching Kylie triple-jump before I leave for the real world. In one way I'm distressed that she's so distant today, and in another I'm relieved to be spared the guilt over leaving to watch real Kylie.

A small group of Pennington girls is gathered on the grassy hill opposite the triple jump pit. One of them is Rob's girlfriend, Jessie. I sit beside her. "Hey."

"Hey," she says back. "What's wrong with Kylie?"

Oh no. "What do you mean?"

"She's got in a thirty-two footer, but her steps are all messed up. She fouled her first two."

"What place is she in?"

"Definitely not first. That girl"—she points to a very tall, athletic girl on the other team—"jumped thirty-five something. And that one"—she points to a different girl—"is in the thirty-twos with Kylie somewhere."

"So she's at best second, at worst third."

"I think so."

Kylie jumped a thirty-six last week, so it's not out of the question that she'll do it again for the win with one of her three final attempts.

Jessie and I watch nervously while Kylie goes to her mark. Her face is haggard. She does her little routine of lean back, up on the toes, lean back, up on the toes, before taking off down the runway. She jumps and lands on the far side of what's been raked in the pit, but as soon as her feet touch the sand, the official hollers, "Foul!"

The spectators from Pennington groan, and Kylie's jump coach holds up a thumb and forefinger to show her the foul was only by an inch. She nods and shuffles back up the runway with her head down. She's not her usual, confident Kylie self. She looks so tired, I don't think she got any of the sleep she told me she wanted last night.

I'm torn. Normally I would go down and say something encouraging. She'd tell me about what she's done to adjust her mark and such, what she'll try next, and then she'd jump and be fine.

But I don't think she wants me to go down. She doesn't even seem conscious of the fact that people are watching her. She just sits on the track and watches her two key opponents as they take a thirty-three- and a thirty-six-foot jump. Now Kylie will have to get in a better jump to place second, or do a season-best to win.

I turn to Jessie. "What does your coach hope for here?"

"He knew about the one girl but not the other. Kylie said he thinks she'll be second but really expects her to win."

Kylie is the kind of athlete who does well under pressure. She's been known to get her very best jump in at the end, but today is different. She compensates for her foul by moving back a whole foot and ends up jumping only a thirty-two from two feet behind the takeoff line.

This time her coach pulls her over for a side session. I can't hear what he says, but he has Kylie nodding every few seconds. She waits there with him as the two leaders jump. Neither attempt is an improvement.

Kylie goes back up the runway and returns her mark to its original position. She puts her toe to it and takes a huge shoulder-raising breath. Lean back, up on the toes, lean back, up on the toes, run, run, run, run, run, run, run, run, run, run, run, run, hop—skip—jump. She sails through the air like she's making a triple jump how-to video and lands perfectly in the pit. It's at least thirty-six, but I bet it's even farther.

The spectators are on their feet, craning necks as if they can measure the jump with their eyes. The official raises his pencil to his clipboard and hollers, "Foul!"

Kylie kicks sand on the way out of the pit.

Her coach tries to talk to her as she passes, but she ignores him. Now I really should go down and see her, and I think Jessie's wondering why I don't. Kylie doesn't watch as her competitors do their final jumps. It doesn't matter now. Kylie will finish third. Eight points for enemy Dunford, one point for Pennington. Not good.

Kylie sits by her discarded warm-up clothes to change her jumping spikes for her racing spikes. She has a one-hundred to run in a few minutes. "See ya, Jonathan," Jessie says as she and the other girls sneak off to watch some other event.

I decide that the worst that can happen is that Kylie will tell me to shove off, so I gather my courage and cross over to where she's tying on her racers. She hears me approach and looks up.

Her eyes are done up in purple and silver makeup shaped like butterfly wings, and her irises glow a bright violet. She was not wearing makeup a minute ago.

I stop cold.

"This isn't a good time," she says.

Something comforting should come out of my mouth, but it's frozen shut. She squints at me, and her long, false lashes dim her violet eyes.

Seven billion fears race through me. Was Kylie really there last night? If not, did my being there, or the creation of the

Kylie dancer, somehow rob her of sleep? I want to clean that slutty paint off her face. I want to tell her it's okay about the triple jump. I want to tell her the truth about everything.

"Great," she says, as if her makeup is perfectly normal, and when I look again, it is. But there are very dark circles under her eyes. "You don't have to make me feel worse."

"I didn't mean—"

"Never mind. I have to get down to the hundred." She grabs her stuff, and I fall into step beside her, anxious to say the right thing, which is tricky because when Kylie doesn't do well, no amount of me saying she did fine or it doesn't matter is going to help.

"I'm sorry, Kylie."

"Sorry for what?"

"Sorry the triple jump didn't go so well." *Sorry I messed up your life.*

"It's done. I'll make it up in the hundred. Just leave me alone till I'm finished, okay?"

She jogs away before I can answer.

Ideally I would leave now for the real world and real Kylie's hundred, but I'm worried about this Kylie. Since I'm not expected in the real world until the relay, I go to the perimeter fence to watch the hundred here. The boys are first, and we do pretty well, a second and third. Then the JV boys run the hundred in several heats because it's the JV sprint race for today.

Finally the girls' varsity race gets on the line. There is tension down here close to the finish. The officials hold their stopwatches up, knowing that their accuracy might be the deciding factor in who gets what points. Kylie steps into lane three, and she puts her hands on the track to back into her blocks along with the other competitors. Once everyone's settled and not moving, the starter raises his gun and yells, "Set!" The runners move into set position, hips in the air. The gun goes off.

Kylie gets a decent, if not awesome, start, but so does the Dunford girl beside her. They barrel down the track to screams of "Go, Kylie!" and "Go, Bethany!" The field falls quickly behind them, but it's impossible to tell whether Kylie or her competition is ahead. Stride for stride they approach the finish and dive with mighty leans across the line. People in the crowd yell that Bethany won. Others that Kylie won. The officials form a tight circle to compare observations and stopwatches. The circle breaks, and the coaches get the news. A cheer goes up from the knot of Pennington girls around their coach. Kylie won. Twelve point six seconds for one hundred meters in April is a good time.

Kylie gets pats on the back from teammates and coaches,

but she's not smiling. The finish was too close, the team win is still in doubt, and Kylie knows her triple jump loss has made it that much harder to win the meet, and thus the conference title.

Since she still has a four-by-one-hundred to run and she told me to stay away, I don't bother her again. If she'd lost the race, I would have had to stay, or condemn myself as the worst boyfriend ever, but the victory gives me leave to visit the real world for a few minutes. I head up to the locker room. It's museum-echo empty, so I quickly exchange my Pennington track uniform for my T-shirt and jeans, reapply some deodorant, and will myself back to the real world.

I choose to emerge in the far corner of the locker room just in case someone is there, but the real-world locker room is empty. I waste no time getting out to the track, which is good because this meet is running ahead of the other one. The boys have started their four-by-one-hundred already. I'll get to see real Kylie run before going back for my girlfriend's four-by-one-hundred.

Kylie waits her turn on the inside of the track at the third exchange. She's looking around nervously and breaks into a sunrise smile when she sees me. I'm caught on the other side of the perimeter fence while the boys come around the turn for their race. Handoffs go smoothly, and our guys are in the lead. Kylie waits the few seconds it takes to watch our boys win, then crosses the track to see me.

"I thought you weren't here."

"I just got here."

"In the nick of time."

"How are things going?" I nod to the track.

"The boys are winning by a lot. I think our meet is close."

I'm afraid to ask, but I must. "How'd you do in your other events?"

She looks down at her foot, which starts playing with a pebble. "I won both."

"That's great!" I have to force myself to sound happy, because the news only makes me more worried for the other Kylie.

"It was okay."

We both turn when an official calls her back to position. "Oh! Gotta go!" She scurries over to her spot in the exchange zone and readies herself for the baton. The starting gun fires, and around the first turn spring Ginny Hamleigh and a girl from the other team. Ginny's having a hard time making up the stagger, and I recognize the Dunford girl as the one who raced Kylie in the hundred in Kylie-Simms-is-my-girlfriend. The handoffs go smoothly for both teams, and the second leg from Pennington, who is usually Mandy but is someone else I can't make out from here, holds her own down the back straight. There is a little warble in the handoff to the third leg, but the Pennington runner makes up the rest of the stagger. Around the corner they come as Kylie and her opponent flex their hands and crouch in anticipation of the baton. The girls approach, and Kylie starts running. Just inside the zone she reaches back her hand for the baton, and receives it perfectly. The Dunford girl doesn't stand a chance. Even from here I can see the finish isn't close.

The usual celebration erupts in pockets around the track. I wait here because Kylie will be back for the clothes and shoes she left at the exchange zone. Eventually she comes, all smiley triumphant, straight over to me instead of her stuff.

"That was fun," I say. "Congratulations."

"Thanks," she says. Her face is flushed with exertion and celebration. "I'm so glad you came."

"Me too."

"Are you staying?"

I'd really, really like to, but I have to get back to Kylie-Simms-is-my-girlfriend.

"I can't, but can I call you later?"

Her smile fades just a little. "Sure."

"It's not that I don't want to stay."

"I understand."

I hope she doesn't mean she "understands" that I don't like

her enough to stay, because that is so untrue. I reach for her hand, sensing she won't mind, and do a quick check to make sure no one's watching. I think we're safe.

"I'm sorry. I'll call you later." I kiss her on the cheek, and she not only lets me, but she gives me a cheek kiss right back. Now I really don't want to go.

"Thanks for coming." She smiles and crosses over the track. She scoops up her clothes and waves at me before making her way across the field to join her teammates.

When I'm confident she's not coming back, I go to the locker room. I strongly consider changing my mind and going out to the stands to wait for the meet to end. I know real Kylie would be happy if I did that.

Instead I switch worlds in the locker room and change back into my uniform as if I've been gone from the meet for only a bathroom break. When I emerge, the four-by-one-hundred for girls is just starting. Kylie stands on her spot already watching the starting line for movement. I hear a gun and run down to the fence to see the race.

Kylie doesn't notice me. She just watches Ginny work on the stagger and pass off to the second leg, who this time actually is Mandy Breuger. The girls' coach in this world isn't taking any chances. I wish I could've told him he didn't need to waste Mandy here.

Mandy passes the other runner easily and executes a perfect pass with her teammate in zone two. The Pennington girl has a ten-meter lead and the stagger to her advantage as she rounds the turn. Kylie wrings her hands and bounces up and down. The lead is so substantial, she gets off her line cautiously, which is better than chancing an early takeoff and a missed pass. Only, she waits so long that the girl passing to her clips her heel and trips. The hand with the baton flails wildly as the girl tries to keep from going down, but it's no use. She lands on the track, and the baton clatters away. Kylie, who is recovering her own balance from the heel clip, hears the noise and turns. She runs back for the baton, but the Dunford team executes their pass perfectly and sails on by her. Kylie misses her first reach for the fallen baton because she's so distracted watching the other team go by. She finally picks it up, but there's too much ground to cover. She makes a valiant effort. She's awesome enough that the crowd thinks she might do it, but the groan at the line tells the truth. It's a disaster.

The mood on the track turns dark. I'm guessing that between the unexpected triple jump loss and this disastrous loss of five unanswered relay points, there's a question now about whether the girls' team can win. Both Kylie and Mandy Breuger were in the four-by-one-hundred, so they can't run the four-by-four-hundred at the end.

Watching the rest of the meet is painful because I overhear a couple of girls talking about what points they need to score from here out to win. It's not going to happen. Pennington will not win the conference title this year.

The girls do well enough to take it to the final event, the four-by-four-hundred relay, but with Kylie and Mandy used up, they have their second-best team competing. After the first leg they're losing, and never catch up. Only halfhearted cheers encourage the anchor leg.

There's the usual flurry of putting equipment away—mats, hurdles, cones, throwing implements, etc. Then the boys' team has the regular wrap-up meeting by the pole vault shed while the girls' team meets dejectedly in the stands. The track crowd thins out pretty quickly after that.

I go up to the parking lot and wait by Kylie's car. The lot empties before she finally emerges, head hung low, gym bag slung over her shoulder. She looks up to see me standing here, and hesitates. I can practically hear her thoughts—*Should I talk to him? Should I run away?* A decision propels her reluctantly forward. I meet her halfway, but she makes sure to leave enough space so I can't reach out to her.

"I'm not in the best mood." She hikes her gym bag a little higher on her shoulder. "I just want to go home."

The dark circles under her eyes are puffy from crying. Her

nose is red, and she hasn't bothered to fix the hair that's come loose from her ponytail. "Let me drive you home," I offer.

"No. I can drive."

"Please let me take you."

"I said *no*, Jonathan. Just because I lost a track meet doesn't mean I can't operate a car."

"The whole meet wasn't your fault. There's plenty of people who could've done better today too. It's a team effort."

"I'm not debating this with you." She backs up a step and makes a wide circle around me to get to her car.

"Can I at least call you later?"

She opens her car door and throws the gym bag inside. She's biting a quivering lip while fresh tears spill down her face, but she doesn't get in yet. "Normally I'd want nothing more than to talk to you all night."

It's awkward to keep shouting from halfway across the parking lot, even if we're the last two people in it, so I approach the car. "Then let me call you."

"I don't want to talk tonight."

"Not even to me?"

"Especially not you." She shakes her head, and more tears fall. "Give me some time to put today in perspective. We can talk tomorrow night."

"Not tomorrow after school?"

"It's only a half day, remember? I might stay home to get some sleep. I promise I'll call tomorrow night." With a swipe of her runny nose on her sweatshirt sleeve, she falls into the driver's seat and shuts the door. She doesn't wave good-bye as she drives away, her car's engine rattling all the way down the driveway.

I'm left burning in the empty lot. I want to hold her tight like she's held me in my misery so many times. Maybe tomorrow night she'll let me. I want to make everything better. I really, really do.

CHAPTER 18

I'VE BARELY BEGUN MY PROMISED PHONE CALL TO REAL
Kylie when there's a knock on my bedroom door.

"Hold on a second," I say into the phone.

If Uncle Joey is upstairs, this is an important moment. I carry
the phone to the door and turn the knob. Tess stands before me
in a shimmery blue blouse and white shorts. I bet our mother
would have been shocked to see where her blouse's neckline
plunges.

Before she can speak, I press an annoyed finger to Tess's lips
so Kylie won't know I have a girl in my room. Thankfully, Tess
cooperates and glides silently inside to take up her usual perch
on my bed. I go out into the hall and shut the door.

"I'm really sorry, Kylie, but that was my uncle. He wants me
downstairs."

"Oh." The disappointment in her voice is unmistakable.

"How late can I call you back?"

"Try my cell whenever you're done."

"I will. I'll leave a message if you're asleep." She must be wondering what my uncle could possibly want that could take so long on a school night, but she doesn't say anything.

We hang up with good-byes, and I storm back into my room. "You knew I'd just started that conversation."

Tess only shrugs. "We have a lot to finish up." She leans forward to scootch off the bed, and I turn away to avoid seeing what her blouse reveals. "Tonight we learn how to close a world and how to move things between worlds. If you're going to merge Kylie all the way, you'll have to move her, and you'll have to close her world."

"What if I don't want to close her world?"

She gives that same shrug. "Then everyone in it goes through the pain of mourning for her. Actually, it will be the pain of her disappearing into thin air. If you want that, keep the world open."

Oh God. More to consider. She has parents and friends in her world.

"Just get on with the lesson."

"First you need to create a world for the purpose of closing it. Think of one you've always wanted to make but didn't."

Tess has to know there's only one world I've always wanted to make. The thought of doing it now turns my blood to ice water. But I can't make any old world just for the hell of it. World-making takes a strong desire for creation, and I've never wanted any world more than the one I've been most scared to create.

"Why can't we just work with one already open?"

"Because I said."

"That's not a reason."

"It's the only one you're going to get."

I think I might hate Tess.

I try to come up with an alternative to the world I most fear. One obviously strong desire of mine is to have a world with a normal, healthy Kylie. I want that world to be the real world, though, and I'm afraid that making yet another Kylie will only do more damage to the two who already exist. I'd like a world where my class credits aren't an issue, but I have that in Kylie-Simms-is-my-girlfriend. I mentally flip through various worlds I've wanted in the past but failed to create—superhero fantasies from being young, an outer space thing, a world even more explicit than Jonathan's-smokin'-hot-dance-club—but if I didn't want these things enough then, I surely don't want them now.

Little by little I steel myself for what is about to come. For the first time in my world-making history, I will a world into being that I don't actually want to be in. It builds itself inside me. I can't bear to determine the details, so I let the world form, as Tess once explained, according to my needs. Parameters emerge like the frame of a house, a skeleton to construct places and events upon. The people simply arrive; the rooms of the house take shape. There is a familiar warmth being sucked from my stomach, and then my bedroom disappears, only to be replaced by . . . my bedroom. How quickly a world is born.

This bedroom is in a much smaller house. The floor, instead of being richly carpeted, is worn old hardwood with a small braided rug. My bed is draped with a thin quilt I recognize but haven't seen in a long time. A computer screen cycles through a screen saver on the desk. The roll-down shades on the windows have rips in them. The clock reads six thirty a.m.

For ten years I've avoided this place, and now that I'm here, it's darker and shabbier than I remember it.

No one is in the room except Tess and me. "Are you okay with this?" Tess asks.

"It's a little late to be worrying about that."

"Come on," she says, and opens the door onto a short hallway. We step out and turn left toward the smell of coffee brewing. The hall ends at an empty living room open to a small kitchen. Mom and Dad sit at the table not six feet away. By reflex my body stiffens.

"Relax. They can't see us or hear us," Tess says unnaturally loudly in the coffee-scented morning.

But I want them to see me.

Even though our parents don't turn at Tess's voice, I'm not sure I believe her. "Why can't they?"

"Didn't we just have a lesson in manipulating worlds? It's a good thing I think faster than you."

Now I feel stupid. How often have I wished I could switch worlds without the stifling, terrifying pressure of being discovered? If Tess isn't lying, I could have been traveling invisibly and soundlessly all along.

We watch my mother raise her mug and blow on the contents. My father writes something on a notepad. She appears to be waiting for him to finish. Her hair is long and black like Tess's, her clothes businesslike and navy blue. When she sips her coffee, her lips purse at the rim, and I think about her flesh being alive, her eyes focused and animated, her hands able to grip the mug and raise and lower it. My father's fingers waggle his pen as words spill out the tip. He has words. He has thoughts. They both are part of a living world.

I have been so used to thinking of them lying in coffins as the world passes them by. So used to pitying them all the experiences they were missing. Sipping coffee and writing words fill this moment with more meaning than any crucial graduation or marriage or grandchildren I pictured them longing to see.

They don't know they're supposed to be dead. I didn't know

how I would feel if I ever saw them like this, alive in one of my worlds. The truth is, I'm finally here and I still don't know how I feel.

Dad punctuates his last sentence and slides what he's written over to Mom. She reads it and raises an eyebrow with a nod that says, *Not bad.*

"Should I leave in that last line?" Dad asks.

"I would," Mom says. "It's nice, especially coming from you." She rises and opens the refrigerator. At that moment I come down the hall. Not me, but The-crash-never-happened me, and I stumble backward a step in surprise. I've never made a copy of myself in a world before, and I didn't consciously make this copy.

I'm wearing jeans and a short-sleeved shirt with a collar, more preppy than I normally dress. My hair is wet and I have a gym bag slung over one shoulder. Despite the slightly nicer clothes, everything about me looks the same except for my face. It is startlingly, disturbingly unmarred by an airplane crash. I guess there had to be an unbroken Jonathan to complete a world called The-crash-never-happened.

Perfect-faced me grabs a banana off the countertop and says, "See ya later," to my parents before walking out the door.

As it clicks shut behind the other me, I want to apologize to Mom and Dad for that thoughtless exit. A little affection, a kiss good-bye or something, seems essential on this day. Emotion swells suddenly in my throat, and I realize just how easy it must be for that other me to take for granted something so simple as leaving my parents' house to go to school. Mom simply dumps the remainder of her coffee into the sink and leaves the kitchen.

The-crash-never-happened Tess barrels past Mom in the hallway. "Bye, Mom," she says, and grabs her own banana. She's dressed in jeans and a long-sleeved T-shirt with "Pennington Tennis" written across a couple of crossed tennis rackets. Over her shoulder is also a gym bag.

When Tess goes out the door, I glimpse the other me sitting in a car in the driveway waiting. The car is no shiny red Uncle Joey car, but it's a clean sedan. Very practical, very safe. For some reason I note that my seat belt is secure across my shoulder.

The door shuts behind tennis Tess, and the house empties of all sound but Dad mouthing the words to whatever he's written on the notepad.

"I hate tennis," Tess says.

"I didn't know that."

"You made me a tennis player on purpose."

"No. I just willed you to be a little less . . ." Her blouse shows so much cleavage, I think she could lose a tennis racket in there. "A little less you."

"Mom and Dad get to be the same."

"Mom and Dad didn't live long enough to turn into tramps."

"You suck."

"Just get on with it, Tess. What do you want me to do here?"

She scans the living room and kitchen while I wonder how accurately I've made this world. It's some part memory and some part desire, but I don't know if it's equal parts each. I wonder if Tess has had more recent experience to know whether I got the details right. "You never told me if Mom and Dad are alive where you live."

"I know," she says, and I swallow a response to her nonanswer with as much loathing as possible. Dad gets up from the table, and for the most irrational second I hope he takes my side and sends Tess to her room. But, alas.

I'm struck by how short he is. Not that he's actually short so much as he's not three feet taller than I am. We are the same height, something just shy of six feet, and his hair is peppered with gray. Dad has gotten old.

What would ten years' worth of changes have done to Dad had he lived?

Tess motions for me to follow him down the hall. As we do, she says, "Pick something in the house to bring back with you." The hallway, as short as it is, is lined with school photos of Tess and me—the earliest ones I recognize from the bins in Uncle Joey's house.

My mom and dad fuss back and forth between their bedroom and the bathroom, brushing teeth, combing hair, finding shoes. I watch them, what they touch, what they pass. If I'm taking an object back with me, I'd like it to be as impersonal as possible. I don't want to look at it and think about how my family lived for ten minutes in a made-up world. I consider a nickel on the edge of the dresser. I could see if it passes for legal tender in the real world. Then I could make a world of money, carry it back to the real world, and be as rich as a computer geek.

Actually, my mom is a computer geek, and she's clearly not rich. But that's not the point.

"What do you think his coach will say?" my father asks. He's tying on shoes while sitting on the bed in front of me.

"No idea," Mom calls from the bathroom.

"I don't want to repeat something."

"If it's a good thing, it bears repeating."

"But what if he says it better than I do?"

"Then he says it better. Jonathan will know how much you mean every word, however it comes out."

"Will he, though?"

Mom emerges from the bathroom sliding an earring into place. Dad watches her cross the room and put on her watch. "I know we haven't seen much of him lately," Mom says, "but it's the nature of his time in life. Graduation is filled with proms and parties and apprehension about college. He spends so much time with his friends because they're all going through it together."

"I know this."

"Then stop worrying. Times like tonight, one tends to remember one's parents."

"And then he'll be gone."

"It's only an airplane trip away."

"It's a six-hour airplane trip away."

"Still the same country."

Dad goes over to the dresser and grabs his keys. "We'll leave here no later than six." There is a note of warning in his voice.

"I'll be home in time. Don't worry."

My mother kisses my father on the lips. It's the quick kiss of two people hurrying off to their separate days, but repeated 365 days a year times ten years, it's a substantial amount of love passing between them.

Mom and Dad leave the house, and I'm left with Tess telling me to pick something already.

I have no better idea than the nickel, so I grab it before I remember there might be something better. "Wait here," I tell Tess. I go back to the kitchen. Dad's notepad is still on the table, his pen casually lying across it. I pick the pad up and read.

Dear Ladies and Gentlemen (or some other intro),

Like any parent, I have always been extremely proud

of my son. I remember that on the day he was born, his

pediatrician came in to do the usual health check. The

doctor raised Jonathan's torso by pulling on his hands.

"He's strong," the doctor said, because Jonathan had

some ability to hold up his newborn head.

At the time I swelled with pride because I took this as a

sign Jonathan would have athletic ability. It wasn't long

before he showed just how strong and quick his little

body was. From the first time he rolled over in his crib to

today, he's enjoyed being active.

As a teacher, I was even more excited the first time

Jonathan recited his ABCs, the first time he added two

plus two, the first time he realized water and ice were

the same thing. Only months ago he topped all that

when he burst into the kitchen dying to show me his

letter from Stanford.

I've never once had to chase after Jonathan to get his

homework done. I've never once had to prod him out of

bed for a Saturday morning track practice. He has an

inner motivation to succeed that pleases me very much.

But what I love most about my son isn't how he

compares against others for class rank or state titles. It's

*the part of him that, for example, when he was eight,
made him use his entire piggy bank to buy his mother
a necklace for her birthday. That same part of him that
stayed all night in a hospital chair when his sister had
her appendix out. The part that leads him to do a dozen
thoughtful things each day, especially when he does
them for me.*

*Jonathan, I stand here today to say you deserve this
student-athlete award, but I don't know what I did to
deserve such a wonderful boy.*

Thank you.

There's a knot in my chest. Tighter and tighter it grows as I scan back over my dad's speech. It doesn't matter that the me in this world is exceptional in ways the real me is not. It doesn't matter that the speech isn't real, that this student-athlete award doesn't exist and could never be won by me.

The knot in my chest is for knowing, for finally seeing on paper, something that I'll never have but always wanted. Something I know I would have had if things had been different. What kind of person would I have turned out to be if I'd had this much love from a father, and a mother, my entire life?

I want this love. I want it so deeply, I ache in my core. To want and want and not to have! My soul screams with all my wanting. I was only eight years old, waking all disfigured from a coma to find everyone gone, begging for them to come back, floundering in the dark unable to adjust to my new life.

This kitchen is filled with evidence of what might have been. Magnets bought at Disney World and New York City hold up papers, pictures, notes, the text of life. In one frame Tess and I stand at the bow of a sailing ship with our arms over each other's shoulders, best friends devoid of hostility, smiles as wide as latitude lines, sunglass lenses winking in the sun, wind whipping Tess's hair across both our faces. In another picture the four of us pose in dressy outfits in a banquet hall, and Mom and Dad are acting like the kids with their fingers in Vs behind Tess's head and my head. There's a note on the chalkboard reminding Tess and me we're leaving tonight for the student-athlete ceremony at six, signed with an "XOXOX Mom." Over the table hang two framed artworks, one featuring a mountain and one a rainbow, both clearly created by the hands of much younger versions of me and my sister.

I have made art in my years at school, and was told, in that thoughtless, general way that teachers announce directions to the class, to "bring it home so your mom and dad can see." All that art I put in the trash as soon as I got home. My mom and dad would never see anything I ever made again, not even the flower bouquet card or the necktie card my school forced me to make every Mother's Day and Father's Day.

My grief is too heavy to support, so I pull out the chair Dad was sitting in a few moments ago and collapse. My head falls into my hands, palms rubbing into my eyes. All my joints ache as if tumors of pure agony will prevent me from ever moving past this moment.

And all along I could have had this world! Ten lost years are found here. All along I could have made The-crash-never-happened, without the other Jonathan, and lived here myself. I could have been the subject of my father's speech. I could have made someone proud.

Instead I am the subject of a truancy complaint dogging my uncle. I will never go to Stanford. Until recent days all my thoughts have been consumed with how I could spend more time with Kylie Simms, not what I could be doing to help anyone other than myself. Now all I want to do is help Kylie, but that's because what's happening to her is my fault.

I was right not to have made The-crash-never-happened before this. If I had, I surely would have been lost to the real world. Or I might have messed it up as badly as Kylie-Simms-is-my-girlfriend, and I never could have lived with myself if after ten stolen years I caused my family's second death.

My life is not a life. It has no meaning or direction. Its only sustenance is a made-up girlfriend's love, real or compelled, and merging that love with real Kylie's strange feelings will change everything, could leave both Kylie and me with nothing at all.

Why have I let it come to this? Why didn't I just join a sports team or make school a priority in the real world? Why did I let my stupid scars, no matter how deep, ruin everything?

A tear drops onto the notepad and blurs the words "wonderful boy." I don't wipe it, for fear I will ruin more words. I look out the half-open curtain into a backyard of trees and grass and a beautiful morning sky. There is a world out there.

Tess's hand appears on my shoulder. It's meant, I'm sure, to be a comforting gesture, but it makes the hairs stand up on my neck. I don't turn to face her, because I need to know, and she won't tell me. "Are Mom and Dad alive, Tess? Is that where you go when you leave me?"

Her fingers clutch and unclutch my shoulder like a mini massage. That strange heat shoots into my arm at her touch, warming the muscle, unsettling me to the bone. "You can have whatever you want, Jonathan. All you have to do is decide what that is."

It's killing me not to know. "That's a crap answer."

She doesn't quip a comeback, just keeps clutching and unclutching my shoulder. I swat her hand away. "You made me open this world to torture me."

"I made you open this world because you want to help Kylie.

I think it's time to finish our lesson." She crosses the kitchen to stand in front of the sink. From her new position she sees the photo of another Tess and Jonathan happily sailing. Her posture and her tone soften out of their normal assault-rifle settings. She lets out the tiniest of sighs. "What are you taking back?"

I hold up the notepad and don't tell her I already know how to do this. I have moved small objects between worlds before. Never a person, though, like I'll have to move Kylie, so I listen to what Tess has to say. She purses her lips as if considering the notepad a bad idea, but does not deny me.

"You can bring anything you want from one world to another, but you must be touching whatever it is. Just like there has to be an element of need to make a world, there has to be need to move objects from world to world. Why would you need this speech?"

To create a new and better life for myself, an improved Jonathan Aubrey. I will use my father's words to fix those parts of myself that have been broken for so many years. Even though she's gentle for the moment, I can't bring myself to say that to Tess.

"That's for me to know," I say instead.

She sighs her disapproval of my keeping a secret of my own.

"Fine. Concentrate on your need and touch the notepad. You

don't have to actually hold it. Any touch will do. Then switch worlds like normal."

I do as she says, concentrate on my need to make everything different, and the next thing I know, I'm back in my bedroom with the notepad on the floor at my feet. Tess appears beside me and picks it up. I snatch it away. It's not like she doesn't already know what it says, but still. It's mine.

"I think you'd better start being nicer to me," she says.

"As soon as you start being nice first."

"I'm giving you everything you'll need to know to help Kylie."

"But not everything I need to know."

She hesitates and doesn't respond. For a second I think I might have hurt her feelings. Maybe she's not being coy or sly. Maybe she really can't tell me what I want to know.

"Put that down," she orders, pointing to the notepad.

I set it carefully in a drawer of my desk, with the intent that as soon as Tess leaves, I'll move it somewhere else.

"Now I'm going to tell you how to close the world."

"Okay."

"Closing a world means evoking desires and imagery for destruction, just as making a world uses desires and imagery of creation. You need to pretend like you're going to move from this world to that one, except, in the split second before you do, fill yourself with the will to have the world destroyed. Any images you can think of—fire, flood, explosion. The world won't actually burn, drown, or blow up, so don't worry. It will just cease to exist in the same way you suddenly made it exist. Got it?"

I nod, understanding, thinking that the clearest imagery I can evoke of destruction is both fire and water, flight 4460 burning and then sinking into the ocean. But as I do what Tess says, as The-crash-never-happened is about to open and pull me through, the destructive imagery evoked isn't of an airplane crash. It's of Kylie merging. Two Kylies stand reaching hands out to each other, mirrorlike. When they touch, both lean back and let out a horrible sound of pain. They crumple to the floor and lie very still. Too still. The-crash-never-happened winks out of existence, and I feel like I wink out with it.

CHAPTER 19

NEEDLESS TO SAY I DON'T CALL REAL KYLIE BACK RIGHT away. My emotions are a thick cloud of crows diving and pecking and tearing me open. The pain is so raw, I almost thrash away into the intoxication of Jonathan's-smokin'-hot-dance-club to dull it, but the dancing girls would be there trying to make me feel good. I don't want to feel good. I want to feel dead.

I consider that Uncle Joey has a liquor cabinet he hasn't locked me out of. I've never touched it, and although I have all the right reasons to drown in a bottle, it's a dangerous precedent to set, just another form of escaping what's real instead of dealing with it. I'm learning that escape is not the answer. When you return to the real world, your problems haven't solved themselves in your absence.

Instead I go downstairs and stupefy my mind with television, finding on every inane channel something that reminds me of my family. I can't even watch the news because there's been a plane crash somewhere in South America. Finally I settle on a rerun of a once-favorite kid's movie and sink into the couch with a throw blanket. Childhood cradles me as the characters do their musical numbers and journey toward happily ever after.

When it's very late, or more accurately, very early, I think it's pretty safe that Kylie is asleep, so I give her cell a quick call, hoping the ringer is off and I'll get credit for leaving a message. Unfortunately, she picks up.

"Jonathan?"

"It's me."

"What time is it?"

Movements crackle on the other end while she presumably tries to answer her own question.

"It's two in the morning," she says. "Are you okay?"

Her voice has that throaty quality of someone who's, well, been roused from sleep by an idiot boy's phone call in the middle of the night. At any rate, if she left her ringer on, she was hoping to be awakened.

"I'm going to bed. I just wanted to let you know I didn't forget about you."

"You don't want to talk?"

"It's late. I'm sorry I woke you. I'll see you tomorrow."

"Okay." She sounds so disappointed, I almost change my mind. "Good night."

"Night."

I hope, like girlfriend Kylie, she's the kind of person who can fall back to sleep pretty easily. Me, I hang up, go upstairs, and spend an hour or two tossing around before finding unconsciousness, and when the alarm goes off at six thirty a.m., my pillow, with my head under it, is at the foot of my bed.

School doesn't stop session because Jonathan Aubrey is having a bad day, so I shower and dress and pack my bag, grab an orange, and perform my daily hike to Pennington High. When I reach my locker, Kylie is standing there.

"Hi," she says. She's blocking the door, so I can't open up and trade books.

"Sorry again about last night," I say.

She doesn't push it by asking what I was doing up until that hour. Girlfriend Kylie wouldn't have pushed it either. It's one of the reasons I love her so much.

She says, "I just came by to make sure you're okay. Are you okay?"

I nod. "You got practice off today?" In Kylie-Simms-is-my-girlfriend, the team has practice off because of the half day.

"Yeah."

"I'd really like to do something with you, if you don't have plans."

She smiles shyly and pops off the locker so I can access my stuff. "Okay. Meet me at my car."

I know a good place where we can be alone and talk. I want to know where her head is at.

I'm not used to Kylie being the driver, since in Kylie-Simms-is-my-girlfriend we always take the red car. Partly I think Kylie likes the sporty awesomeness of it, but mostly my car is more dependable than her two-hundred-thousand-mile hand-me-down.

I direct her street by street, not revealing our destination. I've decided to take her to the local bird sanctuary, a place I last visited with my mom and dad. In fact we have to drive by my old house to reach it, which is probably why I'm thinking of the sanctuary today of all days. As we pass the house, I don't let on to Kylie that my insides rip open at the sight of a coat of brown paint smothering the time-honored green. An unfamiliar car sits in the driveway, and a tree that used to stand at the corner of the house, a tree I used to climb, is now a stump.

I already made her stop at the grocery store so I could run in and get the smallest bag of birdseed I could find and a carton of baggies. They sit concealed at my feet, part of the mystery for Kylie. I look down at them now to avoid noticing any more evidence of strangers living in the place that used to be my world, the place I revisited last night.

When my old house is safely behind us, I tell Kylie to turn up one street and then up another, and right before we reach the sanctuary's driveway, she guesses where we're going.

"I hope this is okay," I say.

"I've never actually been here."

"It's been a while for me."

The driveway is wide enough for only one car, so there are a few turnouts along the way. Kylie ducks into one to let a car heading toward us pass. Then we find our way into the dirt parking lot, and I put a handful of birdseed into a baggie. We go up to the welcome building to pay six dollars for a two-person day pass and are given a photocopied map of the sanctuary. We head for the rockery down the Chickadee Trail.

I don't remember this trail in particular, but my fondest memory of coming here as a kid is of chickadees following through the trees in order to eat seed from our hands. Kylie and I find the entrance to a woodland trail, well cleared and well marked with signposts at the numerous intersections with other trails. The birds start stalking us almost instantly.

We go a little ways down a hill before I put some birdseed in Kylie's hand and take some for myself. A few chickadees descend into the branches just above us and cock their heads as they judge the hands that mean to feed them. One daring bird does a flyby and perches on a branch just out of reach.

Kylie jerks her hand in surprise, which doesn't do much for the chickadee's confidence.

Another chickadee chances a landing on my hand, its gentle claws grabbing hold as it pecks a seed from my palm. Then it's gone.

Kylie stretches out her hand for another try. When a chickadee lands on it, I can see her work to avoid flinching at the touch of the claws, and she manages not to scare the bird away. It pauses a couple of seconds before pecking a seed and taking it to the trees.

Now there are something like a dozen birds chirruping around us. Most of them are chickadees, but there's also one I think is called a nuthatch, and another whose name I totally forget. My mom once taught me the names of birds that came to our backyard feeder, but those names have long since left me.

Kylie is thoroughly enjoying herself. The little black-capped birds dive and peck, and I lower my hand so she'll get all the action. "Hello, little one," she says.

The birds pick her hand clean, so we consult our map and decide to continue on to the rockery. We have to cross a couple of boardwalks to get through some wetlands, and on the way we rest on an observation bench overlooking a pond and a group of foraging ducks. The chickadees have followed us even though there aren't any trees this far out on the boardwalk. They hop along at our feet between flybys. I throw some seed at them. Kylie throws some at the ducks.

"You've surprised me, Jonathan."

"How so?"

"By taking me here. I wouldn't have thought you were the kind of person who gets a kick out of feeding birds."

"I came here because I thought *you* were the kind of person who'd get a kick out of it." I give her the bag of birdseed, relinquishing control of the rations. She tosses a little more at the ducks, who paddle over and dip their beaks into the water.

Kylie's thigh is pressed against mine. Despite the width of the bench, we've chosen to sit so close that we touch. The April sun shines down with that spring reminder, after a long New England winter, that sunshine should feel warm on the skin. I'm ready to talk seriously with Kylie, but I don't dare spoil the moment. We just sit and throw seed.

When the supply of seed grows low, Kylie zips the top as if to conserve for later what's left. Then she goes still. Not stiff-still but quiet-still. Awkwardness settles between us because, with the birdseed put away and the ducks paddling off, we should resume our walk to the rockery, but instead we sit, thighs touching, because this closeness is nice and the air is charged with desire to be closer.

Kylie turns her face to me, so I look back at her. Her eyes

search mine, a strange darting from left eye to right eye and back, as if the two don't match and have to be studied separately. Her gaze flicks to my lips. She wants me to kiss her. If I don't, she might press up and kiss me.

I turn to the ducks. Despite her normal-ish demeanor, something still isn't quite right. Her calm is tinged with a little bit of effort. Like she's trying to be patient. After a second or two of my studying waterfowl, she gets the hint and slouches back down. I want to reassure her I'm not rejecting her, just not convinced she's herself enough to be making proper kissing decisions.

As compensation I stand and offer a hand. She gives me hers, and as we continue down the boardwalk, I regret the offer. Her hand is too warm and her grip too tight. Our steps don't fall into rhythm, so our bonded arms don't swing comfortably to our strides. We alternate leading down the trail, tugging on each other as if we've been glued together involuntarily. I don't have the guts to release her. Her fingers tangle between mine and squeeze. She wouldn't let me go anyway.

We make it over the bridge by the beaver pond, and the pine needles on the trail thin out into pure dirt. The rockery is just ahead, a pile of giant boulders stacked into a two-story mound with a tunnel built through one side and a patio of natural boulder at the top. We spiral through the tunnel and up to the top, where we have an obstructed view of the pond through pine branches. Chickadees stalk us, twittering in the branches, hoping for another meal. The seed baggie sticks out of Kylie's pocket, so with my free hand I tug it out, but can't open it one-handed. Kylie sees what I'm trying to do but stubbornly hoards my hand while pretending her focus is on the view.

I give up on the seed and pretend I'm also interested in the view. Kylie's eyes follow a bird, and she takes a step closer to me as if she needs to come closer to track the bird. Her chest grazes my arm. My body responds with a tremor.

The woods are alive with birdsong and pine branches shushing in the breeze. Sunlight catches ripples on the pond below. The boulders of the rockery stand, ancient and mossy and built as a stage for me to give Kylie what she wants. The rational part of me knows she's not herself, but another part wonders if she might genuinely be attracted to a guy who takes a girl to a bird sanctuary. I didn't choose this place to make her like me. I chose it because it was a peaceful spot to sort out whatever is between us. I don't feel at peace right now.

"Come on, Kylie," I say, and tug her toward the path down from the rockery.

It's like pulling on a statue. She doesn't budge.

"Are you mad at me or something?" she asks.

"No."

"Have you changed your mind, then? About liking me?"

"Of course not."

"You just seem distant all of a sudden."

"And you feel intense all of a sudden."

The pressure of her grip lightens, but she doesn't let go. I now bear some responsibility for keeping our hands together.

"You're giving me such an adrenaline rush," she says, "I can't help it. I'm always thinking about you, and we haven't actually been in each other's presence all that much, so now that we're here, it's just . . . intense for me."

"You don't think that's weird? It disturbed you before."

"I'm still disturbed. It's just that I'm kind of accepting it."

"Acceptance isn't a reason for being together. It would be better if you liked me."

"I do like you."

"If you loved me, then."

"Maybe I do. I've never felt this way about anyone. Don't people write songs about how love just overwhelms them when they don't necessarily want it to? I'm overwhelmed by you. But I'm not sure anymore that's a bad thing."

"You don't know me enough to love me, Kylie."

"You'd be surprised what I know. It's like I sent out a little Kylie spy to study you, and she came back with all your secrets."

This comes so close to the reality of the situation that I

wonder just how much she does know about everything. I clear the lump rising in my throat. "What secrets would those be?"

She blushes. Not just a little pink-cheeked thing but a full-blown scarlet. Her eyes sweep back and forth between mine again. Only, instead of the sensation of being searched, I get the sensation of being told, like she's trying to convince me of what she knows.

She lets go of my hand and pushes my shirt sleeve up as far as it will go, exposing the scars on my arm, scars no one but a doctor has ever seen in the real world. Her fingers caress the skin, easing over the unevenness like it isn't there. She pulls the sleeve down and slides both hands up under my shirt. Only, instead of caressing the old burns, she gives my chest a couple of light taps with her fingertip and leans in to kiss the spot.

I let her do this, even though I cringe that she's chosen to acknowledge the damaged part of me. I search for the romance in her touch, for the evidence that she's with me because she wants to be, not because the merging has made her do it. Her hands are warm. Her fingers slide away from what's scarred and around to my shoulder blades. She pulls me against her. Her chest rises with a breath and presses against my chest, and my hands rather clumsily reach for her lower back.

This is a body I know well but am suddenly unsure how to navigate. A subtle variation in the way she moves makes everything new. I pull up the bottom of her shirt so my hands can rest on bare skin. She seems to like that, so I draw her a little closer and hold her bones and curves against me. We part just enough for our mouths to meet, and plunge into a storm of kiss after kiss. This Kylie is not as practiced as the other, but her passion is more arousing than the other Kylie's skill. We shuffle slowly forward, kissing and moving hands until Kylie's backed against a boulder. She pulls up my shirt and wrestles it over my head, exposing the story of my burns. I hesitate before pulling off her shirt. This is a public sanctuary, and I don't want her exposed where someone might stumble upon us. Although I'm sure she'd prefer otherwise, I leave the shirt on and instead slide hands under it to unclasp and loosen her bra. She responds by kissing me harder, and I'm suddenly afraid of where this is going to lead.

Her hands keep moving, and for someone who hasn't actually been my girlfriend for three years, she knows all the right places to touch. I'm on fire. We move against the boulders, and I've given up the sense of sight for the sense of contact. All I feel is Kylie, her fingertips, her mouth, her hands exploring me, my hands exploring her, my mouth full of her. Breathing is hard, she's moving so fast, and although this feels so exponentially good, little alarms keep ringing in my head. This is not what Kylie would want to do if things weren't all messed up.

"Kylie."

Her hands slide to the waistband of my jeans.

"Kylie."

Our mouths lose contact as she reaches for the button holding my jeans together.

"Kylie, stop."

She hesitates, fingers on the button. Her lips purse in an expression of impatience. For a second I think she's angry at me, her cheeks are so red.

"I'm doing it wrong," she says.

It takes a great deal of self-control to keep talking instead of kissing her again. "If only that were the problem."

"What's the problem, then?" She unfastens the button, and I have to lay my hands on hers to make her stop moving.

"I'm worried about you."

She blinks. Once. Her strange flare of passion sputters, and the red in her face deepens. "I shouldn't have done this."

I don't know what to say. I don't want her to feel bad, but I really don't want her doing something she'll regret later, even though it might be too late for that. I cup a hand under her chin and pull our lips back together, softly this time, hoping I'm not making everything worse. Gently, so gently, we kiss again. And again. Kylie relaxes, and I feel much better about this than the frenzy she was moments ago. Our lips caress cheeks, ears, necks. Our hands slide along each other's skin, but a boundary has been set at the waistline, and I no longer fear we'll end up going too far to find our way back.

I never quite give up an ear cocked for the danger of someone discovering us, but the trees and birds disappear into my rush of being with Kylie like this, and I don't hear them again until the sun has moved and we've sunk to the ground, side by side.

The rock is cold on my bare back, so I reach over and grab my shirt. Kylie fusses with her own clothes to put them aright. We end up sitting against a boulder, knees up, the sides of our bodies touching. Kylie leans her head back against the boulder, eyes to the cloudless sky. I want more than anything in the world to know what she's thinking, because I need her to tell me what to think about this.

The birds have scattered into the treetops. The seed supply has remained in the baggie, and they've given up. Still they chirp in the distance and flit from branch to branch. From where we sit, we can't see the pond, only our stone patio ringed by boulders, like we're sitting inside the tip of a tiny, extinct volcano.

"I'm afraid of what you think of me now," Kylie says.

"It's a little hard to think at the moment." It is. My body is still trying to cool down.

If she were the other Kylie, we would just sit here and be. She would lay her head on my shoulder.

But a familiar intimacy like that doesn't fit with this Kylie.

She brushes some dirt off her knee. "You're not glad."

Is that true? I think it is. I'm not happy that this happened, but I don't regret it either. It felt good and real and important. Just not necessarily beautiful.

"I'm not *not* glad," I say, hoping she doesn't take that as in insult. "Now we know something about each other we didn't know before." This all started with her claim that she had a little Kylie spy feeding her my secrets, so maybe that wasn't the best thing to say. I lean my head back against the boulder along with her. The sky really is the perfect shade of blue. "If there is a next time, though, a candlelight dinner should probably come first."

She makes a laugh-ish sound. "Maybe."

We watch a scattering of chickadees skip through the branches for a bit, before I think it's time to move along. "Do you want to finish the trail around the pond or head straight back?" I ask.

"I think I'd like to finish the loop, if that's okay," she says.

"Then there's a tree I want to show you."

I take her hand and lead her down from the rockery. Her grip is casual now, loose enough to be more friendly than amorous, and I'm relieved. We finish the loop, pausing for a few minutes at the hollow tree I used to hide in as a kid. We clatter along the boardwalks skirting the pond and feed the birds again as we ascend the hill back to the parking lot.

After she drops me at Uncle Joey's house, I wave from the doorway, wondering what emotions she'll indulge when she gets home. It's when she's alone that the pressure seems to build in her, and when she sees me, she releases it. I hope what we've just done will ease her burden, at least for the rest of the day.

I wish she could love me for real. It seems like each day she gets a little closer to that point. Is Tess right that the only way she can reach it is to merge with the made-up Kylie? Do I really want to do that to her? If I don't, will she stay all mixed up forever? A mixed-up love and a merged love aren't the same thing as real love, and neither is fair for Kylie.

CHAPTER 20

I SHOWER OFF THE SCENE FROM THE ROCKERY AND PUT on some clean clothes. For the millionth time in the last few days, I'm desperate to talk to someone. About Kylie. About world-making. About everything. I could really use a mom and dad right now.

I sit on my bed, calling out to Tess every few seconds. She, at least, knows about my world-making, even if she doesn't show much sympathy for my Kylie dilemma. I suspect a heart-to-heart with her won't end up with either answers or reassurance, but I'd still suck it up and talk to her if she'd show. She doesn't.

I've kept Uncle Joey out of the loop for so long, I can't imagine going to him, but I creep down the stairs anyway to see if the light is on in his bedroom. He's home. I could walk right up to his door and begin the conversation, but I just can't think of the words to start.

There's always Kylie. A choice of two Kylies, both of whom

are affected by all this. Both of whom deserve answers as much as I do. The problem is, I just can't bring myself to reveal my treachery yet.

I need to be in motion, and since I'm freshly dressed, I won't go for a run. Instead I fish my keys out of the kitchen drawer and get into my pristine, twice-driven, shiny red car. It still smells like new. The odometer reads sixty-one miles. It starts with a roar and almost drives itself out of the driveway.

I travel aimlessly through the streets of Pennington, passing landmarks like Lacy Pastry and Pine Street Cemetery, hardly noticing them. Fate guides my driving where it will.

I find myself downtown, a few blocks west of Main Street. I pull into a space in a small parking lot and cut the ignition. My car's engine is pretty smooth, but the silence is strong when the engine stops.

Before me stands a church, Auntie Carrie's church. The one Uncle Joey converted to and shared with me for a couple of Easters. The one in which they would have raised the child my aunt was carrying when she died. The idea to come here occurred to me only when I reached downtown, but now that I'm here, I'm afraid to go inside. Too many mysteries behind those doors, mysteries of a faith I don't understand or possess. I don't get why people go to church.

But I get the need to talk to God. I did it so much when I was eight years old. I'd lie in bed staring at the ceiling. Mostly I feared I was talking to myself, but the idea that someone might possibly be listening, that someone who could intervene in matters of death might take pity on me, gave me comfort. Praying was an excuse to dissipate my sorrow into the air, as well as a way to make my sorrow have meaning because God was someone I could blame.

The truth is, I don't think I believe in Him. All the things people say about mercy and love and a Plan where everything eventually turns out okay don't seem to apply to the god of my life.

My girlfriend Kylie, my lovely, happy, perfect girlfriend is falling apart. She wants her space. She blew an important track meet. She cried, for God's sake. I'd never seen Kylie cry until yesterday afternoon.

Real Kylie is out of control. In one day she went from oblivious about my existence to full-blown something, and she can't seem to decide whether her feelings are bad, good, or otherwise. I can't decide either.

If I merge them, it will have to be into the real world, but if there is only one Kylie, which one will she be? Will she remember both selves? Will she be happy?

Something else burns through me, as hot as the question of Kylie. Tess had me open a world of my family last night. I didn't want to do it, but I didn't think it would leave me as starved for parents as I feel today. Setting aside the fact that I wouldn't be having any of these world-making problems had they lived, my parents would have given me guidance about post–high school plans or would have written speeches about me when I won awards. If my parents suddenly returned from the dead to help me through what's happening now, I would expect sound advice, lots of hugs, and the comfort of not being in this alone.

But I am alone.

Except for Tess, whom I'm still not sure about.

Except for Kylie, who needs help as much as I do.

Except for Uncle Joey, whom I know I could turn to because he has been my defender before. It's just that I don't make the effort to include him in my life. So he backs way off, and we're at the point where I can't imagine talking to him.

I want my dad to come walking out of that church right now, maybe with a candle in his hand and a handwritten note from God saying, *Sorry for the ten lost years.*

"Please, God. This is the last time I'll ever ask, I promise." I force my will into a prayer, concentrate all the imagery I have of my mom and dad and life before death, as if making a world or changing a parameter is anything like praying to the Almighty.

"Please, please, God. Give me my family. Give me a life!" *Please. Please. Please. Please. Please.*

If in answer I saw a burning bush or a cross in the sky, I would fall to my knees. If the ground rumbled beneath the car, I would be impressed. If the church bell tolled once, I would be satisfied. If some passerby suddenly turned to me and shook his head *no*, I would understand.

But nothing happens. The church doors don't fling open to reveal Dad with a candle and an apology.

I wait some more, in case miracles take more than a split second, but still nothing happens.

Whatever, God.

It's time to talk to Tess about merging the Kylies. I have a few questions she sure as hell better answer before I decide what to do. I throw the car into drive and pull out of the parking lot. As I do, a pedestrian in the crosswalk steps right in front of me, so I slam on the brake.

I recognize her instantly. She's grandmotherly with short gray hair curled around her ears. She wears plain gray pants that don't reach all the way to her sneakers, and a pair of thick pink socks shows as she steps. A too-big fleece hangs loosely about her arms and torso. She wears a carefully neutral face, and her pace is unhurried.

She stops in the middle of the crosswalk to look directly at me, the driver of the car that might have knocked her flat, and her blue eyes flare with light. Endless sky eyes I last saw when I was chasing Tess at the mall.

I squint away because suddenly I feel like I'm staring into the sun, and when I look up, the crosswalk is empty.

Tess waits in the driveway next to the car that first gave her away the day she stole my shoes. I still don't know why she stole them.

"Why are you driving when you can flit wherever you want?" I ask.

"I like my car." Her voice lowers in pitch, and I think she might actually be attached to her ride. "Get in."

"Where are we going?"

She ignores me and gets into the driver's seat. I am sick of her jerking me around, but I need her, so I climb in on the passenger side. She puts the car in reverse and pulls out of the driveway.

"I have a few questions for you," I say.

"And you will have every answer you need when we get where we're going."

I bite off an angry reply and do what any sibling does when he gives up on winning a family argument. I stare out the window and sulk.

After a few turns I have an idea where we're going. After a few more Tess pulls her car up in front of Kylie's house. I fill with panic. "I don't want to merge them yet," I say.

"Don't worry, my brave big brother. I won't make you do anything you don't want to do. I told you we're here so you can have your answers. Well, really one answer. The only one that matters."

"And what answer is that?"

"Whether merging Kylie is the right thing to do."

She gets out of the car and slams the door so the whole neighborhood will know we're here. I make a point of pushing my door closed so quietly, all I hear is a *click*.

"Get a grip, Jonathan. No one can see or hear us."

Mentally I kick myself. I forgot she could do that. "Is there any way you can turn off the snide comments? Just until this horrible part of my life is over. That would be nice."

"No problem, Bro. How's this: I have taken precautions so we won't be detected. You have nothing to worry your little heart over."

Damn it, I want to shove her.

We end up at Kylie's window. Tess reaches into the dirt and pulls out a familiar butter knife even though I have never broken into real Kylie's bedroom and there is no need for a butter knife to be waiting for us. Tess doesn't use the knife, though, because through the window we can see Kylie inside. She's sitting on her bed with a notebook on her drawn-up knees. She's writing in it. And she's crying rather hard.

"You have such a way with women," Tess says.

I don't respond because I'm numb with the certainty that every teardrop is my fault. I hoped our time in the bird sanctuary would prevent this.

I recognize the notebook from creative writing, so I wonder if she's writing a poem. We watch her tears run while she scratches out her thoughts. She pulls on her covers and wipes her nose. Her crying becomes sobs, larger and larger heartbreaking sobs we can hear even through the closed window. Her body convulses with them as she tries to finish what she's writing. Her face is red and devastated. She glances out the window, and I duck, forgetting I'm invisible, until Tess pulls me up by my collar. Kylie stares, unseeing. Her features untwist, and her sobs reduce to hiccups. She wipes her face with her bare hand and leans back against her pillow. After a while she curls around the notebook and stills.

Tess and I wait. Rather, I watch while Tess acts bored and sits down in the mulch. "Tell me when you think she's asleep, or if she gets up and leaves," she says.

"Why?"

"Don't you want to see what's in that notebook?"

Oh, yes, I do. "Is it going to give me my answer?"

"I sure hope so. There's nothing *I* can say to convince you of what you have to do."

I realize she's right again. Kylie herself is the only one who can convince me. In her own words.

So we wait, and I watch what Kylie will do. She looks like a much younger girl all curled up with the notebook, eyes puffy from crying. It's still afternoon and she's upset, so I give her fifty-fifty odds on falling asleep. She rolls over and back. Her eyes pop open, and she stares into space a couple of times. She never looks to the window, though.

Tess spends the time plucking especially large pieces of mulch from the bed and stacking them into a pile. It's the first time pensive silence has fallen between us. I think about spoiling it with my unwelcome questions, but she surprises me by speaking first.

"I have to admit, I don't get you, Jonathan." The large piece of mulch she drops onto the pile doesn't look like it made it all the way through the chipper.

"What do you mean?"

She spares a glance up from her construction. "I mean all the emotional energy you waste on people. Kylie, your family."

"What do you mean 'your' family?"

"You know what I mean."

"No. I have no idea what you mean." "Your" is a rather disconnected way to describe a mutual mom and dad, plus herself.

"I mean you think these people will make you happy, but all I've seen them do is make you miserable."

"Yeah, well, I'm miserable only because I can't have them in the real world."

"There you go with that 'real world' crap again," she scoffs. "Don't you see? You could be happy if you made a perfect world. All these things I've been trying to teach you have better uses than putting back together a broken Kylie Simms. Now you know how to create and fine-tune the perfect parameters to live in a world just right. You could make an unspoiled Kylie. You could have your family. You could go to college or walk on the moon if you want. Why won't you let yourself be happy?"

"Because I don't think that would make me happy." All my happiness in Kylie-Simms-is-my-girlfriend feels great most of the time, but I've always known that, just like the difference between Kylie's compelled love and real love, happiness in a made-up world isn't the same as happiness earned in the real world. My nagging conscience keeps murmuring that I failed where it mattered and I'm settling for second-best. "Tell me, is that why you've hidden yourself from me all these years? Because you've thrown away your life for a 'world just right'?

And has that brought you oodles of happiness, Tess? Because what I see before me is a bitter, angry person."

"Jeesh. Say what you really feel."

"If living in a cave is so great for you, why come out to help me?"

"That's the question of the hour." Her fingers pinch the mulch pieces at the top to balance them. The pile, with its very skinny base, is getting ready to topple over. "Maybe it's because I know how it feels to lose everything. I know what it is to be damaged goods alone in the universe."

"But you wouldn't have been alone if you had come to me sooner."

"I didn't know you existed until a few days ago."

That is a big, fat admission bordering on an actual answer. I'm stunned. A whole new line of questions stretches in my brain. How could she not know I existed? Did she wash up on some foreign shore with a trauma-erased memory? That day she did the incomplete merging with me, were those oddly echoed memories some clue to her story?

"The truth is, Jonathan, you're the only human being I've had any concern for since . . . since I earned my stripes and became a world-maker. I took a chance on you. And you turned out to be a total nut job."

"*I'm* a nut job? Take a look in the mirror, crazy-face."

"Exactly, Big Brother. We're quite a team." She annihilates her mulch pile with a swoosh of her hand and stands up. "Isn't she asleep yet?"

She dusts the mulch off her butt, then crowds me to the edge of the window frame. Together we look inside. Kylie's arm has slipped a few inches, and the notebook tucked underneath is in danger of plummeting to the floor. For the first time in my life, I'd rather finish a conversation with someone else than rush to be with Kylie.

"I think it's time," Tess says.

"We're not done talking."

"Yes. We are."

I try to feel satisfied that she came clean as much as she did. It's maddening to get so close and have so little by way of answers. I want to know more, but it's clear she's said her piece.

Her arms fold in front of her, nonverbally pushing me away as she says, "I suppose you want *me* to get the notebook."

I know that if I were a good person, I wouldn't be so eager to invade Kylie's privacy like this. If she wrote something in a notebook, it's hers to keep or give as she wants. Maybe it really is a poem and she does plan to give it. There certainly is a precedent for Kylie and me to exchange poetry. Unfortunately, I don't know if I can wait long enough to find out her intention.

"I'll do it," I say. At least if I'm going to be a jerk, I'm not going to be a chicken about it.

I put the conversation with Tess aside. She hands me the butter knife, and I slide it through the screen clips and then carefully open the window, hoping I'm still invisible should Kylie wake. I crawl through and rise softly to my feet. Kylie's room looks nothing like girlfriend Kylie's room, except for the general furniture arrangement and the corner of track medals and trophies displayed on the far wall. Where my girlfriend has animal posters and historical world maps on her walls, this Kylie displays modern art reproductions like the kind girlfriend Kylie disdained in the Fine Arts Museum. Where girlfriend Kylie's bed is done up in blue flannel sheets and a homemade quilt, this Kylie has white cotton sheets and a pink satiny comforter. A pink bearskin-like rug shushes my steps as I sneak over to the bed, whereas in my girlfriend's room, the floor is carpeted in something standard and blue.

Kylie's fingers no longer grip the notebook, but her arm is still draped over it. Gently I pull the notebook up, slide it from under her forearm. She doesn't even stir.

I hesitate, not knowing whether I should look at it here, quickly, so I can return it to under her arm, or if I should take it with me and let her wonder what happened to it. I decide to glance at the contents before making a decision, so I fold back the cover and turn a bunch of pages at once, hoping to get past the old creative writing stuff.

Luckily, she's dated her notes, so I flip as quietly as I can through her creativity and find the poem she wrote about the gravestone right after I mixed up my worlds. Underneath it she's written, *Is the grave for Jonathan's family?*

I flip some more. After some Eckhart notes, there's a draft of the paragraph she wrote about running on the day we posted our sensory descriptions. Underneath this she's written, *Why can't I stop thinking about running with him?*

I turn through several more sheets of notes and poem drafts, all scratched out too messily to make any sense of, though I do see my name in there. Eventually I get to the last page, the one with today's date on it. She was not writing a poem. She was writing a journal entry:

Dear Diary,

I have never in my life written something in a diary, but I wish I had. A long time ago, see, someone had something really terrible happen to him, and I wanted to help and I couldn't. Or rather, I didn't. I wish I had written down my third-grade thoughts, because I am really curious about them now. What did I think about Jonathan Aubrey? Was it a third-grade crush?

The problem is that something's happened with me and Jonathan. A part of me feels like I've been his friend from third grade until now, even though I know I've been no friend at all. I remember being picked by him in fifth grade for teams in tag, and kissing him in spin the bottle in seventh grade, and running with him regularly in high school. The problem is, I've never done any of these things. I have never been running (until the other day) with Jonathan. I have never kissed him (until the other day, but he kissed me. Today it was me who started it.) or been on his tag team. Jonathan Aubrey survived a plane crash in third grade, but when he came back to school, he kind of somehow died anyway, and I didn't know how to deal with that so I stopped trying to be friends with him *gave up on him.*

But I'm having these dreams where we lie in bed together talking at night. Only, my bed isn't mine and he thinks he's my boyfriend. He breaks in through my window, and in my dream I'm happy to see him, which is absurd because it's like he's stalking me. When I wake up and he's not there, I'm disappointed *devastated.*

In school it's just as strange. One day he almost bumped into me in the hall. Lilly said he was leaning over like he was going to kiss me. At the time I wouldn't admit that I was nervous she might have been right, because at the time kissing Jonathan Aubrey was the LAST thing in the world I wanted to do.

Then he got all funny in class about something I wrote and asked to talk to me. Then we went running. Then today. Well, today we went to the bird sanctuary, and I did something I can't believe I did. I needed him so badly. I need to be with Jonathan. It's like when I'm not with him, I go to pieces, and that's crazy because I only just started talking to him a few days ago.

Is something wrong with me? He seems to think there's something wrong about the whole situation. He's holding something back. I know I should be careful around him, but like I said, I can't help how I feel.

The funny thing is, the more I'm with him, the more I think he's a ~~nice~~ wonderful guy and it's okay to like him. He's very likable. It makes me sad he's such a loner usually. At the same time it scares me that these feelings came on so suddenly, like symptoms of a disease. I don't think this is what "lovesick" means. Jeez, maybe it is what it means. ~~I'm sick.~~ Am I in love?

I wish he were here right now. Jonathan, I wish you were here.

I close the notebook. Kylie is liking me against her will. That's clear. It helps that she says she likes me the more she gets to know me, but it feels pretty bad to have someone compare their feelings for you to being diseased.

I shouldn't be too disappointed. I've known from the start that Kylie's problem is the result of my world mix-up. It just sucks to see it in her words. It sucks more to wonder if she might ever have liked me for real if I'd only tried talking to her. It sucks the most to wonder if the other Kylie, my girlfriend and best friend since forever, would write a similar diary entry if the parameters of her world didn't make her love me. I can't stand myself right now.

I don't want to chance waking Kylie up, no matter how sincere she might have been at the end there about wanting to be with me. I place the notebook gently on the ground under the spot where she was holding it. Let her think she dropped it while she dozed. I climb out the window and pull it shut. Tess is sitting in the mulch again. "Done?" she asks.

"Yeah."

"So?"

I think about what comes next. I'm convinced I have to take action, but I'm not going to make Kylie's decision for her. I'm going to talk to the one who has the most to lose—girlfriend Kylie. She'll not only be giving up half of herself, but she'll be leaving her world and everyone in it. Granted, the real world is so much like Kylie-Simms-is-my-girlfriend that it's not like she's moving to another continent. Still, she'll be moving to another world.

"I need a little time," I say. "If you really want to help me with this, can you come when I call for you?"

"Just call my name, and I'll be there."

Girlfriend Kylie promised if I left her alone to sleep in this morning, she would talk to me tonight. Well, I have something to say. I'm going to tell her everything.

CHAPTER 21

I SWITCH BACK TO KYLIE-SIMMS-IS-MY-GIRLFRIEND TO get my own car, and leave Tess alone to drive herself wherever she goes. My sister and I have reached some kind of accord, and I'm grateful.

There's no use putting this off. If I go in the house to prepare a speech, I might lose my courage, and I'm too close to losing it as is.

During the drive to Kylie's my stomach rumbles, which could be nerves or could be hunger since it's dinnertime. When I arrive, the lights are out in Kylie's window, so she's probably eating with her family. I use my newly learned powers to go into stealth mode and enter her dark room through the window. I open the bedroom door, creep down the hall, and find Kylie at the table with her mom and dad. The food smells excellent, some kind of roast chicken, and my stomach rumbles again. If I went back outside and knocked on the door, I'd probably get invited to join them.

I don't do that, however. I hold on to my hunger so I can suffer one tiny fraction of what Kylie is about to suffer. While she dines with her family, I go back to her room to wait.

The red numbers of her digital clock keep me company for twenty-six minutes. I hear someone in the hall before the door opens and the lights flick on. Kylie jumps when she sees me sitting in her desk chair, but thankfully she doesn't scream.

"Jonathan! I said I'd call you. I just finished supper."

I stand and take a deep breath. "I know."

She shuts the door behind her, and I get the distinct feeling I'm not welcome. Her hands rest on her hips as she waits for me to explain why I'm here when I'm supposed to be home by the phone. She looks like she hasn't caught up on any of the sleep she hoped to today.

"I have to do something tonight," I say. "Something that scares me. And I need to talk to you before I do it."

That at least buys me her full attention, even if it is skeptical. "Since I wanted to talk to you, too, I guess we should get it all out at once."

I'm nervous about someone coming up the hall and overhearing us. Kylie must worry the same thing, because she looks to her door. I have snuck into her room like usual, but her parents have never known me to do this. Tonight would not be the opportune time to be discovered.

"Should we go to Lacy Pastry?" she asks.

"Why don't you tell your parents you're coming to my house? I'll meet you in the car. I think maybe we should go to the track."

"The track?"

"Somewhere without people around."

Now she looks über-skeptical, but she doesn't refuse. "Okay."

I climb out the window, which she shuts behind me, and go to her car. She emerges a minute later pulling on a light jacket. She starts the engine, and we're off. Neither of us begins a conversation that will be interrupted by getting to the track, so we ride in silence. My thoughts, though, are anything but silent. I mull over a dozen impossible ways to tell her all she needs to know.

The high school's driveway is well lit, but only the one orange sulfur light shines on the track. To my relief there aren't any dinnertime joggers. Although some cars up in the rotary indicate that something's going on inside the school, the track is deserted.

We pass through the gate, and instead of going up into the stands, we start walking around the night-dark oval. We're not holding hands. Kylie uses lane three, and I go wide in lane four.

"Okay, Jonathan. What's this horrible, scary thing you have to do?"

I keep my voice serious, despite the sarcasm in hers. "I'll tell you, but I thought you might want to talk first."

311

"Nope. You started this conversation at my house. You first."

"Okay. If that's what you want. The truth is . . . I have to tell someone the biggest secret of my life."

She doesn't answer right away. I imagine she thinks she's been keeping her own big secret about the monstrous nature of her recent feelings, which must be the subject she wanted to discuss. In a way she's right. "That someone is me, I assume," she says.

"Yes."

"Uh-huh."

We pace most of the way down the back straightaway through a pause in the witty conversation. Kylie, being Kylie, doesn't push me, and since she doesn't volunteer her own confession, I take my time planning the right disclosure of mine. How do you blurt out to your girlfriend that she's nothing but your made-up fantasy in a made-up world? And what would you expect her reaction to be?

I'm so afraid to speak, but so determined to speak, that my body starts to tremble. I'm cold all over. And nauseous. And glad I didn't eat. It's not like me to have nothing at all to say to Kylie, and I think she finally realizes that something very serious is happening here. She reaches for my hand, and my trembling passes through it into her.

"Jonathan, are you okay?"

We stop walking because it's awkward to hold hands when

an emergency situation is collapsing all over you. "I . . . I . . . I don't know how to say it."

"You don't have to be afraid to tell me. I'm sorry for my stupid attitude lately."

"There's nothing to be sorry for."

"I tried to push you away in the shed, and I did push you away after yesterday's meet. You came for me tonight anyway. I didn't deserve that."

"You deserve so much more than that."

"No, I don't. I haven't been very nice to you."

"Kylie." I'm about to tell her. The confession blossoms in my chest. I need only breathe and form the words, and it will be over. I drop her hand so I won't have to endure her dropping mine when she finds out. "Kylie." Why can I manage to say only her name?

"Whatever it is, it will be okay." My old girlfriend reemerges, trying to make me feel better. If enough of her is still intact, it will help the next few minutes enormously.

"I wish that were true."

"Just tell me. You're scaring me with all this drama."

I rub my face with my hands. What am I going to say? Then, before I can stop them, words come pouring out of my mouth. "Have you ever just wanted to live in a world of your own make-believe?"

313

"What?"

"Have you ever wanted to be in another place, or have other people around you, or things you just can't get in the real world?"

"You mean like imaginary friends?"

"Sort of. Have you ever wanted to, you know, be like Kaitlyn Frost and travel to a world of faeries and mermaids and stuff?"

"Um . . ." Her eyes are scrunching up like I'd better get to my point quickly. "I guess when I was little I wanted to have a house in the backyard. My own house that was me-size where I could live kind of a magical lifestyle. You know, decorated all girlie and stuff."

"You did?"

"Don't make fun of me. I'm just going along with things here, Jonathan."

"Tell me about it."

"What, the house?"

"Yeah, describe it for me."

She purses her lips and furrows her brow in thought. Her eyes gleam in the darkness of this side of the track. The lane lines spread away from us in both directions, as if we've landed in the center of some cosmic roadway. She takes a deep breath, willing to talk about a childhood fantasy for reasons she doesn't understand. Her eyes find mine as if she's checking that I'm serious about asking.

"Well . . . I don't remember what color it was. Purple maybe? Light purple? With a white railing around a long porch. Victorian-looking. When you walked in the front door, there were stairs going up to the second floor. There was furniture, old-fashioned furniture but brand-new. . . . I guess there was a flower garden around it. . . . There were lamps in every room. . . . I don't know what else."

"Where in your backyard was it?"

"Over by the big maple that's not there anymore."

She's given me enough. I wonder if I can do two things at once, make a world and move something into it. The current circumstances mean my will is certainly strong enough. I reconnect with Kylie's hand and draw her whole body to me. She resists at first, but then softens. I wrap my arms around her and focus all my world-making energy on a purple Victorian. I squeeze my eyes shut with concentration, even though Tess said it wasn't necessary. I'm not sure I can do this, so I go with the method I'm comfortable using.

I know I've succeeded when Kylie lets out a huge gasp.

We don't let go of each other, but we're not on the track anymore. The space between worlds rips by, and we stand in Kylie's grassy acre of backyard. Before us is a kid-size Victorian under the wide canopy of a maple tree that Kylie's father chopped down last year. Lamplight blazes from every window, even a small circular one up on the third floor. It's hard to tell it's purple with all the light coming from inside, but the gleaming white detail of the trim shines in the window light. Along the length of the porch railing, flowers trail from flower boxes, and a rose garden around the porch catches the light on a pink rose here, a white rose there.

"Oh, Jonathan," Kylie says. "What did you do?"

I swallow hard. There's a big, fat lump in my throat. "This is my secret. I'm a world-maker."

She scans the whole yard, which I know is exactly like her real backyard. When she remembers to look behind her, it's as if she expects the track to be there, but instead it's her house with the kitchen lights on. Her fingers dig into my arms.

We turn back to the Victorian. "Do you want to go in?" I ask.

She tips her head to see up to the roof and back down to the porch. "Maybe."

"Come on." I tug her sleeve, and we go up the steps. We have to duck to get through the front doorframe. Once inside, the ceilings are barely high enough for us to stand upright. We have to avoid walking into overhead light fixtures.

We tour a sitting room, a living room, a kitchen, a dining room. We go upstairs to see four little bedrooms all trimmed out with lacy bedcovers and tasseled lamps. There are stuffed animals everywhere, which I didn't specifically include, but if the parameter for this world is things a little girl loves, I guess stuffed animals are appropriate.

We go up a skinny flight of stairs to the attic, which turns out to be one long room with a velvet couch at one end and a writing desk at the other. A desk lamp shines down on a pile of stationery and a quill pen.

Kylie hasn't said a word since we entered. She's touched everything, inhaled the varying floral scents of each room, closed her eyes and listened. She looks at me now, her eyes still glistening, but her pupils are wide. I think she might be afraid.

"This is the house," she says. "I couldn't remember all the details, but everything about it is perfect."

"I made it out of your description."

"How?"

"I don't know. I've been a world-maker ever since the crash, or the coma, or sometime shortly thereafter."

"But this isn't real, is it?"

"Yes. It is."

"This is my backyard."

"It's like your back yard, but it's a completely separate world."

Her head moves back and forth, slowly, disbelievingly.

For some reason I'm struck with the memory of how she loved the Arthurian paintings at the Fine Arts Museum. Knights and ladies and horses and castles. I step toward Kylie and wrap myself around her again, squeeze my eyes closed, and concentrate on details, parameters, colors. In barely more than a blink, Kylie separates from me to gape at a looming whitewashed castle in the sun, complete with an open drawbridge and banners hanging from the walls. Tournament horses draped in heraldic colors parade out of the castle. Knights and pages and servants clamor along in an endless line of baggage, weaponry, and high spirits. Tree-covered hills slope gently up and down the horizon.

Kylie's hands smooth over the gown I've given her, blue with a gold fleur-de-lis pattern and gold trimmings. The sleeves almost sweep the ground. Her hair is done up in braids and threaded with gold ribbon. A large blue sapphire sparkles on a gold chain at her neck. I've given myself a simple tunic and tights, leather cap, leather boots, and a bow and arrow. I'm not sure if a graceful lady and a graceless archer would be a passable pair in Arthurian lore, but I've made acceptance of our appearance a parameter of this world.

"How are you doing this?" she asks.

I shrug. "I told you I don't know."

"You're not doing it on purpose?"

"I made this world for you because you liked those paintings so much."

We look to the castle and the parade of chivalry, and I get wistful that before now I never used my world-making powers to craft worlds like this one. I think about the things I could have created out of my favorite stories, out of historical events or speculation for the future. The closest I ever came was Jonathan-is-a-hero, my childish war against alien invaders, but even that wasn't as much about the aliens as it was about having people who looked up to me.

Kylie and I stand just off a road leading up to the castle. A party of nobles with fancy horses and a carriage approaches. "I want to go, Jonathan. Get us out of here." She is beautiful as a Lady in blue and gold. I wish she could see herself in a mirror.

I do what she asks, though, and hold her tight for the journey back. It takes another blink to be re-engulfed by night on the track, and now it's Kylie, not me, who's shaking.

"Are you okay?" I ask.

"That's some secret." She steadies herself by holding on to me, nodding her head as if she's agreeing over and over that my secret's pretty colossal.

"I wish that were the terrible part."

Her head stops as her body stiffens. "What's the terrible part?"

"I don't know how to say it except to say it. But I need you to believe how much I love you, Kylie. I love you more than anything."

"What's the terrible part, Jonathan?"

JEN BROOKS

My leg quivers, like if some part of me's in motion, some-how I can fast-forward past this moment. I have never been so scared in my life, and we all know I've had at least one other pretty big scare.

Her face is in shadow, but I study its contours as if for the last time. Kylie. My Kylie. Her teeth are sunk so hard into her lip, I wouldn't be surprised to see blood. "When I got out of the hospital, I was so depressed that I wished desperately to be in another world. I squeezed my eyes shut, and when I opened them, I was holding a laser gun and shooting at aliens. It was the kind of thing an eight-year-old kid who's played too many video games with his dad might think of. I visited that world every day for a while, but then I kind of outgrew it."

It sounds impossible, even to my ears, but she's listening. She believes I'm a world-maker because she's seen it. I take another breath and continue. "Then I made a world I called Jonathan's-smokin'-hot-dance-club. You know, a growing boy, dancing girls, and all that." I don't like admitting this to Kylie, but I'm not holding that info back when something so much worse is coming.

"Eventually I realized I wasn't going to be happy unless this certain girl I liked was my girlfriend. We'd known each other in elementary school. She had gorgeous red-brown hair. On the outside of her locker, she taped up this collage of music lyrics about friendship and love and happiness, and she never knew it, but I read every single line when I came early to school. She kept a winged-foot keychain dangling from the zipper of her backpack—I heard her say it was a prize she'd won for being "most spirited freshman" on the track team. In the cafeteria she sat in the back corner with a table full of friends and always bought tacos on taco day, so I learned to love tacos and bought them on taco day too. She had this way of drawing people into her circle. While other girls were cliquing around, she managed to be friendly with everyone. Even kids no other popular girl would be seen within a mile of.

"The problem was, I was such a loner that I'd never go near enough to let her talk to me. After losing my whole family and almost dying myself, I was, you know, in pretty rough shape. When other kids made fun of my scar, I couldn't deal. I totally withdrew. By the time I got to high school, I didn't have a single friend. I wasn't an outcast at that point. I had ceased to exist."

Her eyes can't get any wider. This account of me is not the truth she knows, and she couldn't have missed my saying I wouldn't be happy without the girl I liked being my girlfriend. The pieces she already holds of her own experience are falling into place. It's too late to take them back.

"I had never made a world that was like the real world. I never made a world with my family alive, though I wanted it

JEN BROOKS

badly. After torturous years of wanting Kylie Simms to notice me and knowing she never would, I decided my consolation for losing my family would be to have a girlfriend."

"Oh my God," she says. As if her knees have suddenly broken, she plops down onto the track. "Oh my God."

"I'm so sorry, Kylie. I never thought things through to this conclusion. I just liked you so much, and I was so lonely. You're the only good thing I've had in my life since the accident, and there's no way I can explain how sorry I am. I'm so, so sorry."

I fight not to wrap my arms around her again. If she needed space before, she certainly does now. I can't stop here, anyway. There's still the most important part.

"There's one more thing. Kylie Simms still exists in the real world. I got confused one day and thought she was you, and ever since then you've been experiencing each other somehow. All that space you asked for is the distance the other Kylie has. All the love you had for me put pressure on her to like me. The poems, the dreams, all of it is you becoming part her and her part you. It can't be undone. The only way to fix things is to merge both of you into one Kylie."

Her mouth drops open, and she shakes her head. "What does that even mean?"

"It means I take you to the real world to see her, and the two of you become one."

"There's no way I can even begin to comprehend that. Two of us become one Kylie? I'm not even real?"

"Of course you're real. You're brilliant and athletic and beautiful and the best friend I could ever hope for. You're real. It's just that . . . you weren't real until I made you a world."

"But I have memories going all the way back to before you had the accident you say gave you this power."

"I know."

"They're not real?"

"The memories are real, but they didn't really happen. They couldn't have."

Her hands make agitated movements in the air. "I can't believe what I'm hearing."

I can't stand it, I have to touch her. I kneel down on the track and still her wild hands. "I made this world in tenth grade. The first thing we did together was that horror movie party at Mandy's house."

"I remember that."

"Because you were there."

"But not before?"

"No."

I think she's about to wig out. Her breathing is quick and shallow, her skin pale in the darkness. She's not crying. She's worse than crying.

"So this is what's been wrong with me lately? I was happy being in love with you right up until a few days ago. Then all of a sudden, *bam*, weird feelings around my boyfriend. I thought my stupid behavior is what we were going to talk about tonight, but this is the last thing I expected."

She wrestles her hands from mine and stands, backs away from me, begins pacing. All I can do is stand and watch as her arms flail with her words. "I've had all these confused thoughts," she says, "like when you're near, I want to back away. I don't want you to touch me. It's not the opposite of love, exactly. It's feeling uncomfortable around you, like you're a stranger in my personal space. My own boyfriend! At the same time, all I want is you. It's been killing me to try to understand why I want to be with you but can't stand to be in the same room. I haven't slept in three days for the worry, for the nightmares! For not wanting to hurt your feelings but scared that some part of me doesn't care how you feel anymore."

"You can stop feeling guilty about hurting the bastard who's only hurting you."

Her fingers dig into her eyes as she moves. "What's the other Kylie like?" she asks.

It's hard to answer because she won't stop pacing. "Well, she likes science, for one thing, and winter, and wouldn't have picked creative writing if it didn't fit into her schedule. And her room is more girlie than yours."

"You've been in her *room?*" I wouldn't have told her that, but I'm coming as clean as I possibly can. Plus, that gets her to stand still and at least look at me.

"Yeah."

"Have you two . . ."

"No. Not at all. She didn't even know I was there."

"Oh, you were spying on her?"

"I had to know what was going on with you and her. I couldn't just ask."

"Does she know about you? How you make worlds and all that?"

"No. I needed to tell you first."

"Do you love her?"

"I hardly know her."

For whatever reason, that's what finally breaks her. She bursts into tears, big heartbreaking sobs that echo in the night.

"I'm sorry, Kylie." I can't say it enough. She lets me gather her up, and I bury my face in her shoulder while she cries into mine. We hold on tightly, as if an embrace is the only thing keeping us from falling off the edge of the earth. I don't want to lose her. I can't imagine facing the world without her.

CHAPTER 22

"IT'S HARD TO WRAP MY MIND AROUND NOT BEING REAL," she says.

We haven't recovered the strength to stand, so we're sitting on the track, still holding each other. Kylie isn't done crying, but the force of it has ebbed to something we can talk through. She's still trembling, though.

"You're as real as I am."

"No, I'm a copy. You're not."

"One thing I've learned is that you're anything but a copy. I told you, the other Kylie has different tastes, and has made different choices. You and I have been together so long, we have an awesome relationship that the other Kylie doesn't have with anyone. I think being with me has made you develop some differences, but you're right, in all the important ways you're the same."

"Like what important ways?"

"I made you to be her, so everything I loved about her is in you. For one thing, you're the most beautiful girl I've ever seen."

"Oh, please." She shifts and mops some more tears with her sleeve.

"And you both do the same track events, and you do them just as well, with the same personal bests and everything."

"That's just . . . weird."

"You're both honest and have this way of getting right to the point. You're both great at writing poetry and analyzing my poetry. You're both funny and can do a good wisecrack. You're both so kind that you can see through a person's scars right to the person underneath."

"Yeah. You and your scars. You worry too much about them."

"And you hardly notice them. It's the thing I love most about you, and the one thing I didn't know about the original Kylie when I made this world."

"You didn't add traits to me on purpose? To make me better in your eyes?"

"There couldn't be anything better. I just wanted you to want to be with me."

Her trembling is less obvious now, and the desperation of earlier has fallen out of her voice. Her jacket sleeves are wet from wiping her face, but she doesn't reach for her face again. I hope the tears have stopped.

"I'm thinking," she says, "about what you said. About merging."

"You don't have to do it, Kylie. Not if you don't want to. But I'm afraid you'll just keep losing sleep. Or worse."

She slackens her hold on me so she can look me in the face. "You want me to volunteer."

My silence gives her her answer.

"Will I die?"

"The whole point is to make you better so you can live."

"Will it hurt?"

I think of that strange experiment merging with Tess. She said it wouldn't be quite like that for Kylie, but I didn't get the impression it would involve pain. "I don't think so."

"What will happen to my parents?"

"I'll close this world and everything in it. Your parents are alive and well in the real world, an identical world. Nothing will change." Of course everything will change, and she's too smart to believe my overly optimistic answer.

She takes a deep breath and blows it out. "How much longer do I have?"

There's no deadline I know of besides how long I can stand seeing them separately suffering. "It would probably be better, now that you know, to do the merging soon. Otherwise you'll just dwell on it. You have to be together with the other Kylie when it happens, but I can take you there now just to see her and bring you back here first, if you want."

She thinks about it. I can't imagine what it must be like to be her right now.

"No, I want to go home first. Then we'll go see her."

She looks away from me, up at the sky. I find it difficult to raise my eyes to the heavens, so I stare at the lines of the track. "Will we still love each other?" she asks.

It's the most important question in the universe.

"I don't know."

I help her up, and we walk back to the car. Kylie leans her head against the window to stare at the passing world for the whole ride. I want to say something that will make the next few hours easier, but there's no greeting card category that covers merging. My imagination plants me in a grocery store picking out just such a card, and the absurdity of the thought ties my tongue even tighter. The most comfort I can give is a hand on her knee.

When we get to her house, I cut the ignition. Kylie's house is welcoming with its neat landscaping and bright lights at the front door and garage. "Do you mind waiting here?" she asks.

"That's fine," I say, trying to squeeze as much reassurance as I can into two syllables and a soft look.

She gets out and wanders to the front door, straightening her jacket as she goes. And I wait. I imagine her inside, greeting her parents, saying a subtle good-bye, maybe chatting with them in the kitchen or settling with them on the couch for a few minutes of family TV watching.

After a while the light goes on in her bedroom, and I know she won't be much longer. She got all shaken up at the track, but she agreed to everything. Everything. And although I wouldn't say she's happy about it, the what-to-do-next part got decided surprisingly easily. I don't know if she figured her torture was too much to bear for the rest of her life, or if the world parameter that makes her love me is still functioning, still making her compliant when it comes to what I need. My self-loathing surges, but at least it won't be much longer until she's released from my prison of a world.

"Tess," I call.

She appears immediately, standing in the glare of my headlights, which I've forgotten to dim. I do so now, and she stands backlit by Kylie's garage light. She makes no move to get into the car, so I open the door and get out. "We're going to switch over to the real world when Kylie comes out."

"Yeah, I know." She's wearing all black, from her fitted turtleneck to her boots. She's even wearing black gloves. Her hair, unnaturally black, hangs long and loose around her shoulders.

The only part of her that doesn't swallow light is her face.

I say, "I guess we'll take my car back to Uncle Joey's and go from there."

"Should I come with you or meet you?"

"I guess it would be better to meet there." It sounds too much like we're planning a casual dinner.

"She's still asleep, you know. Real Kylie. You can take the other one straight into her room."

"Okay."

Tess shifts so her weight rests on one foot. She regards me for a moment. "It'll be fine, you know."

"Okay."

I'm dangerously close to postponing things because I'm terrified, but Kylie emerges just as Tess winks away. "Who was that?" she asks.

I sigh before telling the last of the truth. "That was the girl I chased in the mall."

"The one you recognized from the crash?"

"Yeah, but what I never said, but should have, is that she's Tess."

"Tess, as in, your sister Tess?"

"She's been helping me, and she's the one who knows how to merge. She's meeting us at the other Kylie's."

Kylie still doesn't argue, despite the pathetic inadequacy

of my explanations. I've already thought of a dozen follow-up questions I would have fired, but she just stands there, willing to take on faith that I know what I'm doing. That sickens me more than anything else. She trusts me despite the twenty feet of physical distance she's left as a barrier between us.

She looks back at her house, toward the drawn curtains of the living room. "Let's go."

Even though I told Tess we'd drive back to Uncle Joey's first, I leave my car in Kylie's driveway. It won't matter if her parents see it parked there. This world won't exist in a few hours.

"Come here," I say, and we step toward each other, raising our arms for an embrace. She feels limp, so unlike the vibrant hugger I've known for so long. I pull her close and move us out of Kylie-Simms-is-my-girlfriend for the last time. Around us rise the four walls of real Kylie's bedroom. Her bedside clock says it's a little after nine p.m., and Kylie herself is fast asleep under the covers. Her hair is tied in a knot at the top of her head, and the puffiness in her face from crying hasn't receded fully. Movement in the corner draws our attention as Tess rises from a chair. "Hi, Kylie," she says. "It's nice to finally meet you." She extends a hand.

It strikes me as weird to be introducing yourself to someone you're about to annihilate by merging them into somebody else.

Kylie doesn't flinch. Her hand goes straight to Tess's. "And you."

"I'm guessing you have some questions," Tess says.

"Yes."

"Okay, shoot."

Kylie takes a moment to study her sleeping double. Except for the little residual puffiness, they are mirror images of each other. She turns and gives me an unreadable look. "I can see what she's dreaming." She turns to Tess. "How can I do that?"

"Well," says Tess. "It's because Jonathan created you to be her. The two of you in the same world is like two walls of the same canyon. Everything you feel or think echoes between you. If she were awake, she'd know what you're thinking. Her dream might even reflect your thoughts right now."

Kylie looks again at her counterpart bundled in the comforter, twitching an arm in her sleep. This whole procedure has been taken out of my hands, like I've become a spectator in the bleachers while Kylie takes the field. "You're right. My thoughts are part of her dream."

She watches sleeping Kylie some more, possibly eavesdropping on her with the echoing canyon phenomenon, before asking, "Will I still be me?"

"You'll have all your memories and thoughts, but so will she. Think of it like updating to a newer version of a computer program. All the original information is there, but some of the bugs get removed and helpful new stuff gets added. The program and the update become one thing. There is only the one program. It might be a little disorienting at first, to have merged thoughts, but it's not like you'll go nuts or anything. Your head will clear and you'll feel just like you again.

"Plus merged bodies don't double in size or anything weird like that. They choose the best cells from each original. You'll wake up physically stronger than you've ever felt before. It's a huge perk, especially for an athlete."

Tess's voice is gentler than I would have thought possible from her. All the sibling-rivalry-esque hostility she's been show-ing me has turned into kindness for Kylie. It's like she's become Kylie's big sister explaining how the first day of school is going to go, and how it's going to be okay.

Unexpectedly our heads turn as one to the door. Footsteps, more than one set, creak along the hall toward us. Girlfriend Kylie draws a breath, but otherwise we all go still.

A weak knock sounds on the wood. The knob rotates slowly before the door cracks open. A head peeks around the door—Kylie's mom's—and checks on the sleeper. Tess must have us in invisible mode, because Kylie's mom doesn't notice that the room is full of people. Mrs. Simms pulls her head back out and closes the door. Voices exchange hushed words, and the foot-steps continue down the hall.

"My other mom and dad," Kylie says.

"Everyone here has a double in your world," Tess says. *Except for Jonathan,* she should add. There's only one me for both worlds, but that one me is as close to being two different people as you can get. Here I'm nothing like the boyfriend she knew in Kylie-Simms-is-my-girlfriend. I'm not in all her classes. I'm not on the track team. I don't have friends. I walk to school. I won't be going to college with her next year. Too many things about me aren't the me she knows, and there will be no world parameter saying she has to be my girlfriend anymore.

Kylie swipes her eyes with her sleeve and blinks back another round of tears. She comes to me and hugs me, a long, tight good-bye. "I love you," I whisper.

She doesn't say anything in return.

When she pulls out of the hug, Tess takes her gently by the arm over to the bed. Real Kylie hasn't moved at all, but her face has smoothed. She looks more serene than she did when we first got here.

"The best thing to do," Tess says, "is to think about what makes you happiest in your life. With you standing this close, the thoughts will fill her, so when you come together, you'll be a little more at ease. Think of it as having your dorm room decorated with your familiar belongings before you arrive."

Kylie nods and presumably beams down warm, fuzzy thoughts to the Kylie she's about to become. I grow faint watching her, and realize I'm holding my breath. The room feels darker and smaller, like the lens of a camera has come focusing down on Kylie and Kylie, cutting everything else from the picture. I'm way out of the shot already, and Tess is disappearing fast. Kylie, by some instinct, reaches out her hand to her sleeping self. Tess catches her by the wrist. "Wait."

Tess peels back the comforter from sleeping Kylie, and I'm struck with immense guilt for never telling the sleeping Kylie her life is about to change. I don't know if it's better to be the Kylie I told or the Kylie I left ignorant, but events are pushing along now, and there's no time to back up and give the other Kylie a choice.

Sleeping Kylie is still dressed except for her bare feet. She wears a Pennington track long-sleeved shirt and pale blue jeans. Awake Kylie's wearing dark blue jeans and a thin yellow sweater. Tess says, "For the sake of the boy over there who's going to watch this, it would be better if you lie down next to her."

For my sake? Kylie hesitates at the directions but doesn't look over at me. Tess gives her a nudge, and Kylie gets into the bed by first sitting and then pulling up her feet and lying back. Before her body reaches any kind of settled position, she brushes against real Kylie, touching her for the first time, and my world turns inside out.

I don't know what I thought it would be like. Maybe two

halves of a deck of cards getting shuffled together. Maybe a magical blue light glowing around them, full of sparkles and peace as they blink from two people one second into one person the next. I am not prepared when blood and skin and hair and clothes and arms and ears run together like the smudge of a wet finger painting. Legs kick out and melt, puddle-like, into each other. Wet slapping sounds. Covers rustling sounds. Another sound like something thick clearing from a clogged drain. A membrane forms around the melted flesh and clothing, keeping the folded colors inside to overlap one another. It's the worst horror picture I've ever seen. My throat contracts like it's ready to vomit. Tess takes my hand. Her strange burning pierces my palm and shoots up my arm. My hand turns to liquid, like my former girlfriend and wished-for girlfriend in front of me. When I look down, I expect to see my hand and Tess's merged, but I see two regular hands.

The pool of Kylies stretches and pulls, and a set of fingers slides down on the inside of the membrane binding it all, five white fingertips in a dark stew. A face pushes up toward the ceiling, squashed by the pressure of the barrier into something vague and featureless. Tess shoots more heat up my arm, spreads warmth through my shoulder into my chest, through my bowels, into my legs. Her compelled reassurance mixes with my natural fear and overwhelms me, distances my horror over the gore in the bed, blurs my line of sight, dulls the pain of regretting the choice to do this to Kylie, the pain of hating myself, the world-maker who destroys.

I can't concentrate anymore on what's happening to Kylie. Tess's comfort thing fills me so completely that all I can think of is Tess, the shape of Tess, the smell of Tess, the sound of her sarcastic voice an inch from my ear. Her mouth really is an inch from my ear, whispering, "It's almost over, Jonathan." Her one hand is firm in mine, but I feel like a hundred of her hands stroke me all over, a hundred of her voices whisper, "It's gonna be okay," while dampening the snap and slosh of the merging on the bed.

A voice buried under all of this cries out for me to pull my hand from Tess's. I should witness every last detail of Kylie's trauma without a filter. I'm losing her. With this transformation she'll be changed forever. The shape on the bed becomes recognizably human, wired with red arteries and blue veins bright against sallow flesh, twice the size of Kylie. My little buried voice cries out once more, and I find the strength to yank my hand to try to free it. Tess yanks back and then lets go, only to grab me from behind and wrap her arms around my abdomen, shooting her warmth down, then up, and I'm utterly lost. I shudder in her arms while Kylie transforms before me, and I have only a vague notion of something seeping through Kylie's forming skin, soaking in a red pool through the bedsheets into the mattress, dripping thickly onto the floor.

I lose the strength in my legs and lean against Tess, dissolving into something not quite me. I try to focus on Kylie, but there's nothing to see. Just a bed with a girl. Tess sets me gently down on the floor. She goes to Kylie, and the absence of her touch clears my head. Anger replaces the warmth.

"You shouldn't have done that to me," I say.

She doesn't respond, just pulls on Kylie's shoulder to roll her over. Kylie is asleep.

"Not asleep," Tess says. "Unconscious. Merging takes a little while to recover from, but she looks okay."

I move to the bed, careful not to come close enough to accidentally touch Tess. Kylie does look remarkably okay. Her face is a warm, healthy pink with no puff around her eyes. She's wearing girlfriend Kylie's yellow sweater, but the Pennington track logo from the real Kylie's shirt is emblazoned on the front. The color of her jeans is somewhere between the pale blue and dark blue of both Kylies' originals. She's wearing the socks and running shoes girlfriend Kylie arrived in, but her hair is pulled up in the knot real Kylie wore to bed.

Tess standing so close makes me feel icky, and I want her to leave. Her part in all this is done. "How long until she wakes up?"

Tess shrugs. "She'll be fine when her alarm goes off." I glance at the clock. Barely twenty minutes have passed since we showed up. "But between now and then you should close the other world."

I forgot about that. "I will," I say.

"Want me to help?"

"No. Just go."

"Are you . . . *mad* at me, Big Brother?"

"You shouldn't have done that to me."

"What, shielded you from the worst of watching a merging happen to someone you love? Made it so you wouldn't think gruesome thoughts every time you looked at Kylie from now on?"

"I deserved to suffer through it."

"You don't deserve any more suffering, Jonathan. You've had enough."

"That's not for you to decide."

"I know what I did was the best way to help you."

"I don't appreciate your brand of help. I've come to associate you with unnatural things."

A flash of hurt changes her face. I've stepped over the line. Didn't she say earlier I'm the first human being she's felt concerned for since she became a world-maker? Shouldn't I be more careful before I blast that carefully placed concern to smithereens? But can she really blame me for lashing out at this moment? The night's events have me so worked up, I don't care. Kylie and Kylie are gone, and it's all I can do to keep from tearing my hair out wondering what will wake up in that new body.

Tess doesn't stay hurt more than a millisecond before something darker replaces it. She smiles—a great, big, feral smile that exposes teeth like a wolf's. Her irises swell and turn black like her outfit. I shrink away from her as she takes her revenge for my selfishness. "I assure you, Jonathan Aubrey, I am the most natural thing in creation." She leans over Kylie once more, bends so close to her face that I'm afraid she'll bite her, or lick her with a big wolf tongue. "She's perfect, Jonathan. You're a very lucky little man." Her words are sharp like her teeth. Her tone entirely satisfied with what's been done tonight.

"I think you should go now."

"What? No 'thank you'?"

"Gratitude might come later. Right now all I know is that you haven't been honest with me."

"I have *never* told you a single lie."

"But you haven't told me the whole truth. Like what happened between the crash and the day you popped back into my life?"

Her lips close and her eyes narrow. "I'll tell you what. You enjoy your brand-new Kylie tonight. Tomorrow I'll give you proof of my honesty."

I do not like the sound of that, but I want her to go away. "Just give me some space."

Is this how Kylie felt when she asked *me* for space? Because I really think another second together with Tess will send me over the edge.

Tess flashes her canines at me once more, then disappears.

In her absence the room's air, which felt stiflingly heavy, becomes easier to breathe. The heat that has built up in my skin dissipates, and I kneel beside Kylie's bed. Her chest expands and contracts with gentle sleep. It's done, and she will never again be in Kylie-Simms-is-my-girlfriend. It's time to close the world that gave me so much and trap myself here to see what becomes of me.

I rise and turn toward Kylie's window, concentrating on the same window in the other world that I was invited to climb through on nights when I needed comfort most. Closing that world tonight is the same as sealing that window forever, and as I pry open Kylie-Simms-is-my-girlfriend one last time, I fill myself with destructive imagery—fire, flood, horrified faces floating in an airplane cabin. Kylie-Simms-is-my-girlfriend yawns open on the other side of a bridge connecting the spheres in the darkness. I almost change my mind and cross over to say good-bye. I never had the chance to say good-bye to my world of childhood in the crash. There is no cemetery for dead worlds.

No place to someday find the nerve to visit and mourn. About to die is the place where I've shared a hundred hot chocolates at Lacy Pastry, where I run seven miles with the guys and place third in track meets, where I walk Kylie to class and get credit for the work I do in those classes, where my teachers approve of me and my coach respects me, where people who pass me in the hall smile and say hello. My foot is raised, but before I can run to my haven from all I've never been able to bear in real life, the world closes and is gone.

Kylie-Simms-is-my-girlfriend is gone. GONE. The ache of total loss is too familiar. I hold it close as penance for the suffering I've put Kylie through. My girlfriend has no world, and she's subject now to the same rules I am. And the same freedom to choose anyone at all to spend her life with.

Kylie lies on the near side of the bed, but there is enough room against the wall for me to climb in beside her. I won't, though. I don't know what kind of Kylie will wake up and see me there in the morning. But I can't leave. I have to make sure she's all right when she wakes.

I pull her desk chair up beside the bed and sit down. After a while I'm too tired to sit any longer and need to rest my head, so I get down on the rug and use a stuffed animal from the shelf for a pillow. I fall asleep to the rhythm of Kylie breathing. And the nightmare of waking up without her.

CHAPTER 23

I WAKE LONG BEFORE KYLIE DOES. NOT THAT MY REST WAS very deep, with all the buzzing in my head and the hardness of the floor. Kylie first rolled over at midnight, and I got up to check on her. Then the night became a series of Kylie tossings and Jonathan checkings until suddenly it's almost six o'clock and I'm wondering if I should let the alarm wake her or do it myself. I can't let her sleep past six, because her mom will surely come in, wondering why she isn't up and getting ready for school.

After hours of pseudo-tending to her, I'm almost sure she's physically okay. Her sleep even seems peaceful. My dreams, on the other hand, have traveled through a wasteland of grief— sepia-toned worlds strewn with the dead, Jonathans calling out in crowds that won't hear, twisted-faced Kylies pointing accusing fingers: *How could you do this to me?*

I didn't mean to do it. I mixed everything up and couldn't sort it out again. I'll make it up to you with all my soul if you'll let me.

The alarm clock reads 5:59, and I decide it's best to let it beep as usual. It will keep her parents at bay if they're accustomed to hearing it get turned off. It will also let Kylie wake up according to her normal routine.

I return to the chair. I want to talk to her but don't want to be the first thing she sees. Seconds pass. More seconds. More seconds. This is the longest minute ever recorded in history.

Finally the alarm goes off. Kylie stirs immediately, lifts her head to see the time, and reaches over to hit the off button. I'm glad to see she doesn't hit snooze. Girlfriend Kylie never hit snooze.

She lies still. Strangely still. I can't see if her eyes are open or closed, since I've positioned my chair against the wall so I'll be out of her view. I'm hoping I've successfully employed Tess's invisibility technique as a backup defense. I've never before watched Kylie awaken when she didn't know I was beside her, so I don't know if this pause is normal. Does she usually take time before rolling out of bed? Is she remembering last night? Is something wrong with her after all?

She shifts position and rolls her upper body so she can see over the bed to the floor where I slept. Her eyes sweep the room, including the chair where I sit. "Jonathan, are you still here?" she whispers.

She sounds normal. She looks okay. No strange tics. No anxiety in her voice. As far as I can tell, she's just had a normal night's sleep like any other.

I still don't know how close she wants me to be, but I let myself become visible and lean forward in the chair. She rolls over onto her back and stretches.

"Good morning," I say.

She yawns and turns her head to me. "You didn't have to sleep on the floor, but I was too tired to say so last night."

"You saw me . . . after?"

I expect her to say *After what?* but she just takes a deep breath, a healthy breath, and says, "I knew you stayed the whole night."

I try to separate traces of girlfriend Kylie from traces of the real one. The shape of her mouth, the movement of her hands, the shine of her hair. All of her looks like the real Kylie. All of her looks like my girlfriend.

As her eyes rake me in return, my body tenses. While I have the same old eyes to gaze upon the new her, she has brand-new eyes to size up the old me. There is no parameter anymore to make her love me, so if one Kylie no longer has to love me and the other never did . . . this could be it for us. Maybe her feelings are confused, since there are two sets of them filed away in there. I wish I knew how much the real Kylie liked me before I did this to her last night.

She slides her legs over the side of the bed and sits up. "I'm going to take a shower. Will you stay here until I get back?"

The total lack of drama in her demeanor throws me. This should be a momentous moment. I nod.

"I'll be quick." She throws back her covers and looks to the back of her door. My girlfriend Kylie keeps her robe there, but nothing hangs from the hook in this world. A fret crosses her face, and she goes over to the closet, finds a robe, grabs some clothes and heads for the shower, closing the door firmly behind her.

I don't know what this means.

While I wait, I inspect the bed. I have a vague recollection, through layers of Tess's interference, of it being soaked in blood and flesh. I touch the sheets, poke under the comforter, get down on hands and knees to peer underneath. Distorted memories accompany me on the search, but I don't find any evidence of trauma. Despite my anger with Tess, I'm glad I can't picture the scene in exact detail. I really don't want to have to think of it every time I look at Kylie from now on.

Kylie is quick returning from the shower. She's wearing a

blue tank top and the jeans she slept in. "You need to swing by your house on the way?"

"On the way where?"

"To school, silly."

Silly? "If there were ever an excuse for a sick day, this would be it."

"I don't feel sick." She grabs a brush and drags it through her wet hair.

I stop short before saying something else. Maybe she doesn't remember what happened last night. Does she think she's still real Kylie? She couldn't, or she would be freaked out that I broke into her room. Does she think she's girlfriend Kylie and we're still in Kylie-Simms-is-my-girlfriend?

She blow-dries her hair halfway and pulls it into a ponytail, then throws on her Pennington track zip-up hoodie. She stuffs some workout clothes into her gym bag and draws it and a backpack over one shoulder. "I'm starving. Mind if we drive-through for hot chocolate and a bagel too?"

Although I'm relieved, I'm waiting for the other shoe to drop. Since I'm still not sure what she remembers, I choose not to rock her boat at this moment. "Sure," I say. "I'll meet you in the car."

"Okay." She shuts her window behind me, and I sneak over to the Kyliemobile using my invisibility trick. Once inside I let myself become visible again but duck down so her parents won't spot me. Kylie comes out a few seconds later and drives me to Uncle Joey's house. I run in and do a superquick shower and change—five minutes, tops—and we get drive-through breakfast on the way to school.

Pennington High's driveway is packed with the usual line of cars and buses, and we have plenty of time to stuff down our bagels while waiting in traffic. When we make it into the parking lot, Kylie picks a spot on the far side. She cuts the ignition and doesn't get out.

The mood in the car changes. Maybe all the casual lightness of getting ready and scuttling off to school was just make-believe. Perhaps Kylie has been stalling while she decides what to do with me. I put my hot chocolate into the cup holder and brace myself. Kylie takes a breath big enough to oxygenate a whale and then exhales slowly. "Jonathan," she says.

We've parked with our backs to the comings and goings of Pennington commuters, so I have nothing to stare at but trees and the bright sky between the branches. Those red buds have swelled into something that will be leaves very shortly.

She shifts in the driver's seat so her whole body faces me. "Jonathan."

I close my eyes. I just can't bear it.

She shifts again, and the next thing I know, her hand is

touching my cheek. Her fingertip tenderly runs the length of my scar. I press my lips together to bite back an emotion, glad that my eyes are closed, because I don't want her to see the desperation in them. A tender touch can't flow from hate, can it? I didn't realize I needed her to touch me more than I've ever needed anything else in my life. She doesn't hate me, and that might be enough.

She clears her throat softly. "We haven't been together much in the real world, and I have to admit my friends have given me a hard time over my behavior lately." Her fingers come up again, stroke my cheek again. Then her hand falls gently away. "I'm not sure what we are now. You know, as 'us.' I remember it being both ways. This world remembers it only one way."

What the world remembers shouldn't have anything to do with this, I want to say, but it's not true. The world and its opinions and under-breath remarks have always intruded on my life. I doubt Kylie will let her friends have the final say on our relationship, but their thoughts will matter to her, especially since she has spent the last week or so incapable of thinking properly for herself.

"I'll do whatever you want," I say. "I just need to know that you're okay. I wasn't sure what you remembered."

She settles with her back against the door. Cars are filling in around us. Students emerge laden with books and bags. The volume of their voices wavers through the closed windows.

"I remember everything," she says, "But it's not as bad as I thought it would be. Of course, I was also surprised to wake up this way."

God, that freaks me out. It's like two heads talking out of one mouth.

I don't want her to make any big decisions right now. I don't want to make her say she loves me or she doesn't, so I don't ask. "Maybe we should just go in separately, like always. I'll see you in creative writing, and you can decide if you want to see me later."

She relaxes a little, relieved. I'm glad I didn't ask, because the answer would have been, *Let's just be friends for now.* I know it. Which would have been fine, except for how I would have felt crushed by a giant mountain.

I don't wait for her to say anything more, just tug on the door handle and let myself out. I ignore the stare of a classmate noticing whose car I get out of, and walk with blinders on to my locker, then on to first period.

When the bell rings, I make the familiar trek to creative writing class. I arrive before Kylie and help Mr. Eckhart arrange the desks in a circle. When the work is finished, I choose a seat. Zach and Emily land in seats opposite me in the circle, and when Kylie arrives, without hesitation she joins them. She gives me a little friendly wave across the gulf between us, though, so at least I can be assured she didn't have a meltdown in first period.

I'm disappointed but understand how she might want to reconnect with the friends she's snubbed the past few days. At least the wave means she still doesn't hate me.

When everyone settles into their seats, the bell rings and Eckhart goes to the board. "Today is free writing day. I'll take suggestions."

The class makes excited sounds, as usual, because most of us like free writing. Even if we don't want to write, we appreciate having a quiet, easy class.

Claude, of course, volunteers a suggestion. "Write about what the world would be like if everyone woke up tomorrow a person of the opposite sex." The class giggles, all except me and Kylie. I wonder how she remembers her transformation in the bed.

Kaitlyn Frost pipes up. "What if the only colors in the world were green and white? Or, I guess, what if the world had only two colors?" Eckhart dutifully writes this on the board.

"Describe your perfect prom night." That's from Janie Majewski.

"Write an alternative ending to *Pride and Prejudice*." That's

Luis Alves. We all had to read *P&P* for Brit Lit this year.

A couple more suggestions, along with Eckhart's additions, make it onto the board. Then the circle breaks. Kylie moves to her position by the window. I, as usual, don't move at all, but I'm nicely placed to spy on her through the whole period.

More than any other time recently, I'm jazzed to write. I don't want to do something heavy. No poems for me today. No explorations of my troubles. After careful consideration and a reminder to myself that no one is forced to share anything aloud during circle time at the end, I decide to write a list of three things I know about each person in the room. I start with Kylie because I want to get it over with.

Kylie Simms: the fastest sprinter at Pennington; graduating somewhere in the top ten (I think she's third in the real world, but I'm not 100% sure); favorite food is chocolate, closely followed by mashed potatoes (I'm not sure if this is true anymore)

Mr. Eckhart: teaches creative writing; is passionate about literature and likes teaching it (wish someday he'd share with us something he wrote); once asked to work with me after school on a story he thought had a lot of

353

potential (I declined—why?)

Kaitlyn Frost: very creative; likes fantasy worlds; makes me feel like I'm not a total loser, because she's nice to me

Luis Alves: prefers mystery novels; plays baseball; tried to talk to me once outside of class— thank you, Luis

Claude Arsenault: writes the funniest stuff in class; went to Alaska over the summer (at least he wrote a spoof about going to Alaska); once complimented something funny I wrote, which helped me out on a bad day

Janie Majewski: popular girl; broke her arm last year in gymnastics; used to have a locker next to mine in middle school and would say hi to me every morning

I find it easy to say three things about everyone, and an obvious pattern develops. Almost all of these people have meaningfully spoken to me at some point in class and in life—*i.e., to them I'm not invisible.* The shock of this revelation stops my pen. Why did I never see this before?

I check to make sure Mr. Eckhart's attention is not on the class, and chance a good look at my classmates. Every one of them is hunched over a notebook writing. Harmless. Following directions. Not ignoring me or pretending I'm invisible, but concentrating on what they have to do. My three-things-I-know list shows that each of them has noticed me, but what incentive was there to keep noticing when they reached out and I never reached back?

For ten years I've been indulging in self-pity over what's happened to me. I've been avoiding the real world like it's treated me unfairly, and perhaps it has, but in many ways maybe my loneliness is my own fault. Kylie-Simms-is-my-girlfriend showed I am capable of making friends. Maybe it's too late to suddenly become Mr. Popular at Pennington High, but after graduation in June, I have schooling to look forward to with people I haven't met yet. I can't assume any longer that people will shun me before they know me.

I was the only one to think I didn't exist. For these people, and surely others in the world, I've been here all along.

My pen's too still, and I have to think of something else to write. Since I'm on a roll about knowing my classmates, I decide to take a risk in my notebook and write down one thing that might happen to each person in the future. I start with Claude: *Someday Claude Arsenault will assassinate a world leader by making him laugh to death.* I skip Kylie because I'm pretty nervous about where I stand in her future, and I'm trying to be fun here.

Kaitlyn Frost will marry an elf and start up a bed-and-breakfast on their unicorn ranch. I'm halfway through the class when Eckhart announces it's time to circle up.

Throughout free writing Kylie has sat, intent either on her notebook or on the view out the window. Technically, staring out the window is against the rules, but her expression has been serious. Every stare outside was followed by something written on her paper.

"Let's get a quick summary of what everyone did today," Eckhart says.

The few people between Eckhart and me give their summaries. When it's my turn, I say, "I wrote three things I know about each person in the room, and then I started forecasting futures for everyone but ran out of time."

A few people raise eyebrows. It's the first time I've ever gotten anything more than a yawn for the subject of my free writing. I bet everyone wants to know what Jonathan Aubrey thinks he knows about each of them. I won't share, though. I never do.

We continue around the circle, giving summary statements. Kylie simply says, "I wrote a poem," which no one finds surprising. When all have made confession, Eckhart opens the floor.

"I want to hear Jonathan's," Luis says. My head shakes *No* in a gut reaction. Luis looks at me with friendly eyes. I don't think he's trying to pry secrets. I think he's trying to encourage me to come out of my shell. He wants me to share because he knows the class is interested and he thinks a little push might give me the courage I need.

"Jonathan?" Eckhart says. His way of giving me the floor.

"Not today," I say. Kylie watches me as I shrink back into my seat. It kills me that I might be disappointing her by being withdrawn. What I've written is harmless but reveals a little too much of what I've discovered about myself this period. "Sorry, Luis."

Luis shrugs. "Maybe next time?"

"Yeah, maybe."

"I'll go," says Claude, and the pressure is off. Claude has a mad lib today, so he takes nouns, verbs, and adjectives from the class and reads a very funny story about a boy who wakes up as a girl.

Throughout his turn, and the sharing that follows, I'm fixated on Kylie. She smiles and laughs and makes eye contact with each speaker, the epitome of gracious listening, but her hands curl around her notebook. Her fingers pinch the pages. She's thinking about sharing, but she's not sure. Time is running out in class.

The circle erupts in applause for a list of the top ten things Claude Arsenault will miss about Pennington High, written by Zach. It's always fun to make fun of the funny guy.

"Thank you, Zach. Who's next?"

There's a hesitation. All the people who were eager to share have had their turn. Now it's down to people who are nervous about sharing but might if no one else does.

Kylie looks around the circle. The top of her notebook lifts from the desk, like she's angling it to read. "I'll go," she says.

"Okay, Kylie. Go for it," says Eckhart.

She slides her chair back and stands, holding her notebook out like it's sheet music and she's about to sing. She looks straight at me, and I know what's coming. The class looks at me too.

She clears her throat and swallows. Takes a deep breath. Begins.

The class falls stony silent. Not a single foot shuffles. Not a single paper rustles. My chest freezes. I will not breathe again until this is over. Kylie's eyes move between her paper and me while she reads.

FOR JONATHAN
by Kylie Simms

A vase broke once.
I tried to glue it together,
But the cracks showed,

So I left it, empty.
It sat on a shelf,
Patient and alone.
I wasn't even sure
It was there anymore.
But today I picked flowers
And needed a vessel
To fill with myself,
Double myself, if you will.
Imagine my surprise
To find that vase
Filled with the sweetest water
For me.

It takes a second for everyone to realize she's finished. Kylie's poetry is often a bit obscure. Now one girl in the circle sighs "Ohhhh," while everyone else gapes openly at me. Even Mr. Eckhart. My skin prickles with something that is not the cold. My lungs open, and air flows in.

Kylie's face is red to her ears, and her hands are shaking, but when my eyes meet hers, she smiles, tentatively. I think what I want to do is run over and kiss her, but that would be a little much for creative writing class. Because it's all I can do, I smile back. I read somewhere that when you're down, if you just smile, it opens up the air passages in your face and you feel better. I give Kylie a smile that opens up everything.

For the first time in a very long time I dare to feel happy. I dare these people to tell me I shouldn't be happy that Kylie loves me after all.

"So you'll pick me up at six?"

We're standing at the track making plans. She wants to tell me about what it was like for her last night, how it felt to wake up this morning. I get the feeling it was not horrific for her, and I wonder if something of what Tess did to me was happening in her. It's all so strange, but we need to talk about it.

"Six o'clock," I say, "If you don't mind the red car."

"First of all, I'd like to meet your car. Second of all, when have I never liked riding in your car?"

Again, two heads, one mouth. She seems to think it's funny, though, and I think eventually, if we're together long enough and we make a single set of memories together, the disconcerting double-talk won't happen anymore.

"It's weird," she says, "that you're going home. I know you're not on the track team, but you've always been at every practice with me."

"It's weird you can be so casual about remembering me both ways."

"Well, you're not on the team now. I'll get used to it. Or you can join."

"I'll think about it."

"Okay, see you at six." She doesn't give me a peck on the cheek or blow a kiss as we part. Girlfriend Kylie would have done that, but it's okay. She seems happy, so there is no reason for me to regret walking home without a PDA.

It takes me twenty minutes. I almost never make this walk after school because I go to practice in Kylie-Simms-is-my-girlfriend. It saddens me to have lost that. It's like another death in the family.

I can't be too sad, though, because I couldn't have hoped for a better outcome with Kylie. I'll go running on my own, and it will be fine.

At Uncle Joey's I go directly upstairs and change into running clothes. My legs are pretty loose, considering all the tension I've had in the last twenty-four hours. I stretch lightly and plan a route that won't take me near the high school or, hopefully, the distance runners if they're on the roads today.

Five miles is a good distance. I start off faster than normal, probably because I'm thinking about being with Kylie tonight. When I hit the first big hill, I tackle it as if it's the only one on the course. At the top I lengthen my stride to keep up my pace. The rest of the run passes in a series of uphills and downhills, main streets and side roads. By the time I get back to Uncle Joey's, I'm eager to get out of my shirt because I'm sweating so much. My watch says I ran about two minutes faster than normal. It feels so good.

I go into the backyard to stretch because it's too nice out to stretch inside. I find myself wishing my uncle had a bird feeder, because the birds would be decent company. They chirp in the big maple tree, but I don't see them. The grass spreads around me, cool and soft, and I lie back in it, letting it tickle my bare back. The sun is low enough to touch the trees, a soft yellowy-white through the branches.

I lie in the grass until the high from my run has left me. My pulse no longer races. My muscles have cooled. There's only so long I can stare at the sky, so I go to my room and shower and change.

I choose tan pants, rather than jeans, for my date with Kylie. I dig through my drawer for a collared shirt like the one I was wearing when I opened The-crash-never-happened. I have to wear sneakers because I don't own anything nicer that still fit. I choose darker-colored socks to make up for the casual shoes.

A few minutes in the bathroom, and my teeth are brushed and my hair is combed. The mirror says a scar still scraggles down my face, but the line is paler. Thinner. The face in the mirror is mine, but I give myself a little credit for being okay to look at.

It's only five thirty, so I have a few minutes to kill. I decide to snack on an orange or something and go through the college and summer school applications on the kitchen counter. I skip down the stairs and enter the kitchen . . . and immediately sense something is wrong.

Although sunlight shines through the back windows, the kitchen has fallen dark. The same icky feeling Tess sometimes gives falls over me. I look around to find the source of my discomfort, but everything is in its place, perfectly clean and ordered, as Uncle Joey likes it.

Except for my college papers. They are not stacked to the side. They sit in a pile in the center of the counter. I approach them and notice that the paper on top does not come from any college or summer school. The header is *Healey House, a Division of North Shore Long-Term Health Care.*

It's a form. It has filled-in spaces at the top. Next to "Patient" someone has typed in "JONATHAN M. AUBREY." Next to "Parent" the line is blank. Next to "Legal Health Care Proxy" is my Uncle Joey's name.

The form's title: *Authorization for Termination of Life Support.*

Two pages of legalese. I flip to the end and see that the papers haven't been signed. They are not dated. They are asking permission to terminate Jonathan M. Aubrey's life. My life.

Under the termination papers, on top of the rest of the pile, is a sticky note. I don't recognize her handwriting because I've never actually seen it before this moment:

> *Here's my gift of honesty to you, Big Brother. Something from the actual real world. I like to call the little place in the universe you think is real "Jonathan-is-alive."*

CHAPTER 24

I CANNOT POSSIBLY DESCRIBE IN SUPERLATIVE-ENOUGH
terms how the earth has been ripped from beneath me.

Or list the memories of my life that flood through me infused
with new meaning.

Or even assign meaning to anything, because I cannot sort
out the questions raging in my mind.

This makes no sense! I am alive! I am real! The whole last
few days have been about making everything real!

"TESS!" The kitchen echoes my desperation back at me.
"TESS, YOU COME HERE RIGHT THIS INSTANT! YOU
HEAR ME? GET. DOWN. HERE. RIGHT. NOW!"

I'm pacing. Absently I kick the kitchen island. It hurts.
"TESS!"

The cabinets whirl as I spin on a heel to pace the other way,
shouting at the ceiling, not sure why I expect Tess to descend
from the ceiling. "GET DOWN HERE!"

There are not enough papers to throw onto the kitchen floor, but I throw them. Not enough countertops to slam with my fists, but I pound them anyway. I open the refrigerator door just so I can slam it shut. The bottles inside clink and crash. "TESS!"

She's abandoned me to slam around the kitchen alone. Terrified and alone.

The lower cabinets make a satisfying sound as I kick them in, one by one. They're sturdy cabinets, so I damage only one door, which slips off its hinge.

The frustration of a hundred thousand attempts to be happy all obliterated in an instant wells up through my core. Tess is LYING. Tess is NOT lying.

I pick up the form from the floor and sit with it at the table in the breakfast nook. I read it again. Every single word. Healey House has been holding Jonathan M. Aubrey for long-term care. Joseph C. Welch, aka Uncle Joey, is Jonathan's health care proxy.

Are these papers recent? If not, they could be from *this* world, unsigned because I woke up ten years ago just like I thought I did. I find no date to indicate when Uncle Joey received them or dates telling how long Jonathan has been in long-term care.

If they're not from this world, it's reasonable to assume that the world where Jonathan is/was in this long-term care facility is the same world where Tess lives. Right? Maybe she's actually nice to this other Jonathan as she sits at his bedside. Or if these papers are old, maybe she visits his grave. I suddenly remember that the first time I saw Tess, she led me on a chase that ended at Pine Street Cemetery.

Tess can't have abandoned me completely. She will come. She has to come. In the meantime I'm supposed to be at Kylie's house in twenty minutes. Time still ticks the same measure it always has.

Yet I feel that the number of ticks is coming to an end. This afternoon, life with Kylie stretched infinitely into the future, but now I listen. *Tick. Tick. Tick.* Each second passes like a countdown. What scares the hell out of me is that I don't know to what end.

I take the life support termination paper up to my room. Tess gave it to me, and I don't want it lying around for Uncle Joey to see.

With the paper tucked safely away in my desk along with my dead father's student-athlete speech, I check myself in the bathroom mirror to make sure I don't look like a wild man. I don't. I look perfectly sane. I look like me. A real, live person, but I'm nostalgic for the person I was in this mirror ten minutes ago.

Am I not real? Can it be true? I don't want to believe it,

but my stupid, know-it-all inner voice whispers, *This world has always been too miserable to be true.*

I leave my room, stand in the hallway, and am seized with the need to open doors. I start with the room at the end, where all the memento boxes sit stacked, full of family moments that possibly weren't lived. I flick on the light, remembering how important all those things have been to me. I don't need to touch them now. I leave the door open and the light on and move to the next room.

I open my second door on emptiness. This room may never have been entered since Uncle Joey and Auntie Carrie bought the house. No curtains hang from the windows, no furniture stands against the walls, not even a stack of bins. A neutral cream paint covers the wall, and a neutral beige carpet covers the floor. A room for everyone and no one. I leave the door open and the light on.

The last room up here, I've seen only twice. The first time it was empty because Uncle Joey and Auntie Carrie were just moving in. The second time was the day I came to live here. I open the door.

The walls are painted pink. White curtains with pink ribbons decorate the windows. The carpet is the same beige as everywhere else, but there is a rolled-up pink area rug off to the side. Auntie Carrie hadn't been close to delivering her baby when she died, but they had known it would be a girl. In the corner sits a rocking chair, and against the wall rest three giant boxes containing a crib, a dresser, and a changing table. I hesitate before leaving this light on, because the room feels more like a tomb than the other two. Although the baby never lived here, this was the only space on earth that was dedicated just to her. She is, of course, buried in my aunt's coffin in the womb she never left.

I decide to leave the light on.

When I get back downstairs, I pick up the papers I threw and prop up the crooked cabinet door. I find the same sticky-note pad Tess used to write her lovely message on, and I jot off a quick note. *Hi, Uncle Joey. Gone on my first date. Be back at a reasonable hour. Jonathan.* I almost write *Love, Jonathan,* but that, combined with leaving a note, which I've never done before, might actually alarm him. I push the stack of college applications back into position at the side of the counter and stick my note right in the center of the empty space I've cleared. Kylie's probably waiting on me by now. I wonder how I'll make it through a dinner date this way.

As I pull out of the driveway, I look back at Uncle Joey's house. The upstairs rooms are aflame with light, and I wince a little to think of my uncle going up there and turning everything off when he gets home. But I like the look. For the first time ever the house shines like life is welcome inside, even though most of those rooms are dedicated to death.

The ride to Kylie's house is so familiar and normal, I feel a little better by the time I arrive. Just seeing her bounce out the door, happy to see me, boosts my spirits as well. She glides into the passenger seat and puts on her seat belt with a neat click. "Where are we going?"

"Do you have a preference?"

"Not so much."

"How 'bout Bella Luna?" I haven't been out for Italian in so long, and Bella Luna prides itself on its romantic little booths for two that will give us some privacy.

"Wow. Sounds great." The wow is because Bella Luna is expensive, but I'm willing to blow some savings on a big date like this.

I bump over the curb as I back out of her driveway. My hands have absorbed all the shaking I'm trying to keep out of my voice. Kylie looks at me like she's assessing if I'm okay. I just put the car in drive and go as steadily as I can to the restaurant.

The wait isn't very long for a Friday, and we get a decent table against a wall, with a crystal sconce to light our dinner. Another crystal fixture dangles above the table. Kylie says, "I don't know if I dressed nice enough."

She's wearing a soft, white sweater and black pants. She's

dressed better than I am. "You look perfect," I say.

It takes Kylie longer than me to figure out what she wants to order. While she searches the menu, I find myself scanning the tables and booths around us. Nearly every table is taken, mostly by couples, but there are a few families with younger kids and a few groups of older adults, their tables scattered with half-empty wineglasses. The couples seem intent on each other, the families on keeping the kids in line, and the groups on drinking and laughing.

We go through the motions of ordering, and when the server brings us lemonades, it's time.

Kylie begins. "So I guess I should start with last night."

"Only if you're absolutely sure you're ready to talk about it."

"Now's as good a time as any."

She is so pretty with her hair drawn up in some kind of half-bun, half-ponytail. Long strands frame her face and sway under her chin. I can't tell if the color on her cheeks is natural or a touch of makeup.

Mostly, though, it's the way she moves, the easiness of her shoulders, the bob of her head as she speaks. The expressiveness of her eyes and eyebrows. She's familiar and unfamiliar at once because she's on the other side of an experience I can't begin to understand.

"There's not really so much to tell. I remember falling asleep crying, and I remember seeing myself asleep while standing in the room with you and your sister. I think I sat on the bed. After that I don't remember much. It felt like . . ." Her eyes shift upward, searching her brain for the right descriptive word. "It felt like sinking into a warm bath, but the water didn't just stay on the outside. It seeped in. Everything went dim and wavery like when you look up at the sky from underwater, except it was warm. It felt kind of good, actually. Calm. Is that what it looked like?"

As if I will ever tell her what it actually looked like. "Something like that."

"The next thing I remember is you standing over me. Were you checking to see if I was breathing?"

"You were very still. You made me nervous."

"I couldn't move at all, and that was scary, but you were there, and I still felt warm, so I drifted back to sleep. I probably drifted in and out a dozen times. Then my alarm went off."

"What was the first thing you thought when you woke up?"

"Honestly? I thought I had missed breakfast, because I was starving. Then I remembered you had been there all night, so I called for you, and the rest you know."

"And how did you—" My eye wanders for a split second to a table behind Kylie. Seated there is a party old enough to be retired, and one of them looks back at me. She has bright blue eyes and an aura of wisdom as visible as the features of her face, and she doesn't fit in. It's a good thing I'm not eating yet, because I think I would choke.

It's the woman from the mall and the crosswalk at Uncle Joey's church.

She must be here because of Tess's note. Not the fact that she wrote a note, but whatever the note means. I don't even get this one last dinner with Kylie. The woman is here for me.

"Are you okay?" Kylie looks over her shoulder to see what has stopped me midsentence. The woman picks up her wineglass and raises it in a toast led by another in the group. She is no longer the woman I fear but a happy, brown-eyed wine-drinker whose flush gives away that she's drunk too many glasses.

I shake it off as best I can. "How did you feel in school?"

At this her face turns grim. "It was hard at first. I miss certain things about the world that's gone. Little differences, like a picture of you and me that used to be taped in my locker. I've barely seen my family to know what's changed. And so many things have double meanings. I tried to remember which things I said to which people yesterday, and I couldn't quite separate what was said in this world from what was said in the other one. I'll figure it out, though."

She's not going to confide how much she suffered, and I've just decided I'm not going to tell her about Tess's note. If Tess is telling the truth, Kylie has sacrificed everything for nothing, and until I know for sure what is real and what is not, until I see proof that no matter what is true, Kylie is happier now than she would have been otherwise, my lips are sealed.

"Thank you for the poem today," I say.

A shy smile grows on her lips. "I was so afraid you'd be mad that I read it out loud."

"That part killed me, to be honest. What did Zach and Emily think?"

She shrugs. "They teased me, mostly. Emily especially thinks it's funny I should like someone I didn't tell her about first."

"Does she disapprove?"

"Oh, I don't think so. Not that it should matter. Emily was the one who was happiest for me when we started going out in tenth grade."

We both look down at our hands on the table. We started going out in tenth grade, but Emily is teasing her now because our relationship is just beginning. "It's hard, isn't it?" I ask.

"Not so bad."

"You keep talking about things two different people did. Do you feel . . . like two people?"

"I feel perfectly myself. Just a little . . . confused sometimes. It's exactly what Tess said would happen."

We grow quiet. The buzz of other people enjoying their

night out sounds perfectly normal, but when I glance over, a woman with wise, blue eyes—I swear she was a girl seconds ago—stares back at me. In a blink she is a girl passing the bread to her mother.

I force myself to look back at my hands, but I can't help it. I look up again, and a sea of blue eyes stares back at me out of a hundred versions of the strange woman's face. Every diner in the restaurant has transformed to create a circus of bizarre clones talking to one another like nothing's unusual. One by one they glance up at me to make sure I'm watching. I try not to show my surprise, because I don't want Kylie turning around again. I catch myself scratching at the table with a fingernail, expecting to peel away the finish and expose the real world underneath. The floor begins to rumble, causing the crystal sconces and chandeliers to tinkle and the wine to slosh, but nobody except me seems to notice. The table remains solid and the earth has trembled, and I need to know. I need to know the meaning of Tess's note.

The restaurant stills. None of the diners is the blue-eyed woman anymore, and the *tick, tick, tick* of seconds passing, one by one, never to be repeated, rings in my ears like church bells.

"I need to know something, Jonathan," Kylie says.

It's hard to concentrate. Her colors sort of fix themselves like paint on a canvas, less real, slightly blurred, an impression of Kylie in dots. "Yes?" I say.

"When did you decide you loved me? Not just had some crush on me. Was it before you made that world? Or was it after?"

I have loved you forever. I will love you always.

The conversations around us intensify, like every person in the restaurant chooses to speak at once and over one another. Not shouting, just voices filling my head as the people themselves slow, their sound deepening. My finger works furiously at the table, a gash visible where I've tried to get underneath. I want Kylie to understand how sorry I am, how much I wish I didn't need her as much as I do, how happy she made me today when she read that poem.

Her hands fall onto mine. Gentle, caring hands that soothe my need. When I look to her face to unburden my guilt, she's gone. My hands are held by a strange woman with infinite blue eyes.

We are not sitting at a table in Bella Luna.

CHAPTER 25

IT'S DARK. SHE STANDS FIVE OR SIX FEET AWAY, SEPARATE, her hands far from my hands. I back up a pace, and trip over a massive tree root. I fall to the ground against the tree that spawned it.

Above me looms black sky pitted with stars. I see no moon, so everything is a shadow, even the woman, who I have no faith looks the same as I've come to expect. Branches sway in the wind, and I recognize the rustle of leaves. They must be newly sprung from their buds.

I'm scared to death. The tree stands, solid against my back, and I can't see that there is a path to anywhere. Only canopy above and clearing below. The darkness thins as my sight adjusts from the restaurant's electric glow to this pitch-dark void of night. As shapes become clearer, my panic rises. Stones stand thrust from the ground at close intervals and in rows. Rows and rows and rows. Gravestones. Oh God, I am in a cemetery. If I'm not already dead, I'm going to die. Of fright if not by the strange woman's hand.

Where she stands, something burns into a glow. A hand clasped in a fist, lit from the inside. Red light pulses through the separation of her fingers. They unfurl and reveal a palm of light, which focuses in a beam that slides along the ground toward me. It's not a palm of light. It's a little flashlight. I think I would have felt better if it were a magic ball in the palm of her hand.

"It's time, Jonathan."

Time for what? But I cannot speak to this woman. I choke on the words in my throat.

She steps toward me. In the glow cast by the flashlight, which thankfully she doesn't shine in my eyes, I see she's wearing jeans and sneakers, whereas I might have thought the occasion called for flowing white robes and a crown of greenery. Her sweatshirt says something about vacationing at the Grand Canyon.

Her eyes, though, are anything but casual tourist eyes. They reflect the light like mirrors. They flash images of myself back at me, braced against the tree trunk. She hobbles as she approaches, then creaks as she crouches to bring her face to a height with mine.

"Take my hand," she says. Her voice sounds grandmotherly,

but it resonates against the shadows around her, like maybe she speaks with a couple of extra sets of vocal chords.

My arm is wooden like the tree, stiff with fright. She reaches down to unlock me, takes my hand in hers and draws me up. Her touch reminds me of Tess, warm and piercing. "Tess?" my wooden tongue manages to ask.

She shakes her head. "You need to see something, honey. Come on."

My hand in hers, we traipse through the graveyard, guided by the flashlight. Corners of granite wink when the beam crosses them. Many of the graves are planted with tiny bushes or laden with mementos of the dead. Some have their own solar landscape lights for comfort. A candle glows, deep in a red glass holder. Christian crosses, Jewish Stars of David, carvings of hearts or flowers or pillars, assorted symbols I don't understand, all illuminated momentarily by the woman's light, but the one thing I can't see are the names. The beam slides by too quickly for me to make them out, until we pull up to one particular stone and she shines it on the final statistics of a family of four.

Mark Aubrey
Christine Aubrey
Jonathan Aubrey
Tess Aubrey

My parents and sister all have birth dates and death dates chiseled into the stone. My name has only one date. I am not dead yet.

A massive shiver runs through me. I have to lean against the stone in weak-kneed relief. Jonathan Aubrey lives.

"Is this the real world?" I ask. But I know it is. Even though it's night, everything's sharper, like a blurred photograph resolved into focus or the sound of a crowd separated into distinct voices. I sense the breathing of the Earth, a hum in the air and its resonance through the trees, through me. In all my worlds, including the one I thought was real, I've never perceived with such intensity. This world, unlike mine, is full of power. It is full of life, despite the graves all around.

The woman's hand covers my shoulder. Soothing warmth radiates down, like a soft quilt warmed by a hearth. It is not the strange half-ecstatic fever of Tess. Not icky, forced comfort but the real thing. "This is the Creator's world. And yes, you would call it the 'real world.'"

"Then it's true. I'm not real."

"Oh, honey, you exist as surely as I do. But no, you were not created here."

I kneel at my family's gravestone and run my fingers over the engraving. The numbers and letters bite, rough and final. My family lies beneath me. Beneath my knees. If I scoop earth for long enough, I can touch them. I pick a few blades of grass for a start. I long to see their faces so I can finally say the good-bye I was robbed of by being almost dead myself. Yet I know that after ten years they aren't really beneath me anymore. If there is a place for souls to travel to, they've moved on. Otherwise, they're just bodies turning to dust.

I want to cry, but my tear ducts are too swollen or something. Sorrow crushes me from the outside in, almost numbing in its effect. I hope this strange woman doesn't mind, but I need to sink into this grass for a moment. Wrap myself in grief and console myself with it. I've wrestled with the question of visiting these graves for so long, it's a relief to see them, really. The names are etched in stone, and somehow I'm not stricken blind by the sight of them. My family is dead, and I want them back, but I can't change any of it.

A prayer comes to my lips, but not to God, who has taken these precious people from me. I pray to them, that they should hear me and know how sorry I am that I've never come to visit them until now. I whisper my love into the grass, a long stream of "I miss you I'm sorry Forgive me I want you back Please watch over me You were the best parents who ever loved a little boy with your crazy jokes and bedtime stories and car trips and camping and Remember when the blanket got torched by the campfire and Remember when you bought me the black Max Rider bike and Remember how excited we were to go to Disney

World I'm so sorry we never made it I wanted to ride everything with you Tess and see all the movie characters and eat the best junk food for a week It wasn't worth losing you I miss you I miss you I miss you I miss you I miss you so much."

If I curled up on this spot, I wonder how long it would take the earth to swallow me. Since my name's on the grave, there is an empty space down there where I could go. Uncle Joey must have been responsible for making the choice to include me on the gravestone. I suppose he considered I'd be joining my family sooner rather than later. Which makes me wonder, "Where is my aunt's grave?"

The woman shines her light on the next stone over.

> Joseph Welch
> Carrie Welch
> Baby Welch

Auntie Carrie and the baby share a death date with my family. Uncle Joey's death slate is as blank as mine. I'm sad about the "Baby." My poor cousin didn't live long enough to get a name, and I suppose Uncle Joey didn't want to choose one without Auntie Carrie.

"Come, Jonathan," the woman says. "We have one more stop before our appointment."

Now that I'm here, I don't want to go. "We have an appointment?"

"One more stop first."

This woman must have gone to the same question-avoidance school as Tess, but then I remember that six-year-old Tess is in the ground. She never became a beautiful, sarcastic teenager. "Wait," I say. "If my sister is dead, who's the girl I've been talking to?"

She gives me a sad shake of the head like she feels bad for me. "She's just another one of us."

"Please tell me what you mean by that."

"I will. I promise. One more stop."

She takes my hand. I feel a little like I'm being led by the ghost of Christmas past. Only, I think it's the ghost of Christmas future who took Scrooge to the graveyard. Plus I think the graveyard came last. The cemetery darkness morphs into neighborhood darkness lit by a goodly number of streetlamps and welcoming porch lights. The houses are small, but neat and tended. The road curves away from us in either direction but is a generous width for kids to get going a pretty good game of kickball.

The woman leads me to one of the houses, an especially well-lit one, and I can only assume she has the Tess invisibility power. I try to do it myself but can't tell if I'm successful. Now that I know this world is the final say on real, I think since I'm not real, I might be powerless in it. I wonder, even though she's never been a world-maker, if Kylie feels powerless in her new world. I wonder what happened to her when I disappeared from Bella Luna.

We go right up to the porch, and the blue-eyed woman opens the door and leads me inside. We must be invisible, because no one turns a head as we enter. The TV blares, and a group of mixed ages groans at some flub their baseball team made on the field.

Four young kids play in the corner with a marble machine. A motorized chain carries the marbles up, up, up to the top, where they begin their run down a complex obstacle course, spinning things and dropping through tubes while the kids watch, entranced. The baseball fans let out a cheer, and I turn to watch the replay with them. Not a grand slam, but a magnificent homer over left field's Green Monster that scores two runs. Beer bottles and bowls of chips fill the tables in the room. Though almost everyone jumped to their feet at the hit, one older man stays planted in a huge, comfy armchair. He takes a swig of his beer. He's wearing a baseball jersey with handwriting on it, the signatures, possibly, of the team.

The blue-eyed woman has not let go of my hand, and now tugs me along the side of the baseball scene through a doorway into the kitchen. The room contains a variety of women sitting, standing, cleaning, putting away dinner. Three older kids, maybe just shy of high school, play cards at the table. The women chat animatedly about someone's vacation, comparing experiences, making wish lists for the future. The eldest woman shuffles clean dishes into cabinets as they come off the line of two younger women washing and drying.

Casual photographs in cheap plastic frames cover the walls. A family of four who made it to Disney World. A family of six by a lake somewhere. Two little kids with spaghetti sauce all over them. On and on the pictures stretch. Most of the people in them resemble one another. This is a family. The older man and older woman are the grandparents, and these are their children and grandchildren gathered for nothing more important, it seems, than a big dinner and a baseball game, but then one of the women pulls a box from the refrigerator and sets it on the table. A birthday cake that reads *Happy April Birthdays! Lauren, Uncle Greg, Nana.*

While someone calls for candles and matches, the blue-eyed woman leads me back through the living room. It's a commercial, so everyone's catching up on snacks and beer. One younger man, barely drinking age, makes a beer run to the kitchen.

We pass the kids with the marble machine. They've pulled it apart and are rebuilding the course. One kid is definitely the main engineer. The littlest one sucks his thumb and lets the others work.

The woman and I close the front door and the screen door behind us. A porch swing hangs to the left, and the woman lets my hand go to sit down on it. She pats the space beside her, so I sit too.

"Do you know why I brought you here?" she asks.

"I'm sure you didn't mean to rub my nose in it."

"I'm not sure what you mean."

"It's the perfectly wonderful family I wish I had."

Our feet touch the porch and rock the swing back and forth. Because my legs are longer than hers, it's a little halting at the top of each upswing.

"You didn't recognize any of them?"

"Was I supposed to?"

"I thought you might, but I'm not surprised you didn't."

"Who should I have recognized?"

"Did you notice the older gentleman in the recliner?"

"Yes."

"The older woman in the kitchen?"

"Yes."

"Think about their faces. Do you remember?"

Now that she mentions it, maybe I did have a glimmer of recognition, but I thought it was me recognizing how wonderful it would be to be these people, with so much love in their house. "Are they my grandparents?" In the real world, my grandparents might still be alive.

"No, honey. I'm afraid not, but if those two people inside could see you now, they would take you in their arms as if you were one of their own."

I don't understand. I really don't understand, and I'm getting tired of all these riddles and secrets and worlds. "Why would they do that if they're not my family?"

"Because, Jonathan, you're the reason they're here tonight, celebrating another birthday. You saved their lives."

"What?"

She touches me again, clasps my hand, except she is not warm this time. In a flash I'm cold, shivering, and in pain. Something drips down my face. Blood. Something stings at my chest and shoulder. Burns. My muscles are tired after pulling from seat back to seat back, climbing, as I did, up the plane, water filling from beneath me. It rises faster than I can climb. I scream with terror as it catches my feet. Everyone beneath me, including Mom and Dad and Auntie Carrie and even Tess, is submerged already. People around me are burned and frantic from the flame that tore through on impact. Smoke still fills the cabin and burns my mouth and nose and lungs. Two people, a man and a woman in the very back seat, farthest from the rising water, hang by the belts. The woman's tears drip all over the place as she and her husband try to undo her seatbelt. His clicks open. Hers is jammed, and she blocks his path of escape. He reaches over her from his window seat, but the way her body presses on the belt, the angle of his reach, and the panic in them both makes him unable to work her free.

The plane groans as it sinks, and water catches my waist as I reach them. The rear cabin door gapes open up ahead, a little daylight coming through with the water, but no one stands in the doorway. Water gushes everywhere, swelling up from the bottom and in a waterfall from the top, soaking me, freezing me, making everything that much scarier because too much water falls into my eyes. I'm going to crawl right past those two people to get out the door. I almost do. But the woman looks up at me as I pass. Her face streaked with tears and fright. I have to help her. I reach over with my small fingers. The water inundates us, the cabin now full past the seat belt. My hands are already submerged. I can't reach the buckle because the man's groping hands maddeningly block the way. He withdraws for a split second, and I slip an index finger under the cap of the belt, and *snap*. The belt springs the woman free, and my world becomes water. There's the door, I'm trying to reach it, but those few seconds' pause mean the doorway has sunk deeper. Where at first water only spilled over the lip, now it pours through the whole opening, and I can't fight the current. I hold my breath and hold on to the woman to keep from being swept back down into the cabin, and when the plane sinks entirely under, the edges of consciousness close in on me. I see the door, push off with my feet and clear it, but the surface of the harbor is too far away. The sinking plane pulls too hard.

That's all I remember. That and the pain. Sometime later the coast guard dragged me to the surface.

My nightmares have involved seat belts lately, so this memory couldn't have been too deeply buried. Reliving it isn't the same as *living* it, but although this memory that the blue-eyed woman has pulled to the surface doesn't come with the physical pain of burning and then almost drowning, it makes me feel burned and drowned.

"Why those two? Why didn't I save my sister, who I thought was behind me? Or my Mom and Dad, who never made it out of their seats?"

"Come here, honey," the woman says. She opens her arms to receive me like I'm a little boy. I slide over and lean in, and her big Grand Canyon sweatshirted arms enfold me. This grandmotherly thing she's doing is strange and good, and again I feel like I should be crying, though no tears come. She rocks us both on the swing. Forward. Back. The chains creak. Forward. Back. Although my feet are still on the ground, I let her do the work.

I let it all rest on her. "Your parents, and your aunt, were dead when the plane hit the water. Your sister climbed only a little ways before the rising water caught her."

I know all this. I've been told it and I witnessed it, but part of what kept me silent and withdrawn that long remainder of third grade was the guilt. People who tragically lose loved ones know this guilt. They died. I lived.

No matter how many times Uncle Joey or anyone else reassured me that my guilt was unfounded, it never went away. This stranger beside me does not say the words "It wasn't your fault," but she makes it clear. I let her reassure me. My face lies against her grandmotherly chest. My body is sunk into her soft bulk. She rocks with me until the surge of guilt subsides, although, as I said before, it doesn't change things.

"I'm glad these two made it," I tell her. "They have a nice family."

"Yes. They do. And you gave up ten years of life to give it to them."

"Those two seconds couldn't have made that much of a difference."

"Oh, honey." She squeezes me tight. "They certainly did."

Inside the house something good must happen in the baseball game, because the family lets out a cheer.

"Come on," says the woman, rousting me from the place

where I've nestled down. "It's time for our appointment."

I would yawn and stretch if I weren't so unnerved by all this. "Our appointment where?"

We walk together back down the porch steps, across the lawn, and into the street. Her pace is quicker now than it was when we arrived.

"You're going to meet your creator."

CHAPTER 26

THE ROOM WE ARRIVE IN IS DIMLY LIT. A NURSE FUSSES over some equipment next to the bed. Cute little cartoon doggies cover her pink uniform. The loose pant legs sway as she steps.

My eyes are drawn to the bed. The nurse blocks the patient's face from my view, but I can see the outline of legs under the crisp sheets. A blanket, knitted with fringe like an old-fashioned shawl, is draped over the feet. A shift in the nurse's position, and I see a hand, fingers curled in on themselves, wrist bent forward as far as I've ever known a wrist to go. The only sounds are the nurse's shuffling feet, a mechanical hum, and some soft music. Lullabies. Piano notes drifting up and down. Not the *beep, beep, beep* I always think of when I picture hospital scenes.

The door behind us opens, and another nurse comes in. He checks the patient's blood pressure as the first nurse steps away to pull up the shawl-like blanket. When she does, I see the face, and although the identity is not unexpected, it's painful for me to see.

The real Jonathan Aubrey is a hollow boy. Smaller than I am. Gaunt. Tubes snake under his covers. Both of his elbows are bent, and his crooked hands rest near his chest. He wears a hospital johnny, the ties at the neck undone and straggling along his shoulders. No tubes are attached to his face, but I think I would have preferred tubes to the half-open mouth and eyes just short of being closed. White slivers glisten under the lids that tremble as he breathes.

"I heard he signed them," says the male nurse.

The female nurse puts a shushing finger to her lips and points to the unlit corner of the room. Someone is sitting there. He sleeps with another one of those granny blankets drawn so high on his chest that his shoeless feet lie uncovered. "Yes. They'll do it tomorrow," she whispers.

"Poor guy," the male nurse says.

My heart melts. The sleeper in the chair is none other than Uncle Joey. He's older-looking than the Uncle Joey I've been living with, his face drawn and lined, hair thinner at the top. Next to him is a long radiator shelf covered in stuff. Papers, folders, crates for files, a laptop closed but plugged in. To his other side is a table piled with books. I can't read the titles from here,

but I recognize the cover of the one on top. *Le Morte d'Arthur.*
There's a bookmark in it. A pile of newspaper lies on the floor. A
bag crammed with T-shirts pokes out from under the chair. This
is not Uncle Joey's first visit. He's been here every single night.

The male nurse finishes his work and leaves the room. The
female one apparently was stalling until he left. She now goes to
the bed and places a hand on the comatose boy's crooked arm.
"Good night, Jonathan. Godspeed." Her lips press together as
she watches him for a moment. She pats him on his blanketed
feet and leaves.

"Sit, Jonathan." I jump, having forgotten about the woman
who brought me here. It's quite shocking seeing yourself in a
coma that's lasted nine years and nine months longer than you
thought it did. She guides me to a chair and takes her own seat
on a footstool, since there aren't any other chairs left.

"I thought we were going to meet my creator," I say.

She looks to the bed.

"Him?" She must be speaking in riddles again. If she's not,
I'm terribly disappointed at what her answer means.

"Yes."

"I thought I was going to meet God."

The woman can't help herself—she laughs and doesn't stifle
it fast enough. Now I feel like an idiot.

"Never mind," I say. "I know there's no such thing as God."

"Now wait a minute. I never said that."

"Then why did you laugh?"

She gets all serious, really serious, and for a moment I think she's about to tell me *she's* God.

"I forgot, despite all the power you have, that you're just a novice. I'm sorry. God means different things to different people. Meeting God means different things to different people. To me, meeting Jonathan Aubrey is very far from what I believe meeting the Creator would be like. No offense, honey."

"None taken." Though her laughing about it stings a bit. "How do you picture meeting God?"

"I hope someday to discuss the broader and finer points of my religious beliefs with you, dear, but the truth is, we don't have that much time."

"Why, because my uncle signed the papers?"

"Tomorrow morning at eight the real world will say good-bye to Jonathan Aubrey."

We take a moment to look at him, tubes, curled hands, and all. The piano lullaby fills the silence.

"If he's my creator, what will happen to me when he dies?"

"That depends."

"On what?"

"Jonathan, I think you know why I've brought you here."

It's hard to think it, but I do know. "I have questions first."

"And I promised you answers."

"Okay, then." I settle in my seat and fire off the first thing that comes to mind. "For starters, who are you?"

Her blue eyes sharpen, ready to deal plainly at last. I get this shiver of excitement and total dread. "My name is Rosemary. I'm a world-maker, same as you."

Okay. A fair start. "How'd you, you know, get to be a world-maker?"

"Let's just say I married a pair of angry, whiskey-lovin' fists. They landed me in much the same state your airplane landed you."

"Oh." Suddenly my hands demand for me to look down at them. "I'm sorry."

"No worries. That part of my life, thankfully, is well past."

"So why are you here? What's your interest in me?"

"You needed help. And you deserved to be helped." She shrugs like the answer is obvious.

"Why would I deserve to be helped?"

"Think about it, honey."

"The two seconds with the seat belt?"

"Yes."

"That makes no sense. I would have left those people behind if I hadn't been able to get the belt undone."

"You had a generous heart in those two seconds. More

generous than most people have over a lifetime."

I didn't mean to be generous. It seems silly to make such a fuss over reaching across and giving a click. "Things wouldn't have ended any different for me if I'd passed those people by."

"Oh, but they would have."

How could she possibly know that? I can only believe what she says, since there's no way to disprove her. None of that matters now anyway.

"Plus," she adds, "even if there were never any seat belts, you've suffered enough. I believe in mercy."

The room's doorknob turns. We hear voices on the other side, indistinct words, and brace for the speakers to enter. The window beside the door fills with the back of someone's white lab coat. The coat shifts. Dark hands flip the pages of a clipboard, and the voices move away.

I let out a breath I didn't mean to be holding. "So who is Tess?"

The old woman nods. An expected question. "Another world-maker. Her true name is Whitney. She thought it would be easier for you if she put on the appearance of being your sister."

"Is she normally so . . ."

"Abrasive?"

"Yeah."

"Risqué?"

"Uh-huh."

"Her heart's in the right place." She leans back on the foot-stool, forgetting it's not a chair, and flails for balance. I stand to catch her, but she rights herself quickly enough and shoos me back down into my chair. "Here's the basics, honey. There aren't many world-makers walking the earth, so we make a point of knowing one another. There's some who prefer not to get involved much beyond that. There's some, like me, like Whitney, who meet on a regular basis. A support group, of sorts. That doesn't mean we all agree or even like one another. Whitney, for example, doesn't believe in the Creator. She's as scientifi-cally, non-spiritually oriented as they come, and not a big fan of this world. For her, people become world-makers because some trauma they've experienced changes their brain or some such—all chemistry and biology. She thinks world-making is a personal escape you should keep secret and enjoy. She doesn't understand why you don't want to live happily ever after in the world you made with Kylie."

"How could I live happily ever after if the Jonathan who created us dies? Wouldn't our world explode or something?"

"A world once made survives the death of its creator."

"Then maybe I do want to live happily ever after."

Rosemary shrugs. "That's your right."

"But you don't agree."

"I believe in God. And I believe world-makers exist as part of His plan. Jonathan there"—she gestures to the bed—"can't be part of God's plan if they pull the plug on him. You can change that."

"How did you even know I— How did you know Jonathan was a world-maker? It's not obvious from looking at him."

She draws a deep breath and blows it out, preparation for an explanation. "It was Whitney who found you first. You've seen the worldscape when you change worlds, haven't you? All the spheres and corridors connected? Whitney's made a practice of lingering in the worldscape watching other world-makers cross back and forth. Last week she noticed two worlds moving toward each other—your world and the world you made with Kylie—something none of us had ever seen before. By the time she told me about it, she had already identified both you and Jonathan, had researched the crash, and had found Jonathan here.

"I don't know why you mattered so much to her. She's never taken an interest in anything beyond hunkering down in her made-up world and watching others do the same. Maybe she simply felt sorry for you, but my guess is that she was plain old lonely, which I know you understand. Loneliness drives a person to do anything for another soul to talk to. Whitney probably picked you because you're young. I don't know of any other world-makers in their teens. Whatever the reason, she came to the hospital and partially merged with Jonathan to see what he still had inside. It turned out he had a lot, but there was a big jumble where the plane crash should have been." At that she reaches behind her chair, and like magic—world-maker magic—she retrieves something.

My silver shoebox. She holds it out to me, and I take it into my lap, but not before checking that my shoes are still inside. She says, "Whitney stole this from you because it had survived the crash. One thing you'll learn if you stick around is how to recreate a world from an object that was in it. She wanted to experience your plane going down."

"Why in heaven would she want to do that?"

"Because she wanted to understand the trauma that made you a world-maker, before she got involved. Again, all of this happened before she told me. She had discovered from Jonathan that he knew your uncle was preparing to sign his life support termination papers. The colliding worlds were his reaction to learning that all hope was lost. Can you guess what day that was?"

It doesn't take a rocket scientist to figure that one out: the night I snuck into my girlfriend's room feeling like there had been some cosmic shift, the night before I almost kissed the real Kylie. "So I didn't mix up my worlds after all."

"I don't know what really happened that day, but if you mixed them, there was something else going on to share the blame."

"Where is she—Whitney—then? Why hasn't she shown herself tonight?"

"I've already spoken too much on her behalf, but . . ." She hesitates. She takes another deep breath and sighs it out. "I think she finally told me what was happening because I followed her. She'd been even more secretive than usual, so one day I watched her travel to a world that wasn't hers. Turns out it was your Kylie world, and she was spying on you at the mall, still trying to decide what to do. She asked for my advice. I told her if she didn't want to help you, I would do it."

"If she wanted to help so much, why did she leave me that horrible note?"

"Whitney can be . . . spiteful. Life hasn't treated her any more fairly than it has treated you, and she's got a bit of a hardness in her. An inability to forgive. It was only right that you should know about the real world, for your sake and Jonathan's. She said she'd tell you, and she knew if she didn't, I'd do it myself. When you dismissed her after she helped you merge Kylie, she took her revenge by breaking the news in the worst way possible."

I knew at the time that I'd gone too far with my anger. It was a very hard day, but that's no excuse. Now I feel supremely awful. Whitney took a lot of pains to help me. I remember the strange memory echoes of our partial merging and realize she was feeding me memories she must have taken from Jonathan.

Since I thought she was Tess, I assumed the plane crash had made her a world-maker. Now I wonder what other trauma gave her the power while making her so angry and eager to shun the real world. After all, her made-up world was a sunny vacation on a tropical beach. With zero people. Whitney gambled on me when she got involved. Maybe I could have saved her right back, restored to her a little faith, but I was too focused on myself.

The hospital-ness of the room is starting to get to me. Like life is vanquished here instead of rescued. Like sickness is normal.

"If you were supposed to break all this news to me," I say, "why didn't you do it as soon as you found out? Why let me go through all that?"

Rosemary smiles. On any other face I'd say that smile was condescending, but on her it looks only kind. "Sitting here, now," she says, "having gone 'through all that,' I hope you agree I did you a good turn by waiting. You learned some things, Jonathan. About your family, about having friends, about how to make a life, not just a world. Things you can apply to whatever world you live in."

I look at my double in the bed. I don't want to be in that

curled, pale body. I don't even understand why it's so important for him to wake up. Would it be so bad if they ended his suffering tomorrow by pulling the plug?

"Whatever world I live in," I repeat. "Why would I give up my world with Kylie, to be here? I won't have Kylie, and I *still* won't have my family." I feel awful about Uncle Joey as I say this, since it's obvious he's given up a lot for me. "Everything will be different. I won't even have gone to school for ten years."

"The difference between this Creation and your creation is, to use an art metaphor, the difference between Michelangelo painting the Sistine Chapel and an eight-year-old trying to copy it. I believe the Creator made this world. An eight-year-old made yours."

"That eight-year-old did a pretty good job." But is that true? I wonder if this is the source of my yearning for what's real. For ten years I've been anything but happy in the world he made for me. I had to make my own happiness in other worlds.

But he gave me the ability to make that happiness, and I don't mean because he made me a world-maker like him. He gave me choices about how to live life in the world he made, and I mostly made the wrong ones.

"What happens tonight is entirely for you to decide," Rosemary says. "You can go back to your world and have great happiness with Kylie. If you merge with your creator, however, you will have a different kind of chance to make life good. The Kylie in this world hasn't known you these ten years, and she'll have little opportunity to know you. But other opportunities will appear to replace the ones you've lost. You will be a miracle, and the world will put a claim on you."

That's not exactly the best argument to get me to stay here, but I see her point. "I need some time to think about this."

"You have until morning, but it would be best not to wait until the last minute. There will be too many doctors and nurses busy on the floor." *Who might witness the spectacle*, she leaves out.

"I understand." She gathers herself off the footstool. It looks like her old bones don't cooperate as much as she'd like. I realize that for her this looks like the conclusion to ten years of waiting, even though to me it's only hours since I got my news.

All in all, Kylie handled things much better than I did.

Rosemary doesn't blink out of the room. She uses the door, closing it gently behind her without any parting words of wisdom. This really is up to me. She passes by the window and is gone.

I have no idea if I'm still invisible. I'm not so much worried about Jonathan on the bed knowing I'm here, but Uncle Joey could wake and see me. He's not snoring or anything, so it's hard to tell if he's in a deep sleep.

It can't be deeper than the one real Jonathan is in. I go to his bedside, careful not to touch him, and watch the slight rise and fall of his chest under the sheet. It's not a robust breathing, but apparently it's enough.

Is Kylie still at the restaurant, sitting at our table, wondering when I'll be back? I want to ask her what she would do if she were me, but given how easily she agreed to her own merging, I can guess her answer. Then again, I'm working under the theory that she did it because I made her love and trust me. The new Kylie might have a different answer.

Still, favorite seasons and college majors aside, Kylie wasn't being asked to give up as much as I am. Her life isn't that changed. It's my role in that life that was always the question mark. I would be giving her up for a future I can't even begin to picture. Is my body strong enough to pull this Jonathan's out of a ten-year coma? Assuming so, what will it mean to be a miracle?

I explore Jonathan's life a little by taking in the room. I start with the stack of books topped by *Le Morte d'Arthur*. Underneath sit some Harry Potters, a mystery novel, some books I read in middle school and elementary school, like the Hardy Boys. All books I've enjoyed, and I wonder if the reason why is because my creator heard the words read to him night after night by Uncle Joey.

I find it strange that real Jonathan would give my world the books my uncle reads but not Uncle Joey himself. How many nights did I wish my uncle were home, and in the real world he was here? I'm sure of it. In this hospital room. Did real Jonathan want to keep him all to himself?

If real Jonathan—a merged me and real Jonathan—wakes up, how will that change my uncle's life? I mean beyond the obvious time he'll get to spend not in this sad room. He is a father needing a son, and I am a son needing a father.

The tears that have been reluctant all night let me know they're there if I need them, gently pressing against my eyes.

If what Rosemary said is true, merging will not mean I lose my world-making ability. I turn over her words about God having a plan. It's hard to think that putting me through all of this could be for a purpose. It really doesn't seem fair or benevolent. Although I can't quite get myself to embrace or deny the idea that God exists, that doesn't stop me from wanting to make my own plan. How could I put my world-making powers to good use? Could I be like Whitney and find another coma victim to bring back to life? Could I help people who aren't world-makers?

Of course, I learned only recently what I can truly do, from closing worlds to changing parameters to moving things from world to world. I'm not sure how any of that could help someone else, but a very needy part of me is attracted to the idea of trying. I have wondered for so long what I should do with my life. Maybe my failure to receive a diploma and my obscure college plans are all because I have a rather nontraditional destiny. If I choose to merge, my first concern on waking up probably won't be what college to attend.

It will be how to live without Kylie.

The thought of it is an ache in my soul, if I even have a soul. Can I have one if I was created by an eight-year-old coma victim? If I merge with him, will we get to keep his soul?

Now I'm getting too deep. It's too much to comprehend.

From this side of the room I notice something I didn't notice before. A bin. It's shaped exactly like the ones in Uncle Joey's house in the room at the end of the hallway, and it's hiding under the hospital bed. A piece of duct tape slapped on the front says "Jonathan." I slide the bin out as quietly as I can so as not to wake Uncle Joey. The lid peels off easily.

The same things in the bin back home fill this one. Toys, games, clothes. I paw through it all, removing stuff that makes too much noise to sift through. At the bottom is a pile of papers I don't recognize. I work them free.

On top is a series of newspaper articles, yellowed and thin, about the crash. Of course I never collected these, so I suppose my uncle did. The pictures are horrific—all the emergency vehicles in the water, the body bags lined up on the shore. I start to read one account and stop after a couple of paragraphs. It's too painful. I skim through the rest until I find mention of an eight-year-old survivor flown to Mass General along with two other people. Arlene and Philip Pearson of a large and happy family in a little house with a porch.

Beneath the clippings lie hospital papers dated and signed by Uncle Joey detailing some of the care I received. Beneath those are some papers I did in third grade. A times table with a perfect score. A report about the dissection of a cow's eye. Beneath that is a manila envelope.

I flip the top and reach inside. I draw out a piece of yellow construction paper folded in half. A Crayola rainbow spans the sky over a building with the word "hospitel" printed above it. The inside of the card has a drawing that looks like a tree with flowers. *Get well soon your frend Kylie.*

My tears are streaming before I can stop them. I try to cry quietly, but it's not easy when I'm this upset. This part was real. Kylie reaching out to me in third grade was 100 percent real. Jonathan never made it back to school, so they never had an indoor recess with crayons, never had anything at all after the crash, yet he made *me* to love her. Did he do that because, before the crash, he was already in love? I picture Uncle Joey reading him Kylie's card, even posting it on the wall. If he didn't already love her—and can one be in love in third grade?—was this get-well card, this unlooked-for kindness, the motivation for his making my world with her in it? All this time has my love been as compelled for Kylie as I made hers for me? What is the true story of Jonathan and Kylie's love?

In one night I can't make sense of all this and come to a decision about what will make me happy. About what will be the right thing. If I choose to merge with Jonathan, it can't be undone. If I choose not to, he will die, and that can't be undone.

Piece by piece, tear by dropped tear, I replace the contents of the bin and secure the top. My nose runs everywhere, and I swipe it with my shirt. As I slide the bin back under the bed, Uncle Joey stirs. I freeze.

He rolls to his side but doesn't wake. I use my shirt again and wipe my eyes. Out of tragedy, a miracle.

I can't go through with a merging if my world is still open and Kylie exists, but since I wasn't the one who created it, I don't know if I can close it. I test, like dipping a toe into the ocean, to see if I might be able to transport myself back there, and the world peeks open. Kylie, my ever-patient Kylie, still sits at our table in Bella Luna eating pasta without me. She is so lovely. A beautiful person inside and out. The fork rises to her lips.

I love running beside her, mile after mile on the trail, through the trees, under the sun, breathing the glory of creation. Her hand is perfectly fit to mine. Her body graceful sprinting around a turn, walking through the halls, holding me. I wish I had brought my creative writing notebook, because in it I've kept all her poetry. Every beautiful word she's ever written in the world.

I think I'd better just close things now. Then not merging won't be a choice anymore. Without that world, I'll have to move forward with life as a resurrected Jonathan.

Still, I hesitate. I closed Kylie-Simms-is-my-girlfriend under Tess's guidance, and now that I know who Tess is, closing that world seems like a worse choice than it did at the time. So what if taking girlfriend Kylie out of that world would have been a tragedy for the people she left behind? They were still people. Like me. Real. Real enough. I created a bigger tragedy by blinking them out of existence as though they'd never lived. I brought the apocalypse on those people. My creation.

I can't let Kylie, my Kylie, die for good.

I don't have to do this.

I could go right back to Bella Luna and finish my meal.

No. I can't. I need to close my world.

I fill myself with destructive imagery, which at this moment is picture upon picture of me losing Kylie. The images rise up, and I am a conductor gathering my arms for a crescendo of destruction. Music fills me, but it is softer than it should be.

Tiny piano notes traveling up and down a scale. Lullabies from the radio by comatose Jonathan's bed.

The music changes everything. A lullaby is love—a baby boy in his mother's arms, an uncle crying night after night in a hospital room. My just-begun imagery of colliding worlds and crippling loss combine with flash after flash of all my ways of knowing life, springing from every corner of me. Grief, bliss, pain, health, fear, love, childhood, family, breath. A glance at a scar in a mirror. A high five at the finish of a race. The pine scent of a forest trail. The roar of my shiny red car. All the lights ablaze in the house. My father's speech. Lips touching, arms enfolding, hearts racing.

Death and life merge in a white-hot world-making . . . No, world-destroying . . . No. The images grip me so hard, I'm not sure anymore. All I can do is watch them and hear them and smell them and feel them. I don't want to destroy the life I've lived. I don't want to destroy the only love I've ever known.

Kylie deserves more than a last meal at Bella Luna. What she did for me deserves as much sacrifice on my part in return.

Once the idea comes, it's impossible to deny. I can change parameters. I can manipulate things. Kylie sips on her lemonade, the last one I will ever see her drink, and I focus my raging life-and-death power into her world, my world, the world in which I became me.

She puts down her glass and looks up. Smiles. A great, big sunshine of a smile. It seems egotistical to give her me, but that's what I do. If only I had thought of that for Kylie-Simms-is-my-girlfriend. If only I'd given those left behind a Kylie identical to the one I took.

Another version of me takes the seat across from Kylie as if he's been gone to the restroom. At least that's where he thinks he's just been, and that's the direction I've made him come from. He smiles back at her, and I identify his emotion. The thrill of being with Kylie is like soaring in a sky made of joy.

Good-bye, Kylie. Oh God, Kylie, good-bye.

I'm burning out with the passionate effort of changing parameters and leaving that world forever. My hold slips, and the doorway closes. The last thing I see is Kylie laughing. Somehow the other me has already done something to make her happy, but it makes me cry.

I've fallen to my knees, gasping for air as quietly as I can between sobs. I think of Kylie and I think on this: world-making comes with a greater responsibility than an eight-year-old child can understand. It is an awesome power. A world-maker made me real enough to feel love so deeply that I suspect these tears that fall are less for loss than for the magnitude of what I have done. What I can do.

All this power came from somewhere. Maybe, as Rosemary

says Whitney believes, it is something unlocked by a trauma-tized brain. A body can discover all kinds of strength it never knew it had, when the strength is needed. Like at the end of a long race, when you're tired and sore and can't suck the air fast enough, but you have to pass one competitor in the final stretch—then your legs and lungs and heart find something that wasn't there before, and that extra strength is victory.

Anything is possible, but I'm tempted to believe it's some-thing else—God, fate, love—watching over me.

> *I see a lighthouse on the shore.*
> *I've never seen it lit before.*
> *Today, however, it is bright*
> *With guiding, misty lighthouse light.*
> *The boats go by it one by one,*
> *The fisherpeople having fun.*
> *They leave on time like floating clocks*
> *But do not dash upon the rocks*
> *Because they have the lighthouse lit.*
> *They're safe because they pass by it.*

If I could change one thing about my life, it would be this: how long it's taken to understand just how much light has been in my life, and by extension in Jonathan's life since he gave me mine. Dad, Mom, Tess, Uncle Joey, Kylie, Luis, Kaitlyn, Mr. Eckhart, Mr. Diamond, Coach Pereira, Whitney, Rosemary, doctors, nurses, my rescuers in the harbor, and whatever mercy in the universe gave Jonathan, and therefore me, our power. All of them have been beams crossing the darkness, giving us just enough guidance to find our way home.

Terrible things have happened to me, and that is life, but I have never been utterly alone.

I breathe and sob for a few minutes more. Hunched over, I can't help but trace the lines of the floor tiles while I slowly calm down. When the last of the fit is over and I've used every last dry spot on my shirt to wipe my face clean, I'm finally ready. My feet drag like cement blocks as I labor back to the bed. The clock on the wall says it's almost eleven p.m. A very quiet hour. One of Jonathan's tubes twitches. He has suffered long enough.

I don't bother taking off my shoes. I place one knee on the bed, taking a last look and seeing with a shock what I can't believe I missed before. Real Jonathan, for all his sickly, hollow appearance, is entirely without a scar. His face is smooth and perfect from his brow to his cheek. I touch my own scar, wondering why he put it there, wondering how it will be to ask this of myself when I awake.

"Jonathan?"

I didn't hear him stir, transfixed as I was by the missing scar.

Of course I've made enough noise to disturb his sleep. I turn to my uncle. His eyes are wide with wonder, and I want to run to him. All this time he has loved me and cared for me in a way no person should have to endure. I want him to know how grateful I am before I'm no longer myself, or become more than myself.

I don't move, though, because blue-eyed Rosemary in her Grand Canyon sweatshirt and jeans has appeared behind him. Her hands hover over his shoulders, ready, as Tess's once were for me. I truly hope her touch is better than Tess's. I think it will be.

I can't do this without saying something, so I blurt out exactly what I'm thinking. "I wish so much Auntie Carrie had lived. And the baby. I'm sorry I made things harder, but I love you so much for watching over me. All these years."

His shoulders move when Rosemary's hands descend on them, and I hesitate only long enough to make sure I'll fall without spilling over the bed rail. Kylie was right. It's like sinking into a warm pool. The water seeps inside. Almost pleasant. Divine.

Kylie . . .

EPILOGUE

IT'S ONE OF THOSE EARLY MAY DAYS WHEN THE GRASS IS greened from spring rain and sunshine. The colors of the world blossom in pink and white tree buds, yellow daffodils, and the yellow-green of new maple leaves. Pastels. Like a painting everywhere you look.

I sit under a tree facing Dartmouth Hall, a classic white college structure full of classrooms and professors' offices, flanked by similar old, white buildings. Baker library stretches to my left, the Hanover Inn to my right. All around the Green stand the beautiful brick halls of Ivy League academia. The bells of Baker Tower chime the noon hour, and I'm people watching instead of studying. Dartmouth students have a million places to go.

My phone vibrates with a text notification. I texted Whitney with the info on a world-maker meeting that's just been announced. I wondered if she was coming. *That's for me to know and you to find out! j/k We'll both be there.* ☺ She's spending a

year in the Caribbean with Rosemary, who's helping her redis-
cover the importance of peopled beaches. I've seen her only
twice since I woke up. The first time was awkward since we had
to bandage the hurts we'd caused each other, but the second
time, we went hiking in the Grand Canyon while Rosemary
took pictures from the rim. Our frequent texts keep us up-to-
date on how we're dealing with all the choices we're making in
our new lives.

In truth I don't feel much different. My childhood memories are stronger. I remember ten years of life I gave myself in
another world. I also remember being in the coma and a strange
series of semiconscious moments spread over ten years. With
perfect clarity I heard the decision finally being made to terminate my life support. It's hard to scream when you're locked
in a coma, so I did the only thing I could and tried to combine
worlds. I don't know how I expected that to save me, and I'm
not sure it wasn't just some primal instinct to do something,
anything, for my buried voice to be heard. Thank God Whitney
noticed and found the other Jonathan. Found me.

All my worlds are closed to me. I haven't made a new one
in the time that's passed, but I now have this: Jonathan-goes-
to-college-in-the-absolutely-positively-for-real-this-time-real-
world. I got here by waking up a miracle and proving myself
on the SAT I and SAT II. That plus the year I spent earning an

equivalency diploma. One year behind for ten years lost. All in all not too bad.

The biggest obstacle to my attending college wasn't my health, because I could run almost as soon as I woke up. It wasn't my brain, because I could read the day I opened my eyes. Just like with Kylie, my merging took the best of each Jonathan. It wasn't the newspapers, or the crowds of the faithful, or the nonstop appointments with political and religious officials. It wasn't Dartmouth itself, which opened its arms to me as soon as I proved I was more than capable of doing the work. It wasn't the doctors' tests upon tests upon tests on every element of my being.

The biggest obstacle was me. Deciding what to do with myself.

Some members of the track team meet for lunch at the Hop after class on Tuesdays and Thursdays. I like Hop fries, so I make a trip there on Tuesdays and Thursdays too. I slide the book I was reading, *The Origins of Religion*, into my backpack. There's much I have to learn if I'm ever going to understand the gift I've been given. Someday I hope to use it again.

The New Hampshire air is almost warm when the wind pauses and the sun shines down. As I cross the Green, most people succeed at not staring, but because I'm the famous miracle coma-boy, I can never go anywhere without someone's glance lingering a bit too long. Since waking up, I have been anything but invisible.

At the mailboxes, as usual, I meet up with my friends—Lyle, Julia, Marcus, who are all philosophy and religion majors. We pass into the café area and put our stuff down to claim a table before getting in line. The track people are already eating, a clique unto themselves, full of their own camaraderie.

When my friends and I finish eating, we clear our table and go our separate ways. I have a poetry writers' meeting to go to when I say good-bye.

I walk toward the track table, nervous, as always. She sees me coming and rises, says good-bye to her friends. We meet at the recycling station, where she sorts her lunch debris into appropriate containers.

We walk and talk together all the way down to the River Cluster dorms and into the common room of French Hall for our poetry writers' meeting. We don't hold hands. We've never kissed. We've never written a poem to or about each other.

She is beautiful with her long red-brown hair swinging in a ponytail as she walks. She is more familiar to me than the sun, more life-giving. She is not in California at Stanford. She is not at UMass Amherst. She plans a premed English and biology double major, and she is the reason I applied here.

And she doesn't have a boyfriend.

Yet.

ACKNOWLEDGMENTS

I cannot overstate the importance of my experience in Seton Hill University's Writing Popular Fiction Program. The SHU WPF community is intelligent, inspirational, and above all, supportive. Thanks to Dr. Albert Wendland, Dr. Lee McClain, Dr. Michael Arnzen, and Dr. Nicole Peeler for their creation of and commitment to a program that taught me so much. Thanks to Anne Harris and Diane Turnshek for their praise and encouragement of my thesis projects. A very special, head-bobbing thank-you to Timons Esaias, who had the patience and persistence to guide me through the first manuscript I ever wrote, and who taught me lessons about how to be a writer as much as how to write.

At SHU I met Rhonda Mason and Diana Botsford, now my critique partners for over ten years, now two of my very best friends. Thanks for being sounding boards sometimes, critics others, and cheerleaders always. You are my favorite authors in the world.

Thanks to Alexandra Machinist for choosing to champion this project in its first stages. Thanks to Stephanie Koven for choosing to champion it through the latter stages and beyond. I am very lucky to have the advocacy that I do.

The person who has had the greatest influence on this project is my editor, Christian Trimmer, at Simon & Schuster BFYR. Christian, for your wisdom, competence, support, very long phone chats, and all-around bright attitude, I thank you. Most importantly, thanks for making the effort to understand my vision and to find all the best ways to support it while shaping this project into the best book it could be.

Thanks also to every hand at Simon & Schuster that touched this book, especially Justin Chanda, Catherine Laudone, Lizzy Bromley, Michael Frost, Bara MacNeill, Hilary Zarycky, Katrina Groover, Michelle Leo and her team, and Audrey Gibbons. Your dedication to the work of publishing has helped to make my dream come true.

My beta readers provided essential feedback through many revisions. Thanks to Amy Huff, Greg Cushing, Jamie Frank, Sally Bosco, Shara White, Michele Korri, Alicia Kleinman, and the guy who stayed up late so many nights to talk things out with me—Chris Vale. Thanks to Jake Smith for sharing the journey, and to Tom Steckert, who, as my very first critique partner, remains one of the most positive influences on my work I've ever had.

I've been lucky to be part of some wonderful YA debut groups—the Fearless Fifteeners and the Class of 2K15. I want to say a special thank you to the Freshman Fifteens for taking me in at a time when I really needed friends in the same boat. Your wisdom, humor, and support have made this publishing journey so much easier. And so much more fun!

And of course, a great deal of inspiration for this work came from my time teaching at Tewksbury Memorial High School. TMHS is a place full of devoted educators who I loved to work with and miss very much. From my English and creative writing classes, to the cross-country and track teams, to groups I advised, to every other student that I had the privilege of getting to know, thank you for sharing your high school years with me, which helped me to become the person who was able to write a book like this. Bob MacDougall and Steve Levine must be singled out as special mentors. Your influence on my life is immeasurable. Thank you, thank you, thank you.

I've enjoyed encouragement and support from friends and family all around me, people too numerous to name, but you know who you are. I am deeply grateful for each one of you who has read my book, or asked about my writing, or cheered me along the way.

And finally, to the people who mean the most to me in the world—Marietta and David Brooks; Amy, Connie, Kristi, and their families; Chris and Lucas. If I could make a thousand worlds, you'd be the first people I would put in each. Your love for me is everything, and I love you so very, very much.